RICOCHET

Alan Forsyth

HAYLOFT PUBLISHING LTD
CUMBRIA

First published by Hayloft Publishing Ltd., 2014

Hayloft Publishing Ltd, South Stainmore,
Kirkby Stephen, Cumbria, CA17 4DJ

tel: 017683 41568 or 07971 352473
email: books@hayloft.eu
web: www.hayloft.eu

Copyright © Alan Forsyth, 2014

ISBN 978 190 452 4977

A CIP catalogue record for this book is available
from the British Library

Apart from any fair dealing for the purposes of research or private study
or criticism or review, as permitted under the Copyright Designs and
Patents Act 1988 this publication may only be reproduced, stored or
transmitted in any form or by any means with the prior permission in
writing of the publishers, or in the case of reprographic reproduction in
accordance with the terms of the licenses issued by the Copyright
Licensing Agency.

Designed, printed and bound in the EU

Papers used by Hayloft are natural, recyclable products made from wood
grown in sustainable forests. The manufacturing processes conform to
the environmental regulations of the country of origin.

To the Recce Lads
Who are Far, Far Away

All characters appearing in this work are fictitious.
Any resemblance to real persons, living or dead,
is purely coincidental.

PART I

Summer 1946

Chapter 1

Sinai

THE blazing white heat kept the horizon bubbling in a constantly changing outline, playing the fool with my screwed-up aching eyes. The map which had looked so competent and full of authority as I clipped it into place under the transparent cover of my mapboard, back in the cool shade of the Orderly Room, was now a hideous examination paper composed to expose my woeful ignorance. Every complex of creases obscured possible features in otherwise barren areas of cartographer's guesswork. There was nothing in the map or in the pitiless waste of rock and dust in front of me that coincided, and my mind groped wildly for something that could be identified. I slid slowly into the state of mild panic where reason was blind and impotent into the intellectual fog which a quadratic equation on the blackboard and the impatient sarcastic voice of the maths master always induced.

'God damn you for a stupid half wit, damn you, damn you,' I swore at myself. Somehow I must remove the cloud panic wraps round the brain. This much I had learned. The sound of the truck engines, ticking-over roughly because they were too hot, was acting like a metronome, or the blackboard pointer slapping against old Watkin's leg. I could almost hear him.

'Come along Wade, Spring is on the way and none of us are getting any younger while we wait for you.'

I turned round, and when I could see that Crompton was watching me from his seat in the second jeep, I signalled for the engines to be switched off. I felt very much on my own as I imagined the looks being exchanged between the men in the four army vehicles at the bottom of the Wadi, and the age-old common soldier's bewildered misery when suffering at the hands of a still shiny, newly hatched troop leader. I could imagine their comments, remembering my own brief service as a trooper.

'Gor, what's the stupid runt effin' around at up there. I'll bet the silly effer's lost us.'

When the noise of engines had died away, I called down to Crompton and told them to brew up, then sat down in the minute patch of shade behind a rock to flog the map into submission.

*　　*　　*

The sense of urgency had gone, and as the cheerful roar of the petrol stove and the murmur of men's voices broke the leaden silence, reason began to re-assert itself.

I dug back into my memory to recall the moment when we had turned off the track to skirt a sand dune which had drifted across it. We had turned onto a bearing which was exactly 90 degrees to our original course, looking for the southern end of the dune. That had been between a bend in the track about a mile prior to the turning and a series of Wadis on the map. The trouble was that there were Wadis everywhere on the ground.

When we had reached the end of the drift, the speedometer had read another five miles. Allowance for the wheel spin when the jeep had bogged down once reduced this by half a mile. Then we had turned west and stayed on that heading for a mile before turning north to regain the track.

We had gone two miles beyond where we should have crossed it. Had we driven over it without knowing? Instead of running across the track on top of a slight crest, we had begun to enter the bottom end of a shallow Wadi which was curving away more to the north, and would lead us up into the low foothills which I could see through the binoculars. They would be somewhere off the edge of my map.

If I had wrongly estimated the position where we had turned off the track, and in fact we had been making better time and had been nearer the northward curve which it made to go up the long Wadi, we were going in the right direction. I realised that this could be the answer, that we were still on the correct bearing, but approaching a track which was curving away from us locally, and separated from us by a series of deepening rough Wadis. A short walk to the boulder strewn crest of the ridge gave me a vantage point, and now being certain where I had to look, I saw the track, marked by old oil drums about a mile or two away.

To rejoin it would mean re-tracing our route for two miles of rough going to the bottom of the Wadi, and driving up the east side of the troublesome dune, whereas the plain in front of me was firm and hard. I looked at the map and saw that the track curved and meandered through the Wadis, where presumably the occasional shade for camels and donkeys had determined its course, whereas we could save ourselves those long difficult miles by striking out in a dead straight course over twenty miles of sand and salt flats. I decided that we would reach the track easily by 18:00 hours and bivouac early in one of the Wadis about twenty miles from Akaba and save ourselves at least ten miles. This would leave us an easy run into camp next morning to mark the end of my first small command. Although I would have preferred to finish the journey without a night out in the desert because of the 7,000 Palestinian pounds which we were carrying, it would be better than ending the journey in the dark.

I drew the new route onto the talc and stood up to make my way back to the trucks. The sound of the scrabbling footsteps up the side of the hill and the clatter of a Sten magazine against rock heralded the arrival of Sgt. Crompton.

A thick film of fine grey dust covered his lean face, apart from the clean pink area round his bloodshot and red rimmed eyes where they had been protected by his goggles now pushed up onto the front of his tank beret. Rivulets of perspiration had curved muddy tracks in the dust of his face and throat. He was breathing hard after the exertion of the short steep climb and irritably slapped away the flies that crawled round the corner of his lips.

'I can't think what these little bastards find to live on out here sir, but every time you stop, there they are.'

He nodded towards my mapboard.

'I gather you've got a fix sir.'

'Yes sergeant, but I'd like your opinion as well, where do you reckon we are?'

He looked uncomfortable, lips pursed and frowning.

'Well to tell the truth sir, I'm damned if I've had much of a clue since we made the second alteration of course, but I saw you taking that first bearing, so I assumed you knew.'

He was at least ten years older than I was but this was just not good enough, and I had to remind him that he ought to have kept a second check on our route all the time. He took the reproof like the professional soldier that he was, without discussion or even a change of expression, but his eyes were focussed at a point just above my eyes.

I found myself wondering how crooked the badge was on my cap as I had under the eagle eye of the troop sergeant just a month ago while still a cadet. Like a waiter who has won a prize on a football pool and immediately joins the ranks of the privileged diners in an expensive restaurant, I could feel the professional eyes looking beyond the signs of office to the insignificant flesh and bone masquerading as a leader.

In wartime the differences between us would pass un-noticed, and would certainly not matter, but now, the old hands were grasping the reins again. The peacetime leaders would all speak with the same accents once again, without provincial corruptions they would all have the same haircuts, the same nostalgic tailoring and carry a suitable religious label.

'Give me your mapboard sergeant, and I'll mark our position, you can follow from there.'

He handed it to me, and I saw at once that he knew perfectly well where we were. It was ringed in red chinagraph. There was no trace of a smile of triumph on his face, but there was no doubt who was leading this particular match. I handed it back to him without comment unable to suppress a grin at the ridiculous situation building up between us.

'Well that's enough faffing about for one day Sgt. Crompton. It's about time we sorted one or two things out. Firstly I've got a hell of a lot to learn, I know it, and so do you, but whether you or I like it or not we're going to work together. I don't doubt that you know your job, and you do it to the best of your ability, and I intend to do the same. We're going to have the best troop in the Squadron just as soon as you realise that it needs two of us to do it. Now let's go and have some tea and start the job properly.' He responded with a salute, so correct but completely out of context there in the middle of that blistered wilderness, it could only be ironical.

The chatter died down as we reached the circle of soldiers relaxed round the now silent cooker on which a billy can of steaming tea was sitting. Eleven faces watched us silently as we approached. Dusty faces, some very young, some approaching middle age, but all strangers. The lance-corporal, Marshall, chased one of them off to get my mug from the jeep. Someone had already one for Crompton, and handed it to him. He waited until I had mine before he drank.

I looked into the tin mug which was three-quarters full of mahogany coloured, scum ringed tea which smelled strongly of petrol and condensed milk.

'That looks a pretty powerful brew, Oh well to hell with our socks.' Marshall neighed dutifully, Crompton smiled with half his face, politely and the rest were silent, absorbed in their own thoughts.

''ave we got far to go sir?' asked one of the troopers in a slow south country drawl.

'No, not very far,' and I explained where we were and where we were going, modelling a little relief map in the sand at our feet.

'Wouldn't it be better if we went back first sir'' asked the pimply youth Gregg, 'then we'd be sure where we was.' Before I could answer Crompton whipped him back into line.

'This isn't a bloody discussion group Gregg, Mr. Wade, at great trouble to 'imself and quite unnecessarily is telling you what's 'appening so cut your cackle, load this cooker and start up.'

'Yes sergeant.' said the offender against propriety, and leaped into action.

'Sgt. Crompton,' I said, 'I'd be pleased if you would ride with me in my jeep. It's about time we got to know each other.'

'Yes sir,' he said, but his face remained a mask, and sat beside me as I settled myself behind the wheel and drove off up the Wadi.

'It's not the usual thing for officers to drive themselves sir,' he hinted, 'not that I want to interfere sir.'

'That's alright. I'd be very grateful if you would keep me on the rails, and I look to you for a lot of guidance. I want to drive now though, mainly to find out what a jeep can do on this stuff. I could be wrong about this, but I think that a junior leader ought to be able to get the best out of any vehicle and any weapon otherwise he doesn't know what can be done with them.'

'Is that why you carry a No. 5 rifle sir?'

'No it's simply because it's reliable, and I can use it better than a hand gun. I just can't shoot with a Webley, and I don't think a Sten is much better than a shotgun, well at least it isn't in my hands.'

'You seem to take your soldiering pretty seriously sir – by the way you've still got the four wheel drive in.'

I'd done it again – made a damned fool of myself while holding forth on some subject of which I've no real experience worth mentioning. I found myself blushing like a schoolgirl, and brought the convoy to a lurching halt while I sorted out the gears. The next ten miles passed in hot, dirty uncomfortable silence.

'Can you stop a moment sir?'

I looked at Crompton who was staring ahead while be fumbled for his binoculars. I coasted to a halt, gently and applied the handbrake as he focussed his glasses.

'Could you switch off sir?' he asked.

'What is it?' I asked. He had stopped breathing as he concentrated.

'I don't know sir, but I just spotted a small dust cloud at the foot of the Djebel about 2,000 yards away over there,' and he pointed. I focused my own glasses but saw nothing except heat shimmer, irritated that 2,000 yards meant nothing to me in this flat country.

'Perhaps it's another convoy,' I suggested but knew as I said it that I was talking nonsense again. We both knew that there were no more troop movements planned during these three days. He made no comment. This was probably a little scare to see how I would react.

'It's most likely an Egyptian frontier commission patrol, or some oil company people.'

'Too far north for oil men sir, although they are most likely locals. We could treat this as a sort of exercise sir, it would give the boys something to think about instead of just sitting on their arses.'

'Good idea sergeant, we have to join the track beyond that point and it looks like a low col so we'll have a spot of defile drill. Orders group now.' This was a situation made for me, giving me a chance to get a tight grip on it and show them that I could at least cope with a simple tactical situation.

Feeling slightly smug I watched passengers in jeeps become soldiers and click into their roles. Corporal Marshall's jeep with the Bren screamed off as point car heading for a low, rock strewn hill a couple of hundred yards off to our right front, while we covered his drive over open country. Through glasses we watched him arrive and set up the Bren to cover our dash to positions in the broken ground within 500 yards of the mouth of the defile, formed by the shoulder of the hills between two wadis and a long low hill covered with scrubby camel thorn and boulders. Sgt. Crompton moved over to the three tonner leaving me with the jeep, and a reminder that we were due to make a check-call to B Squadron in half an hour's time at 17:00 hours. A last dig at me, presumably because he felt that he was losing his grip on the present situation.

When Marshall signalled that he was settled, we drove off in an exhilarating sprint over the wind rippled salt flats. Swerving between boulders and thorn bushes which were becoming more frequent, I drove the jeep to its limit. A quick look at the crew, showed that they had woken up, enjoying themselves in this game of cowboys and Indians. The three tonner was bouncing and jolting about like a wild-west prairie wagon. The men hanging on to the tilt and grinning like children. The boulders were getting thicker and bigger and the sand and salt surface had changed to dried and cracked mud, curling up at the edges like potsherds. This was far enough. I pulled into a group of rocks and skidded to a halt. Fellows, Caffin and Holbrow were out and in position among the rocks looking for targets on the defile sides before the dust had settled.

This is better, I thought watching them settle into position, set their sights and slip off safety catches. Finding myself a comfortable firing position, I set my sights at 800 yards as I found a possible target area. Fifty yards to our left I saw Crompton and his men go to earth in a fold in the ground.

I focussed my binoculars on Marshall and saw that he was

watching me. I waved him on and saw him acknowledge my order before sprinting with his three men to his jeep. A puff of blue oil smoke from the car's exhaust pipe and a spurt of dust from its back wheels and they were off on the dash to their last bound which would cover my move into the left flank on the defile. I settled down to wait and searched the hillsides with my glasses. The sun was lower, throwing long blue shadows from the little rocky outcrops on the rounded flanks of the hills, and deep blue and mauve pools of shade in the dark sandstone wadis, running deep into the Djebel on our left.

The sweat collected between my shoulders and stuck my shirt to my back, and the dust gritted between my teeth. My head was throbbing with the heat, and the brilliant sunlight; I never thought that the light would bother me so much. I looked at my watch, five to five. Hell!

'Caffin, switch on the set, and listen out on today's frequency for our tuning call, I'll join you in a minute.'

He scrambled over to the set withdrawing the round from the breech of his rifle and pressing it back into the magazine while he closed the bolt, carefully covered it with the trigger squeezed and applied the safety catch. Just as carefully and deliberately he switched on the set and let it warm up. From twenty yards away I could hear the whine of the power pack, and the sudden flow of mush from the spare earphones. A thin tinny voice grew from the background, 'Easy Baker Oboe One, Easy Baker Oboe One, Easy Baker Oboe One, Tuning Call Ends, Hear netting call, net now.'

I worked out my position, encoded it, and waited nervously like a proud ballerina for my first solo performance. 'Netting Call Ends, Hello all stations East Baker Oboe, report my signals, Over.' Eventually the ordeal was over only my operator and control must know how I felt.

'Have a fag sir,' said Caffin.

'No thank you Caffin, I don't smoke.'

'What about a beer sir?' he looked at me with slightly raised eyebrows.

'That's cruelty to dumb animals, laddie.'

The dusty mask with bright white teeth and white goggle

protected patches, broke into a huge grin and without saying a word, pulled a pint bottle of Stella beer out of his bedding roll.

'You first sir,' he said and hooking the edge of the bottle cap over the edge of the shovel clipped to the side of the jeep, he slapped it open with the palm of his hand, and handed it foaming to me.

Who was I to tell him that I had never tasted Stella, but after the first shock of its flat stale flavour, it was magnificent. Suddenly it occurred to me, I was hungry.

'Come on Marshall keep moving.' The little jeep in my glasses was leaping and bouncing urged on by the corporal's crusading zeal. I must have a word with him he's driving his boys round the bend, and he's inclined to creep a bit. I must do it discreetly without discouraging him, or perhaps leave it to Crompton. Once again the jeep stopped and the little figures hopped out and disappeared like rabbits.

'Sgt. Crompton,' I called.

'Sir.'

'We'll go about 200 yards into the defile, take cover on the flanks and bring up Marshall, then you can press on to find a leaguer.'

'Very good Sir.'

'Right move now!'

We mounted and reversed out of the rocks before setting out at a brisk pace for the mouth of the defile. I was surprised to see how high the hill on my right was, and by the length of the defile which curved away down to the right. The three tonner was dropping back a little but I kept my foot down on the accelerator. Tracks appeared from the left and disappeared ahead into the low scrubby trees which grew at intervals. I took a quick look back over my shoulder and saw that we were still well within sight and range of Marshall's Bren group but saw the Dodge closed up behind me. I must look for cover soon, just beyond this rock outcrop, I thought. A rain gully on my left became deeper and forced me to keep into the hillside. The track was getting narrower.

I changed down to third, when suddenly I saw the regular disturbed patches of earth ahead – the swept hand marks in the sand – and footprints. Cold terror gripped my guts, like a frozen hand. My feet slammed onto the brake and clutch and the jeep slewed first to the left and then the right as I fought to keep it straight yet stop it.

'Get out!' I yelled to the crew, and froze onto the controls as the jeep broadsided slowly and inevitably before it slid with wheels locked, backwards onto the mines.

The world dissolved into a mess of noise and flame and screeching metal, until I found myself lying bemused, face down in soft sand with my ears ringing, my whole body quivering like a ferret frightened rabbit, and I felt a distinct inclination to cry. What the hell am I doing here why has this happened to me? Suddenly I was aware of the noise, the kerthump and crack of rifle bullets and the long stutter of a Bren gun. Peeping out of my right eye I got my bearings, the gully was six feet to my right and what was left of the jeep in a steaming inverted heap, half in it and half out of it. The wheels were still spinning, and someone was lying trapped under it.

I gathered my arms and feet under me, and hurled myself sideways into the gully where I lay breathless for a moment. A ragged volley of fire thumped into the bank over my head. I belly crawled to the man under the jeep, it was Caffin, and he was dead. My rifle lay under him, and without exposing myself I got it out and wiped off the blood and sand. Under the mass of bedding rolls and jerry cans, I found the box of 36 grenades and detonators and spent the next five minutes arming a dozen of them while I checked where everyone else was by calling their names.

The three-tonner was on the side against the hillside to the right of the road, and Crompton and two of his crew had survived the initial ambush. Holbrow and Fellows were with him in a clump of rocks and scrub twenty yards away from me.

Are you alright sergeant?' I called.

'I have stopped one in the knee sir, and Holbrow's got one in the gut, what about you sir?'

'I'm bloody hungry sergeant,' and I meant it, for my stomach was rumbling and bubbling horribly although this was partly from fright. He called something back but it was lost in an outbreak of erratic fire from my left, directed at the three tonner, and I saw the muzzle flashes. Two riflemen. I looked carefully, and saw a movement and a white blob. Four hundred yards. I settled my cheek comfortably against the smooth butt and lined up the sights. The blob and a dark patch behind it floated into line, and holding my breath I squeezed the trigger. A tiny doll like figure jerked backwards, arms flailing from behind a clump of thorn and fell on its face in the sand. He's dead. Who the hell have I killed? Was he a Jew, an Arab or what? We're not at war with anyone – all this is nothing but unlicensed murder. Oh well they started it. Where's the other bloke?

A second figure started to run towards me dodging and weaving like a drunken boxer. Two rapid shots and they both missed. Taking my time over the third shot I was beaten to it by one precise shot from Sgt. Crompton's group, which brought down the running man like a marionette whose strings have all been cut at once. Someone turned their attention to me, two through the floor of the jeep already riddled with splinters and the other into the earth by my head, throwing dust into my eyes. Away to the rear, Marshall's Bren and two riflemen kept up a steady fire, until suddenly they were silent.

'What has happened sir can you see?'

*   *   *

'Can't see a thing sergeant, my bloody glasses are broken.' Suddenly, to my horror, I heard a jeep engine whining hesitantly up the road. The enemy held his fire and the jeep came on into the defile.

'That stupid twit, he's coming in,' called Crompton. 'Is he trying to win a bloody VC?' Crompton fired five shots rapid which sent the jeep and its crew scuttling for cover a second before the enemy opened fire.

'Good work sergeant!' I called. 'I hope to God Marshall has had the sense to send a contact report, my radio has had it.'

Suddenly I caught a glimpse of the top of a head about twenty to thirty yards away up the track and heard the click of steel against stone. I took a grenade, and with trembling hand pulled out the pin. The knuckles of my right hand were white with anxiety as my fingers held down the lever. I couldn't throw it from a lying position, and hope to clear the jeep with certainty – I must stand up and leave my snug little hole in the ground for a fraction of a minute. NOW, and a good long strong throw, then back to earth. A pop as the cap fired, and the little black wobbling ball was away to drop ten yards over. Another quickly, as the first went off with an orange flash and a hollow bang. Whining splinters hit the jeep. The second fell on target and spread bloody ruin.

'Bloody good effort mate,' shouted an anonymous soldier, before renewed fire from the front killed conversation.

'Sir,' called Crompton, 'I'm on my own now Holbrow's dead, and so's this other lad, I'm coming to join you. I've got four smoke grenades, I'll set one off it you give me covering fire.'

'OK sergeant whenever you're ready.'

'Now Sir,' he called and hopped at speed across the track while I emptied a magazine in rapid fire down the wadi at the flashes in the gathering gloom.

'How do you feel? You seem to have collected a few splinters in your face.'

Until then, I had not noticed them, the excitement having acted as a sort of anaesthetic. Now the feeling of security which the proximity of a friendly human being allowed the stinging pain of a number of small face wounds to make itself felt.

'We've got to get out of this somehow and if possible stop our enemy of the moment from getting the weapons and ammunition from the bodies as well as the money from the three tonner. Sergeant as I'm still mobile, I've got a suggestion.'

'What do you want me to do sir?' he asked.

'You know where we are now don't you?' I asked and he   nodded assent. 'Well we are strictly speaking off our route but you could easily regain it by doing a detour to the south of this hill on our right and you could be in Akaba in a couple of hours if that jeep of Marshall's still works. But before we can consider that I'll have to secure the hill so that you can get away as soon as the sun goes down. Whoever ambushed us either did it off the cuff or were waiting for someone else so they daren't hang about too long, so I should be able to hang out until you get away and make contact with the Squadron. There is no alternative, so the sooner we get started the better. Now I'm going to see if I can get down as far as Marshall's gang of cut-throats and see if they can contribute a driver.'

Two hours had passed since the ambush and our tormentors seemed to be prepared to bide their time, which was puzzling.

Marshall was dead, lying on the track between the jeep and the ditch. Two of his men, Davies and Waterton were still alive although Waterton was badly wounded with three bullets in the body, and kept losing consciousness. From where I lay the jeep seemed to be intact so I told Davies to be ready to make a run for it as soon as night fell and take Sgt. Crompton with him. I hoped that something, anything might remove the necessity for their leaving but nothing happened apart from the occasional sniping.

As the sun dropped lower in the sky, it began to grow cold. The blue shadows of the hills and the thorn bushes grew longer reaching out over the bottom of the wadi. Lying prone, we dug ourselves into the dusty and stony earth working alternately while the other provided a pair of watchful eyes and a ready trigger finger. Further back down the track, the chink of steel on stone indicated that our other survivors were doing the same. I wondered who else was still alive, but we could not call out because of the risk of revealing our weakness to the enemy whoever they are.

'Who do you reckon these characters are sergeant? You don't suppose they could be our own people do you?'

'I shouldn't think so sir, not even the Air Force are as trigger happy as these bastards were. I reckon they're Irgun and they knew that we were carryin' all this money.' he replied.

'What I can't understand, is why they are hanging about and haven't come in for the kill.'

'Oh I reckon they're waitin' for the dark as well. After all we've got quite a few of 'em and the remainder can't get past us out of the wadi in daylight, not in vehicles anyway.'

'Look sir, we can't leave you like this, let's take a chance and all run for it, you've done your best and we can set fire to the jeep and truck,' said Crompton. But as much as I wanted to believe him I knew that he was only speaking half the truth. No-one would get away unless that hill was cleared and held.

'This is going to sound daft sergeant, but if you get out alright and I don't, will you go and see my Father and tell him what happened. He'll probably say 'that's the stupid sort of thing he would do, get the chop before he even joined his regiment, off his correct route in someone else's battle altogether' and he'll be right, but tell him that I did try and I'm very grateful to them both. My Mother will never understand.'

'OK sir, with a bit of luck I'll see you tomorrow. Here you'd better take our water bottles, there's a couple of jerry cans of water in that jeep and you might find some grenades useful up there.'

Somewhat self-consciously, I fitted Caffin's bayonet to my rifle. The whole situation was becoming stupidly and embarrassingly melodramatic and I wanted to get away before we started shaking hands.

'Let's have some rapid fire sergeant, while I sprint for it.'

At the first shot I was out of the ditch and running like a fool hung about with water bottles and grenades up the astonishingly steep slope of the hill. Someone was shooting at me from behind and to my left, but the top of the hill was my goal and I could think of nothing else. I was tiring and my rifle seemed to be growing heavier when a startled man scrambled to his feet ten yards in front of me and looked at me with his mouth open. God, if only I could run faster, I must get him before he collects his wits, I thought and levelled my bayonet for his stomach. To my astonishment he dropped his carbine and held out his hands palms towards me, but it was too late, and my bayonet took him low in the belly while he clawed at it with his bare hands.

'You lousy bum,' he screamed as I pulled it out and shot him.

Staggering on exhausted I fell to my knees fifty yards away from the summit as a rifleman in the rocks opened fire on me, and I fired three wild rounds towards him. He staggered out bent double, and I hit him again with a deliberate shot from the hip which dropped him where he stood.

I half crawled the last few yards and stood to look onto the wadi. A violent blow hit me in the left side and another tore my left leg from under me sending me sprawling between the rocks. I lay with the breath knocked out of my body while the initial shock wore off and the pain came flooding up from my leg. I rolled over onto my right side and ripped my trouser leg to expose the wound which was slowly exuding blood while bits of white bone splinter stuck out of the ragged exit hole below the back of my knee. I tied it up with a field dressing, and turned my attention to the neat round blue hole in my left side between my diaphragm and hip, there was no exit, so I still had that one but it was strangely unpainful.

I re-loaded the rifle and crawled to the edge of the escarpment. The whole story lay before me in the fast gathering gloom. The ambush party had three civilian trucks which were hidden in the trees about a mile beyond the ambush, and the rifle flashes showed that at least ten of their party were still active. Picking the nearest one I fired at the flash, then chose the next and fired again. Slowly and painfully changing my position after each two or three rounds until nearly all the remaining fire was drawn to the hill top.

The sun went down and I heard the whine of the jeep's starter motor and a flurry of shots from the valley and the far slope. Between the noise and flash of my own shots I heard the jeep rear away, its exhaust blaring through a perforated silencer. Later I heard it motoring across the desert to the south of me clean away, I could have yelled with triumph but lay still and listened.

The boy whom I had shot just as I reached the peak was groaning quietly but I daren't relax and go to him because I could hear people moving about in the valley, and climbing noisily up my hillside. As the moon came out, I could see two figures moving up the slope towards me, and I groped hurriedly for a grenade. Pulling the pin smoothly now with confidence, I lobbed the grenade softly into space. One of them shouted a warning to his companion and threw himself flat. His friend did not hear, but asked him something instead as the grenade exploded. He staggered and rolled away into cover. Spasmodic firing went on from all sides in all directions for another hour, then suddenly stopped.

Some time later their trucks started and drove off and the night was still except for the rasping breathing and delirious moaning of the wounded boy. I crawled over to him. He heard me coming and tried to drag himself towards the machine pistol, lying just out of reach of his grasping hand. I pushed it further away from him with my bayonet.

'Lie still laddie, you'll damage yourself. I won't hurt you.'

He said nothing but lay curled up on his right side with his face towards me.

*   *   *

'Where are you hit?' he still did not answer. 'Come on don't be bloody stupid, I'm trying to help you. Do you speak English?'

I looked closely at his face and saw that his eyes were open, and he was staring at me. Both his hands were grasping his left thigh, and groping with my fingers I found that his knee was shattered. He must be applying pressure to the femoral artery, I pulled his hand away, and a rush of blood spurted from his wound.

I took the cleaning bottle out of my rifle butt, and made a tourniquet out of the pull-through and the oil bottle. He had lost a lot of blood from his leg and kept fainting. He had another wound in the chest which he seemed to have plugged himself. I took a clean handkerchief from my hip pocket and tied it loosely round the remains of his knee.

The night was getting cold and the moon shone brilliantly in a clear star sprinkled sky. I looked at my watch but it had stopped and the glass was shattered. My mouth was dry but I daren't drink because of the wound in my guts.

'Hey what's your name? It can't do any harm to tell me because it looks as if we're going to die here together.'

To my astonishment he was smiling.

'Well I'm glad you think it's amusing. What the hell's the joke?'

'Jacob Bernstein, son of a kosher butcher from Liverpool and by the trace of scouse accent creeping through your British Army type voice, I'd say you were almost a neighbour.'

'Hell's teeth, how did you get out here?' I asked.

'My Father took his demob out here, and we all came to join him.'

'Well what the devil had I ever done to you to make you want to kill me and those boys lying down there?' I asked.

'How long have you been here?' he countered.

22

'Just a month,' I said, 'but what's that got to do with it?'

'Well just ask yourself what right you have to be here as part of an occupying army.'

'Simply because it's my job.'

'And I would give you the same answer,' he replied, 'so why don't you finish me off?'

'Here have some water and stop talking balls – I daren't touch the stuff.'

I flipped my water bottle towards him. I heard him laugh, but he took the bottle, and drank. A jackal or dog of some sort was yelping and howling down in the valley. I reached for my rifle and checked that it was fully loaded and cocked.

'I don't know your name,' he said, 'but whoever you are don't let those bloody animals get at me. I know I'll hang for this when your police get their hands on me but anything's better and cleaner than those bloody Pi dogs.'

'Forget the dogs, if I look like croaking, you can have my rifle, but what's all this about hanging, surely you'll be a POW?'

'POW? Do me a favour wacker. I'm a bloody terrorist according to the Pal. Police – it's the long drop for me.'

I was beginning to learn the limits of my equipment for this job. Perhaps they're wrong, but then perhaps so were the French and Polish Resistance movements. Now we're playing the German's role in the play with the same protagonists, only this is a damned sight worse, we are fighting Englishmen. Why the hell were we hanging on to the Mandate anyway? I suppose it is simply because the Arabs are frightened of the idea that the Jews would make a bid to dominate the Middle East, and we have to keep on the right side of the Arab because of our oil supplies. We're a back number in the world politics now so why do we bother. Meanwhile the pawns never learn the lesson and go on dying dutifully. I for example have just expended nine men's lives for a few rifles and seven thousand pounds. That's a piss poor bargain.

I must have been getting weaker. I found myself on the verge of crying like a bloody soft kid. I must get a grip on myself as I couldn't even sort out my own ideas without cursing – inarticulacy is a professional soldiers' badge of office. It must have been written into my flaming commission somewhere.

Why did I want to become a professional soldier? I must have thought about it somewhere or at some time. Comradeship? That must have been the key, and devotion to an ideal and suppression of my troublesome ego. The prospect of glory still had a big part in it, but the main thing was the ability to apply oneself to a series of well defined and clear cut objectives without thought of self. It was a sort of faith where the qualities of the disciple are blind obedience and the admiration of physical courage applied to a continuing track. There was also a great tradition of faithful service to emulate. Where has it got me? Two years of service as a trooper, a year of cadet training, six months of commissioned service and now this.

I had lost my first little command, knew better than the book and cut across country off my route without reporting it, run slap into an expert ambush and got wiped out. On the credit side, I was still just about alive, the money was still in the three tonner, Crompton and Davies were clean away and we must have got at least half a dozen of the enemy. We should have had help long ago though. The sky was beginning to lighten behind the low line of blue hills to the east and the stars were fading. My God it was cold, and the pain was rising into jagged raw peaks every few seconds.

'What is your name?' Bernstein asked.

'Peter Wade, I'm from Liverpool as well in a way – although I lived most of my time in Wales.' Talking took too much effort, so we both retreated into silence, until he seemed to slide into unconsciousness, while I struggled to stay awake in case he was faking and just waiting for me to close my eyes. I used the time to consider what had brought me to this place and condition, trying to remember times and dates and conversations.

We had moved to Denbighshire in 1938 when my Father decided that he was really meant to be a farmer and not an engineer. By the same queer sort of reasoning, he decided that I ought to be an aircraft engineer and apprenticed me to De Havillands at Hatfield – no questions or discussion, it was just done. I wanted to be a soldier and the war was on, so I sneaked off at the end of the second year and joined the Recce Corps as a trooper. Faced with a *fait accompli*, he seemed to be all for the idea, and claims that engineering was my idea from the first. The trouble is that he never knows where his thoughts end and other peoples begin. It's probably the result of working in industry all one's life, pinching other people's brainwaves, and losing your own by the same process.

Talking was hard work but kept my mind off the pain. I asked Bernstein if there was any water left in the bottle, but there was no reply although he was still breathing heavily and at times noisily. I realised that I had begun to voice my thoughts, but even without an audience, it kept my mind on duty and sleep at bay.

'Now I'm twenty, reluctantly and dimly engaged to a girl I've known since we were both knee high to a grasshopper, and now, well I'm probably due to be Court Marshalled for incompetence and conniving with the enemy.' I became aware that his eyes were open and he was staring at me.

'Twenty,' said Bernstein, 'so am I, in fact it's my birthday today – if I had any sense I'd be back in Jerusalem sitting...'

*   *   *

'Quiet a minute, I heard a truck engine.' We lay silent, hardly breathing. There was nothing to hear but the buzzing of the flies that were beginning to gather. It was growing lighter, quickly, and already the air was getting warmer, but I could hear nothing.

The silence was like something solid pressing down on all sides, thick and jelly-like, smothering me. The semi-molten disc of the sun, distorted by the low haze, climbed erratically into the yellow and turquoise sky. As I watched it through half closed eyes it seemed near enough to touch. Hundreds of little feet ran over my lips and eyelids, buzzing like circular saws inside a tent made of heat and silence. My hands felt too thick to lift and brush them away, and the sun was getting higher and hotter.

My tongue would not move to speak and Jacob was silent. I could hear noises in my head and I was floating about in the air. The noises are outside my head now, then in front of my nose, like spirals and helixes of noise, catherine wheels and balls of wool, whining and grinding noises. Men shouting and running, kicking stones. If I could only open my eyes, but they seemed to be stuck. I felt for my rifle with my right hand, the comfort of it was like a dummy to a baby. With some effort I rolled onto my back, and dragged the rifle across my chest resting the butt on the ground. I pushed the safety catch forward and squeezed the trigger. The report and recoil jerked me back to full consciousness and reality. There was complete silence after the echoes had died away, then I heard a man shout.

'Hold your fire whoever you are, we're civilians.'

This didn't make sense to me so I lay still and waited while they walked about and searched the hillside, calling out to each other as they found the dead and wounded. Then they found us.

'Jesus,' said one, 'these two are a mess, are they dead?'

Someone was kneeling beside me feeling for my heart. I tried to speak and raise my head without much success.

'Take it easy old son," said a second voice. 'Take a mouthful of this water, but don't swallow it just swill it around and spit it out.'

Gentle hands washed my eyes, and someone gave me an injection and after a while they carried me down into the cool shade of the wadi. I could look round and saw a truck carrying the Shell sign and the men, two Americans and a black European who were the crew. Four of us seemed to have survived, Jacob, two soldiers whose names I could not remember and myself. One of the men was sitting on the running board of the Shell truck speaking into a microphone to report their find. He switched off the set and came over to me, his face split in a wide grin.

* * *

'They know all about it suh, your sergeant had just got in, and a patrol is about five or ten miles away now, so if you don't mind we'll push off and leave you tucked up comfortably.'

'Thanks,' I said, 'leave me your names, who's the boss?'

'I am,' he said, 'Reuben Macloud and sort of British really, from Trinidad.'

'Where are you heading for?'

'Haifa.' he replied.

'Do you know what will happen to this Jew boy when our police get him?' I asked.

He knelt down beside Jacob, who was unconscious again and looked at him closely.

'I didn't know he was a Jew,' he said, 'but I suppose the poor bastard'll swing.'

'Probably,' I said, 'if you happened to take him with you and left him at the first kibbutz you passed, he'd stand a good chance, and I couldn't stop you in my shaky state of health.'

I closed my eyes and said nothing more, but I heard him giving quiet orders to his two colleagues, heard one offering feeble protests which did him no good, and heard Jacob being lifted quietly from beside me and the heavy steps of men carrying an inert burden.

Reuben came back, and spoke to the two troopers whom they had carried up to join me on the hill, offering them cigarettes and telling them that help was coming. One didn't answer him and the other seemed cheerful enough.

'Thanks a lot mate, I'll buy you a beer for this when I see you, I thought we'd bloody had it. But what are you doin' with that kid?'

'Don't worry about him man, he's just croaked we're going to lay him out over there with his mates, he'll only attract flies to you – cheerio and the best of luck.' The others called goodbye, and the truck drove off, sounding like a grand prix car as it screamed up through a seemingly never ending train of gears.

'Roll on bloody demob,' said a sad voice on my right.

I opened my eyes and turned my head till I could see him. 'How are you feeling?'

'Oh hello sir. I thought you was out for the count – I'm alright just a nick in the arse and one in me foot, but I thought I was the only one,' he laughed quietly. 'Where was you wounded Jack, show us yer wound they'll say when I get back – pity you don't get a medal just for a wound like the Yanks sir, I'd get the Purple Arse.'

It seemed unusually funny to us both, and I was beginning to feel light headed again. I slowly dragged myself into a half sitting position against the rock behind me and pulled my rifle across my knees. Now I could see what was happening. The dust kicked up by the Shell truck was rapidly receding over the north western horizon. Slowly as I watched it go, the desert slid sideways into darkness and my senses gave up the struggle, spiralling off into dreamless...

CHAPTER 2

Sarafand

1946

IT WAS a process which took a dream-like form, and, as far as I could tell, may have taken days or weeks before I could exercise any control over my thoughts. Until the day when I saw the light bulb, dreams and words and music had flowed through my mind, but they were words that had no memorable meaning, only the empty feeling of fear, and the music was sometimes only half heard above the roar of the sea and at other times so deafening that it could only be endured. The light bulb became the centre of my universe and everything else slowly came into focus around it. A ceiling which was sometimes as remote as the sky and at others as close as a box around my head, moved above me. One day, it was still. That was the day that I heard voices and saw, without a great deal of interest, faces and hands for the first time. After more sleep and dreams, the voices began to make sense. My body felt as if it weighed a ton and would never move again. Cool, starched, brisk and rustling nurses moulded my new half-existence to a nursery routine, until the day when someone must have thought that I was fit enough to be exposed to a controlled view of the outside world again.

I awoke from a dream of trout streams and pollarded willows, to the harsh reality of oppressive heat and the sound of flies, and became aware of someone sitting beside me, I tried to turn my head to see who it was, but it was too difficult.

'That's all right old man, just relax. You've had a bit of a rough time but they tell me that you're going to be almost as good as new soon. I say, can you understand me?'

My visitor's face floated into my line of sight, and registered itself as the sort which might be worn by a professional cavalry-man of about 50 years of age. I tried to nod assent, but my head refused to move. In spite of this he seemed satisfied.

'We've not met formally yet Wade, but I'm your Colonel.' He examined me closely.

'You're damned lucky to be still alive 'n kicking y' know, luckily Crompton is a very experienced soldier, and a plucky one. It must have taken a lot of guts to drive that jeep so far with his knee so badly smashed. If he hadn't got to Akaba and given an accurate map reference of your position... well I dare say we'd have lost you all.'

A nurse was hovering respectfully behind him trying to attract his attention. 'Colonel... excuse me!' He ignored her, but I wished he would just go away and let me sleep and sleep.

'Yes we were all damn lucky – but a bit rough for a first job... still you did pretty well... and you were lucky to have a good sergeant... put him in for the MM.'

'Colonel please, you must leave... he's got to have rest.'

'Yes, yes!' he stood and moved out of my line of vision but his voice was still there saying something to the nurse. 'No dammit, no one else, least of all the SIB... I don't care what they say...' and he had gone.

There followed a period of sleeping and waking and operating theatres and pain then another visit from the Colonel which was largely a duty call. This time however, I was able to take a little more part in the proceedings. He told me that the Brigadier was quite pleased with the result of our action but somehow there seemed to be a subtle reserve in his manner which had not been present at our first encounter.

The pauses in the halting conversation, which mostly seemed to be a valiant series of attempts on his part, to feed me with an indigestible recital of cricket results, grew longer and longer. Finally, without preamble and like someone having to tell the Pope that he would have to announce that the birth of Lenin had really been the Second Advent, he told me that I had a Military Police guard on permanent duty outside the door and that the Assistant Provost Marshal wanted to talk to me. He advised a policy of smiling, courteous non-cooperation.

The nurse, who once again had been trying to attract his

attention, finally told him plainly that he must go, as there was another visitor, a young lady waiting to see me. This surprised him, but it surprised me even more. I tried to sit up but there was no power to raise my body, or my head from the pillow, only pain. The Colonel looked as if he had been about to protest but looked at me, raised his eyebrows and pulled down the corners of his mouth and slowly stood.

'D'ye know I've flown all the blasted way from Fayid today just to see you thinking that you were a sick man in the midst of heathen foreigners, and what do I find? Hordes of young gels running about after you.' Leaning closer he muttered, 'I rather fancy the Sister myself, wait till you see her – I had thought of shooting myself slightly in the leg, but I probably wouldn't do her justice even with only a little wound. We've written to your parents, and if you want us to, we'll fly them out to see you, how do you feel about it?'

'That's very good of you Colonel, but it will only throw them into a panic, perhaps one of the nurses will write a letter for me and explain that there is nothing seriously wrong with me.'

I thanked him for calling, and watched him go, stopping to speak to a Palestinian Policeman and a Military Policeman in the corridor. The realisation that the Shell men might have handed Jacob over to the police and reported the incident filled me with panic. I suddenly became aware of the nurse's voice asking me if I felt well enough to see another visitor, but before I could answer a stocky red faced officer with staff tabs was walking backwards into the room arguing furiously with the Colonel who was trying to order him out.

'If he's well enough to see that woman, he's well enough to answer a couple of questions,' and ignoring the Colonel who was trembling with temper he turned at the end of the bed to face me.

'I'll bloody well see about this,' said the Colonel and walked rapidly out of the room. I examined my exalted visitor. He looked badly assembled and overweight. The band of his battle-dress blouse stuck out over the top of his very long webbing belt which carried a pistol in a holster at the right hand side, butt to the rear. I wondered how he could possibly get it out in a hurry, with the press stud flap closed, in such a high position. One presumed that he had never had to, or he would not be here now.

'I'm the Assistant Provost Marshal' he said, 'I want you to answer a few simple questions.' A bespectacled Signals corporal came in and sat beside the bed with a note pad and pencil poised expectantly.

The APM launched into a series of disjointed routine questions about the action, the wheres, whos, whens and how manys which calmed my fears somewhat. The pace of the questions had begun to slow down, when he suddenly said.

'When did you last see this young woman?'

'What young woman sir?' I asked.

He looked irritated. 'The one outside of course, who is waiting to see you.' It was my turn to be irritated.

'I've no idea who she is unless it's one of the officer's wives from 1st Armoured Div. HQ and I can't think that any of them would come to see me.'

He began to look as if he was going to have a heart attack.

'Look here young fellow, you may think that you've fooled everyone into thinking that you were a bloody hero, but neither the CID nor I are quite sure – in fact we think you're making a bit of a young ass of yourself – so stop being a smart alec and tell me the truth. When did you last see this woman?'

The Colonel came back into the ward with the matron and an RAMC Major. The matron told the APM to get out, and he went, his stenographer trying to put away his notebook, pass the nurse, matron, Colonel and Major and salute all at once.

'You will have no more visitors today,' said the doctor. 'This young woman can come back tomorrow,' and having said this he turned on his heel and left with his retinue. The Colonel smiled smugly at me as he closed the door.

The nurse tucked in the bedclothes quite without need, and told me to go to sleep like a good boy. She must have been every day of 24-years-old, and very regimental. She told me that I was on a drip, whatever that was and that some repairs had been done to my guts the previous week. Apparently I had been the subject of some interesting surgery and bone grafting during the past ten days since

I had been flown in. Trooper Clements who had been badly wounded was operated on by a Jewish surgeon in Haifa and flown from Lydda to Blackbush for a major operation at St. Thomas's in London. His story was in all the daily papers, but for some reason the story of our little battle was being suppressed in the English papers. *El Misri* carried the full story as did *Le Monde* and the *Daily Tribune.*

Next day, the doctor came to see me and told me that I would be in hospital for at least a month but should be out on sick leave for my birthday in September. He warned me that my left knee would never have its full movement again, and that they had taken away my left kidney. Apparently heat exhaustion and loss of blood was the main reason for my present condition. I slept for most of the morning, but awoke to hear the Matron saying.

'Just take a seat dear, he will probably wake up soon – Oh hello Mr Wade I've brought you a tonic, your young lady.'

A girl in a white cotton dress was standing behind her in the passage, not smiling, just standing looking at me.

'Please come in and sit down,' I said and was surprised as she came into the room to see how tall she was. I failed to notice that the Matron had quietly left and closed the door. The girl was carrying three yellow roses in a sheaf of white paper, she stood looking round the room.

'Where can I put these?' without waiting for an answer she put them down on the locker beside the bed and smiled at me.

'What's the matter Mr. Wade, has the cat got your tongue? I heard you were more than usually talkative for a British Army Officer.'

'Well,' I said, 'I'm not used to being visited by beautiful and mysterious young women bearing roses.' She knew my name – but who could have told her, I don't know. I wouldn't have thought it possible – so far from home.

She laughed, 'Thank you kindly sir,' she said and bowed slightly from the waist, her hands resting quietly together in her lap. Her air of calm, self sufficiency was faintly irritating, but her large steady brown eyes and the long dark lashes reduced me to silent admiration. She was young, probably about seventeen or eighteen with a beautiful slim body and lovely shoulders and arms. Her face, the top of her shoulders the outside of her arms and the backs of her slim hands were tanned to a golden brown. Her jet black hair was braided and coiled round her head. She wore no jewellery or make-up apart from a little lipstick and a faint perfume vaguely suggestive of lemons. Her face fascinated me, big dark eyes in an oval high cheek-boned beautifully modelled face with a mouth like the famous head of Nefertiti.

'I've got it,' I heard myself say, 'I know where I have seen you, you're a walking Modigliani – but what is your name?'

She said nothing but smiled, and pulled the chair as close to the bed as it would go.

'My name is Deborah and I and my family owe you a considerable debt.'

'I don't understand you,' I said, but only half meant it, because there was something about this girl's voice and manner which reminded me of Jacob Bernstein. She saw that I was half way to understanding her and said quietly.

'He is only my half brother, but I couldn't think more of him if he were my real brother, and now thank God he is safe and is going to live. My father said that you must come to see us so that he can thank you for giving him back his son, even though he has sworn that no Englishman should ever sit at his table as a guest. This must sound strange, but we feel very deeply about things and are apt to become a bit emotional. He's very old now and almost blind and he's a little inclined to forget the present. Israel has always been his promised land, and he brought us out here at the end of the war and left the butcher's business in Liverpool for his partner to sell. His partner was a Jew, but he was married to a Gentile woman. Well, he wrote to say that he was having trouble selling it, and business was bad. Three years went by, then he wrote offering to buy Father's share in the business at its original valuation. Father sold it, and then we heard that the business was booming and his so called friend had opened another two shops, not kosher but self-service groceries for Gentiles and he had become a Christian himself.

'I was studying painting at Liverpool, and Father could not go on paying for me so I came out here. The day I arrived, after hitch-hiking across Europe, Mother came to meet me at Haifa, there was some shooting in the street outside the station, and a man in bush jacket and shorts came running past us through the crowd and pushed a pistol into the hands of an old woman beside my mother. The old lady put it in her handbag and walked away. Everything was very confused and there were soldiers and police everywhere. They shut the station and kept us all inside. One policeman came through the crowd towards us, looking from side to side as he walked. He stopped in front of us and looked briefly at Mother, before he turned and shouted to another of them.

'Here's the old cow Sarge,' he seized her arm and pushed his way out of the crowd towards the Rail Transport Officer's office. When we protested, I was taken as well and we spent the next eight hours being questioned. Her heart always was a bit weak and the heat and the fear of it all killed her. That was my introduction to Eretz Israel, and why my Father thinks that all Englishmen are his enemies. You have upset his simple view of soldiers and he thought you might have an ulterior motive, but you have been investigated and he wants to meet you.'

What could I say to this flood of unsolicited and embarrassingly frank information.

'Don't you think you have taken a hell of a risk coming her Miss Bernstein?' I asked.

She looked startled, and leaned forward, 'Please just call me Deborah,' she said. 'My real name is Weinstock, I would not have dared to come using the other name. You see both my brother and I are very well known to the police. Will you come?'

'Of course,' I said, 'How could...' The door opened and the Matron came in.

'Time to go Miss, you can come again tomorrow if you want to.' She smiled and held the door open.

Deborah turned and nodded to her, then looked at me as she stood up and picked up her handbag. She stepped up to the edge of the bed, stroked my hair back and kissed me on the forehead.

'Bless you and – thanks,' she said, and walked quickly out of the room without saying a word to the matron or acknowledging the MP's, 'Good afternoon Miss.'

The matron walked over to the bed and without comment, picked up the flowers. 'I'll put these in water for you before they die of thirst.'

For the rest of the day I was in a daze and the irritating hospital routine scarcely touched my consciousness. People came and went, I took chicken broth and injections and cascara and thought only of the possibility of her coming again tomorrow. I also had time to do a little worrying about the interest being shown in me by the Provost Marshal's department. Deborah's appearance on the scene had hardly been helpful. The next day came and went, but she did not come. The next two days, Friday and Saturday went, and Sunday only brought the APM again.

He arrived just before lunch was due, and repeated his questions but I just pretended to be sleepy and closed my eyes whenever I felt inclined. In an obvious fury he left after about an hour, and I made the mistake of thinking that I had won the first round. Immediately after lunch, a large sergeant of the Palestine Police came in, and settled himself comfortably on the seat beside me. He took a notebook out of his pocket carefully opened it at a clean page and licked the point of his pencil.

'Good afternoon sir,' he said.

'Good afternoon sergeant,' I replied and closed my eyes.

'Would you mind telling us sir how long you've known the young lady who called earlier this week?'

'Not at all Sergeant, do you want the exact time or an approximation? Well I would say about five days and 47 minutes or perhaps 48.'

He sighed, 'Look sir, I've just got a job to do and I'm trying to do it to the best of my ability, trying to be awkward isn't going to help either of us.' He had not recorded my answer.

'I hope sergeant that you are not implying that I am lying. Because if you are, I will take up the matter with your superior.' My God, I thought, that was more than a bit priggish.

'Well let's put it this way sir, wouldn't you think it sounded a bit unlikely – a young woman you don't know, have never seen before, walks in here, to a Military Hospital, asks for you by name two days after an ambush in the middle of the Sinai desert, which hasn't been publicised. Moreover she gave you a smacking big kiss before she goes, and calls back as regular as clockwork the next two days and today.'

I tried to conceal my elation, she had come and was here now.

'Sergeant why has she not been allowed to come in?' I asked.

'Well sir, I believe the doctor said that you couldn't answer questions, and you kept falling off in a doze whenever the APM asked you a difficult question, so it didn't seem right to allow too many visitors.' I could have hit him for the look of smug satisfaction on his face.

'Sergeant you can get yourself out of here as fast as your great feet can take you, and tell the APM he can get stuffed. You're a pack of incompetent idiots.' As soon as I had said it I felt ashamed of the outburst but it was too late, I was committed.

'Get to hell out of it, no bloody wonder the Jews manage to bump you off so easily, you must keep your brains in your backsides. Why don't you damned well earn your keep by just checking the posting records and duty rosters since I've been in this stinking country. You'll quickly find out the only people I've spoken to here are the other people in Div. HQ, their wives, a couple of shopkeepers in Beersheba and Julis and now you second rate sleuths.'

He went pale under his tan and was shaking with impotent rage. When he spoke his voice was unsteady. 'I must report this conversation sir, and I'm afraid my orders are to stay here until I'm relieved at 18:00 hours tonight. I've spent ten years in the Metropolitan Police sir, and three years here, and I've never before been spoken to like this.'

'Well if these are your orders sergeant you had better make yourself comfortable, but I intend to protest in the strongest possible terms to my Colonel about this nonsense. Do you realise that no-one has yet seen fit to tell me why I am being subjected to this treatment?'

'I didn't know about that sir, but you're not being particularly co-operative and that's not helping you or us. We've been here a lot longer than you sir, and we know what we're doing. You've been badly shot up by these bastards most of your men were killed, didn't you want to see someone swing for it? Just try co-operating sir, and we'll get the rest of those who got away.'

There was a knock at the door, and the APM came in, followed by a young man in a light tweed suit. He was about 30 to 35 years old, and was wearing a pair of expensive fashionable sunglasses. He walked to the end of the bed, picked up my temperature chart and looked at it. The sergeant was standing to attention; he normally did not do this for the APM and the APM himself looked ill at ease.

The newcomer casually walked round the room, looked at the magazines and newspapers on the table, sniffed the three roses and when he reached the chair, lowered himself, languidly into it, and crossed his legs. He sighed.

'Isn't all this a most frightful bore? One shouldn't have to work in this heat,' he looked towards me.

'Do you know who I am?'

I didn't know him from a crow, and said so, but I hazarded a guess that he must be a superior sort of bluebottle. He raised his eyebrows slightly, 'err, bluebottle?'

'A policeman sir,' the sergeant volunteered.

'Or a scuffer, a rozzer, or a policeman, take your choice,' I added. A flutter of irritation showed on his face.

He unbuttoned his jacket and put his hands in his pockets. I noticed that he was wearing a Rifle Brigade tie and idly wondered why he was not with his regiment now. He should be a captain and possibly a major and would almost certainly have served with them in North Africa and Italy. Was he with the Palestine Police CID? I wondered, but tried not to let my speculation show in my face.

'I am Major Warrender of the Special Investigation Branch and I'd be extremely grateful if you would throw some light on a few small points for me, you see this case is now my responsibility.'

'Well I'm grateful to you for one thing so far sir,' I said. 'You have just said this case, which seems to indicate that there is some reason for the interrogation to which I have been subjected since last week. Just what is going on? What do you want to know?'

He looked quietly at the APM who seemed ill at ease; and

asked him to bring the transcript of the questioning. He turned to me and said.

'Why were you not using the route to Akaba which you were given at Julis?'

I told him about the diversion to avoid the sand drift across the track, and unlike the APM he seemed satisfied. He sent the sergeant down to the office of the hospital to get my maps, which so far no-one else had thought of checking. For the next hour he went over the details of my route, and its timing and, when he had apparently satisfied himself that I had been where I said I was when I said I was, produced two typewritten sheets of HMSO foolscap and asked me to sign at the foot of the second sheet when I had read it.

The sheets were a statement and were headed 'Summary of Evidence for Court of Enquiry into the Action between a convoy of the 10th Dragoons and a Haganah detachment at Ref: 836549. The text told the story of the incident in stilted military jargon, and was apparently dictated by me. I looked at Warrender to see if an explanation was going to be given to me.

'Am I supposed to have written this?' I asked.

'Yes,' he said, 'why is there something wrong with it?'

'Well in the first place, it is not very accurate, and contains a fair bit of embroidery which is not mine, and secondly I would like to know what the title of this document means. What is the Court of Enquiry for? Who called for it, what was a Haganah detachment doing down there, and how do you know they were Haganah anyway?'

'Do you mean to say that you haven't been told all this?' he took off his sunglasses and looked at me intently.

'I haven't been told a damned thing sir, but it's all beginning to fit together,' I told him.

'Well,' he said, 'I'd better put you in the picture.' He took another transcript out of the file and read it to me. It was a statement by Sergeant Crompton which corroborated what I had said up to the point when I went up the hill on my own. It went on to state that, 'Mr Wade went up the hill under our covering fire, and after some minutes we heard shots which were directed towards the enemy. After about half an hour we managed to start the jeep and left.'

There was no mention of my encounter with the two men on the hill crest but then it is possible that he did not see it and the noise would be covered by their own gunfire. It concluded by describing how the fuel had run out about five miles from Akaba and they had been picked up by a relief column coming out to us.

He handed me other statements to read, from the officer commanding the relief column, Major Howe, who was to be my Squadron Leader, the Medical Officer with him and the APM's evidence after he examined the scene of the action.

Most of these were routine stuff, but the last one gave the clue. From the end of the first paragraph it was apparent that he had an axe to grind. Although I had not been told, it had been the intention to send with me, the pay for the two Royal Marine Commando units and the second battalion of a Highland Regiment which were paying a courtesy and training visit to Trans Jordan. It had apparently been decided that it would be safer than sending it up through Palestine and over the Allenby Bridge to Amman. Having found two wounded Jews and persuaded one of them to talk, he discovered that it was a Haganah detachment which had ambushed us.

He could find out nothing more from his prisoners, but an examination of the scene showed quite clearly by tracks and heaps of expended cartridges that they must have been about twenty strong and very well armed. From all this he concluded that we had been expected, and run into a deliberate ambush. Because a Haganah unit and not Irgun had been involved, he quite wisely advocated discretion in releasing news of the incident. He suggested that although we turned a blind eye to the theoretically illegal military training which the members of Haganah received because it was quite obvious that the Jews would have to defend themselves against the Arabs should we leave, a special investigation was warranted in this case.

The last sentence recommended that all junior officers and NCOs should be given the severest reminder that discussion of proposed troop movements with unauthorised persons was an offence which would be dealt with rigorously. The implication was obvious, and the absence of a statement from the Shell lorry reassured me. They only suspected that I had been guilty of careless talk.

'You look relieved!' Warrender said.

Trying my best to look as naive as possible I said, 'Well of course, I was beginning to think that you were going to accuse me of massacring a Haganah training school and causing embarrassment to the Mandate!'

He looked startled and stopped in the act of replacing the sheets of evidence in the folder.

'Well I'm damned,' he said. 'If I had been on this case for ten years, I doubt if I would have come up with that one. No wonder you and the APM have been at cross purposes.' He stared at me shaking his head slowly from side to side, a look of mock wonder on his face.

'It's really not fair to turn you laddies loose over here until you've cut your milk teeth!' I felt my face flush but held my tongue.

'Well I'll get this statement amended to fit the facts as you've told me and I'll send it back to you for signature by tea time. By the way we're not entirely convinced that your girl friend was unknown to you before this incident, but you're not such a fool that you wouldn't understand that it's necessary for us to investigate her. Bear that in mind, and remember time is on our side.'

I opened my mouth to speak but thought better of it and simply wished him good afternoon. His manner had been pleasant throughout the interview, but now he switched off all semblance of politeness wished me good day and left.

I looked down at my hands which felt as if they were trembling and saw that they were. I was not out of the wood yet. What did they really want? What did they suspect?

They would probably have checked my evidence about my friends and contacts before the action, the engagement itself, and my relationship to Deborah. I had no need to fear the truth, but the weak link was the reason for Deborah's initial visit to me. I decided to tell them that it hadn't occurred to me to wonder why she had come beyond the reason she had given me. I intended to imply that she had read about the action in *El Misre* and being English and perhaps discovering that I was a fellow Liverpudlian had realised that we were almost ex-neighbours; so came to cheer me up. Perhaps she came again because we got on rather well together. It sounded simple enough and would probably have allayed any layman's suspicions, but not a professional police-man's clinical examination.

It failed even to make sense to me as I very much doubted that the Egyptian Press would know the names of our casualties or even the unit involved, let alone that even one of the soldiers involved came from Liverpool.

The whole situation was getting out of hand. I felt that it was someone else's life that I was living. I was becoming involved in things that were no concern of mine. Suspicion was beginning to grow, infecting me in some way which was apparent like leprosy, until my few friends here would avoid me. These few hours in my life had turned my world upside down. For years, as long as I had thought about being a man in fact, I had wanted to be a professional soldier. My Father and both of his brothers had served in the First World War. My Father had commanded B-Squadron in France and Italy before being so badly wounded that he was invalided out with a disability pension. He was chairman of the Old Comrades Association and whenever the regiment was back in England before the war, we visited them. I had almost grown up with them and expected my father to be pleased when I told him that I wanted to stay in the Army when the war was over.

He said nothing at first, so that I thought he had not heard me or not understood what I was saying. As I started to repeat what I had said about not returning to engineering but remaining in the Army, he stopped me.

'I heard you Peter, and I'm not really surprised to hear you say this, but I would prefer to see you wait until the war is over, before you make a decision about it.'

We were sitting on the wall in the sun outside the White Horse at Llanfair and it was the last day of my leave. The next morning, I was to return to Bovington for my final month at OCTU and it seemed to be a suitable time to bring up the subject. We were having our customary drink before walking back up the hill to the house for lunch.

He carefully refilled his pipe while I went into the bar to get another two pints of bitter. As I came out backwards carrying the two glasses, and closing the door with one foot, I hear him talking to someone against the background sing-song of cheerful chatter of people coming out of the chapel gates which opened onto the gravel covered pub forecourt. I turned and saw that he was talking to Gwen and her Father, church-dressed and wearing their Sunday morning chapel faces.

'*Deawch*! that looks good to a man who's just been giving his all to six hymns with six verses apiece.'

'What will it be?' I asked him.

'The usual Guinness if you don't mind Peter.'

'Gwen?'

'Well you didn't take me to chapel this morning and you didn't take me out last night – I'll have a large brandy and soda.' She pulled the sides of her straw hat down till she was looking at me along a tunnel and put her tongue out.

'You'll have a bottle of light ale and like it.' I told her and put down the two full glasses.

'That's it *bachgen*, start as you mean to go on, a good firm hand on the rein, a woman, a dog and a walnut tree, the more you beat 'em the better they be!'

*　　*　　*

'I'll help you carry them,' said Gwen and followed me into the pub. Inside the cool dark hall she linked her arm with mine and sighed.

'I wish you didn't have to go tomorrow Peter, you do love me don't you? Just say it once before we go into the bar.'

I said it, and wondered if this was really love. It certainly had been, and had grown slowly and gently as we had grown up together until during one long hot hay harvest before I was due to leave and start my apprenticeship at Hatfield, it had burst. All the friendly bantering and rivalry, the childish horseplay and un-self-consciousness had gone and we were bewildered and enchanted and perhaps a little frightened. To be separated even for a few hours, was torture and yet together we had been shy and clumsy.

One day we had been working late and Gwen, Guido an Italian PoW and I were taking the hay cart back to the stack with the last load. I was silent and probably sulking because we had quarrelled about a village dance the next night. Gwen wanted to go, and I did not. She was resentful and feeling spiteful, so amused herself by flirting with Guido. She was sixteen and had ash blond hair and brilliant blue eyes. Her father was an independent quick-witted and quick-tempered man who didn't give a damn for anyone, and Gwen was the feminine of the species. When she turned her sparkling effervescent charm on, she was in my frame of mind, infuriating, particularly as it was not directed at me.

I stabled the horse and was in the loft forking down some hay into its manger and could hear her laughing and chattering in Welsh to the Italian who was trying to learn it. This made me even more furious because my inability to learn the language was always a subject for teasing. I heard her say '*nos dach*' to him and call after him in English as he left, 'Tell mam I'm going to Peter's to collect my bike, I'll be back by ten.'

She came running up the ladder and I heard her stop. I could feel her eyes looking at my back as I put back the trap door over the stable.

'Come on sulky boots, or have you decided to be a hermit, and turn your back on the world?' I could just see her outline in the gloom, standing in one of her arms akimbo attitudes which were specially calculated to act like a primary charge to my high explosive temper.

The evening was warm and still and the house martins were twittering under the eves of the stable. I could only stand and listen and try to hold on fast to this little piece of pure bitter sweet interlude before I could call her name, and leave my protective shell of loneliness. Without saying anything she came towards me and took my hands in hers and I heard myself telling her in a shaky voice that I loved her. It was true. This new devastating emotion, that stripped off all our affected adolescent barriers of selfishness and abruptness brought us together simply and humbly.

Her firm young body strained against me, her restless hands stroking my neck and head. Suddenly she pulled herself away from me buttoning the front of her dress with trembling hands.

'Not now Peter – now here. Come to me tonight. I'll leave the front door unlocked.' She ran her fingers through her hair and tried in vain to remove the hay from it. She laughed quietly.

'You're a bit of a character, I bet you have done this dozens of times.' I kissed her quietly, and did not reply, suddenly self-conscious and not knowing the right answer. If I said yes she might be angry or jealous, and if I said no she might think I was lying and not be to be trusted because of ignorance.

She turned and ran down the ladder and across the cobbled yard. She stopped at the stile and called. 'I'll race you to the porch, the last one's a softee.'

'Cheat,' I called and ran after her the farm collie Rex falling in beside me joining the chase. The sudden violent physical action was a relief from the last hours' tension. The turf was deep and springy under my flying feet and the whole valley was full of the golden evening sunshine and heart bursting happiness.

'Look out Gwen, my shadow's almost on your heels.' She had reached our orchard wall and was over it and running between the trees up the last steep slope to the edge of the lawn. My Mother was kneeling weeding the rose bed.

'Oh Mrs. Wade save me!' Almost out of breath with running and laughing Gwen tottered on tiring legs over the last few yards. I caught her, and we fell in an untidy heap at my Mother's side, the dog running and barking around us.

'Children when will you grow up?' Mother brushed her hair back out of her eyes with the back of her hand leaving a smear of soil across her forehead. Gwen, lying on her stomach propping her little elfin face in her hands, looked at her and said, 'It doesn't suit you Mrs. Wade.'

'What doesn't dear?'

'That oblique smear of Denbighshire across your forehead, clashes with your otherwise cool elegance.'

Mother concealed her irritation with one of her faint cocktail party smiles and got to her feet.

'The midges are beginning to bite, and it's about time to get supper ready so here endeth gardening for today, will you eat with us Gwen?'

'No thank you Mrs. Wade, we have only just got the last load of hay in and we have been working since half past seven this morning so I don't think that I'm fit to be seen in public until I've had a bath and changed.'

'Well come tomorrow evening then before you go to the dance.'

Gwen looked at me and smiled with a new gentleness, that I had not seen before and said, 'I'd love to come for supper thank you, but we've decided not to go to the dance.'

The rest of the evening dragged by, my Mother trying to interest me in getting together clothes for my departure for Hatfield two days later. My Father was fuming about the reverses which we were suffering in the Far East. I sat listening to the sound of their voices and made appropriate noises at the right moments, and watched the moon come rising over the thick creamy banks of cumulus clouds that were building up.

My Father opened the French windows and stood on the terrace looking out over the valley towards the Berwyns. The clouds were thick and black behind the rounded shoulders of the mountains and their undersides were illuminated by occasional flashes of lightning. It was too for away for the sound of thunder to reach us. He turned to me with a wry smile and said.

'You are soon going to see a demonstration of why engineering is a better bet than farming. At least three quarters of the farmers in this valley are going to spend a sleepless night worrying about their hay lying out in the fields. A year's work ruined by a few minutes peevish ill temper by the Almighty.'

'Arthur there is no need to be blasphemous.'

He laughed, 'Do you know why it's still lying out there dear? Because they're afraid of what the neighbours will say if they work on a Sunday. They are a pack of damned hypocrites, why even old Vaughan is as bad as the rest. If Gwen and Peter hadn't worked all day he'd have lost the lot. Old Pugh the sidesman saw a fox stalking his best goose on Sunday morning as he was going out to the closet, but shoot it – not on your life, the neighbours might hear about it – 'shooting on a Sunday Daniel Pugh, Deawch.' If I go to see the old devil on Monday and slip him a fiver, judiciously, and he will find the best part of a newly killed black market pig for me or supply me with enough petrol to take Peter to Hatfield. They are a pack of selfish narrow minded – it fills me with wonder that old Elwyn Vaughan and his dried up bitter as vinegar family could produce Gwen. That girl is the shining golden hope of this valley.'

I could hear my Mother knitting like a machine in the dusk. She grunted. 'The shining golden hope smelt like a stable when she was here earlier – and your son and heir was not much better.'

She always referred to me as 'your son' or 'your Father's son' when I was out of favour. My Father laughed and dug me in the ribs with his elbow.

'True, young Don Juan didn't smell much better before he had a bath, and the regulation five inches of hot water have not done much for him now.'

'Arthur there are times when you are unbearably coarse. Why don't you come inside and close the windows so that I can light the lamp.'

He didn't answer but sat sniffing the air like the little boy in the Bisto advertisement. 'That fox is about again Peter, we can't afford to let him get the chickens. I think I'll sit up for him tonight.'

I took the cue. 'No don't bother, I'll sit up, you have to work tomorrow. As a matter of fact I think I know where he lies up in the daytime, and I might be able to catch him on the way home.'

'Oh alright, take the twelve-bore, but for God's sake don't let anyone know if you get him, my name will be mud, a fox shot on my land!'

'Are you worried about what the neighbours will say?'

'I suppose I asked for that,' he said. 'Well that's what becomes of being married to a Welshwoman, aye mam?'

My mother sniffed vigorously, folded up her knitting and said, 'If you are going to sit in the dark, I'm going to bed. Don't lock yourself our Peter, and put plenty of warm clothes on. Goodnight dear, you won't be long Arthur will you?'

When she had gone, my father went to his desk and opened the top. He took out a whisky bottle and two glasses, poured himself a stiff tot and a smaller one for me and brought them out onto the terrace. We sat in the two old wicker chairs. He stretched his long legs out in front of him and raised his glass, 'Cheers!'

'Cheers!'

It was not an evening for conversation, and whenever a subject was exhausted I did nothing to revive it, or find a new topic. This ability to dull a conversation into frozen silence and send a tedious guest about his business, was a useful, if anti-social, trick borrowed from my mother's armoury of non-violent weapons. Eventually he took the only course, and stood up.

'You know, it's a queer thing Peter,' he said, 'but we never get around to talking about the things that matter. It was the same with my own father, one always felt that there was time to talk about things, tomorrow perhaps, but then he was dead and, well d'you know what I mean?'

'Not exactly, but –'

He ran his hands over his face in the way that a tired man does.

'Well you wouldn't of course, but one of the saddest things in life to me anyway, is the way that we fail to really get in touch with people who matter to us. We waste all our efforts trying to impress the wrong ones. You see, tomorrow, you're going off to start your own life, and you're going to make the same stupid mistakes that I made and get hurt in the same way. You'll probably hurt other people in the same way that I have always done as well, by stupid neglect and thoughtlessness.'

He walked past me into the house. I heard him stop half way across the room. 'I've only one bit of advice for you Peter, I'll spare you the rest. Just hang on to your integrity. Hang on 'till Hell freezes.'

'Goodnight.' He left me with the feeling that I should have said something and that a not-to-be repeated opportunity had been lost. I wanted to tell him that I had no enthusiasm for the career that lay ahead of me. Quite suddenly the prospect of being an engineer, tied to factory hours, desk and slide rule and only occasionally in contact with the hardware of my profession filled me with a sense of foreboding. Apart from anything else I did not feel that a boarding school had done much to fit me for living in a world with real men and women, but I didn't know what the answer was, and had missed the opportunity of seeking help.

I felt as if I had taken the first step in a very complicated and formal dance on the wrong foot. I waited until the sounds of running tap water, opening and closing doors and my mother's querulous sleeping voice, were stilled, then went to my room to change. The house was quiet, and moonlight poured into the kitchen as I opened the door into the yard. I picked up the shotgun from behind the dairy door, and put eight cartridges into my jacket pockets.

The threatened thunderstorm had still not come to a head although there was still an occasional flash of lightning over Denbigh Moor. Each field smelt, and felt, and sounded differently. Top Meadow with its newly cut hay felt warm as if it had absorbed the whole years sun and was quietly exuding its heat. Long Quarter, wedge shaped and thirsty, was tussocky and pocked with rabbit warrens. The water meadow was cool and tricky to negotiate with wide drainage ditches and areas of almost pure marsh. The river formed the boundary between our land and Vaughan's and because of the dry summer was only ankle deep.

It was another half mile to the farm, and although it was still only early I found that I was walking faster and faster. I stopped by the yard gate to get my breath back, heart pounding and knees shaking from exertion and tension.

The kitchen and bathroom lights were still lit but apart from the sound of a heifer lowing in the fields beyond the farm, all was quiet. Half an hour later the kitchen light went out, then the one in the bathroom. I wondered where the dog was, and felt in my pocket for the bag of rabbit scraps which I had brought her. The bag had burst, and filled my jacket with sodden brown paper, fat, bones and blood. My fingers groped about in the ruins while my mind ran on to imagine my mother's reaction – and questions next day.

Shotgun in hand, and ruinous dog-bribe in the other I made my

49

cautious way into the treacherous slough churned and befouled by the passage of thirty milking cows four times a day, which Vaughan called a yard. Where was that damned collie? An unpredictable beast, with the temperament of a prima-ballerina. She might be lurking almost anywhere, just waiting for the right moment to rush out and attack me from the rear, or just as likely, she might be off on one of her poaching jaunts.

'Here Bess, here Bess' I called, and was horrified by the unexpected hoarse and shaky bellow which I made. There was no reaction from the house. No lights, no opening windows and still no dog. The blood from the meat was beginning to drip between my fingers.

I arrived, stealthily like a burglar, at the front door porch, and was just wondering what to do with the disintegrating mess in my right hand when Bess appeared like a ghost beside me wagging her tail. She took my offering, like a wolf, and in two gulps disposed of it paper and all, then licked my fingers clean. I hoped that she would know when to stop.

'Go on girl, huss, good girl!'

She stood and looked at me, her feet apart and poised like a boxer, panting but she didn't move.

'Go on you damned fool,' I whispered hoarsely, but she didn't move an inch. I didn't feel inclined to turn my back on her knowing her temperament, so I propped the gun against the wall and groped behind me for the porch door handle. She shifted her weight and growled softly.

'Good girl, there's a good girl,' but she was not amused and I saw her teeth in the moonlight as she curled her lips in a rumbling snarl. I fished around in my pocket for any bits which may have fallen out of the bag and found what I hoped was some bacon rind and a piece of fat. While she took them I opened the door and quickly stepped inside.

She went crazy, barking and running about in circles. A sash window squeaked open upstairs. Old Vaughan hurled abuse at her in Welsh and slammed the window shut with a bang which made the porch rattle. I felt a childish desire to stick my tongue out at Bess, now whimpering with suppressed rage on the other side of the door. Occasionally she would sniff at the cracks in the door and push it with her fore-feet, but after a while she seemed to go away.

I cautiously got to my feet and stretched my cramped limbs. My watch said 1.30 am. My boots were muddy, so I sat on the step and took them off. The laces were covered in mud, and so in a few moments were my hands. I tried to see how dirty they were by the light of the moon, and as they came close to my face, I smelt gun oil, earth and stinking meat. A search of the porch revealed nothing with which I could clean my hands. Cutting my losses, I wiped them on my jacket, without a great deal of success.

The practical problems of the situation were beginning to obscure the reasons for my being there at all. I took off my raincoat, folded it and put it on top of my boots. My heart was beginning to thump again as I turned the front door handle. I felt like a burglar as the handle would turn no more and I pushed the door gently. It did not move. I tried again, and the letter box rattled, but the door remained firmly closed.

Gwen may have unlocked the door, but she had not reckoned with her father's mania for extra bolts, she must have forgotten one. It was hopeless, so I put my raincoat and boots on again and was about to leave when the dog, still on guard, began to snarl.

'Blast,' I said, and she growled again, only louder. This was a hell of a situation. I could just imagine the consequences of being found by Vaughan in the morning when he called for the day to collect the cattle and found me there. The questions, and the gossip, and my mother – my God!

I was driven to desperate means. My raincoat was stout. If I could only get out of the porch quickly and wrap it round the dog's head before she had time to bark or bite me. I had no choice, so I had started to take it off when the heifer started bellowing again. This time it was insistent so I waited to see if anyone was woken by it. A bedroom light went on, and the porch became almost as light as day. Blackout didn't mean a thing in this part of the world. I waited anxiously to see if he would come out of the front of the house, but my luck held. I heard the back door open and close, then his bad tempered, sleep laden voice calling for Bess.

The fool animal yelped and rushed about outside the porch reluctant to give up its catch, but torn by a well developed sense of duty. At last the sense of duty won and she ran round the side of the house to join him. I was out of the porch before she could change her mind. Pausing only to pick up the gun I fled from the scene before the fates could get their talons into me again – already preparing my alibi in an imaginary conversation with Gwen.

'Well yes, I probably could have got in through the kitchen door after your father left, but actually, I tripped in the yard and I broke my ankle. No, no it doesn't hurt at all really. Of course, I couldn't tell the family, they'd wonder how it happened,' and found myself limping most realistically down the Home Farm lane. I stopped at the edge of the willow thicket and settled myself down in the hollow formed by the eroded root system of the fallen elm tree to wait for the fox. The night was full of sounds and scents and the first light behind the Clwyds came quickly and almost unnoticed at first.

A dog barked in the village, and another nearer until by a chain reaction they were giving tongue up and down the valley for miles. I waited for the dawn chorus, and was just about to change my position when I saw him. He had stopped at the edge of the path one forefoot poised above the glistening grass, scarred grey flecked muzzle upwind turned away from me. The gentle wind dragging its fingers through the trees above his head masked the sound of the safety catch clicking into the 'fire' position and the rustle of my raincoat as the butt came into my shoulder.

Squinting along the gleaming steel valley between the barrels, his outline was indistinct, but as he began to move, my finger squeezed against the trigger. The recoil kicked me back to reality, while the rearing barrels saved me from the ugliness of his dying.

The flat echo of the shot sent a pair of wood pigeons crashing out of the far side of the trees above me and rushing away in headlong flight. The fox lay on his side on the path. His muzzle was scarred, his ears ragged and his brush was flecked with grey.

I opened the breach of the gun and ejected the warm and stinking cartridge, together with the live round from the choke-barrel. The smooth wood and warm steel in my hands, the shining bores and the dead blood-spattered fox filled me with a hungry brand of sadness and a feeling of identification with the animal which I could neither understand nor discuss.

The broad, ragged wings of a cloud of rooks beat the air in silent procession over my head. I put two fresh cartridges into the breaches and snapped the gun shut. Death was in the air, in my forefinger curled round the front trigger – the squeeze of a finger between the fox and me.

The sun was coming up behind the Nant-y-Garth pass, and my last day at home had begun. Tomorrow, next year, everything would be quite different and nothing would ever be so important or deeply felt. I had put on my first piece of armour.

CHAPTER 3

Suspicion

FOR SEVERAL days after Major Warrender's visit I was left in peace, and apart from a duty call by the C of E padre, I saw only the doctors and nurses. The padre posted some letters for me, and left some magazines and English daily papers, having satisfied himself that the hospital had furnished my bedside table with a Bible.

Nearly every other day there was a letter from either my mother or father, Gwen's letters which had begun to diminish in number the longer we were apart became more frequent, stimulated by news of my wounds no doubt. It was now commonly accepted that we would one day marry, by everyone that is except my mother, who probably had vague ideas about pushing the family up to its previous minor eminence by an alliance with at least a General's daughter. She made all the dutiful gestures to Gwen, but the barriers were never lowered, and she never referred to her in any of her letters to me.

In fact Gwen and I had begun to drift away from each other as our interests widened and we made other friends. She was naturally sociable and liked having a good time, and I had become more absorbed with my work and engine tuning during my training at Hatfield. Aircraft and engines fascinated me. The resin bonded plywood structure of the Mosquito filled me with a new excitement almost bordering on religious zeal. The very boldness of the conception and its fantastic strength to weight ratio represented the biggest technological success of the war to me, but this was before we saw the Gloster/Whittle jet. During my last year before I joined the Army, I was in lodgings with a Rolls Royce engine representative who used to race a Bugatti at Donington before the war, and it was from him that I heard of the Issigonis, Austin special and John Bolsters' Bloody Mary, both these cars used wood as the basis of their construction. Weekends when I was expected to go home or to meet Gwen in London, I spent working on a sprint special which used everything that I had learned about aircraft structures.

I went for help to the people at High Wycombe who developed the resin bonded plywood to a point where it could reasonably be used for a 400mph aircraft. Although they told me nothing about the chemistry or production methods they told me where I was going wrong and one of their directors pre-fabricated sections of the chassis for me. Using the lightest sections of plywood and light alloy doublers with large numbers of high tensile cadmium plated steel bolts at points of high stress concentration, at the end of six months concentrated spare-time work, I had a chassis of which I was very proud.

Our section leader in the Drawing Office was very interested and gave me a lot of practical help, saving me a lot of time by checking and correcting my calculations. The landlord and his wife had very mixed feelings about The Thing, which they were sure would be the end of my romance with Gwen and probably the end of me.

Gwen only came down once, and when she found that the car was to be a monoposto affair and not something which could be used to take her out, she was furious. When she found that I had just spent the remainder of the years' allowance which my father made to me, as well as my pocket money for the week, to buy an unsavoury looking 1100cc supercharged Jap engine, we had our first major row. She had the idea that we might be able to spend the weekend together at a pub somewhere on the Thames. She only had a couple of pounds left after the rail fare from Wrexham so she had to share a bedroom with my landlady's daughter on the Friday night, and went home on the first train on Saturday after lunch.

On Monday morning there was a telegraphic money order from my father, and a letter in the next post telling me in no uncertain terms that I had behaved boorishly and would report home on the following Saturday morning to humble myself before Gwen. So it went on, partings and reconciliations, then I joined up and everyone wagged their heads sagely and said.

'It'll be the making of him and bring him back to reality.'

Gwen suddenly realised that her old standby was in danger of escaping altogether and began to talk of marriage with increasing frequency. The idea of marrying before I had achieve anything or had been anywhere seemed ridiculous, but my conscience told me that this was selfish and that I should think of her. Accordingly we became officially engaged the day I was commissioned and I got hilariously drunk for the first time in my life. I now had a breathing space because officially we could not marry without the CO's permission before I was 25, and I was only 20. A very wise rule.

Our ideas about so many things were changing and in the last four years we had become very different people. I had always been used to succeeding in whatever I did, and generally getting my own way. I had never liked large group activities and crowds of people, parties and school games and was perfectly happy to spend a complete day engaged in some solitary job on the farm like hedging or ploughing. Gwen on the other hand was happiest in a crowd and was captain of her school hockey team and rode with Flint and Denbigh hounds. Although we both loved horses the hunting set irritated me. Because of my father I would have been welcomed by his friends and associates in the hunt. It always annoyed Gwen that I would not go to meets with her particularly as people always asked her where I was. We were both fond of show jumping as were our parents as this was a common interest which brought us together.

The Army threw me into a barrack room and taught me to live with masses of people and even to like it. It gave me self-confidence in dealing with other people, and made me a leader before I had learned that arrogance was not an attractive feature. Gwen in the meanwhile had gone to Bangor University with the intention of becoming a vet and judging from her letters was enjoying her extra-mural activities.

Reading her latest letter, I saw that the dominant emotion behind every phrase which referred to me was not love, but pity. The realisation shocked me although I knew that I deserved nothing more. It also reminded me that this was my life, that I was still alive and that there was no need to be pushed about by the odd currents and side winds of existence. There was no need to drift aimlessly into a marriage that would in time become a chain tying us together. There was no need to lie here and have my career in the Army ruined by one disgruntled military policeman with a bee in his bonnet. I decided to get my mind onto some new track altogether and picking up the Bible beside my bed, opened it at random to begin reading. It fell open at Zachariah and my eyes focussed on verse seven of chapter two:

Deliver thyself O Zion that dwellest with the daughter of Babylon. For thus saith the Lord of Hosts; After the glory hath he sent me into the nations which spoiled you; for he that toucheth you toucheth the apple of his eye. For behold I will shake mine hand upon them and they shall be a spoil to their servants, and ye shall know that the Lord of Hosts hath sent me.

The complete passage was precisely underlined with red pencil. I rang the bell for the nurse, and a military policeman opened the door.

'What do you want sir?'

'I would like to speak to Sister Antrobus'

'Right sir, I'll get her.'

He picked up a telephone from a wall shelf beside the door and rang through to the sister's office. She came in almost immediately.

'Yes Mr. Wade, what do you want?'

'Can you tell me who put this Bible here Sister?'

She looked at it. 'Yes it was a new one and I took it out of its wrappings when it arrived. Why what is the matter with it?'

I showed it to her. 'That passage was underlined Sister, and if you remember that is the same text that was pinned to the body of the two Palestine police officers found hanged at Haifa.'

'I remember it distinctly – it was in the newspaper report, but shortened a bit.' She looked puzzled, 'I don't understand.'

'Neither do I, would you mind finding out for me, without telling the police, where it came from and who actually brought it in.'

'Well I don't think I ought to, it seems more like a job for the police to me.'

'Please Sister, these damned policemen seem to think that I'm in league with the Jews so I can't expect much help from them.'

'So that's why you're under arrest is it?'

'Who said I was?'

'Well there is always at least one MP and sometimes a Palestine policeman on duty outside. As far as I'm concerned you're on your own.' She slammed the Bible down onto my bedside and strode out. For the first time fear touched me.

If the Stern Gang or the Irgun had decided to get me, no-one here was going to lift a finger to stop them. One MP with a hand gun wouldn't stand a chance, particularly if his role was to make sure that I could not try to run away. Who the hell could help me or would even want to? Not the Colonel, he had gone back to Fayid and that was hundreds of miles away. Certainly not the police they probably still believed that I was working with the Zionists, and this warning would only confirm their suspicions.

It looked as if my alleged accomplices were just reminding me not to talk. Perhaps they were! Perhaps it was someone else trying to frame me? My mind raced over all the possibilities. Perhaps Deborah substituted this Bible for the first one? Perhaps she had been detailed to kill me, after all her two brothers were in the Irgun or something similar.

'My God boy, now you're really in the mire,' I said it aloud and it sounded funny. I said it again and laughed at the lunacy of it all. The door opened and the policeman looked in. 'Do you want something sir?'

'Yes,' I said, 'I would like you to contact Major Warrender for me, I'd like a word with him.'

'Who is he sir?' This was a little puzzling.

'The chap in civilian clothes who was in here earlier this week. I'd like to know where the statement is that he is preparing for me to sign, and if possible I would like to see him as soon as he is able.'

'Well I will pass on your request through the APM sir, but I don't know the officer you mean, is he one of ours?'

' He told me he was an SIB man.' The policeman looked even more puzzled.

'I know most of them sir, and there isn't a Warrender of any rank, that I know. Are you sure you've got it right? What did he look like?' I described him, but drew a blank.

'He must be either a new bloke or a Pal CID man sir. Sergeant Meredith is having a cup of tea with Sister Antrobus in her office now sir, shall I ask him to come up?'

'Yes would you please?'

A few minutes after the policeman closed the door, the sergeant came in, he was the Palestine police sergeant with whom I had crossed swords earlier.

'Come in Sergeant and sit down will you?'

'Afternoon sir.'

'Sergeant first of all I want to apologise for being so rude to you the other day, it was very wrong of me.'

'Thank you sir.'

'You probably heard since why I was so annoyed. No-one had told me what was going on or why I was being pestered in spite of being so ill. Even now the hospital staff seem to think that I am under arrest for collaboration with the enemy. Put yourself in my position and imagine the rest.'

'I quite understand sir, but you did lead off a bit. Here is the statement from Major Warrender for you to sign.'

'He seems to be a very nice sort of chap,' I ventured. 'I didn't realise that he was with you at first and not the Army.'

'Who said he was sir?' I looked up after finishing the sentence I was reading. This almost brought us back to the dead end.

'Oh it must have been something he said or implied. Do you think I could have a word with him?' I signed the statement.

'I'll get him for you sir.' He went out and spoke to the MP who picked up the phone and asked for a number. The sergeant came back into the room

'About this arrest business sir, the guard is for your own protection. They are there night and day, and they're armed for the same reason you have no visitors except the padre and us. We think that you inadvertently let slip some information to someone who is passing information to the Irgun and in your case a Haganah group which was getting a bit Barbary.'

'Now whoever this person is, and they are probably in one of the two organisations, they would no doubt like to get rid of you in case you can give us a lead to them, and you might you know. Someone in your circle of contacts perhaps? Because you haven't been here long, you're very valuable to us because that circle is still quite small. Are you with me sir?'

'Yes I follow.'

'Previously we have had other leakages of information which have led to successful attacks on us, and the one common factor is 1st Armed Div. H.Q. Now do you see where you fit in?'

'Yes I do Sergeant, but why the hell didn't someone tell me all this before?'

'Quite frankly sir, because the APM was convinced that you were the Irgun informant, particularly as you already had a Jewish girl friend.'

'But that is crazy, if I had been passing information none of my supposed Jewish friends would be stupid enough to visit me knowing that I was surrounded by police.'

'Well I realise that sir, but the APM isn't 100% convinced.'

'What about Major Warrender, surely by now he has checked all my circle of contacts, such as it is. My social life here hasn't been anything, to rate a report in the *Tatler.*'

'Well he's coming along to see you sir, I should ask him your-self, but in the meantime if there is anything you want just let me know.'

'Has Miss Weinstock been again?' I asked.

'No sir, but she rings each day and asks how you are. Would you like to see her?'

'No it doesn't matter really, but I would like you to let her know that I am alright and the doctors say that I should be up and able to sit in a chair in a week or two. Perhaps they will allow her to come and see me again then if she can spare the time.'

'Yes certainly sir if you like I'll call and deliver the message myself.'

'Very good Sergeant, thank you. I suppose you know where

she lives, because I don't.'

'Yes sir I know, I'll call on my way home tonight and bring you any message tomorrow.' I thanked him and he left.

When Major Warrender called, I was being washed before lights out. The doctor on duty was reluctant to let him in but he persisted and sat down patiently in the corridor until the nurses had finished with me. When he came in, he asked how I was and if the statement was correct, and we chatted about hospitals generally.

I handed him the Bible opened at Zachariah. 'Where did this come from? The sister won't tell me because she hates my guts, thinks I'm a traitor.'

He called the policeman in and told him to get Sergeant Meredith to check how the Bible got to me, at the double. He looked visibly shaken.

'You don't think this is genuine?' I asked.

'No,' he said 'not at its face value but it does not mean that it's a joke either. I think someone is trying to give you the shits. It looks to me like the heavy handed methods of the military police, but we'll know when Meredith finishes his investigations, he's an excellent man. The APM is keen but rather inclined to panic measures and he probably hopes to make you talk by frightening you.'

I smiled, but held my tongue. This was more dangerous than the APM's bluster.

'What do you think?' he asked.

'I think that I am an inert pawn in a game which I don't understand, and whatever happens, I stand to lose. When you people have finished playing cat and mouse with me and finally decided that I am just a Cornet in a tank regiment trying to get fit so that I can get back to work, no-one will want to know me. Everywhere I go people will know half the story and guess the worst as they always do and I will be followed by mutterings and rumours. I can just hear them now, 'there's no smoke without fire.' It would just kill my father if he knew what the hospital staff think.'

'You're over-dramatising the situation. They have too little to do here, and gossip fills in the time. Besides I understand your recommendation for an MC has gone through and has been endorsed by the divisional commander. As soon as you are fit to be moved,' he went on, 'they are going to take you to the British Military Hospital at Fayid in the Canal Zone away from possible reprisals. Then you can convalesce at their place at Gineifa on the lake, and believe me it's very pleasant there. You will be near to your Regiment and your friends can visit you. In the meanwhile, you sleep. The guard will be strengthened from now on and you will only be visited by Sergeant Meredith and me, so go to sleep and stop worrying.' He wished me goodnight and went.

The following morning both he and Sgt. Meredith were there soon after the day staff came on duty. Warrender sat down beside the bed and stared at me, Meredith stood at the foot.

'That Bible was bought in Jerusalem by the APM himself and put beside your bed on his orders by the man on duty three nights ago. He bought the Bible from a NAAFI shop and they are in the clear. It's almost certain that he marked the thing himself. He has also been shooting his mouth off about having caught the informant and although he hasn't mentioned your name, it was implied. He is pointing the finger at you, and everyone is now waiting for you to be arrested. Last night he traced your Jewish girlfriend and found who she is. Now what do you think he will do next?'

'Why should he do anything?'

'You know damned well – she is the half sister of the Bernstein brothers and they are two boys we've been looking for, for a long time.'

'Why do you suppose she came here then?' I used every bit of self-control to hide my feelings. A lie detector could have given me away, my heart was beating like a trapped rabbit and my mouth was very dry.

'I believe that she was sent here to incriminate you and divert suspicion from someone else who was more useful to them. It seems a risky thing for them to do though, and she is a very brave young woman to try it. Now if everything goes to plan, my suspect is going to try and cook your goose finally today, and when he tries to come and see you we will finish our search of his quarters. We have almost enough evidence for a case now, but if possible I want the names of his contacts and his letter box addresses. His bank account and Mess bills are pretty damaging, he is spending twice as much as he is officially earning already and he has no private income.'

Just as he was speaking the door opened and a middle aged civilian in a light grey lounge suit came in.

'Hello John,' said Warrender, I thought you were watching the Curtis menage.'

'I was, but there doesn't seem much point in it now. On his way back in this morning he caught sight of one of our boys watching the house and recognised him.'

'O hellfire,' said Warrender. 'What happened?'

'Nothing then,' said the newcomer, 'except that he gave our man a rocket for being so bloody obvious, he seemed to think it was funny, then he went inside and blew his brains out with a Colt automatic.'

'Did he leave any note?'

'Not a damned thing, we've searched the bungalow from top to bottom but there's not a scrap of evidence apart from a little more than 500 Palestinian pounds in between the pages of Kings Regulations in the bookcase and the best part of two dozen empty whisky bottles in the kitchen under the sink. His liver must be in a hell of a state.' Warrender stood up wearily and stretched.

'Oh well here comes another day, roll on bloody demob.'

They seemed to have forgotten me, and began to discuss the final report on the case quite openly. I had served my limited purpose. The APM, poor devil, had tried to set me up as a suspect to direct enquiries from himself. He had thoroughly blackened my name and left me to clear myself. I don't suppose I even crossed his mind in the few seconds before he pressed the trigger and solved his own problems.

Sgt Meredith saw me watching them and spoke to Warrender. 'What about Mr. Wade sir?'

'Oh yes Mr. Wade.' He turned towards me. 'Mr. Wade can return to his role of temporary acting local unpaid hero, on paper anyway, although I doubt if his friends and comrades will see the sun shining out of his arse as brightly as he does.' He smiled at me, with as much warmth as a November sun.

'Perhaps after he has been here a little longer he will get as tired as we are of being set up as targets for the Irgun and either crack up like that poor bastard, or just perhaps get a weeny bit sick of the sight of Jews, even female Jews.'

The bitterness of this attack was something new to me its savagery and injustice leaving me speechless.

'When you next see her, if you ever see her again, you can tell her that I have been hunting her brothers for the last two years and if it takes me till the end of the Mandate I'll get them and send them home to her old Jackal of a father, in a sack.'

Both the sergeant and the CID man looked embarrassed and turned away to leave. Warrender went out quickly pushing them aside.

Meredith came over to the bed. 'Don't take any notice of him sir, we all have our off days here.'

I held out my hand to him and he took it. 'Good luck sir, I hope you are soon better.'

'Thank you Sergeant and I suppose goodbye.'

They left and collected the MP from the corridor as they went. He put his head round the door and waved. When they had gone, I suddenly realised that I had not had breakfast. I was hungry.

Although the SIB and police were no longer interested in me, and the sentry had been taken off my door, he was replaced by changing teams of plain clothes Palestine police. No-one other than medical staff came to see me in the weeks that followed. Being in a private ward, I saw none of the other patients, and they were apparently not even sufficiently moved by curiosity to visit me. I knew that B Squadron were still at Akaba and would still be running the patrols across the Negev, so I had hoped that someone from there might call. There was to be a polo tournament at Sarafand at the end of August so there would be a chance of someone finding the time to visit me then.

I occupied my days by writing letters and trying to remember what Gwen looked like and how her voice sounded. My mind would not produce a clear image. It showed me Deborah instead.

I told myself that I was being stupid, that she had probably come to see me out of a sense of duty. At the most I had only seen her for half an hour of stilted self-conscious conversation. It was only love for her brother and gratitude that made her come, and pity that brought her back. Perhaps it was not pity but a chance of turning me into a genuine traitor. It seemed obvious the more I thought about it, but it seemed inconceivable. I found myself making excuses for her and wishing that she would come again. On Sunday morning, 1st August, I was allowed to sit in a chair and the Padre called to see me with a letter from Sgt. Meredith.

In it he told me briefly that he had called to see Deborah but her father would not let him into the home. He had however spoken to him in the garden, and he had agreed to pass on my message. Deborah was apparently in the Canal Zone attending an interview for a job with a French engineer's family – but would be back sometime at the weekend. I looked up at the Padre and he was smiling.

'Well, I never thought that you were going to smile again,' he said. 'This is a distinct improvement.'

I felt myself blushing and the more I told myself that I was being a fool, the worse it became.

'It's simply that I thought all my friends had deserted me and I was beginning to think like a defeated man, but right at this moment I don't give a damn!'

He laughed, 'It must be love or drink, and as they don't allow alcohol in here, it must be the other – but what has the estimable Sgt Meredith got to do with it?'

'I don't know that 'love' as such enters into it, Padre, it is probably a bit of homesickness crystallised by the appearance of an attractive girl from my own part of England, just when I was feeling ill and at loggerheads with the world. Meredith is no way involved, except that he delivered a letter for me.'

'That sounds reasonable, but not wholly convincing. You couldn't see your own face when you read that letter. I suppose you already have a girl at home waiting for you?'

'Yes, I'm afraid I have Padre, and moreover we are engaged.'
He sighed and looked at me reproachfully.

'The best thing you could do would be to leave here without seeing her again. I presume that it is the young lady of the Jewish faith?'

'Yes it is Padre, why?'

'I understand that her family are not exactly well disposed towards us, and the difference in faith is a considerable barrier.'

'No-one is talking of marriage Padre, I have only seen her once, and then briefly. If I don't see her again the fleeting memory I have of her now will be like the face of a beautiful woman seen in another passing train. You will never see her again or know who she is or what she is like. It would haunt me for the rest of my life, but if we got to know each other better, the chances are that the illusion would not stand up to a searching examination. The difference between us would kill it.'

He looked dubious. 'That sounds like a cool appraisal but it isn't you know, you have made up your mind, and you are probably wondering how you can tell your girl in England that you are going to run off with a Jewess.' He stood up to go.

'But before you say it, it's none of my business really, I will go. If I can help, let me know. Don't forget that you have to ask the Colonel's permission to marry and in this case it might not be forthcoming.

'Padre, once more, I don't even know the girl, and in any case, I have no doubt that her family would be more against the idea than the Colonel. Thank you for calling though, and your offer of help.'

After lunch had been cleared away, I was put back to bed, and got on with writing to Sgt Crompton about the boys who were wounded and asked him for the addresses of the parents of the dead. I could hear a little more activity in the corridor as visitors for the other patients passed.

I was just sealing the envelope when Deborah came in. She was wearing a plain white linen sleeveless dress and sandals with short heels. She stood in the doorway holding the door open for a moment without speaking.

'You look lovely Deborah – you've robbed me of my last shred of manners. Please come in and sit down. No, here where I can see you without breaking my neck.'

'I can easily see that you are better. In fact I don't feel too safe. How are you really?'

I told her that I had been out of bed and asked her how Jacob was. He was apparently in hospital under another name, ostensibly the victim of a bad motorcycle accident. The conversation flowed along as if we had always known each other. She had brought me fresh fruit and a pair of slippers from Egypt and told me about the job she had just got with the Lapointe family at El Kantara. I asked her why she had gone to Egypt for a job, and why as a governess. She looked at me and raised her eyebrows mockingly.

'And why should I not, Mr. Wade? Did I omit to obtain your permission? If you really want to know it was so that I can make sure that you are being properly cared for, we feel a little bit responsible for you.'

'How can you care for me when you are in the Canal Zone and I'm in Palestine?' I wondered how she knew, because this move was supposed to be for my protection.

'Because my dear Peter, as you probably well know, you are going to be transferred to a little hospital at Gineifa which is just about a couple of miles away from the dutiful Deborah's new job.'

'Who the hell told you?'

'It was important to me to know what was happening to you, there were police all round you and the rumour was all round the hospital and the garrison that you were under close arrest. There were some people who wanted to know why of all people the British should arrest you. There would have been more sense in it if they had given you a medal. Naturally we were curious, and I was particularly curious, so set out to ask some of our friends to find out for me.'

'Who –'

She leant forward quickly and put her fingers over her lips. Her lips were close to my ear, and she whispered.

'Please don't ask any more questions Peter, this room might well have microphones and I've been very indiscreet already.' I kissed the fingers on my lips. She sat back quickly.

'The sooner you and your fiancée are together again the better it will be for her.

'Who told you I had a fiancée?'

'A young man I know.'

'What else did he tell you?'

A nurse came in with a tray carrying tea and sandwiches. She smiled at me, then said 'The sandwiches are cheese and tomato,' and turned to Deborah 'there is no ham.'

Deborah smiled. 'How considerate of you nurse.' When she went I turned to Deborah.

'I'm sorry about that, she must have a bit of a mood on.'

'I'm sorry for you Peter, I didn't think when I came to see you what people would say. I won't come again.' Her face was very pale.

'Please Deborah come again – it's only because of the rumours. You know there's no smoke without fire, it's nothing to do with you personally. Besides I want you to come, more than I have ever wanted anything else. Will you?'

'Don't start getting any silly romantic notions about me. You're engaged to an English girl and I am a Jewess and an enemy. Apart from any other consideration I just can't afford to get involved. I just feel sorry for you anyway.'

'How brutal can you get? But never mind. I'll settle for a little sympathy at the moment as long as you carry on coming to see me. Will you?'

'Well I start my new job in a month, and I don't suppose that I will get a lot of free time between now and then, but I'll see if I can find the time.' I looked at her hands, which were not as calm as her face.

'I am sorry, I shouldn't have asked you like that. It isn't fair of course, because your own people will not like it. Forget it.'

She flushed, with what I wrongly supposed to be embarrassment. 'Peter you are a fool, you know nothing about people, you're not safe to be let out without your mother. Just leave me to do the worrying. Let's drop the subject.'

'I am sorry.'

'For heavens sake stop saying you're sorry, you'll drive me mad!' She was twisting her gloves into a rope and untwisting them.

'While you are biting my head off lassie, the tea is going cold.'
She laughed.

'You make me feel as if I am at home, I mean in England, when a crisis seems unavoidable, make a pot of tea.'

'Do you still think of it as home?' She handed me my tea.

'When I talk to you, it reminds me, and I feel a little homesick. Israel is a very different thing for me compared with a survivor of Auschwitz. I see no point in all this killing. You are bound to get out eventually. To me, as a woman it seems particularly horrible to work up all this hatred and bitterness to rob families of their fathers and children and husbands when we all know that in a few years we will probably need you as business associates or even allies. I resent your being here, carrying arms but the idea of you dying as a political gesture, is inhuman. You belong to a pig-headed race Peter, you have never acknowledged defeat and it's a very good thing for Europe and us that you didn't, but now it's just that self same stiff-necked conviction that you are right that is keeping you here. The same stupid attitude that's getting you killed.'

'You are as English as I am and you must have been on Merseyside during the Blitz. Did you think of yourself as anything but English then?'

'No, I suppose not, but circumstances change, we must keep to our convictions and our faith.'

'Don't you mean that you must keep in step with your kind, because it's easier?' She looked at me quickly.

'You don't have a very high opinion of my character do you. Do you think a decision to leave a comfortable life in England and come out here was easy to make?'

'Oh I appreciate that it must have been a terrible decision to make, to leave dirty, smoky, scruffy bomb-blasted Liverpool and that good-for-the-soul rationing, for the ordeal which all this glorious sunshine and wide open Mediterranean coast must be. It shows great patriotism.'

'Peter, you're a pig. You're laughing at me – don't Englishmen have ideals?'

'Not until they retire, there isn't time for it. After they stop working for a living, their repressed ideals come creeping out. They all retire to the country and try to stop progress by protesting whenever anyone tries to straighten a road or bring in electricity or abolish hanging. If anyone shows signs of letting his ideals get out of hand before 65 he's labelled an eccentric, possibly a revolutionary and certainly someone to be avoided. Not ostracised, just avoided.'

'Look at me for example although no-one knows it yet, I have stepped right out of line. Every movement of my life as a professional soldier in the British Army is ordered from the moment I get up to when I go to bed, or die. It's like a damned great ballet, every step worked out. How I should act in any conceivable circumstance already has an acceptable precedent. It is almost without doubt the most humane and downright common sense Army in the world today. The trouble is that it takes a hellish long time to adapt itself to change and it is not allowed to anticipate trends. If I said to my troop, I don't want to be called 'sir' every other minute, call me Peter, or we'll abolish lights out, although these things will happen one day, it's no use trying to hurry them along. Anyone who does rocks the boat. He won't be wanted. I don't say that I have a great urge to do these things, I don't probably because I don't have the strength of character or the courage of my own convictions, but these are lines over which I will not step. I think that this is true for nearly every British soldier.

'You couldn't take a troop of soldiers and say there are twenty Jews who are probably terrorists make them dig their own graves, then shoot them. You can't do it because whatever training you give an Englishman he knows what is right and fair and unless he is already a villain won't break his own personal code. Apart from anything else you can't push him around. For the same reason, I didn't stick to my lines in the play, although it would have been easier and it would have done me a lot of good professionally. What I have done is wrong you know Deborah. I know it and so would any soldier. In effect I have captured one of the enemy's weapons and instead of destroying it, given it back to them to be repaired. Now it may kill other British soldiers and I will be responsible.

'It may even kill me; so as a professional soldier I have failed in my first job. If I had done the same thing with a rifle, I would have been court martialled, cashiered and served at least two years detention. My mind boggles at the present possibilities. But, if I had done what the book says, I just couldn't have lived with myself. I don't want to be that sort of man so you see the rot has set in. I have stepped out of line and because I am too soft-hearted to allow the commonly accepted rules to sort out my problems, I'm probably doomed to failure in everything I do.'

'Peter, for God's sake, the three in one Judge, Jury and Accused.' She pointed to the ceiling and mouthed, 'We may have an audience.' And then as she walked over to the window, 'You just can't win and certainly not when you're in this self-destruct mode. What can I say to help you?'

'You can ask me to have another cup of tea,' I said and looked at my watch.

'Good Lord look at the time it's six o'clock, the sister must have forgotten us. How are you going to get home; wherever that is?'

'My father brought me, he's got an old Plymouth and we have a house in Ben Yehuda Street in Jerusalem. Any more questions?'

'Yes for heavens sake, do you mean that he has been sitting outside in that blazing sun all this time?'

'Oh no, he went on to see some friends at the kibbutz not far from here. They are on the 'phone so, I will ring him when the sister throws me out.' She took my cup and smoothed the turned over sheet.

'How do you get petrol? Aren't your movements restricted?'

'Ask no questions, and you'll be told no lies,' she said and patted my hand in mock reproof.

I caught her hand and held it between mine and to my astonishment found that my heart was thumping wildly with excitement. Instead of taking it away, she gave me her other hand as well and smiled.

'It's obviously time for me to leave, before you start getting amorous and step even further out of line.' She withdrew her hands and stood up pulling on her gloves, then walked over to the door.

'I'm going to see a friend of yours tonight Peter and I'm going to remind him of his obligations to you. I might even persuade him to retire from active service altogether. Will that make you any happier?'

When she had gone, I lay back and tried to analyse why and how she was beginning to occupy so much of my mind. Perhaps I would be able to get things back in perspective when I saw more people and could get up and get on with my duties. I had nothing else to do here but lie and think, and she was my only visitor.

On each remaining day of that month she came and stayed as long as she was allowed. We talked about our lives before we had met, and the people we knew and each day that passed made me more depressed to think that we would not be seeing each other after Saturday, for heaven knows how long. I gave her my home address and agreed that if she wrote there her letters would always find me and she gave me the El Kantara address and telephone number. We were both irritable and depressed possibly by the oppressive heat and in my case by the news of the latest bomb incidents and murders. About ten minutes before the end of visiting time, she asked if she could bring her father in and I said that I would like to meet him. Just as she was going out to him, she stopped as if she was going to say something then went.

To my relief, he was even more ill-at-ease and unsure of what was expected of him than I was. We both noticed this silence simultaneously and it broke down the barrier. He was short and swarthy with a shock of iron grey hair and large black moustache streaked with grey. He must have been somewhere between 50 and 60 and looked bronzed and fit. The conversation was formal and trivial until he mentioned Deborah, then he looked serious.

'Mr. Wade, I must talk to you simply and come to the point without preamble. I and my family hope that Deborah will settle down here in our country and marry a Jewish boy. She is still very young but she has a mind of her own and these days particularly in our country we want people who can think for themselves and who have their roots here. We are very grateful to you, but that does not mean that we will allow you to play fast and loose with Deborah.'

'But...' I began.

'Please let me finish even if I am wrong. We want her to be happy, but I know from experience that even if you consider marrying her that this is no good. It cannot work. It would be hard for you both and even more hard for your children. If I forbid you to meet, I am a fool. I am sending her to be near you at El Kantara, and you can talk about these things and you will see in time that it is impossible. If you still want each other, it will be without my blessing but I will not interfere.'

I looked at Deborah, but dared not say anything to her because she looked as if a kind word or a cross one might equally well reduce her to tears. I turned to her father.

'I think too much of Deborah to make her unhappy, but it's pointless to talk about the future now. I'm in no position to predict my own future yet. I don't even know if I am going to be fit enough to stay in the Army.' There was a strained silence broken only by the whine of the fan and the ceaseless buzzing of flies.

'We will go now Deborah,' he said looking towards her and standing up. He shook my hand and said 'Thank you' before going. Deborah stayed until he went through the door, then walked towards me.

The sister came and stood holding the door open. 'You must leave now Miss Weinstock.'

'Yes sister,' said Deborah, and turned to me. She was trying hard not to cry.

'Did I do wrong to tell him Peter? You see I had to get him to persuade Jacob not to go back, it was for you. I have tried not to let this happen to us, but I don't mind if you don't.'

'Oh Deborah, you glorious crazy girl. There are no problems. No problems at all. Nothing can go wrong now. Look after yourself till I get to Gineifa, don't smile at any strange soldiers and don't forget, 'up the scousers'.'

She was embarrassed by the presence of the silent, watchful sister and blew me a self conscious kiss before she turned and went. The situation looked distinctly brighter.

The weeks rolled by until a few days before I was due to be packed off to Gineifa, three of the officers from my regiment and Sergeant Crompton came in. One of them was the adjutant Captain

Wood who told me that Crompton's decoration was through. Apparently another officer had been given my troop at Akaba and I would have to be a spare body for a while, probably acting as Intelligence Officer and stay at RHQ in Fayid. The other two officers were leaders from B Squadron John Cooper and Pip Hugill who was Senior Subaltern. The three of them looked fit, efficient and self confident and very professional. Their visit further helped to boost my morale, and I was eager to get away from the little cell-like ward which had been my prison for so long.

I had been particularly pleased to see Crompton who although still on crutches was mending rapidly. He would probably be down-graded but this would not exclude him from the Quartermaster Sergeant job which was shortly about to become vacant – winning an MM within a few days of re-joining had sent his stock soaring.

They had come to Sarafand for the Polo competitions and were confident that they could beat the nearest opposition, the Arab Legion Team which was captained by an ex-Dragoon Guard.

Giniefa

Three days later, I was on the train, rattling across the Sinai desert to El Kantara. I felt like a troglodyte, dragged out of its cave in pyjamas into the daylight and bustle of the train and stations. The world looked strange and the faces of its people seemed ugly and menacing when viewed from a stretcher. The noise, the turmoil, the dust and heat and the flies as well as the stink of people and the lurching movement, made my new little hospital ward seem cool and welcoming.

So this was Gineifa. It smelled the same – ether and carbolic soap, new paint and the strange sickly sweet smell of Egypt, sucked in through the Venetian blinds by the same old noisy table fan.

It looked the same, cream and green paint, the iron tubular bed, the red blanket and bedside table – but what was this. Three yellow roses. Roses in Egypt are not so common that they would be put in a stranger's room. Perhaps they belonged to the last patient who occupied this bed I thought. But it seemed unlikely that they would just leave them. The RAMC orderlies who carried me in gossiped and laughed with the Irish nurse who tucked the bed-clothes in until they were rigid and immovable as sheet steel. The sound of music came in waves through the open windows. It was a Beethoven symphony.

'Where is the music coming from Sister?' I asked.

'It is a German POW symphony orchestra rehearsing for tonight's concert at the sports stadium. If it bothers you I will close the windows.'

'No for goodness sake don't do that, it's lovely. Beethoven isn't it? What is it, the 4th?'

'I wouldn't know dear, but while I remember a young lady called yesterday asking for you and left these roses. Are you always welcomed like this?'

'Not always Sister, in fact quite the contrary but I think that my welcome here is rather better than the one Sarafand gave me.'

She smiled. 'We always try to do our best for our customers. Now after you have had a drink you must sleep.'

The next morning Deborah came to see me. Neither of us mentioned her father's visit, it was as if he had never been, or even as if he did not exist. As the days of September came and went we saw each other every day until by the end of the month I was able to walk in the grounds of the hospital with her. Although there were always people about and we were never on our own, as soon as she arrived we occupied our own small world, and other things and other people no longer existed for us. The hours and minutes and seconds of being together were precious and we were jealous of intrusions and hated the creeping fingers of the clock.

On the 2nd of October, I was sent to the Convalescent Home for three weeks and we knew that I would soon have to face the Medical Board. I tried to avoid thinking about it, because I knew beyond any doubt that I loved Deborah, and the Board's decision was probably going to decide our future together. If they down-graded me I would be finished as far as my career in the Dragoons was concerned, although I might be found a less active job, but I hoped that it might be possible to get something that would keep me in the Middle East. An administrative job in England or Germany would be out of the question, I might as well join the Inland Revenue. Either way would trap us together in the soulless nine to five routine of home-buying, commuting as well as the rat race for promotion and favours in a land where the sun seldom shines and Jew was still a guilt-ridden word. It would be like planting a rose in a coal mine.

If they kicked me out I would be free to go anywhere and although my minute private income of £200 a year would keep me as a beachcomber in Cyprus, it wouldn't support two of us. The only other alternative would be for me to finish my training as an engineer in England, and then look for a job. That would mean waiting for another three years before we could think of marrying. The idea of resuming an apprenticeship at the age of twenty after such an interval of time didn't appeal to me but it might have to be done.

One day Deborah called in the Lapointes car, and drove me down to the French club to meet her employers. She seemed more like a member of the family and I was surprised to hear her conversing fluently and easily with them in excellent French. It made my own halting efforts sound like a German comedian imitating an Englishman speaking French.

When they discovered that I was fond of sailing, they insisted on lending me their eighteen foot clinker built boat which was at permanent moorings on Lake Timsah. Deborah had never sailed before, but as there was little or no wind and the boat was Bermuda rigged and designed for single-handed sailing, this presented no problem. For the rest of the afternoon we sailed gently about the lake the sound of the water rippling and bubbling along the planked hull, while the sun sank lower over the tree fringed western edge of the lake.

I turned up into wind and sailed close hauled towards the anchorage some three miles away. Deborah leaned back against me and rested her head against my chest. I put my arm round her and held the mainsheet with the tiller hand.

'Deborah has it occurred to you that in a very short while my future is going to be decided by the quacks and that they might send me back to England?' She pulled my arm tighter round her body and shivered.

'I have been expecting you to say this for a long time, and trying to remember that I am a Jewess and that you have a girl waiting in England for you. Whichever way you look at it there is no way out, you will have to go sooner or later.'

'Whether I go or stay there is one thing that you must know. Although I've never said it, you must know I love you. Whatever happens to me, I'll always love you.'

She turned to me, her arms about my neck and we kissed. The round of the jib slapping as the winding spilled out of it brought me back to reality. The boat had come up into the wind and the boom swung over, like a pendulum nearly collecting our heads as it went by. Deborah lay in the bottom of the boat laughing while I got the boat under way again in the freshening offshore breeze.

'First he tells me he loves me, then he kisses me in full view of the clubhouse and then still in public tries to knock me into the sea. What other little surprises have you in store for me?'

'Well I was about to ask you to marry me.'

'It's just as well you didn't, I'd have accepted you my love.'

'Deborah! Do you mean it?'

'Yes you adorable idiot.'

'My God, what will we live on?'

'Let's worry about that tomorrow, tonight we'll celebrate.'

'Well right now wench, you're going to learn to pick up moorings – be serious. There's a time for everything.'

She was kneeling at my feet her arms about my waist and her face upturned to me what could I do but kiss her. It was getting dark before we picked up our moorings and rowed ashore in the dinghy.

Madame Lapointe had come down to the boat house in her own light 15 Citroen, and was the first to hear our news. She hugged Deborah laughing then held her at arms length and looked at her.

'I suppose you have both thought of the difficulties – you know, religion, your parents, the army and everything and of course the inescapable fact, you're both children still!' Deborah looked at me.

'There are even more difficulties Madame Lapointe, but none of them are insuperable.'

'Don't you think that it may affect your career?'

'I don't see why it should. I hope that I will be judged by my ability, but if it does make a difference, then I will get out and do something else.'

As I said it, I knew that I was putting into words, something that had been going through my mind for some time, and it was something that disturbed me. The next few weeks would tell me whether my feelings of foreboding were justified. Writing to tell Gwen had been the most difficult task, and my parents the next. We thought that it would be better to go and see Deborah's father together, and although the prospect was not a pleasant one, he at least was expecting it.

Gwen's reply came by return of post. She always found letter writing difficult, and this one was one of her worst. In every way but this, she had grown into a very attractive and polished young woman, but her letters were full of women's magazine purple passages which looked so insincere and mechanical in print. I always felt embarrassed by them and sometimes wondered whether she used sections out of her weekly magazine. Her letter left me with mixed feelings of guilt, embarrassment and relief, but I felt free.

My mother replied to my letter, as I thought she would, the subject being outside my father's experience, and therefore to be avoided. She hoped that I would not do anything rash, that I would think of my career and remember that these infatuations were apt to go as quickly as they came. I lied to Deborah and told her that she approved and sent her love.

The following week, I left hospital and joined the regiment at Fayid, and then it became obvious that my brief popularity with the Colonel had finished. My duties kept me almost permanently in camp, and although my brother officers were co-operative and friendly on the surface, the sudden silences which greeted my arrival in the mess, were depressing.

I was given a troop in C Squadron and this kept me very busy occupying my mind for the hours between dawn until the end of the training at mid-day. We had taken over four new Comets, and as most of the troop had just come out from training regiments in England there was a great deal of work to be done on troop tactics driving and radio training. At the end of two months we were better than most troops in the regiment, mainly because I had to prove something. To watch the four tanks efficiently pitching and thrusting their way through a tactical advance, trailing a boiling cloud of dust behind them as they went, gave us all a great sense of team spirit and power. We aimed to practice all the possible moves in the book until they could be performed like a crack rugby football team in action. We split the troop into two pairs of tanks and stalked each other using the ground to hide us and our dust, changing duties within the tank and within the troop.

After three months, the squadron went out to train as a complete unit, and we earned our first crumb of praise, but it had also become apparent that I was physically well below standard. Each day left me in pain and exhausted. Climbing onto and off the tank was difficult but getting in and out of the turret was becoming harder and harder and as physical training with the troop and the daily run were impossible, it was becoming obvious that I was becoming a handicap.

The regiment had a considerable social life but apart from one cocktail party to which Deborah came, we took little part in it. We could only meet at Lapointes or at the sailing club, and we were never alone together for more than a few moments. Although they must have thought that they were doing the best thing for Deborah, they made it almost impossible for us to see each other and kept telling her that if we married, my career would be finished. This was in itself irrelevant as my medical board result made plain.

The strain began to tell, and although we never quarrelled, one day I had to tell her I was being sent to Jerusalem having been declared unfit for active service. We had just finished a miserable dinner at the Union Club in Suez, during which nothing had gone right. It had been her nineteenth birthday and the dinner had been a surprise, but the food was poor and the night was cold and damp. Arthur Howe and the MO were going to join us for drinks after dinner, and I hoped that Arthur would be bringing the good news that he had been able to get a bungalow for us at Fayid, that the Colonel had given his formal consent to my application to marry and the Jerusalem job was going to be short.

We had taken our drinks onto the verandah overlooking the street, when Arthur arrived on his own. He was a stocky cheerful little man of about forty who normally looked as if his uniform had been built onto him but this evening he was in a shapeless Donegal tweed suit which would have looked more at home on the Curragh than in Suez.

'Blessings be upon you my children, and a very happy birthday to you Deborah.' He stood with his hands on his hips and looking down at her while I stood to welcome him.

'She's too damn good by far for you Peter, no wonder you keep her tucked away so carefully. Some of our shining white hopes of the debs mums might start getting notions, and come to think of it, so might I!'

But she looked pleased. Only Arthur and I really knew the truth, that I was thought to be irresponsible for even considering marriage to Deborah, although what they really thought of her as a woman was something else altogether.

The Egyptian waiter who knew him well, appeared with his usual brandy and soda. He raised his glass. 'Here's to you Deborah.'

We drank to it, but we were waiting for what he had to say.

'Well alright, let me get me breath back,' he said, but he didn't seem too happy. 'Briefly, I've got you a flat, there's a bloke from the RAF in it now, but he'll be out by the end of this week, then you can have the key. It's furnished after a fashion, it's small and it's on the third floor, but it's cheap, alright?'

'Alright,' said Deborah, 'it's wonderful, how did you do it?' for the first time that day she looked happy.

'What about the old man?' I asked.

'Not so good I'm afraid Peter, he's not at all keen, he waffled away about your youth and the glamour of the East – and oh you know the rest and wound up by saying that he would re-consider it in six months time.'

'My God, what are we supposed to do now?' I looked at

Deborah. To my astonishment she looked amused. Arthur looked apologetic and uncomfortable.

'Oh I'm sorry Arthur, it must have been a lousy job coming to tell us that. Let's have a damned big drink.' I called the waiter and ordered three doubles.

'What's worrying you Peter?' Deborah asked me. And before I could reply she said, 'If our parents don't object I really don't see what it has to do with anyone else, not really. Besides we can't be married in either your church or mine and it will have to be a civil wedding anyway. My people won't regard it as a wedding at all really, and I'm not sure that I will, so where's the problem?'

'Simply that the army will honey, and they in the person of the Colonel have said no.'

She smiled and shrugged, the palms of her hands turned upwards. 'Alright, so we don't get married then no-one can be offended and the problem is solved.'

'Well I'm darned if I can see any joke in that, particularly as we now know that we have somewhere to live.' She took my hand and looked at me pityingly.

'I'll make you a proposition in return for your proposal – on condition that the parents don't object to a marriage – in theory anyway.' Arthur looked a bit more cheerful. Deborah looked at him slyly.

'I don't think your toffee nosed Colonel would object to that would he, a Jewess as a wife is no good, but a mistress would be correct. Oh I'm sorry Arthur that was unfair to you, you've been so kind to us, but it's true.'

'Before you both rush off and live in the proverbial sin, just listen to the rest of the news. Your medical board met yesterday and you've been downgraded to C3 and that means that this posting to Jerusalem is the immediate result. Someone has been pulling strings, because the whole thing is damned irregular. The Doc is at Fayid hospital tonight trying to find out what the exact position is. We think that you will be posted as a permanent instructor to the Arab Legion, because the Staff Captain at Canal South District was on the blower this afternoon just after you left camp, to ask if you could speak Arabic and if you had experience with armoured cars. When I told him you were in the 38th Independent Recce, he was tickled pink and said that you would fit into your next job very well.'

'But this is bloody awful Arthur, I don't want to go to the Legion, it's just as awkward getting in and out of an armoured car as a Comet apart from which although I'll be escaping from the Colonel's clutches, I don't suppose an Israeli wife would be too welcome in Trans-Jordan.'

'Well I'd suggest you meet that one when you get to it Peter.'

Deborah looked at us both. 'I don't know what you are going to do, but I'm taking two days holiday from tomorrow to make a long weekend and I'm going home to see my father and prepare the ground for Peter. As you're going to be in Jerusalem darling we might as well get it over. I've written to your mother today and introduced myself.'

I had been thinking as she was talking. 'Deborah I've made my mind up. In one month's time I'll be twenty one, let's get married then and to hell with 'em all.'

'Are you sure you know what you're saying my sweet, and it's not just the brandy talking?'

'Stone cold sober and sure, one month today come hell or high water, in Jerusalem.'

'So be it,' she said, and leaning across kissed me.

'Amen' said Arthur and emptied his glass. 'You two will end up in a bloody kibbutz plantin' spuds an' raisin' kids and imagining you're happy and what'll I be doin' still waiting for my divorce to come through and mopping up Mr Hennessey's rot gut.'

At three in the morning it was organised, and all the other guests had gone. The moon was round and yellow like a great cheese and frogs were croaking and squelching in the ditches along the Sweet water canal as we were driven home up the Treaty Road very slightly drunk, in our own private world.

It was a week before my posting was confirmed, a week spent handing over the troop to my successor and packing my kit, my mind only partly engaged with the day's events. Being idle while trying to look busy was more trying than a normal day's work and I became more anxious to get away from the regiment as the days passed. It became increasingly obvious that the regiment was equally anxious to be rid of me. Even, Arthur, who had been so helpful, seemed relieved as he called me into the Squadron Office to collect my Movement Orders and travel warrant.

That evening, before I left, we had a quiet farewell party at the Fayid club during which we exchanged home addresses, promised to contact each other if and when we were posted home – and promptly forgot.

In the morning, an hour before Reveille, the duty driver was outside the door of my hut with his 15 cwt Bedford. An hour and a half later I was on my way to El Kantara station, my feelings wavering between relief and anxiety about my future. Only the prospect of seeing Deborah again and our marriage added any warmth to the landscape of my thoughts. I had written to her home to let her know when I would be arriving and she had replied by telegram to say that she would wait in Jerusalem for me. She gave me her telephone number to ring on arrival.

We had spent our last night, or what was left of it, at Lapointe's house. The family were visiting the Nile temples with the children so we had the house to ourselves. We slept together like two lost children, hiding in each other's arms from the harsh reality of the hostile world created by our love, reality in the shape of the inexorable sun and the cacophony of the waking streets awoke us.

That morning she had left for Jerusalem while I went to cancel the arrangements which Arthur Howe had made for us to take over the bungalow in Fayid. This had not been such a sad task as I had supposed because it was small, dark and dirty and looked exactly what it was, a barrack block in an old POW camp which had been 'converted' into married quarters.

Palestine

The train to Palestine crawled across the coastal strip through the heat of the day, packed with troops and their equipment, its windows closed and protected by wire netting. The heat was stifling and the train's progress after El Arish was slower and interrupted at intervals while the line ahead was searched for mines.

Between Gaza and Ashquelon we were held up for over two hours, sitting in frustrating inactivity and listening to the spasmodic rattle of small arms fire and the ear-splitting crack of a Daimler armoured car's two-pounder somewhere among the orange groves ahead of us. The unreality of the situation did not seem to strike the three Grenadier subalterns who were the other occupants of the compartment and who had apparently written me off as a crank when I had turned down their offer of a game of bridge.

Eventually, and without further incident we arrived at Beersheba where I was to be picked up. To my surprise, when I reported to the RTO a Palestine police constable who had been sitting on the bench of the office reading a magazine, stood up, dropped the magazine on the seat and walked over to me.

'Mr Wade sir?'

'Yes.'

'I've been detailed to pick you up and take you to Jerusalem. The jeep's outside, and if we get a bit of a move on we can tag onto the RASC convoy which left a few minutes ago. We should catch them before they reach Ramlah, and I'd rather travel in company if you don't mind.'

He looked solid and capable, but I took his point and picked up my grip. The orderly who had loaded my trunk and loose kit onto the porter's trolley, followed us out into the Dannert wire protected compound where a police jeep was waiting. Another policeman was sitting in the back of the jeep, a Sten gun across his knees, its sling around his shoulder and buttoned under an epaulette. He looked relieved when he saw us and without saying anything swung out of the seat and helped to load my baggage.

A little while later we caught up with our convoy on the Ramlah to Latrum road, much to the undisguised relief of the driver who had spent the first few miles of our journey telling me of the growing confidence of the underground factions. Fortunately for us, there was still a considerable rift between the regular Haganah detachments and both the Irgun and Stern Gang.

I was glad when we arrived in Jerusalem, but was surprised to find that I was to be housed in a Military Police training school with a room of my own in the instructor's block. The bed was made and there was a supply of fresh towels and a manilla folder on the pillow, it contained my briefing notes, including domestic arrangements and an outline training programme. As I read through page after page, it became obvious that the Army had abandoned me and even though it had also promoted me to Lieutenant, command was not part of my future. I was to be removed from the regimental family and employed in some, as yet unspecified role, as an individual specialist. I went to the noisy, canteen-like Mess and dealt with the immediate problem of hunger.

After breakfast, I reported as instructed for my introduction to a new but isolated life, in second-rate civilian clothes, with the difference that a shoulder holster was also provided to accommodate a .45 Colt automatic pistol. There was no alternative but to follow the programme and hobble through the days and nights until I was deemed to be ready for my next task or rejected.

The stack of books about Islam and its culture, Arabic and the Koran, dictionaries and grammars all indicated that I was not about to enter a period of relaxation so I decided that I could either use it as an opportunity or be defeated. This was a chance to be grasped and was a form of free education.

At no time was I allowed time on my own and was expressly forbidden to make contact with anyone, either directly or indirectly. Each day, together with my personal instructor, we moved from camp to camp and all conversation after the first week was in Arabic. Every day, at apparently random times, we would spend at least an hour at a live firing range for more and more realistic pistol practice; in a fully furnished village, where potential targets would appear for less than two seconds. Generally, they would be unarmed civilians, but sometimes they would be a crouching gunman about to fire with the photographed face of a known wanted man. As the practice became more and more demanding, the target would appear from an alley or room full of cut-out figures of ordinary people going about their everyday business. The stress level increased day by day, with more classroom work on civil as well as military law and fresh intelligence to be absorbed between supper and bedtime. Even the latter provided no escape, as range time was extended during the hours of darkness.

At the end of the second week, there was a review of progress with my immediate instructors, who persuaded me without too much difficulty, that I was beginning to be too confident for my own good. Together with my ex-Arab Legion 'minder', we moved over the Jordan to a Frontier Force outpost, with an indoor pistol range and a thriving village community around it, where we would live with a farmer and his family. Our city suits were replaced by less conspicuous local robes and gelabiya and with more time spent drinking coffee, exchanging gossip and discussing the news, the strain was taken out of the intensive learning process. With the greater relaxation came colloquial Arabic, as well as improved performance on the range, so after ten days, we returned to the CID training unit over the border.

After four more days of assessment and classroom work, I was declared of sufficient competence, to be allowed to take part in one or two excursions into bandit country as the back-up man to a working officer. The fact that I had been instructed not to shave since beginning the course had resulted in a somewhat juvenile beard, and meant that my mother would probably not have recognised me and further disguise was superfluous. Although no major events were triggered by our days of wandering the narrow street, markets and coffee houses of the old city of Jerusalem and of Bethlehem, the final appraisal was that I was ready to be gainfully employed.

What I was not prepared for however, was my next meeting with Sgt Meredith, who told me that Warrender wanted to see me on the following morning, but until then I was not to make any outside contacts at all. In particular, there must be no contact, even by 'phone with Deborah. When I asked him the reason for this, he suggested that it would be obvious to any working copper, but there was new intelligence which I must hear and until then, he was simply relaying an order. He left me with an intelligence summary which reduced the forces of government, administration and all forms of opposition to numbers of people, time and resources, without names. I could see where I was going to fit in, with no room for compromise or personal freedom of action.

At the end of the summary, after the instructions for its burning, was the simple detail of the time and place for my meeting with my controller, Warrender at the terrace bar of the Kyrenia Hotel in Ben Yehuda Street at 10:12 am next day. I was to be in civilian clothes, still unshaven, wearing sunglasses and a trilby hat and carrying a copy of the *Herald Tribune* and of course, armed.

After a shower and having made the excuse of an attack of the usual upset gyppy tummy, with frequent trips to the latrines, my watchdogs gave up and I was able to find a 'phone so that I could call Deborah. Some unknown woman, who spoke no English or Arabic answered, so there was nothing to be done but leave my name and get back to my room and bed and hope that the call was not bugged. I was not in the frame of mind where sleep would come easily and the dawn brought no relief.

I knew that I had lost immediate control of my life. Even if I were to be employed at a desk, on staff administration or as an intelligence analyst, I would still be in an impossible situation in relation to Deborah. As my initial training would suggest, something more active seemed to be indicated and in any case there was nothing in my short career to date which would positively qualify me for a desk job. My analysis of the situation did little to improve my appetite for breakfast, in the otherwise drab and ill-lit Mess, where the only other occupant was a solitary Arab waiter. I pushed the cool and greasy kedgeree around the plate for a while before settling for a piece of toast and a coffee.

I knew that the only realistic course would be to resign my commission at the first opportunity and in the meanwhile ask for a job, anywhere else other than in Palestine. Jordan would seem to be a possible location, but I could not see any way that I could be much use to the organisation in which I was currently employed. This in itself was probably not much of a problem in an organisation like the Army, which had a special genius for finding jobs for the most unpromising candidates in the most improbable roles, particularly to avoid any sort of confrontation which might become public.

As I walked through the crowded sun baked streets of the Old City, I had come to the outline of a plan which would only begin when I had some idea of what my new boss had in mind for me. Because the first meeting of our new relationship was to be in a very public place, it would not be a particularly good moment or location for any sort of confrontation. In fact, he probably was deliberately trying to make the first encounter as relaxed and informal as possible. Not being in control meant that I would be wise to sit and listen before introducing my own problems.

By the time that I walked into the welcome shade of the Kyrenia Hotel's lobby, I had thought myself into a calm and receptive frame of mind, where I had put introspection on hold. Warrender was sitting on his own at a table under the sun awning which shaded the patio, close to the street, he was reading *Le Monde*.

I approached him from the inside of the hotel and asked him if he would mind me taking the other seat at his table. He nodded assent, so I sat down and ordered a coffee, meanwhile he returned to reading his own paper and watching the passing people and traffic. After the men at the next table left, he turned to me and asked if I had finished with my newspaper and would I consider exchanging with him. It was easy to open a conversation when I explained that my command of French was not up to reading his, but that he was welcome to mine.

After a few minutes of general chat that two strangers might have about harmless subjects, which of course began with the weather, he ordered more coffee. Then without any discernable change of tone or expression, the conversation became more to the point.

'Well Peter, that was not a bad start, on time at the right place and you didn't give me a chance to see you first. In fact I'd no idea there was a way into this end of the patio from the hotel.' I sat and watched him while he tested his coffee for temperature. 'From now on, my name is John and although you will see very little of me in the immediate future, I'll be taking a close interest in your progress – as I do now in fact.'

While talking he hardly looked towards me, but when I failed to reply, he looked at me closely. 'Well?' There seemed to be nothing much to say, except 'OK' and join his people watching.

'Now the downside, as I understand it, is that you were given clear instructions not to make any sort of contact with your local girlfriend, yet you 'phoned her home last night. Why might I have the temerity to ask, did you directly disobey an order, well?'

Although the question was not totally unexpected, I had not thought that it would be asked at this time or at this place.

'It will sound pretty feeble I know, but I did not think of it as an order in the ordinary way, but I just wanted to let her know that I was still alive and had not deserted her. At the moment, I don't quite know where I am, what I'm doing, who I'm working for or what is going to happen to me in the future. I only know that I am totally out of my environment and that I would only feel a sense of relief if you were to tell me that I'm sacked.'

All that I could read in his carefully controlled expression was disapproval and perhaps contempt. After a brief silence, filled only by the chatter of the passers-by and traffic noise, his eyes turned to the street.

'Happily for you, although your 'phone call was picked up and recorded badly, the woman who answered was the housekeeper who has been on our payroll since you led us to this particular viper's nest. No, don't say anything, you might regret it later. Apart from her, the whole lot have just melted into the landscape, luckily before you called them.'

The heat and noise, the dust and pressure of events were robbing me of reasoning power and there seemed to be nothing to say. I could only shrug my shoulders and hope that I would sooner rather than later, find a quiet, cool place to think. I finished my coffee and found my mouth full of grounds and sugar. I was just reaching for a glass of water, when a car, slid to a tyre-screeching halt at the kerbside and the crowd began to run in all directions to get away.

Someone in the back of the car flung the door open and lobbed something towards us, over the potted plants at the edge of the terrace. As those occupying the other tables, looked around, half stood and in some cases, ran. Warrender screamed something and flung himself down and sideways as the grenade exploded. I had dived below the tables and rolled down some steps into a half basement, and was able to come out, pistol cocked and ready from the next flight of stairs, as two gunmen had begun to open fire at anyone in the place where our table had been. I managed to get off a couple of shots at the car as it raced away, doors swinging open, then made my way back to where we had been, to look for Warrender among the dead and dying.

I was just about to make my own way over to where two soldiers of the Parachute Regiment, were reloading their Stens, when a second car without glass in its windscreen or doors, came along the street in the same direction, with three or four people in it. It was not in any hurry and would seem to have been sent to complete the job, whatever it was. Both soldiers quickly opened fire from the cover of the doorways and as the driver floored the accelerator, he was hit and the car careered off to the right and smashed into a parked van. Both vehicles burst into a mass of flames and oily smoke as I finished off a magazine at one of the two men trying to get out of a jammed door. Two others managed to get out of the opposite side, pursued by Warrender, firing as he ran, past one of the paras who had been hit. As I ran into the street, I overtook John who had slowed to a jog as he reloaded.

The two escaping gunmen split up, one running into a side street was bleeding heavily and I went after the other who, although limping, was still moving quickly into an area of small workshops and yards, pushing people out of his way as he went. Occasionally he would turn and fire a snap-shot at me, but he was certainly slowing down. We ran into a side street, down a long shallow flight of steps with stone pillars at intervals, now in cool shade. At the bottom, he shoulder charged a half opened double door and disappeared inside. Wishing that some help might arrive, I quickly fitted a fresh magazine and flung myself flat inside the doorway to adopt a prone firing position. The yard was a storage area, dirty and in shade, half covered by a tin roof. There was total silence and no sign of movement as I made my way silently and with senses keyed to a brittle edge, into a random series of packing cases and old car tyres. Apart from the sound of my breathing and distant traffic, all was silent. Then as I turned a corner, he was no more than twenty feet away, whimpering like a frightened child, feet in a pool of blood trying to reload his pistol. I hit him with three or more rounds of the five which I fired, the last as he tried to get up onto his knees to take one last shot at me.

As the echoes of this last shot died away, Warrender and a small crowd of locals and Palestine police had arrived. My legs seemed to have run out of energy and I was only interested in getting away to somewhere where I could get a bath and a long cool drink. It was not to be however as Warrender was enjoying his big moment. He walked over to where a policeman had been trying to administer first aid to the gunman and had rolled him onto his back. He called me over.

'Well Peter, you seem to have hit the jackpot, the leader of the team which was hunting me and it would seem, you as well. It's Jacob.'

I had run out of light conversation, so bent down to pick up Jacob's pistol and immediately saw that he had tried to feed a new round into a separated case. It was useless. As I looked down at him, I felt the fear that must have gripped him as he tried, desperately to clear the jammed feed. Warrender signalled me to follow him, as the uniformed police took control of the scene and began to search the compound to see if there was a particular reason for Jacob to choose it.

Sgt Meredith was waiting with a taxi in the lane, which had been cleared of people. He handed me a kitbag, containing the arab clothes which I had been wearing during my training. As I changed into them, he put the suit, tie and shoes into the bag and held his hand out for Jacob's pistol. I had been trying to clear the breech, but my hands were wet with blood and my own perspiration and were shaking too much to be effective. He wiped the weapon dry with a piece of rag, removed the empty magazine and grasping the knurled rear of the slide between thumb and finger, jerked it back swiftly so that the problem cartridge spun away in a clean arc, leaving the split case in the breech.

'There you are sir, a nice souvenir' he said as he replaced an empty magazine handed the weapon to me, butt first. Warrender, who had changed into a blazer and straw hat, nodded his approval and got into the front passenger seat.

'Make your way back to the rear of the Kyrenia, taking your time, but use another route and keep your eyes open for anyone taking a very close interest in our activity at the crime scene. They are going to be very curious about how this big op went so very wrong. Just watch and listen, but for God's sake, no heroics, apart from keeping your own skin intact.' He looked at me closely. 'Are you about to be sick?'

I was, for the first time since I was ten years old. He wound up his window and left me with my own problems, the first of which was how to get back to the main thoroughfare by some other route. One of the policemen who had been searching the yard, showed me a gate hidden behind an old cart which had been propped against the back wall. It was unlocked and gave access to an unmade lane, where life was going on as usual, with pedestrians, load carrying donkeys and goats in profusion. I became just one more member of an anonymous moving throng as I made my way back by a series of lanes and alleys between two and three-storey white-washed houses and street markets. When I came to the cordon of police and soldiers who had sealed off the whole area round the hotel, I had no wish to advertise myself by seeming to have a special dispensation by showing my identity card to an officer.

Luckily, one of the local residents was passing through with his extended family and neighbours as he was moving home. Plenty of hands were needed to carry the mattresses, boxes and suitcases as well as all the kitchen equipment, so two more were welcome. After accepting their thanks, but rejecting the offer of refreshments, I arrived at the rendezvous, hoping that I had not been forgotten, but the police on duty had been told to watch for me and took me into the manager's office where Warrender was waiting for me. He had just finished dictating his report and ordered a couple of beers for us before swivelling his chair round to face me and indicating that I should sit down.

'Well, although you may take a somewhat different view of this morning's work, I think that we have done a reasonable job. Our team, one para with two non-lethal bullet wounds, three dead civilians and half a dozen with blast and splinter injuries, the baddies, lost all but one of the whole team, one in the second car with Sten and .45 rounds in him, in hospital and due to croak any minute now. The one I was after, although I'd winged him could have disappeared into the crowd, but they gave him a working over and finished the job for us. A bit messy, but job done as he was one of the pair, you having nailed little brother.' He looked at me closely and waited for a response, but there seemed to be nothing to say, so he continued.

'Now, did you note anything on the way here?' I told him about the masked exit to the yard and said that beyond the properties on the other side of the lane, there was scrub land and a narrow wadi, beyond which the new houses were probably owned by Jewish families. Apart from which, there had been nothing else of note to report. He smiled and nodded slowly.

'Just before you got here, the police searching the yard found a cache of four suits of Arab clothing, down to the last detail, as well as four wads of used bank notes. All part of the getaway kit. I think that after we've fingerprinted them, it would be rather a nice touch to send the dosh to a Jewish children's charity.' I could not but agree, without comment, for I was tired of talk, but he had not finished.

'As I have said already, although the family have disappeared, apart from our tame housekeeper and you will probably not want to waste any more time on someone who has not been entirely truthful with you, you may wish to pen a suitable farewell when you feel up to it.' Still watching me he went on, 'When you have done it, plain envelope, just her given name on the outside, give it to Meredith, very trustworthy chap, he will find a way of delivering it. We have routes of communication, generally via the God botherers, so that once we've all stopped filling graves, the politicians know who can talk to whom. OK?' I nodded assent and asked if he had finished with me.

'Almost,' he continued, 'I suppose you realise that both you and I are no longer of much use here, because I've been in the game locally for too long and today was the result of a very major effort to settle my hash for good. Roy Farron was shipped out pretty jildi when his cover was blown and I will be due for the same treatment. If you had been even slightly discreet, no-one would know of your part in today's exercise, but as it is, you've moved yourself right up to the top of the naughty-boy list by playing happy families with a local godfather and his brood. As for the here and now,' he looked at his watch and frowned, 'we've just got twenty minutes, before the big Boss arrives, – told him about you and he wants to take a dekko at his new hot-shot and tell you what the system has in mind for you, – which reminds me, your suit, covered with blood, shit and corruption – had it cleaned and just good enough for today so we'll get you a new one which can mean a buckshee de-mob suit for you. So get yourself smartened up a bit before the old man arrives.'

I did as I was told, having been given the keys to a vacant suite. The main street outside the Kyrenia still being closed, Warrender and I sat at the back in what passed for a garden and awaited the coming of the Great One. Almost exactly at the appointed time, a Humber staff car flying a four star General's flag, drew up in the car park and Warrender walked over to speak to the passenger before beckoning me over and getting into the seat beside the driver. The driver came around the car and indicated that I should get in beside the gilded, mahogany complexioned, real-life General, complete with red tabs and the shoulder badge of a Lt General. Leaning over from the front seat, Warrender introduced me. The latter looked me over with cold blue eyes, without any sign of approval and offered me a limp hairdresser's hand. 'How d'ye do sir' I offered in response, and he continued to regard me with the sort of look which a Master of Foxhounds would reserve for some pretentious bounder who had the temerity to pass him when the hounds were in full cry.

Warrender was smiling, without warmth and to my astonishment addressed this all-powerful being by his Christian name, apparently continuing a conversation which my arrival had interrupted.

'Let's face it Charles, it's not a nice way to be doing things, but today has probably saved the lives of a few of your soldiers. I don't bloody well enjoy it you know and I can assure you that Wade isn't overcome with enthusiasm at playing the part of the goat tied to a tree to bring the tiger out of the jungle.' Light was beginning to shine in dark places.

'Beside which, we think that one of them escaped, so we're both targets now. Ergo, we need to get Wade away from here pretty smartly, can you fix that?'

The General turned his attention to me again.

'You've done a damned good job young fella, but you'd have been better off with the regiment doing some respectable soldierin' instead of this blessed hole-in-the-corner stuff buggerin about with policemen. However the harm's done now so we'll get you flown out tonight and tuck you away in a UK transit camp until we figure out what to do with you. New name, for a while anyway, new passport, bloody complicated, but John will fix all that stuff. As far as recognition goes, your Colonel has approved a mention in Dispatches for the Sinai affair, not quite an MC but less publicity and I am going to talk to my bosses about a Civil List honour for you, it won't be for a while and the dust has settled.' I thanked him and said that I hoped the latter would not be posthumous. That appealed to his sense of humour and after he had stopped laughing, he slapped his booted calf with his cane and lent forward to Warrender.

'Are you thinking what I'm thinking John? That would solve two problems in one.'

'You're ahead of me Charles – what do you have in mind?' I had begun to catch the drift and did not like the direction very much.

'What if we report the death of young Wade here, recommend him for a Civil gong for services to the Civil Administration in one of the Mandated Territories and let the modest press release do the rest?' John thought it a brilliant idea, Charles beamed with pleasure at being one step ahead but to me, it felt like being present as the undertakers discussed the unmentionable details of preparations for my interment. The decisions seemed to have been made and the General took control.

'Right driver, back to HQ Mess.' He turned to me, 'You fellas had better come back to the Mess with me for a bit of scoff and a burra peg, a sort of Wake what?' And before I could answer him to thank him he imperiously eased himself over onto his right buttock and broke wind loudly. Warrender had the temerity to lower his window. The General continued the briefly interrupted conversation by asking after the health of John's wife Betty and the children. All seemed to be well in that department and I was free to deal with the turmoil in my mind, which kept me largely silent through a long but excellent meal. Afterwards, the General was surprisingly affable towards me, perhaps because his sudden bright idea had transformed me from a problem to his project. I was found a room at HQ for the night, a replacement suit arrived and a batman packed my kit for my departure for Cyprus in an old and dirty Curtis Commando.

One engine failed on landing after running hot during the descent and the ground crew decided that both engines would need a major overhaul. As there were still enough examples of the Commando to start a new airline or two, she was towed to a quiet corner of the airfield to rot away in her own time. The next flight, which was in a Lancastrian being relocated back to Lyneham via Rome, was not scheduled as a passenger flight, but the controller was able to add me to the crew list because of my special status. The pilot was not encouraged to ask any questions and the crew who were going home on leave from Rhodesia were wildly incurious, so I was left with my own private thoughts on the long, cold and noisy flight to Ciampino.

I had plenty of time to read the letter which I had written to Deborah and had been made redundant by my supposed 'death'. Much as I desperately wanted to see her, I knew that this could never happen and slowly and carefully tore it into smaller and smaller pieces to discard or burn at the first opportunity. Even as I did so, I knew that this love was never really going to go away.

PART II

Summer 1960

CHAPTER 4

England, 1960

IAN was just getting over an attack of mumps and we had given him a box of photographs to play with. Sitting in the moving speckled shade of the apple tree in an old armchair, he carefully picked them up, one at a time, and examined them, his calm grey eyes absorbing each detail. As I lay on my back in the sun, watching him through half closed eyes, it seemed difficult to realise that he was my son. There was, of course, no doubt about the facts; but there were times like that moment when the sun, burning its way through the fabric of my shirt to my skin, and the sound of the breeze sensuously stroking the leaves of the tree overhead, were more real to me than my relationship to Gwen or our families, or my work, and even at that moment, Ian, my three year old son.

I had no cause for complaint, he was growing into a fine looking boy, with a straight back and a solid little body which was just beginning to lose its baby dimples. His hands were learning to follow his mind's orders, careful and precise in their actions giving me a strange detailed pleasure as I watched them building and assembling more complex structures as the seasons passed. His probing fact-hungry mind kept his tongue working from waking to sleeping, asking questions, singing half-heard and superficially remembered jingles. His mind was as straight and single-purposed as his mother's, allowing no complications to stand in his way of his intentions.

What was he looking at now? His eyes were raised from the photographs, focused somewhere above and beyond me, brow knotted in a slight frown.

'Mummy,' he called and jumped off the chair scattering box and photographs and ran as fast as his short legs could propel him. Seeing only Gwen and thinking only of her, everything else driven from his mind, his foot slipped across the surface of the nearly finished chassis drawing that I had been working on. The thud as his body hit the grass beside me snapped my mind back to the present. He was on his feet again, ink on his feet, socks, knees and right hand. His face began to crumple ready for tears, a word of sympathy and he would lose control. I watched with admiration, the well-timed diversion, the face saving line of escape that Gwen produced for the little boy who wanted to seem a man.

I realised with irritation that I must look more than slightly idiotic as Gwen introduced her two companions. Half past ten on a Spring Saturday morning, khaki shorts, bare feet, long thin whiskery legs and an old Aertex shirt didn't exactly fit me for the role of husband to cool, bright, straight out of the bandbox Gwen, mother of my son and heir. With a slightly sick feeling, my invariable reaction to an embarrassing situation, a right hand to my chin to stroke it revealed a twenty-four hour stubble. Hell, I must look more like the village idiot.

'Darling, do you remember me telling you about Pam who used to be at St. Hilda's with me? Pam this is Peter and number one son Ian.'

Pam smiled, employing the barest polite obligation of a facial disarrangement and turned to gush over Ian. Her husband, a smoothly-tweeded middle-aged man, stockily built stood quietly waiting for an introduction and dutifully echoed the ends of Pam's gurgling sentences of child-worship. As the introduction did not seem to be coming he leaned precariously across the rose bed and offered me his plump well manicured hand.

'Charles Green' he said.

'Oh how frightfully rude of me,' said Gwen. 'Peter, dear, do see if we've got any drink in the house.'

Oh my God, I thought, why does she fool herself. I know we haven't, as she does and I'm damned sure these people can tell, if only from the state of the house, that we're not likely to have even a bottle of beer.

'I'm pretty certain that we haven't,' I said 'but I'll look.'

'I've got a better idea,' said Charles. 'Peter and I can go off to the Ring-o-Bells for a quiet pint while you girls natter about your school days. We can bring something back with us.'

'Why can't we all go?' said Pam in an irritating little girl voice and pouted. I wondered how long she had been doing this particular act, and tried to imagine seeing this performance once a day for the rest of one's life. It was difficult enough to live in Gwen's world of shining perfection, keeping up the grand facade of success and pretending to her friends that my moth-eaten appearance was really an eccentricity but at least she didn't have any hysteria-inducing mannerism.

'I'd love to Pam, but young Ian will be roaring like a bull for his food in about an hour, so I'm tied to the cradle – some other time perhaps, when we can get a babysitter. Shall we have some coffee instead until the boys get back?'

'Oh scrummy,' chirruped Pam and clapped her smooth plump be-ringed hands together. Charles rolled his eyes upwards and held his hands together in a position of prayer.

Ian looked at her from about four feet away with an expression of frank astonishment. Oh Lord, what is he going to say now I thought, and caught Gwen's anxious expression, she had wondered the same.

'I'd better go and change if you'll excuse me,' I said quickly, 'Come on Ian, help me to get dressed.'

'Daddy isn't that lady funny, why has she got pink hair, is it real?'

'Come on you little horror,' I said and propelled him into the house out of earshot before his questions became any more intimate. From the bathroom above the noise of running water, I could hear Charles' guffaw.

Ten minutes later we were outside the house admiring his new car, a Ford Zephyr which he had apparently only bought recently. As he settled down behind the wheel, he turned to me and smiled sheepishly.

'Fast cars are my real weakness, but Pam likes bulky rather flashy coloured ones, so I bought this thing, she loves the tomato colour and she chose these foul leopard skin lose covers; I had the guts of the car worked on and a Raymond Mays conversion done to the engine. Do you like fast cars?'

'I suppose I must, because they are the reason why we never have any money, I could make more as a fitter in an aircraft factory than I do now.'

'What do you do?' he asked.

'Well I design and race unsuccessful cars, buy and sell second-hand racing machinery and in theory anyway, run an agency for Maserati in this part of the country. Of course, no one around here can afford to buy a 4.9 coupe, but it's fun and it keeps my bank manager off my neck.'

'Heavens above, I'd no idea you were the same Wade. I remember seeing you race at Oulton Park last year, and we were at San Remo when you drove an Osca there. Didn't Osca offer you a works entry for Le Mans this year?'

'Yes they did, but I made a balls of it and ran out of road at Tertre Rouge on the second lap, not an impressive performance. Gwen is beginning to drop less subtle hints that I've had it, that I never did make the grade and never will. What's the use though? It's the only thing that stops me from going round the bend, and we still eat regularly. I've been trying for years to get the Society of Motor Manufacturers and Traders to back the design and development of two or three promising formula one cars for the current formula but they won't play.

They couldn't see any further than the ends of their toffee bloody noses; do you know they won't even allow us to use the Motor Industry Research Association circuit, although Jags and Triumph do? Motor racing in a few years time will be in the doldrums unless something is done pretty smartly. It's becoming too expensive and the development of piddling little GP cars which have no power is making it all a gamble where the hamfisted amateur can do almost as well as the maestro. What we want are hairy great cars using big production motors – Brian Lister had the right idea – which will be noisy, fast and need real drivers. I've stuck my neck out a mile and built one – would you like to see it?'

'I would very much but what about this pint first?' He started the car and drove off down the hill like a man pursuing a thirst.

'Oh I've done it again' I said. 'If you get me on the subject of cars out comes the old soap box and my sense of proportion takes a holiday.'

'When can I see your car?' he asked.

'Well it's at Oulton at the moment, two of the boys are down there with my boss doing some carburettor and plug tests and I'm going down after lunch to do a few laps to see if it goes round corners. Would you like to meet me there at 3pm? We have the circuit until about six'

'By golly yes. Oh but we've got visitors.' He looked as excited as a schoolboy. He left the problem in my lap.

'Bring them with you if you like – but no dogs please, although I'm sure you wouldn't anyway, and no cameras. We're going to race in a formula libre race at Aintree this next Saturday and we want the Pig to be a complete surprise to the opposition. Providing you don't get too enthusiastic there might even be time to try your Zephyr on the circuit. Would you like to?'

'I would love to, but I would also like to go round with you driving or am I presuming too much?'

'What are your tyres like?'

'About half worn I would think, but I can get a new set on before we come and run them in on the way down if you think that would be better.' He looked anxious to please.

'I gather you are not afflicted by money worries, but I don't think that will be necessary as we won't have too much time available to waste your rubber.'

'I'm sorry,' he said, 'but I wasn't trying to show off.'

He parked the Zephyr neatly against the wall of the pub's garden and we went inside. The barman knew him and began to pull a pint of bitter in a pewter tankard as soon as he crossed the threshold.

'Morning Mr Green' he said.

'What will you have Peter?'

'A bitter please, just a half.'

'No, no, you must have a pint.'

'No just a half thank you.' I began to feel irritated and embarrassed.

'Would you rather have a Scotch?'

I tried to hold my rising temper. I had only the price of a

couple of pints at the most in my pocket and had to be careful. Someone else walked up to the bar behind me and before I could remonstrate further a double Scotch was in my hand and I was being introduced to two newcomers. They were apparently fellow golfers, and the conversation was completely beyond me within a few sentences. I watched their rapidly emptying glasses with growing apprehension while, my fingers explored the seldom used ticket pockets of my old infrequently worn suit for the forgotten coin or – faint hope, bank note. Nothing but fluff, scraps of paper, and a bus ticket rewarded my quest as the moment of truth drew nearer.

'What are you boys drinking?' I suddenly asked golfer number one whose name I had promptly forgotten in my embarrassed and pre-occupied state of mind.

'No, it's my round.'

I protested feebly.

'I wouldn't hear of it old chap, you're our guest. Are you visiting the district?'

'Same again Henry,' he said to the barman without waiting for an answer.

The nightmare continued and I steadily became drunk, unused as I had become to alcohol. The talk buzzed on monotonously and I seemed to float on the fringe of my sight. Sometimes my eyes would see but my brain didn't know what it meant so that in the end I gave up and sat quietly drinking. I suddenly heard myself saying. 'What the Hell am I doing here?' and became dimly aware of the silence and the faces turned towards me. The conversation broke out again with everyone talking at once about the weather, or golf, or sailing.

'Balls to the lot of you,' I said with some difficulty and walked out with what I imagined to be dignity thinking to myself, 'You bloody oaf, you bloody oaf, some of those people are Gwen's friends and the parents of some of the kids Ian is going to grow up with.'

'What the hell, they're not real. I'm me and I'm my own man.' I let myself into Charles' car and almost immediately went to sleep.

When I awoke we were driving home, and I felt very cheerful.

I looked at Charles and tried in vain to get his face into focus. But no amount of mental effort could make it anything but a pink jelly. When I moved my head to look at the road in front of us my eyes trailed sluggishly in its wake, they seemed to be full of dust and inclined to close. My mind turned in on itself, spiralling inward and downward into uneasy sleep, only climbing out into the awareness of sunlight when the motion of the car had stopped. The door at my side of the car opened and a hand grasped my arm above the elbow.

'Come on old man, we'd better get you inside, you're a bit under the weather.'

I shook the hand off and swung my legs out until my feet touched the gravel of our untidy drive. The sun was bright hurting my eyes and I only wanted to get into the cool of the house and get the weight of my body off my feeble and hard-to-control legs.

Gwen must have seen us arrive. She had opened the door and stood aside, holding Ian back out of my erratic path. Her face was a cold white blur in the gloom of the hall.

'I'm sorry you had this bother Charles, what happened? He usually never drinks these days particularly when he has any driving to do.'

'It's alright Gwen, perhaps he's not well. Anyway, I'd let him sleep it off.'

I hear their voices and understood, but could not trust myself to say anything, so climbed carefully and steadily upstairs and lowered myself towards the bed.

Feeling cold and very thirsty I awoke and raised my arm until I could see my watch.

'My God,' I said aloud. It was half past three and I had arranged to be at Oulton Park at half past two to start our final tests with the car. Even if I started now and got there through the Saturday traffic in half an hour that would leave an hour at the most before we had to clear the circuit before the GMT team arrived.

I staggered to my feet still bemused by sleep and alcohol and quickly changed into driving boots, slacks and shirt and ran downstairs calling for Gwen to get the Anglia out. The house was silent except for the kitchen sink tap which needed a new washer, its monotonous drip marking the passing time.

'Gwen' I called, but only a wasp and the dripping tap broke the silence of the hot still afternoon. I sprinted out to the garage and opened the doors, the car had gone.

'Damn and blast.'

My next door neighbour was poking about in the flower bed in uninterested fashion. He pointed down the road with his pipe stem when he saw me looking towards him.

'Went out an hour ago with the nipper, in convoy with a very super Zephyr.'

'Oh thanks John, I wonder if I could be a damned nuisance and ask you to run me down to the garage in your bus, I can take out one of the hire cars.'

'Yes, just a tick and we'll get the old heap out.'

It seemed to take a year for him to urge his old Morris out of its comfortable den, where it was sleeping peacefully dreaming about its pre-war youth amid the comfortable smell of old paint tins and sawn timber.

When we reached the garage, the boy who was looking after the pumps, told me that every car was out – but there was a motor cycle which was still taxed and insured. I had always hated riding a strange second hand motor cycle until I had checked its mechanical condition but beggars can't be choosers. He wheeled it out of the showroom and checked the fuel, oil and tyres while I rather self-consciously put on my helmet and tucked my slacks into my socks.

It was a BSA Road Rocket which some enthusiast had been using for clubman's road racing and was fitted with narrow clip-on handlebars and a dolphin fairing. It started easily and the engine screamed upwards at the gentlest opening of the throttle. A gentle touch was going to be called for if I was to get to Oulton Park at all, as it was some time since I had ridden a motor cycle, let alone a projectile like this.

After the first few miles of exploratory and gentle motoring, the Chester road straightened out before me, I opened the throttle cautiously until the road became a sinuous pouring torrent of tar macadam and the cats eyes on the curves flickered towards me like tracer bullets. The roar of the wind deflected over my head by the small curved screen on top of the fairing drowned the song of the twin-exhaust pipes as the needle on the revolution counter hovered around the yellow warning mark.

The miles rolled behind me and the other traffic now beginning to make its doddering way back from the Queensferry bridge and Wales, was left as if stationary.

By the time I arrived at the Bailey Bridge at the park and road round the barrier I was stone-cold sober and ready for action. When I replaced the barrier while still sitting astride the motor cycle its engine stalled and I stood up to restart it. As I did so, the noise of the Pig coming up Clay Hill stopped me I propped the machine against the side of the bridge so that I could watch unimpeded. The crackle of its twin-exhaust echoed between the trees of Druids as he shut off and braked before changing to second. As the driver accelerated round the corner the scream of the car's tyres tore through the rising engine noise and the car shot out into the sunlight like a pale green shell. Changing up to third as he thundered under the bridge, he kept well over to the left of the road to get into line for Lodge then he went down into Deers Leap and he was out of sight. My heart was pounding with excitement at the sight and sound of this car that had cost me so much, and at the idea of anyone else driving it. It particularly irked me that he was driving it so well.

I rode over to the pits in a flurry of dust and fury to where the cars of Gwen and Charles as well as Crompton's were parked. They did not recognise me at first, only Crompton looking up from his stop watch recognised the motor cycle and said something to the others as I walked towards them taking off my helmet. Gwen walked quickly to me telling Ian to go to Pam.

'Darling are you alright?' she asked.

'Why the devil didn't you think of asking me that before you left?' I said. 'Who the hell is in that car?'

'You've no need to speak to me like that, it was for your good and ours. You would probably have killed yourself if you'd tried to drive. In your state you could hardly walk. You've been very rude to Charles and Pam and you've been treating Patrick like dirt for the last six months. You must try and remember that he is your boss whether you like it or not and he only keeps you on so long as you are any use to him. If you break the car and maim yourself what do we do then? Heaven knows we're not exactly affluent now and this 'old comrade' stuff isn't going to make him go on paying you a salary for doing nothing. Please remember Peter before you say anything to him.'

'I'm sorry honey, you're quite right, I'm bloody impossible, but boss or no boss Francis Patrick Crompton isn't going to let any Tom, Dick or Harry drive that car. It's not all his anyway. The second mortgage on the house and two years of my useless life have gone into that beast, so just let me deal with him my way.'

I could hear the car coming through Lodge again so I picked up a black flag from behind the pit counter and walked out onto the track holding it out. The driver saw it as soon as he came into the straight and pulled in dutifully to where Crompton was sitting with his legs dangling over the counter. Crompton was watching me, holding out his stop watch so that I could see where the now stationary needle stood.

'That wasn't exactly a flying lap but it was still under the one minute fifty seconds' he said. 'You'd better look to your laurels mate.'

The driver was climbing out of the cockpit and taking off his helmet and goggles. I did not recognise him but he was very young, no more than a schoolboy.

The tell-tale on the rev-counter was 500rpm over the limit that I had set. I held my tongue with difficulty.

'You might as well meet your understudy Peter. This is Simon Aaronsen, who will drive our other car.'

We shook hands and I looked round for an explanation.

'What other car, can't someone tell me?'

'We've got a backer laddie,' Crompton was grinning. 'He thinks that your Formula Junior car design is a good one, as well so we're going to build it, or to be more accurate it's going to be built for us.'

'But good Lord Patrick, there's design and development time on this car yet apart from the Junior. It'll not run this season after Saturday, so what do we need another driver for yet?'

'Simple, he's going to relieve you of the driving so that you can get on with the design of the new car.'

Before I could answer, he jumped down off the pit counter and led me towards the workshop van gripping me by the elbow with a not too gentle hand.

'Before you say anything Peter, think – you'll realise that this is sound common sense. This geezer's putting lolly into the company, lolly we need, and in return we let his nipper play Grand Prix driver. Let's face it, you're 34, you're married and you've a kid, there's nothing in this game for you, certainly no future anyway. Doing things this way, you get a steady job and a salary regular as clockwork once a month.'

'Just a minute, what are you leading up to? Are you suggesting that I should sell out my share of the business? I know it amounts to damn all compared with your holding, but it gives me a small feeling of independence.'

'That's just your bloody trouble Peter, independence, you seem to think that you don't need anyone else to live, but everyone else needs you. Let me tell you something, as far as I'm concerned you're not worth a can-lad's wage, you don't even sell petrol. You've just got us deeper and deeper in the damned mire with your wild schemes for importing impossible cars and building even more useless and unsellable crates like that bloody thing there. Even as a racing driver you don't exactly send me, or anyone else, in fact most racing fans think you died long ago. They imagine you were one of Dreyfus's mates. Now to make matters worse you're getting old and staid and to crown it all you can't even be relied on to turn up to a practice session without getting stewed.'

'At this moment Crompton, I am stone cold sober and if your protégé hasn't taken the edge off it I would like to get on with job on hand and drive my car, assuming of course that I have your gracious permission.' I felt sick, cold and angry and was conscious of the underlying truth in what he had said. Without further comment, he turned and walked back to the car. I heard him giving orders to refuel the Pig and change tyres and could not help but admire the vigour and drive of the man as he stripped off his jacket and got to work with them.

'I'm going to have a look round the circuit on the bike. I'll be back within five minutes ready for a few laps,' I called, and Ron the chief mechanic waved his hand in acknowledgement. As I walked towards the motor cycle, Charles followed by Gwen and Pam came to meet me. He looked concerned.

'Are you sure you feel fit enough Peter? I believe we only have the circuit for another half hour before the GMT boys arrive and it looks as if it might rain soon anyway.' He looked like a grey haired Boxer dog with stomach ache.

'You worry too much Charles, leave that to me. I always feel as if I'm about to have an attack of gastro-enteritis before I get into a car but there is no need for you too. Look at Gwen she doesn't give a damn.'

I saw Aaronsen out of the corner of my eye walking towards us so started the engine and moved off onto the circuit before he could get within speaking distance.

I took my time and looked at all the corners riding round what would be my car line. Just for the hell of it, I came out of Druids flat out in second selecting top as I came under the Bailey Bridge before the pits and did a flying lap. I stopped at the end of the pits, leaned the motor cycle against the counter and walked slowly back to where the car was standing. Ron was in the cockpit running the engine. As I reached the front wheel he cut the engine and stepped out.

What had Crompton said, 'one minute fifty seconds?' I had never driven a monoposto car here before, only small capacity production sports cars, so in fact, this time was far faster than I had ever circulated on this circuit.

'I'm going to do a couple of slowish laps Patrick then if all is well I'll do a few quicker ones, OK?'

'Sure you're the driver, only don't overdo it, we'll want it next weekend.'

I slipped the gear lever into second, dipped the clutch and switched on the ignition. The electric pump ticked twice and silence descended. The sun went behind the cloud and the colour went out of the trees.

'OK?' asked Ron.

No-one else in the small crowd of spectators moved or spoke. 'OK let's go.'

Two of the mechanics and Crompton began to push. The car began to roll, the men's feet pattering on the tarmac. I engaged the clutch and eased the throttle open and the engine burst into a clean hard roar. Keeping it in second and taking it up to 7,000rpm, I held the car over to the left of the straight to get into line for Old Hall, changed into third out of the corner, into fourth briefly, then down through the gears to second for Cascades. It was going like an engineer's dream, smooth firm, precise and with clean power output all the way round the revolution counter after 3,700rpm. Frightening myself for a moment coming out of Esso Bend by being a little too heavy footed, but regaining confidence with each bend, I arrived back at the pit straight for my second slow lap. Coldly determined, watching the road and my line round the two and three quarter miles of the circuit, I completed the second lap, passing the pits at 7,200rpm in fourth gear.

The road was a river of molten tarmac flowing towards me in a torrent the exhaust note hard and clear behind my left ear. Brakes, a burst of throttle down to third, toe and heel down to second, power on round the right hander, clipping the apex of the bed, drifting out a little left, lock on, up into third, then fourth through the avenue. Over the crest of the hill, Cascade in front of it, down to third, second and on with the power to maintain the revs and the angle of drift. Up into third. Up into fourth and flat out into Island Bend. A rough corner and sharper than it looks, the air rushing over the low screen blasted past my head. The cockpit was getting warmer and smelled of warm engine. The gear lever sliced cleanly into third then second for Esso and I was pressed down hard into the tight, tailored-to-my-backside seat as I fought it round on to the line for the wild flight over the crest of the hill, down to Knicker Brook.

The roar of the wind grew, the flood tide of the road became a flashing torrent as the engine screamed up through the gears into top for an ecstatic quarter of a mile. Over the left of the road, brakes, toe and heel down through the box cleanly slicing rhythm, the same narrow band of effective power pouring out to the urgent thrusting wheels and cat-clawing tyres. Flicking it into a drift, cautious on the throttle to hold a delicate balance between toboganning progress and screaming mangled disaster, we, the car and I hurtled into the forward slope of Clay Hill. Under the bridge, a blast of sound hit back from the bridge and the club members stand. Through the fading sunlight filtering trees into Druids, the moment of truth. This should be taken in one long clean full bore drift, all the way round in a continuous sweep making a single corner of two. The unbroken falsetto scream of tyres and the steady re-counter needle testified to success.

Up into third and then fourth, under that damned low Bailey Bridge – people on it, always duck my head instinctively. Well to the left for Lodge down through the gears to second and starting to accelerate alongside the pavilion, gently with delicacy and elegance, then all the power available up through Deers Leap to the Pit straight.

As I tore past the pits, I looked quickly and saw them click the stop watches, but now I was in my stride and for three more laps I clipped successive seconds off at the corners. When I came past for the seventh lap, the GMT van was unloading and Crompton was talking to a newcomer who had put the watch on me as I drew level. I finished the lap slowly and drove gently over into the paddock behind our van. While I climbed out of the cockpit and took off my helmet Aaronsen came running over.

'My God, Mr Wade, that sixth lap was one minute forty exactly, that's just over 99. Your wife couldn't stand watching any longer and is sitting in the car, I don't blame her. She said you were angry and wouldn't be content until you'd set a time that I couldn't match. Is that true?'

'No, not at all, I'm afraid that I don't care enough about anything any more to want to do that. I just wanted if possible to show that I was not past it, a back number. It was nothing to do with you or anyone else and in any case, I enjoyed it. Now I know that the old Pig is a good piece of machinery and that I can use it, I'm content, it's all yours.'

He looked at me in astonishment, his expression varying uncertainly between disbelief and faint contempt.

'When you can do what you have just done, why don't you go on and use your ability?' I felt tired and hot and people were bearing down on us. He was waiting for an answer, but I felt too drained of interest, and embarrassed by the coming questions to answer honestly.

'That my dear Mr Aaronsen is the sixty four dollar question, but look at us both and you have the answer.'

His quick brown eyes, with the open natural arrogance of youth examined my open necked shirt with the faded frayed collar, the coming out at the elbows grey pullover and baggy Government Surplus Store corduroy trousers. To my astonishment it was his turn to look embarrassed, as if he were ashamed of his immaculate pale blue racing overalls and silk scarf.

I felt my face break into a smile in spite of itself and as he grinned with relief, the tension broke and we formed an unspoken alliance against the exploiters of racing drivers.

I was about to join Gwen, who was getting the picnic basket out of our old Anglia, when Crompton called me to meet someone. He was walking towards me holding his companion by the elbow in his usual irritating manner.

The man with him was a stranger to me, but when young Aaronsen greeted him as 'father', it became obvious that he was our new owner. He was tall, slightly over six feet with a mass of crinkly grey hair and a heavy fleshy face laced with a network of tiny red blood vessels. His cheeks had tufts of dark grey hairs under his eyes and his lips were full and slightly apart as if breathing through his nose were difficult. This seemed strange because he seemed to have ample nose for one man.

Although it was hot and humid, he wore a beautifully cut but heavyweight dark grey lounge suit and waistcoat as well as an Anthony Eden hat.

'Peter, this is Mr Aaronsen, – Peter Wade.'

'How d'ye do Mr Aaronsen.'

'Very well thank you Mr Wade, and I observe that you were doing very well a few minutes ago. I must confess to being somewhat surprised though, to discover that you are not the hair brained and dashing young whippersnapper that I expected from that exhibition. I like to see my money being put to good use and I was given to understand that you were the technical brains behind the car and you were looking for a talented young driver. It seemed that an investment would be well used by you to build a new car which my son could drive and be the forerunner of a marketable racing car, but it looks as if you will be too busy teaching my son to drive as well as to design cars.'

'But Mr Aaronsen,' Crompton interrupted, 'I am sure that Peter agrees, your son is quite competent to drive right away, after all he has had quite a lot of experience driving on the Continent and he was trained at Taruffi's school so Mr Wade can carry on with his design work.'

'Steadily, steadily Mr Crompton, let me finish. Mr Wade shall go on driving for as long as he wishes, but he must select his design staff and train Simon, so that next season we can field two cars. It is better that Simon should be a top class Formula Junior driver than a third class Formula One pilot, what do you say Simon?'

'I think that we ought to talk about this over dinner tonight, rather than here. Anyway Mr Wade's wife is waiting with a cup of tea for him over there, and the boss of the GMT boys is trying to catch his attention as well.'

'That's sensible, very sensible we meet you at the Blossoms tonight eh? Bring your beautiful wife and brighten up our dull lives. My wife and her little girl are away on holiday at the moment, so the sight of a pretty face will cheer us up, ay Simon? Seven-thirty in the lounge then,' and without waiting for an answer he raised his hat to Gwen, bowed slightly and strode off to a pale bronze Rolls which was parked by the deserted competitors bar.

Simon waved goodbye and followed his father, leaving Crompton. I joined Gwen and Ian. She was quite tense, and I knew that a wrong word would provoke an argument. Today I could do no right. 'Gwen, I don't know who this character is who is coming here, but before he arrives we are expected to have dinner with Aaronsen and his boy tonight, as well as Crompton, so we must get home soon. I'll send the bike back in the van and come back with you.'

'Where do you think that we can get a babysitter from at this time on a Saturday evening? You'd better go on your own, besides I've nothing to wear.'

'But honey, we haven't been out for heaven knows how long, it will do you good. Perhaps Pam will sit for us?'

She looked close to tears, and looked down at her now empty beaker, rolling it between the palms of her hands. I longed to put my arm round her shoulders to comfort her.

'Mr. Wade?' I turned and stood up.

'Yes, what can I do for you?'

'My name's Hall and I manage the GMT team practicing now. We were watching you drive a short while ago and were quite impressed. Have you any plans for the rest of this season?'

I looked at Gwen who was putting a sweater on Ian, but her face only showed polite interest and concentrated on the immediate task of struggling to get a too tight polo-necked sweater over the wriggling elusive head. This was her way of leaving a potentially tricky problem to me, concerned with anything other than a simple matter of entertainment.

'Well we have some rather nebulous plans, and they are not entirely under my control. Why what have you in mind?'

'Formula One reserve, and the odd Gran Turismo event, does it interest you?'

Five years earlier and I would have responded immediately with real enthusiasm, but I felt strangely detached.

'Will it mean much travelling away from home?'

Gwen was tidying away the picnic hamper and its irritating collection of odd coloured plastic beakers and plates which always seemed to make tea taste like soup and were always reluctant to be fitted back into the space from which they came.

'We may be short of a pilot for Monte Carlo and the Nürburgring if Peter Hemingway doesn't change his plans about getting married in the middle of the season, and we are certainly short of someone for Aintree next week unless Iredale will drive for us. That will be all the events this year as far as I know. So what about it, assuming of course that you and the car get on? There will be a trial of course, at Aintree next Wednesday morning. Well?'

'Can I let you know tomorrow?'

'OK, I'm staying at the Blossoms, just give me a ring between nine and half past tomorrow. Cheerio.'

With a lack of immediate interest in his proposition which seemed surprising to me, I watched him as he returned to his team. When he had gone I went over to Crompton and asked him to take the motorbike back in the transporter as I intended to drive the Anglia home. He nodded towards Hall's broad duffle-coated back.

'What did matey want?'

Affecting even more indifference than I felt, I told him. He pursed his lips.

'You'll take it of course?'

'I'm not sure, I think I'm a bit too old to be a new boy, but I would like to try the car anyway, so I'll take a trial run on Wednesday.'

'D'you know that's typical of you Peter, you're mad keen to do a thing until the chance arrives, and when it does, you find a hundred and one reasons why you can't. You are going to say, you've got to think of Gwen and Ian, and you're getting too old, you can't afford the time and so on, but the real reason is that you're terrified of perhaps finding out that you are only second rate. Rather than discover that, you'd miss the chance. You're spineless.'

To cover my rising embarrassment at hearing what sounded uncomfortably like the truth, I laughed. 'True Patrick perfectly true, but I still prefer to be second rate but harmless than an effective but selfish bloody moneygrubber like you with all the speciality salesman charm that you can turn on at will. We'll see you later.'

His response was a lop-sided grin and silence.

Occasional heavy spots of thundering rain were falling so we each sought the shelter of our respective cars without further sparring.

'Wipe your feet before you get in dear, I cleaned the carpets this morning, and please don't drive too fast on the way back it makes me feel sick when it's thundering like this.'

'Would you rather drive?' I asked. It was raining heavily now and the windscreen was covered by a sheet of water. The inside of the windows were beginning to cover with condensation. It was in the nature of a gesture rather than a serious question, and as I drove away towards the paddock exit she failed to answer but continued her search in the glove box for the travel sickness tablets.

I looked quickly at her face in profile, and realised with a feeling between fear and irritation that she was beginning to look middle-aged. Her hair, although naturally blond was beginning to look dead and dull, and her neck to show the tell-tale circlet of wrinkles that spell thirty-five-plus so clearly. Every day of unhappiness, anxiety and insecurity was beginning to make its cumulative effect apparent, and made it more difficult for me to reach her. Mutual need, affection and pity held us together like an invisible cobweb, and the little love of which we were both still capable was centred on Ian. With Gwen who was always inclined to possessiveness it was becoming an obsession, and this together with my lack of business acumen combined to act like a wedge between us that was slowly driving us apart. It was happening almost imperceptibly, but at moments like this I sensed it and felt as if I was waiting to go into an operating theatre smelling the sickly pungent ether.

Ian was standing behind my seat as I drove, his plump strong little arms around my neck.

'Leave Daddy alone dear while he's driving,' Gwen said, and turned to me.

'What on earth can I wear tonight? I simply can't go Peter I haven't a single pair of stockings without a ladder in them.'

Her face looked punished and grey, and her forehead was gathering itself up into a maze of wrinkles.

'What about the dress your mother gave you for Christmas?'

She was obviously just registering a protest because she ignored my suggestion, and sat nervously twisting her wedding ring around her finger. The weekend traffic was getting thicker as we got nearer to the outskirts of Chester and took the Birkenhead road.

'Why does he want us to have dinner with him?' What is so special about today?'

'How the devil should I know? As usual I am the last person to be told, after all, I didn't even know he existed until today, and while I was on the subject, your friend Pam and her pompous husband were on friendly terms with him. How much did they have to do with all this?'

It had suddenly occurred to me that Gwen was more than usually nervous. How much part, I wondered had she played in this deal?

'There is no need to be rude about my friends Peter, anyway what has been done, was done for your good and mine.'

'Perhaps so Gwen, but I'll bet you a pound to a penny that Crompton comes out of it better than we do. What has been going on anyway?'

'Will you promise me not to be angry if I tell you now? It was meant to be a surprise.'

'Oh for heaven's sake Gwen, get on with it, what have you done?'

'We've got you what you always wanted, that's all.'

'And what have I always wanted?'

'Oh Peter please stop being so prickly, you make me feel as if I've done something awful. You've always wanted to build a Grand Prix car, and produce a Formula Junior car for re-sale well now you can, Daddy has lent me a thousand pounds, and Mr Aaronsen is furnishing the rest to start a new subsidiary of Crompton and Wade and you have a free hand to get on with it. Well what do you think?'

'Does it matter what I think? You seem to have made all the decisions already, but because you did ask, this is what I think. I think that as usual someone is making a mug out of me. Just let me guess how it is to be organised.

'Chairman of parent company Aaronsen, vice-chairman and managing director of Crompton and Wade, Patrick Crompton who is unqualified but astute, I will be off that board and a joint director with you in the subsidiary organisation. Now if they run true to form we will be a separate thing financially so that if we go down the drain we don't cause them too much trouble, but at the same time Aaronsen will be our chairman and I will just be the managing director with a microscopic salary and no bread and butter business. How is that for a guess?'

I looked at her quickly, and saw that she was frightened and worried.

'Please Peter don't bait me, but you're almost right about the organisation. The only thing is that they suggested that you ought not to be worried with too much administration and have decided to let Crompton manage it with young Mr Aaronsen as chairman and responsible for sales and competition.'

'Jesus wept, what am I supposed to do?'

'Oh you will be in charge of design of course dear, as technical director.'

'And what do you think that means Gwen? Be your age, it only means that I'd do the work and act as the whipping boy. I'll just be a bloody draughtsman. How in Hell did they get you on their side? What have you signed?'

The thought of the endless confidential cosy chats that must have gone on to get to this stage without anyone telling me anything filled me with cold disgust.

'What does Charles get out of this? Our friend Mr Green? Was that why he took me out and got me tight this morning?'

'Alright if you want to be rough Peter, yes he took you out and got you tight deliberately, apparently on the smell of a barmaid's apron, so that we could prevent you from killing yourself in the Pig, and so that we could discuss the reorganisation. You're past driving in competition as you should know best of all, and you're no business man, so for our own good and mine, you're going to be pinned down to the drawing board where you are some use. They've been decent enough to give you a directorship and allow me to buy an equal shareholding to Crompton with 1,000 one pound shares in a newly formed subsidiary.

'Just a minute, Gwen, where the hell has Crompton suddenly got a thousand pounds from, or for that matter, where can I find that sort of money?'

She shrugged her shoulders and said nothing.

I began to feel cold and tired, and wished that we had not agreed to go back to Chester, but it was too late for regrets. It was far too late. We finished the journey in silence.

While I put Ian to bed and told him a story Gwen went round to ask our neighbours if they would allow their sixteen year old daughter to baby sit for us.

Ian was too excited to go to sleep, he wanted me to tell him about driving the Pig over and over again. His little room was still bright with evening sunlight which found the gaps in the curtains and he couldn't understand why he should go to bed while the sun was still shining. At last his battered knitted golliwog with one eye touched his cheek, and his thumb found its way into his mouth. Heavy eyelids, blue veined, closed over his tired eyes and I was able to detach my first finger from his left hand and tiptoe out of the room.

Gwen was walking about our bedroom in bra and pants trying to dry her newly applied nail varnish by gently waving her hands about in the air. She looked over her shoulder at me.

'Don't stand there grinning like an ape, it's seven o'clock already, and you haven't even started to change.'

'Honey, if you only could see yourself, you have just restored my sense of proportion. Walking about in a state of semi-nudity waving your hands about like a Victorian preacher. The thought just occurred to me that there must be millions of such women all over the world, black, white, brown and yellow, fat, skinny, old and young all wandering about in the noodles doing the same thing. A sort of pre-prandial act of worship.'

She only looked exasperated.

'There is a clean shirt in the linen cupboard, your cuff links and studs are on the bathroom windowsill and your black shoes are under the stairs.'

I began to take off my clothes as I turned on the bath.

'For goodness sake Peter, there's no time for a bath if we have to be there by seven-thirty.'

'Mr Aaronsen can stuff himself with olives while he's waiting and Crompton can just worry. I have been doing some thinking while I was putting Ian to bed, and by the time I've had a bath I'll have it all sorted out, so stop worrying. I'm tired of being pushed around by everyone all my life. The worm is about to turn. Have we any money?'

I lowered myself gently into the hot water, fascinated as always by the way one's nerve endings reacted violently to the pain at first, then almost immediately set about accepting them enjoying the warmth.

'What do you mean, have we any money?' Do you mean now, in the house?'

'Yes dear now, who knows we might end tonight by paying for our own dinner, and we will certainly have to pay for the odd round of drinks as well as paying Janet for babysitting.'

'Hell,' said Gwen. 'I didn't go to the bank this morning because of all our visitors what did you use for money at the pub?'

'The less said about that the better my love, what about the milk money, did you pay him today?'

'Oh no, of course not, and I didn't pay the grocer either so that will be about £2. I left it in the old teapot in the kitchen. I'll look through your old suit pockets shall I? That might be fruitful.'

'I doubt it, but you can try.'

She rushed like a tornado down the stairs into the kitchen in her stocking feet so as not to wake Ian. As she came back upstairs she looked into the bathroom.

'Success, £2-9s-6d in the teapot, 25 shillings in the telephone box and 1s-6d in your raincoat pocket.'

The search moved to the wardrobe, the sound of rattling coat-hangers and the squeaking door indicated her haste.

As I was dressing she came in again. 'For goodness sake Gwen what is the matter now?'

Her face was cold and angry.

'How long have you been carrying this photograph around with you like a silly schoolboy?' She held out a crumpled old picture of Deborah that was my last remaining token and had been in my wallet until about a month before when I had mislaid it.

'About twelve years I would say, and it looks like it doesn't it, did you find any money?'

It was no use trying to fool her, she knew perfectly well that I was terrified of losing that picture, it had become my last link with Deborah and the idea of it being destroyed or lost filled me with a strange superstitious kind of dread. This faded and creased little picture of a laughing girl at the helm of a dinghy, her hair long and straight and wet, frozen into a mood of perpetual happiness without a thought for the black and bloody days before us. If I lost this, I would only remember her face as I last saw it, as I saw it in dreams by night and day during the last twelve years.

'You needn't look so worried Peter, I won't harm it, although God knows, nothing would give me more pleasure. I just wondered when all this nostalgia for your lost youth is going to end. Most women are faced with a bit of competition after the first few years of marriage and I could cope with a flesh and blood rival but I can't fight ghosts. I have watched you on numerous occasions, you see one woman on a train or a crowded street, that looks a bit like her, and you become deaf to anything I am saying. The awful thing about it is that the girls that attract your attention, your ghost Deborahs are all a good ten years younger than she will be now. If she is alive, she will be getting on for middle age like us and like most middle aged Jewesses putting on a lot of weight. Start thinking of her as a flabby-breasted, big-bottomed momma stuffing cream cakes into her voluptuous mouth, and surrounded by screaming kids and I could be spared hearing you talking to her in your sleep. It's a pity she can't –'

A knock at the front door cut her short in mid sentence, and she thrust the picture at me before going to answer it. It was the babysitter and Gwen took her through into the living room before putting some supper on a tray for her.

Five minutes later we were on our way to Chester, driving out of the cheek by jowl modern, three bedroomed semi-detached all mod. con. speculative builders jungle in which we lived. I hated every damned brick of the place, the deadly smallness of it all, and the conscientious orderly nine to fivers who lived there. Sunday morning, washing the car, roast and two veg for lunch with apple pie and custard to follow, out for a nose to tail drive to the coast or Wales in the afternoon and to queue with thirty thousand other families in the evening to get back to Wirral or Liverpool over Queensferry bridge. Home to Renedane, or Arcady, or Dunroamin with a cartload of irritable tired children, buckets, spades and sand to Westmoreland Avenue. 'Where shall we go next week mother?'

The evening had grown cold and the car heater had stopped working, so by the time we had parked and walked to the hotel through the rain-glistening streets we were both beginning to feel chilly. The bar curtains were drawn and the lights on. The barman stood, white coated and bow-tied in front of the glittering backcloth of mirrors and multi-coloured bottles like a circus star about to perform seemingly impossible tricks. No doubt he would during the course of the evening injecting his victims painlessly with small but regular doses of alcohol and spiriting their crinkling folded money out of well stuffed creaking wallets, into the management till and his own pockets.

I imagined him saying, 'Nothing up my sleeves ladies and gents, but a pair of well trained quicker than silver cocktail shakers. Now my next trick will be to smile, to smile I say, at this definitely-not-out-of-the-upper-super-income-tax-bracket lady and gentleman.' Acknowledging his smile, I looked round for Aaronsen and his party.

'Are you Mr. Aaronsen's party' he asked, thought reading.

'Yes, are they in the lounge?'

'Yes sir, I think they are waiting for you.'

He lifted the bar counter and led us through the hall past the expensively stuffed jewellers glass showcases to the small lounge. Aaronsen, Crompton and Green broke off an earnest conversation to rise and greet us.

They looked as if they had been deciding just how they were going to skin me. As we stood and made small talk about the weather, Simon Aaronsen came in with the head waiter.

'Hello Peter, just in time to order, what will you and Mrs Wade drink before we settle down to reading the menu?'

He ordered drinks, and the conversation began to flow quickly and easily. I looked at the clock, its fingers were approaching eight o'clock and it occurred to me that I was very hungry. At intervals I made contributions to the conversation but mostly I watched the others and listened. Simon Aaronsen had brought his girlfriend who was obviously wildly out of her depth, and was making frantic stabs at the too easily murdered art of small talk with fatal results. In between sallies, she tried vainly to persuade her too short skirt to reach her knees and drank gin and tonic as if the next oasis was going to be a long way away.

Simon occasionally sent her a private look, but otherwise seemed to be ignoring her, although it was apparent that he was taking careful note of her gin consumption. As her intake grew so her attempts to preserve her modesty became less frequent, and her elaborate beehive hairstyle began to look like a haystack in a force eight gale.

Simon was agreeable to listen to, with a pleasantly pitched voice without affectation, and an easy flow of anecdotes. He seemed to have the gift of persuading other people that they were gifted conversationalists and so had Gwen telling the story of our one continental holiday.

I ordered a new round of drinks while Gwen continued her story leaving myself out of it because the Aaronsens and Green were drinking double Scotches and it was going to cost rather more than I had bargained for. When the drinks came, there was a gap in the conversation, and under the professional gaze of the waiter as well as seven pairs of eyes, I had to take out my wallet which was falling to pieces, pull out too few notes and find the rest out of small change, cleaned from three separate pockets. I felt my face getting red.

'Aren't you drinking Mr Wade?' asked Aaronsen senior. 'What's the matter? You're not a Muslim are you?'

Everyone laughed dutifully. He looked round at his audience beaming.

'We must all enjoy ourselves tonight, we are celebrating what I hope will be the beginning of a happy and fruitful partnership. We must start as we mean to go on ay?'

The head waiter materialised at his elbow and announced that we could go to our table whenever we were ready. I leaned over to Gwen and asked her what part Green was supposed to play in the new organisation. She said that she would tell me later and finished her drink.

The meal was lavish and bore very little resemblance to anything described on the menu. Conversation was limited to food and wine and clothes, all apparently favoured Aaronsen subjects.

We retired to a private room forming part of the suite which Aaronsen had taken for his visit to Cheshire and drank coffee and liquers.

'Come and help yourself to more brandy Peter,' he called from where he was re-charging his glass at the sideboard.

'Perhaps you would like to try this one, it is made by a Greek Orthodox community in Israel, and uses as a base a very old Greek brandy. It's orange flavoured and quite smooth although dry.'

He took a clean glass and gave it to me to hold while he poured, the rich amber liquid which looked thick like liquid glass. As its fumes reached my nostrils, I remembered that I had drunk it before, one summer evening in Suez, at the Union Club with Deborah and Arthur Howe. Rolling it over my tongue and feeling the fumes rise, took my mind back to that night, to the long moonlit drive back to El Kantara and the cool night-time smells of Egypt, away from the stuffy cigar smoke filled little sitting room and its chattering occupants.

'What did you think of it?' Aaronsen added, and he looked genuinely interested in my opinion.

'It made you smile.'

'It is a beautiful liquer but it has romantic qualities more suitable to a young man's palate, I had quite forgotten it.'

'So you have tasted it before, how disappointing. I always like showing people new and pleasurable things and it gives me a lot of simple pleasure to see their expressions of astonishment and enjoyment. But you looked first puzzled, then a little startled and finally rather dismal. Did you taste it in Israel or Greece?'

'No, it was in Egypt, and I only drank it once then, but of course one could never forget it.' He was looking at me closely.

'Were you there on business, or was it in the services?'

'It was when I was a temporary soldier, at what was supposed to be the beginning of my career.'

'Oh yes of course, Crompton told me that you and he were in the same regiment, didn't you get a medal?'

'Yes, but so did Patrick, you'd better get him to tell you about it. It's rather dull and much better forgotten. I certainly would prefer to forget it if I could but the absence of one kidney, a half useless leg, and this brandy act as reminders. I don't want to abuse your wonderful hospitality by boring you to death with stories about things that don't matter any more. Won't you tell me why you decided to take an interest in our small and not too successful business.'

He looked as if he would have liked to know more, but restrained himself.

'Surely you know it all?' he asked.

'I know nothing apart from what Patrick told me today that you were the new boss, and your son would be driving my car in future because I was past it.'

He looked hurt and a little annoyed.

'This is not at all right, someone has misrepresented the case to you, let me explain. My son is very keen to race, someone must teach him. He also wants to learn car design, he must be taught. I would also like him one day to take over a business that is suitable, and this could be it, so I have put some money into it and I'll help you and Crompton with some professional and financial guidance. You benefit in the meanwhile, and because I know that you know your job I think it is a good investment.'

'How do you know that I know my job Mr. Aaronsen, and why don't you send your son to a university to take an engineering degree first?'

'First you, I know a great deal about where you have been and what you have done in engineering, the Army bit doesn't add up to much. The press seem to have picked up on a *Gazette* announcement that you had died from your wounds on the flight back to hospital in England. The next two or was it three years, seem to be a bit of a blank, except for the 'posthumous' award of a mention in dispatches or an MC, resulting from an earlier event in Sinai. You next pop up several years later, when taking voluntary redundancy from a desk job in Rome with the Foreign Office. So one presumes that is where earned you the CMG and learned Italian.

'You stayed in Italy for four years, and worked with Maserati, then when you heard that your father had died you came back for the funeral and worked with the BRM team till you had a row and left. Next you went as a private driver and designed a new Grand Prix car for yourself with a Maserati engine, but this it would seem, came to nothing. While you were at Le Mans driving an Osca your mother died and you came back home, met Gwen again at the funeral and a month later you got married. That was about four years ago.

'The same year you met Crompton again when you were looking for a garage in Cheshire and he offered you a partnership in his. You got the Maserati agency and started to design and build special racing cars and sports cars to individual order. You're not making any money at this because Maseratis are both expensive and unreliable and you can't afford to put in the plant and jigs you need to build your money-making idea .'

'What is that?' I asked him.

'Once again I'll tell you. It is a twin cylinder aircooled engine driven three wheeler sports car with a low drag body and because of its simple design very cheap to build, am I right?'

'More or less Mr Aaronsen – you seem to have done your homework thoroughly.'

'What you don't know yet Peter, and neither does Crompton, is that I have had Brumwell's market researchers to work on this and they say that there is a demand for this type of machine, if the price is right and we can produce in the right numbers.'

'Did they tell you how big the potential market is?'

'Yes, they reckon that favourable insurance and tax would allow it to take a large slice of the motorcycle market. Insurance rates are going up on the big bikes so that is a big factor, also of course the weather protection is so much better.'

'How many do they say we will have to produce per week, and where do they suggest that we buy our engines when the motorcycle boys realise that we are using their best motor to steal their bread and butter?'

'I thought you were not the business minded partner yet you ask me these questions and they are very relevant.'

I made what I felt to be an ironic bow in acknowledgement of this patronisation and caught a quick glimpse of Gwen talking to

Simon. She was sparkling with relaxed good humour letting her uncanny gift of making other people dedicate their confidences to her. What used to be a failing, the inability to make conversation about everyday incidents and trivia, she had turned to her advantage by becoming a co-operative listener. However long or dull the story, she would hear it out never competing for a worse operation or a better bargain at a sale, but collecting an audience with her and adding a little colour or corroboration to help the by now, intoxicated speaker with his Odyssey.

Aaronsen noticed that I was looking at Gwen.

'Your wife is a wonderful woman Mr Wade, had you known her long before you were married?'

'We almost grew up together,' I said, and told him briefly how our families had been neighbours. He sighed.

'You are a very lucky man. To make a perfect marriage is the greatest of good fortune, and you should realise this. My first wife died ten years ago, she was Charles Green's sister and she too was a fine woman, but simple and very gentle. Such people I feel are too good to live with the rest of us, and are only lent to us to show us how we should be. Simon, her son, is more like me, he knows what he wants and he takes it. Most men hate him, and all the women think he is just a nice boy, but a little naughty and of course, that makes them happy. They like to try and reform him or so they tell their friends, and just as they used to do with me, they find themselves in bed with him. Everything is too easy for him you must make him work very hard and I should keep him away from your wife.' He laughed and slapped me on the shoulder. I could feel him watching me closely and on impulse decided to give him a verbal, but totally unwarranted kick in the teeth.

'If I were you Mr. Aaronsen, I would advise him to stay away, or I will kill him, by accident of course,' and smiling amiably walked away. To my astonishment he let out a roar like an angry bull and hurled his glass down at his feet and stamped on it.

'You, you bloody crazy man you're sick in the head,' he shouted, red in the face with fury. 'You're not fit to be out alone, you're no gentleman, you insult me in my own home!'

'Father for God's sake, calm down what's the matter?' Simon

put down his glass and walked over to where his father was standing, feet apart fists clenched and eyes staring.

He looked unbelievably ridiculous and I could hardly prevent myself from laughing but the enormity of what I had done and its fantastic result shocked me. I realised that I must be a little tight, but the situation had to be restored. The room was silent, everyone seemed to have stopped breathing.

'Yes what is the matter Mr Aaronsen?' I asked concentrating on breathing slowly and regularly to maintain my calmness and sobering rapidly.

'You just repeat what you said to me then, just tell them go on, tell them, tell everybody.'

I looked puzzled and shrugged my shoulders.

'Surely you don't want me to repeat all our conversation do you? Do you want me to repeat your last remark, even though you've had a drop too much to drink, it would scarcely make good listening with ladies present.'

I thought he was going to have a fit, he just stood clenching and unclenching his fists with his mouth wide open, saliva dribbling from the corners. Simon persuaded him to sit down on the settee. He sat staring at me as if he was looking at a ghost. Everyone began to talk at once and began to say how late it was and how they had to be up early in the morning. Crompton was looking very agitated and was hovering around the old man making noises that were obviously intended to be understood as apology and disassociation from me and whatever I may have said. He glowered at me over Aaronsen's head. I gave him a friendly oafish smile in return.

Gwen had collected her coat and I held it out for her. Her face was set and her skin had taken on the pale green waxy look which indicated tightly controlled fury. Pam Green hurried over to her and took her hands in hers.

'Don't worry about it Gwen, he's obviously a bit slewed and he's very hard to get on with anyway. He probably misunderstood what Peter said to him.'

'I don't care what Peter or anyone else said to him, he's behaving like a savage. Who the devil does he think he is anyway?'

I went into the hall to get my coat. It was cool and free of cigarette smoke. Simon followed me out.

'I'm sorry about that ridiculous scene Mr Wade. I hope it won't affect your decision to continue our business association.' He looked genuinely anxious.

'We'll see how it looks by the cold light of day, then we can decide,' I suggested, and took Gwen's arm as she came out.

'Goodnight Mr Aaronsen, and thank you for asking us to your party.' Gwen gave a dutiful smile and we left.

As we passed the residents lounge someone called my name, so I stopped and looked inside, two or three figures were sitting in almost complete darkness, staring, hypnotised at the last few hundred frames of a cowboy epic. One raised himself to his feet and came out into the brightly lit hall blinking. It was Hall the GMT manager. I introduced him to Gwen.

'Well, what about it? Are you going to drive for us?'

'I would very much like to Mr Hall, but you will want to see me drive the car first, I presume.'

'Well you know time is getting a bit short for trials, but if you can get to Aintree on Wednesday the boss will be there as well so we can settle everything at once. OK?'

We settled the time of our meeting and because it was obvious that Gwen was impatient, we said goodnight and left.

CHAPTER 5

Rachel

THE streets of Chester were glistening with the rain and reflected the shop and street lights as a galaxy of splintered stars of all colours. If it had not been for Gwen's almost tangible anger, which could never be easily dispelled, the mood of depression which had been settling down uncomfortably around me like a black Merseyside smog during the course of the day, would have gone.

To drive a closed warm car through the deserted but brilliantly lit streets of a city at night, without the thrusting jostling, noisy people and cars was like being the only man in a make-believe world of leisurely plenty. The last survivor of a civilisation, with time to waste, to stop and look at the miracles of craftsmanship in the jewellers windows brought to life by the electric light. To look at the deep glossy patina of old furniture, and the sleep inducing luxury of the displays of thick soft woollen blankets was to be able to indulge in the pure sensual appreciation of texture, unspoiled by a desire to possess the objects themselves. All this without the distraction of other people with eyes and tongues demanding attention and competing for living space and ownership.

One had to be alone, without communication for brief periods like this to regain one's sense of individuality. Otherwise any real sense of personal purpose or identity would be lost. Things and events, coincident cycles of men's and women's lives happen in such a way that they take control and involve them in a lunatic charade, each player absorbing a little of the others and matching the rhythm of his existence to theirs. He is only real while he is acting, he is still nothing more than a rag-bag of different impressions to the other actors, each of whom is trying to be bigger and truer and more real than his private image of himself. For every event in which he is a hero to himself, he is someone else's villain.

'It's all a matter of where you are standing,' Gwen said.

After some five years of marriage to her, I should have given up being surprised each time she echoed my thoughts. She was smiling when I looked at her, and she squeezed my left knee affectionately.

'What was that for?' I asked.

'Because,' she said and I wondered why I could feel nothing but comfortable domestic affection for this woman who was the mother of my son and who endured my selfishness and stupidities for five years while I wasted a small legacy which my father left me on the pursuit of technical wild geese. A mixture of self-pity, nostalgia and guilty conscience had made me propose to her and before I had realised what was happening the juggernaut of wedding preparations was under way. The enveloping net of undemanding affection, forgiveness and a physical desire with which she bound me to her, left no time for thought.

To make the trap even more inescapable, universal family approval was added, and frequent massive injections of alcohol donated by the enthusiastic bystanders. Marriage seemed to be like a cold swimming pool, those who had fallen in or had been pushed, could think of no greater joy than to drag in some more non-swimmers. The day came, and a feeling of numb resignation carried me through the formalities until the night.

We had stopped at an old half-timbered inn at Ludlow on our way to Devon for the first night of our honeymoon. It was a November night and the fog had been thick between Shrewsbury and Craven Arms. We were both tired and were told that dinner had finished and the chef had gone home when we arrived at the inn. The landlord cut some beef sandwiches and brought them into the cold lounge for us. The three other residents, two old ladies and a salesman, sat in complete silence and watched us struggle with the thick gristly beef and dry bread, until I could stand it no longer and went to look for a chip shop. Fortunately there was one open, so we had the rare pleasure of bringing some back with us and eating them out of greasy old newspapers in the saloon bar. The landlord's air of professional rigid disapproval added to his debit account in our estimation and brightened our evening.

The hotel's hot water system, although complex, was useless and a bath was out of the question, so we had to share the contents of a kettle from the kitchen in order to wash.

I became conscious of Gwen, she was speaking to me,

'Darling did you hear what I said?' Gwen's voice harpooned my wandering mind. We were almost home.

'No, I'm afraid I was thinking about something else.'

She sighed. 'I said that this association with Mr Aaronsen didn't seem like such a good idea now.'

'I don't think it ever was Gwen, but Crompton is ambitious and he can't afford to pay me or find the money we need for research and development so Aaronsen, or someone like him, is a necessity. What he doesn't seem to have considered though is that Aaronsen is going to do the whip cracking, and it's no use waiting for him to die in a few years because there is another ready-made Aaronsen to take over. If he looks around a little more, he will probably see uncles, aunts, first cousins, sons and daughters in law, all well qualified to take over duties in the business. In a few years time it will be a big organisation, just as Crompton wants it, but he will probably wind up as a depot manager or chief clerk. It's the money that counts, not know-how. They can always buy brains and experience.'

'The trouble with you Peter is that you're anti-Semitic, just can't stand the thought of working for a Jew.'

The thought had not entered by conscious mind.

'I don't think so Gwen, it would be just the same if he were a Gentile. The whole thing is really that if we're not to go bankrupt in the near future, we need him now and luckily, he needs us. I will go and see him on Monday and apologise.'

'You'll do nothing of the sort. I won't have you crawling to him or anyone else.'

I remained silent, but I had decided that if Hall's offer to drive one of his team's cars did not materialise I would apologise to Aaronsen. Gwen had suffered too much already for the mistakes of marrying me, and the least that I could do for her would be to earn a living for her. She seemed satisfied that my silence indicated assent, and left the subject alone.

When I parked the car in the garage and switched off the engine, I became aware of the fact that I was physically exhausted. It required a great mental effort to drag my reluctant body out of the driving seat into the cold night to close the gates and garage doors and to climb the short flight of stairs to bed.

Gwen had paid the baby sitter and sent her home before I had got in. She was getting ready for bed to the accompaniment of the tinny traditional jazz from her transistor set sitting among the almost empty pots of face cream or hand cream and general debris which littered the top of her dressing table. She saw me watching her in the mirror and pulled her dressing gown over her body to hide her bare breasts. I pretended not to notice, and undressed, anxious only to wash and get to sleep, before she came to bed.

Respect, affection and loyalty I could feel for this strange woman who still looked like my first love, but no great physical affection. We had always really been out of step with each other and it had only been within the last year that I had noticed how the strain of loving and getting nothing in return was beginning to show in her face and her manner. I could make love to her but without involvement. It was as if my mind disassociated itself from the sprawling undignified fevered bodies. The ability to love was dying of neglect.

An obsessive detachment was cutting me off from other people until the only moments of feeling which approximated to happiness or exhilaration were when I was alone in a fast car. At other times when I was alone, at my drawing board, or at the bench, the memory of Deborah would invade my thoughts and lead them away to the sun and blue skies of Israel. The thought of her smooth black hair and golden skin, and her voice took me away from the corrugated iron roofed wooden shack which was my office, and the eternal stink of petrol and dirty overalls, to the hot white gleaming sand and the royal blue sea. As the days and the months and the years went by it became harder to remember her face, but the loneliness and the longing for her grew. It was like being held prisoner in someone else's body, living a different life.

I went to sleep as I did each night with the feeling that perhaps tomorrow she might walk up to me in the street. My mind never went further than the moment of meeting. To do so would be like walking under a ladder.

On Sunday I went into the garage and worked, finishing a re-boring job on a customer's Land Rover before completing some detailed drawings for the three-wheeler. Without help and working in the evenings at weekends, I would be able to finish all the manufacturing drawings before the autumn and this would coincide reasonably well with the end of the racing season. Whatever Crompton and Aaronsen arranged, this was my project and was going to pay for Ian's schooling and wipe out some of our outstanding overdraft.

There was plenty of work to keep me busy, and as Crompton was away in London talking about contracts to Aaronsen's solicitors the inevitable brawl about the incident at the party was put off.

Wednesday morning came coldly and wet, and Gwen had one of her regular streaming spring colds that reduced her to a waxy faced ruin with red nose and bloodshot eyes. I took her a cup of tea to bed, while I was getting my own breakfast. Ian paddled about the kitchen in his bare feet ostensibly helping me until it was time for me to leave.

I turned in to the Aintree circuit at nine o'clock and parked beside Hall's Lotus Elite behind the members stand. As I walked toward the group around the car they stopped talking for a moment and turned to look at me. There was an air of irritation and impatience about the group. Hall looked pre-occupied and was peering into the engine compartment of the car which was a much modified Formula One Lotus with a flat four swing valve engine and wire wheels.

'I don't give a monkey's what-not what you think,' he said to Burroughs the chief mechanic, 'I think it's an air leak in the inlet manifold. You've changed the fuel, there still can't be water in it.'

'I gather you have troubles, would you like me to go away and come back later?'

'That's alright old son, you stick around. It's just missing a bit at the top end of the rev counter. We'll sort it out for you. Go and have a look round the circuit while you're waiting. We're only

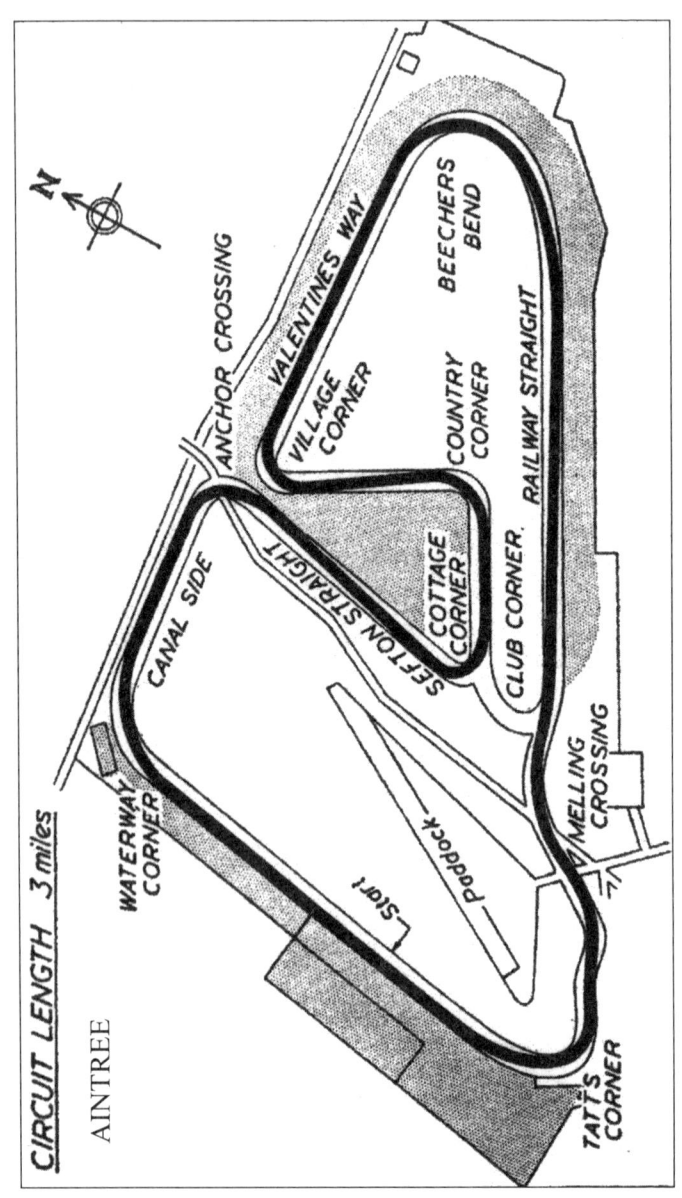

CIRCUIT LENGTH 3 miles

AINTREE

N

WATERWAY CORNER

CANAL SIDE

ANCHOR CROSSING

VALENTINES WAY

VILLAGE CORNER

BEECHERS BEND

COUNTRY CORNER

COTTAGE CORNER

SEFTON STRAIGHT

CLUB CORNER

RAILWAY STRAIGHT

MELLING CROSSING

Paddock

Start

TATT'S CORNER

allowed to play on the Club circuit I'm afraid, so when we've finished our plug tests here on the finishing straight we are going to bring the car over to the short circuit. I'll meet you in the Picnic Loop in about half an hour. There are a couple of hopefuls out on the circuit at the moment in one of the track GT cars, tell them who you are and try a few laps in it. Don't overdo it though, the car's getting a bit clapped and we've only got a small first aid kit.'

It may have just been the oppressive greyness and lack of colour that always surrounds Aintree and the stench of synthetic putrescence that the nearby chemical plant exudes, but my enthusiasm for this enterprise was spiralling downwards into my water logged boots. The rain had settled into a steady drizzle that tickled the face and dribbled off the ends of our noses. Hall's wife was holding a yellow and red golf umbrella over the car's open engine compartment to give some shelter to the mechanics as they worked, backsides up in the air and heads down on the silent steaming engine. The rain sizzled and spat like fat on a hotplate as it hit the exhaust pipes.

Mrs Hall, tied bunchily into a lumpy fawn gabardine, a sodden garish red and blue souvenir of Monte Carlo headscarf wrapped round her greying hair, was examining me curiously from head to toe. She seemed to find me faintly amusing, and as I turned away to pick up the Anglia and drive over to the other half of the circuit, I heard her say in a hoarse stage whisper, 'a bit long in the tooth for a new boy isn't he Chris?'

I felt myself blushing like a schoolboy but pretended not to hear.

'For Christ's sake Hetty shut up will you' – the rest was lost as I walked away wondering what the hell I was doing here and why it still mattered. If I had any sense I would be in a steady job by now, perhaps earning fifteen hundred a year as a section leader in the design office of De Havillands, with spare time that was my own and no worries about anyone finding out that I was getting my Competition Licence renewed each year by fiddling my medical. There would be no worries about what would happen to Gwen and Ian if I were killed or maimed.

It was too late to go back although I only had to get into the car and drive home to put an end to this nonsense. If I went home I would have to find another job and who would take me on now after so many years out of the aircraft business; no I had no choice but to go on, using the winters to try and find a backer for whatever car I had dreamed about during the summer, until I had to find a job for the summer as well. That day would come when the young men began to brake for the corners later than I had done, when I began to want to live and go on living.

When I arrived at the Club circuit, the GT car, a much modified hard topped TR3, was sitting beside the circuit surrounded by a colourful group of young men and women. A mechanic in pale blue overalls was changing the back tyres. No-one seemed to be very interested in him, and my arrival only caused a brief interruption of the conversation. I fitted the offside wheel while he lowered the quick-lift jack.

'How's it going? I asked.

'Oh not too bad mate, although God knows why because these two buggers are a wild pair. The long legged 'erbert with the blonde 'air 'as spun off twice at Country Corner already, an' the cocky littl'n was bloody 'opeless to start with, but e's improvin'.'

He nodded towards the spectators. 'They've brought their frippet along with them and they're not 'elping much.'

He stopped and looked at me anxiously. 'They're not friends of yours are they?'

'No, I've never seen them before – just here for a trial like them. Have they finished with the car yet?'

'You'd better ask 'em,' he replied, thrown off balance by the discovery that I had not just been sent over to help him.

'I say, haven't you finished that wheel change yet? We're getting most frightfully wet.'

The tall blonde youth who was dressed in an immaculate suit of blue nylon overalls and an American style 'bone-dome', opened the off-side door of the Triumph and sat in the off-side seat, tucking his long thin legs into position. I pointed out that I had also come to take a trial and would like an opportunity to find my way round the Club Circuit before the Formula One car arrived. He shrugged and climbed out with a noisy sigh, but made no comment.

One of the three girls, a brunette with heavily made up eyes and a thin scarlet gash of a mouth, pouted and took both his hands in hers. 'Oh Jimmy darling, what a shame, – just as you were getting into the swing of it and Clive has hardly had a go yet.'

'I'll try not to keep you too long,' I called. 'I just want to get the shape of this circuit, then you can have it back.' They ignored my gesture and walked over to their cars to wait.

Under their battery of critical eyes, I adjusted the seat to suit my shorter legs and tried to settle myself into this strange car, which felt and smelled alien. The inside of its cockpit was bare untrimmed fibreglass and aluminium, roughly finished in matt black paint, with scuffed off high spots on the transmission tunnel and the floor in front of the pedals. I could hear the chatter of the group by the cars.

'For heaven's sake what is he fiddling about at in there – who the heck is he anyway?' No-one seemed to have any ideas on the subject except the smaller man who suggested that I must be one of the boss's relations. The mechanic leaned into the car.

'She should go on the button OK. Just keep 'er below six – five and take it easy on Club Corner – 'specially now you've got new tyres on, OK?'

'OK' I said, and pressed the starter button. As soon as I moved away the old hard familiar hammer of the engine spirited away my self-consciousness and apprehension. After two laps I began to try a little harder, and the corners began to flow smoothly.

Coming out of Beechers Bend at six thousand in second, I caught a glimpse of the transporter with a convoy of private cars draw in beside those already in the Picnic Loop, just before I changed into third, then top down Railway Straight. Braking for Club Corner, the tail of the car twitched, then as I came to second for the corner itself, it tried to break away to the left. I caught it in time and turned the power on smoothly for the tight seemingly endless loop, so that the rear outside wheel just flicked the dirty grass at the exit. A short sprint into third before braking and selecting second gear for Country Corner. Something felt wrong, but before I could do anything there was a bang from the front off-side and the car spun violently to the right. Cars, grass, sky, mud and water flew past the screen as the Triumph spun off the apex of the corner and lurched to a soggy halt.

'Hell's flames, of all the times for this to happen, in front of that damned audience.' The engine was still running, so I engaged bottom gear and tried to motor back onto the circuit, but the driving wheels spun helplessly on the wet turf.

I switched off the engine and got out. My head was aching and my mouth dry. The rain had stopped and the grass was steaming as the sun began to warm the earth. The mechanic and Hall were running over to where the car had come to rest – Hall looked furious, his blue eyes staring out of his red veined face.

'What in the name of heaven do you think you were doing. Didn't I ask you to take it easy?'

I unfastened my helmet and trying to stop my voice from shaking with the blazing anger that was welling up inside me, suggested that he should look at the front off-side brake. The mechanic who had been with the Triumph when I arrived was already under the wheel arch. He whistled.

'I can't see properly but there's brake fluid all over the bloody shop – the brake housing's missing and there's bits of alloy everywhere.'

Hall joined him on the ground, while I walked back to the Anglia. A cup of coffee seemed very desirable, so I sat down to enjoy it while the post mortem went on. One of the three girls, no more than thirteen or fourteen-years-old, walked over to me.

'Jolly bad luck, but I'm glad you're alright.'

'How very kind of you,' was all I could find to say. 'Would you like some coffee?'

'Oh yes please' she said, and got into the passenger side of the car. She was shivering.

'You look frozen to death. I'll start the engine and get the heater going. Motor racing is no sport for spectators in this climate.'

Her serious little face relaxed into a half smile.

'So I gather. This is only the second time I've seen any racing – I think it's cold, boring and frightening. It even frightens you, doesn't it?' She turned a pair of large, round brown eyes on me, eyes that would allow no evasion.

'I suppose it does, but it's wonderful when you stop.'

She laughed, and the coffee slopped over the rim of her cup onto her obviously new tartan trews.

'Oh blast!' she said and looked round ineffectively for something to use as a mop. I gave her my handkerchief and held her cup while she tried to repair the damage. Handing back the sorry ruin of a handkerchief she said, 'Your wife will tell you off for making such a mess of it. You'd better tell her it was my fault.'

'Of course, I'll just tell her that I was drinking coffee with a young lady whose name I don't know, when –' She saw the point.

'Well, you can say that the young lady was a schoolgirl called Rachel, playing truant from a school mountain craft course. Would that help?'

'Hardly' I said, trying not to show my curiosity.

'Not even if I told you that my other name is Aaronsen?'

She certainly did not look much like old Aaronsen and he had said that his wife and daughter were away on holiday.

'Your father must be the famous Aaronsen's biscuits –'

'Stepfather, my own father's dead.'

'I'm sorry, very sorry. That was stupid of me.'

It was apparent that I had exposed a small gap in her protective armour. Her silence filled the confined space around us, with oppressive unease. A lock of smooth black hair swung out from under her head-scarf and brushed across her cheek, its end resting against the corner of her mouth. My hand, following an unrealized instinct, began moving to brush it back into place, but it stopped halfway and I self consciously turned its half completed arc into a stuttering gesture towards the dispersing group of people round the Triumph. She flinched slightly as if I had been about to strike her and tucked the stray lock back into place with an easy grace which seemed to be characteristic of her.

'Well I suppose I had better see what's going to happen next – if anything. Hall seems to be looking for someone, it might be me.' I roused myself from the half dreamlike sequence of feelings and actions which was turning over the stones in the corners of my mind, like the sense of having heard a conversation before.

'Do you have to drive? Do you earn a living doing it?' she asked.

'Heavens no, but if these people decide that I'm good enough – I might. A great deal depends on today, – more than you'd ever realise.'

She smiled and showed me her crossed fingers.

'Bless you I need all the luck I can get. If I don't make the most of today's opportunity, I don't know what will happen.'

Hall had walked over towards the car and stood beside me as I got out.

'Sorry I was so abrupt with you Wade, but that Gilhooly was just about the last straw. I owe you an apology. We'd been a bit over enthusiastic in our lightening programme. The brake housing has failed where it joins the torque flange, so you got maximum brake on one side and none on t'other – sorry.'

'A bloody good job it wasn't a road circuit,' I said, and thought a great deal more. If I was going to drive for these people, leaving the maintenance in their hands would be disturbing. He must have guessed what I was thinking.

'This is the first mechanical failure we've had in three seasons.'

I laughed, 'And with my luck it has to be me driving. Well, what happens next?'

He looked back over his shoulder at the group round the GP car and gestured toward them with his thumb.

'I've promised the long laddie first crack at the Formula One car, he'll do twenty laps, then if all goes well it's yours.'

'Is he good?' I asked.

'Oh, he's a bit wild, but with team discipline he'll improve.'

'You know him pretty well then?'

'Yes, he's driven sports cars for us already and has started Formula Junior this year. I'd have thought you'd have known him.' The spluttering roar of the car's engine saved me the trouble of answering and we walked over to watch. Hall leaned over and shouted into my ear.

'Providing he can keep his mind on driving and off the assorted skirt that follows him around, he'll be a top rank driver one day. Just look at him now.'

He was pulling on his gloves while one of the girls fastened his helmet straps. Hall walked up behind him and grasped him, none too gently by the shoulder.

'Come on John, stop playing about we've got work to do, and little enough time in which to do it. I want you to meet Peter Wade, Peter this is John Kenning.'

Kenning looked slightly puzzled.

'You're not the Wade who used to race a Maserati Special and Oscas are you?'

'Yes, why, does it seem unlikely to you?'

'Oh no but I would have thought that you would have been much older, that was a long time ago wasn't it?'

'Probably before you started I would think, but not long ago really. All things are relative.'

The mechanic who had been sitting in the cockpit got out. Hall was restless and the rain was beginning to fall again. Kenning wriggled his long nylon sheathed limbs into the narrow cockpit, and nodded to Hall, who hustled mechanics and spectators off the track, and waved him away.

Watching his rev counter, head inclined Kenning built up the engine speed and fed in the clutch. Back wheels spinning, steam and smoke spurting off the blurred outline of the tyres, the car surged away leaving a cloud of spray and oil haze behind it. The blast from the open exhaust pipes sent back pressure waves that the chest felt as distinct blows. My mind, hands, feet and will drove the car away down the straight to the first corner, and the tension relaxed. This feeling, almost bordering on ecstasy always held me in its grip at the start. Cold concentration took over during the race, or boredom if I was watching. I went back to the Anglia to watch. Rachel was still sitting inside.

'Boring isn't it? I asked.

'When he drives, yes, but not when Simon or you do. John Kenning is always thinking about how he looks. You and Simon are different. You're not human of course, you're too cold and dedicated, like priests'.

'How do you know?' I asked. 'You've only seen me drive once, and that wasn't for long?'

'It was enough, and it frightened me. Do you know Simon?'

'Yes, I met him on Saturday, he drove my car at Oulton Park, very well too.'

She hooked her heels up onto the edge of the seat and hugged her knees in an unselfconscious schoolgirl pose.

'Isn't he a pet, don't you think he's handsome?' Before I could answer, she was off again. 'Why was he driving your car, does Daddy know?'

'Have you finished?' She nodded vigorously, eyes round and full of unspoken questions.

'First, yes I do, second, because my partner invited him to try it, as he is about to become a very active member of our little company and lastly, yes your father does know, he was there.'

'Golly', she said, 'where are they now? Father will give me Hell when he finds out that I'm not staying with mother, and she'll do the same if she discovers that I'm not with the school. As I said I'm supposed to be on a sort of outward bound course for young ladies at Coniston for the whole month, but I've skipped this weekend.'

'Where have you been staying then?'

She sighed and looked at me sideways.

'I don't know why I'm telling you all this, but you seem pretty reasonable.' I smiled and bowed slightly from the waist.

'No, don't fool about, it's serious really. I've been staying with Helen, that blonde girl, she's a friend of Simon's and she has a flat at Newsham Park. They live together at times you know.'

She was watching me in the mirror to see if I registered shock, and seemed a little disappointed by my lack of response.

'And where is your mother the while?'

'Another damned baby of course, what else? I've never seen a more prolific family than the Aaronsens, they breed if they just hold hands.'

'Well you'd better wear a label round your neck when you grow up, 'Danger Aaronsen"

'You forget I'm not one of them,' she interrupted, curtly.

'I'm sorry Rachel, I keep opening my big stupid mouth and hurting people, without thinking and certainly without intending to hurt anyone. Do you remember your father?'

'No, he died before I was born, a bit of a mystery man – probably one of those gunmen who used to go around bumping off soldiers – but nobody talks about that now, least of all to me. He can't have been a hero or someone would have told me, so there's just a sort of gap. Let's talk about something else, your family for instance.'

I told her about Gwen and Ian and was going on to explain how we had become involved with her stepfather, when the car came round the circuit on its third lap, motoring slowly and misfiring badly. It seemed to clear itself passing the pits, then cut out and coasted to a halt. Only the hissing of the rain in the grass broke the silence outside.

'Oh dear, what on earth has happened to the thing now?'

She looked bored and exasperated, 'Doesn't this sort of thing drive you round the bend? Something always seems to be going wrong.'

'Yes it does, I'll probably go quietly crackers one day, motor racing is rather like war, one helluva lot of preparation and build up of tension and waiting, waiting, waiting, – then nothing very significant happens because the blessed thing won't go, or else the opposition has done its preparation even better.'

'Haven't you forgotten something else, the risk bit?'

'Half the risk wouldn't be there if only the real opportunities happened more often. We just have to take the odd chance once in a while, otherwise there would be no competition – nothing for the paying public to watch. A procession, even at Indianapolis speeds can be very dull for the spectator. I must go and see if there is anything I can do to help. When are you going back to school by the way?' She sighed.

'Tomorrow if Simon will take me, otherwise on Saturday after the races, why?'

For some reason, perhaps a disturbed conscience, I was beginning to feel some responsibility for this child. She could have been the daughter of Jacob, his brother or any one of the men we had killed in the Negev.

She told me that she had to get to Coniston where the course was based for the fell walking and sailing week. I suggested that if Simon could not take her, Gwen and I would take a day off and drive up with her, probably spending the night at the Vaughans' cottage near Torver. She promised to ring later that evening after she had seen Simon.

John Kenning and his entourage were walking back to their cars and one of the girls called to Rachel saying that they were going home. As they left together, Rachel was obviously discussing me with Simon's girlfriend.

The group around the Grand Prix car looked resigned and it was apparent that they had decided not to waste any more time on it. It squatted sulkily in the sodden grey-green grass beside the track, a raincoat thrown over its empty cockpit. Hall turned towards me and made a thumbs down sign.

'We're packing up for lunch Wade, are you coming with us?'

'It depends where you're going.'

'We're taking the cars back into town, and we thought we'd have a snack at the Phil' lunch counter.'

It sounded as if it might suit my pocket and certainly would be better than standing around in the steady downpour with the water soaking through the holes in the soles of my shoes. I gave them a thumbs-up sign and called that I would meet them there.

After some beer and sandwiches, the ice was broken and we went to the garage where the cars were stabled. The Grand Prix car had been wheeled into the development shop, which had the well lit and clinical air of an operating theatre.

Hall sent the two mechanics to work on the two team cars for the Saturday meeting and asked me if I would like to try and find out what was wrong with the car we had been using during the morning. I rang the garage and Gwen to tell them where I was and we got to work.

There was no real mystery about the failure of the car to run well, but it took half an hour's checking ignition and fuel systems to discover a hair line split in the plastic pipe to the second tank which had allowed air into the system, with consequent fuel starvation. The cylinder heads had to be taken off to discover what damage the excessively lean mixture may have caused. To do this meant taking two longitudinal tubes out of the rear end of the chassis frame.

There was considerable evidence of overheating, including badly burned exhaust valves. We worked on, forgetful of time until Mrs Hall came in carrying a tray which held three cups of tea. She set them down on the littered bench. She was still loosely parceled in her old Gaberdine and headscarf; the bedraggled remains of a cigarette between her lips its smoke curling upwards, caused her to screw up her eyes as she bent over the naked bones of the chassis to see what we were doing. I watched the cigarette anxiously as it quivered between her nicotine stained lips, poised over the exposed valve gear. Hall looked up, unconcealed irritation showing on his face.

'Hetty, in the name of all that's holy, why don't you give some thought for the shareholders even if you don't give a damn for yourself or us, these tanks are full of one hundred octane fuel and the drum behind you with nitro-methane!'

She giggled foolishly. 'And worth a guinea an ounce!' but she carefully crushed the stub end out under the worn down heel of her shoe.

'I suppose you know that everyone else has gone home and that it's almost six o'clock? What are you doing anyway?'

I finished fitting the cam-shaft covers and tightened the water hose clips while Hall explained how we had become involved in doing more than we had intended. We stood and drank the tea in the pool of light round the car.

'What does your wife think about being married to a motor car Mr Wade?'

'Probably much the same way a doctors' wife feels about her husband's patients I would think.'

'That's hardly an answer to my question, but being a man that's just what one would expect.' She paused and looked round the workshop, 'I feel about these damned things the way any wife would feel about her husbands' mistresses, six of the bitches. Just look at them, all expensive, dangerous and more exciting than me!'

I said 'I see your point,' and left it at that, but she went on.

'I hate them, yes I'm even jealous, who wouldn't be if their husband forgot that it was their birthday today?'

'Like Hell it is Hetty, that's the third time this year that you've tried it on. At this rate with three birthdays a year for the twenty one years we've been hitched, you must be knocking on for eighty three instead of forty one. You poor misunderstood old bag, come and have a drink.'

She dug him sharply in the ribs with her elbow, smiling at him like a toothpaste advertisement as she did so, then fled for the door. He reacted by flinging his empty tin mug at her. She paused long enough to put out her tongue, and closed the door behind her.

'The Liver Club in ten minutes, table for four at eight!' he called out hopefully in the direction of her fading footsteps.

The outer roller doors clattered down and we heard her drive away in the Elan. Hall carried on with an earlier conversation about the team as if there had been no interruption. He suggested that as I had been unable to try the car during that morning's session, I should continue with my original plan to drive the Pig on Saturday with a reserve place in his team.

I asked him about Monte Carlo, the next major race on the calendar, and to my surprise, he suggested that I should drive one of the Formula Junior entries, Kenning taking the other.

We washed, and went in my car to the Liver Club which was in a pair of converted houses near Gambier Terrace. It was in an area of Liverpool which had been built when the city's prosperity was at its height and the slave trade was providing the solid financial footing for the great shipping companies. Some of the houses were suffering from financial malnutrition with slates awry, odd panes of glass missing from beautifully proportioned windows and assorted litter lying in the basement areas. The stucco was peeling off the fronts and grass showed over the edges of the gutters.

Number twenty showed a brave face to the world with new pale blue paint, carriage lamps and a portly brass-bound commissionaire at the door. Yet another seven day wonder club, destined for brief success while the novelty lasted and the celebrities came. Then in their wake would follow the too-moneyed youth and their girl-friends too easily conquered. The in-town-for-a-couple-of-days business men with unquestioned expense accounts, their buying officer guests, and the scavengers. The scavengers with well developed senses who can detect an expense account two streets away, with the well developed ability, like a chameleon, of taking on the colour and form of something female, desirable and just sympathetic. Dim lights, smoke, gin, noise and freedom leading to drinking after hours, the frankly out-for-business girls, the forgotten member's book, and yet another club would go down the city drain. Phoenix-like, it would struggle out of its ashes, one step down the social scale as a worker-of-the-world type coffee club with a tape recorder, coffee, free love all round, even if you only can go through the emotions, and members who stink. All hellishly innocent, boring and insanitary.

Just for kicks, the occasional reefer would appear then the odd bottle of gin, or red-biddy, then once again the rozzers, and the cycle is repeated. One day someone would probably start a very good jazz club there, or more likely it would become a half-hearted brothel. For the moment though, it was enjoying its period of prosperity and respectability

As if by telepathy Hall stopped at the doorway, and said, 'I'd give it two years, what would you say?'

'I'll let you know when I've met the owner.' He laughed, and we went into the cloakroom to hand our raincoats to the miserably thin girl in fishnet stockings, who was trying to do her best to look interesting in spite of the evident goose-pimples on her bare arms.

As we went through the dining room to the bar, the blare of conversation, heat and cigarette smoke enveloped us. We made our way through the crowd which was a mixture of evening dressed men and women and provincial beatniks with scouse accents. Hall turned to me.

'Have you ever spotted how little notice anyone ever takes of people who pass them in a bar after they've had a couple of drinks, just watch.' He continued his progress, passing two young women who were talking at each other at once, smiling politely but vaguely. He put out his tongue at the one facing him, and passed on. Her expression did not change. Passing another, plump middle-aged but attractive woman, he stroked her little round tightly-girdled bottom, and walked on. Without pausing in her story she took half a step forward towards her fascinated partner, who was apparently looking for something which was hiding down the front of her dress, and continued talking.

Hall looked back at me, 'Marvellous isn't it?' As he reached the bar, the barmaid recognised him, and ignoring a man who was trying to remember a long and complicated order, asked him what he wanted. He took her hand kissed it, and held it out for me to do the same.

A voice from behind me said. 'When you two dirty old men have finished cavorting, perhaps someone will get me a drink.' It was Hetty.

Three double whiskies appeared as if by magic. Several drinks later, someone took hold of my elbow and asked what I was going to have. It was Simon. I introduced him.

'Does this mean you're leaving us Peter?'

'No not necessarily, but I thought it was a reasonable precaution to take as your father does not like me and he will soon be in a position to kick me out of my own company.'

'Who said he doesn't like you, even if he didn't, the business can't run without you.'

'Don't fool yourself Simon, no-one is indispensable in any business. Not even your father in his. There are always at least two men who would move into his position at 9 o'clock tomorrow morning given half a chance. No, I've no illusions.'

He laughed. 'You've got the dreaded boozers gloom, have another and bring your friends over to join our party.'

'That's very nice of you, but we are going to eat soon.'

During the next half hour, we joined Simon and his friends including the blonde Helen, and I discovered that Simon would not be taking Rachel to the Lakes next day. He said that she was going to 'phone my home to arrange about where I would pick her up. I remembered that I had not told Gwen about this arrangement and thought of the frigid silence that would greet my return later. What the heck I thought, I'm enjoying myself for the first time for a very long time. Simon was teasing Helen about something which obviously amused everyone else. She looked annoyed.

'I know damned well why she doesn't like me Simon. It's because I'm a Gentile and she's jealous because I'm younger than she is. The trouble with you is that you fancy her yourself you little billy goat, and she's half as old as you again.'

He wagged his finger at her admonishingly.

'Whatever other vices I practice, incest isn't one of them, besides, I don't think Oedipus Aaronsen sounds so good.'

Hall looked interested. 'You're not talking about your glamourous mother are you Simon?'

'No Helen was, she's a damned clever woman really, apart from being a beautiful one, because she acquired a grown-up family when she married my father and although I was all set to hate and resent her I don't. I think she is the finest woman I have ever met, and I began by classifying her as a gold digger. Make whatever you like of that but that is my opinion.'

Helen was looking at me.

'What do you think of this paragon, Mr er, Wade.'

I shrugged. I can only judge the lady of by the little I have heard. I've never met her. I have an idea that her daughter feels a little put out by the idea of a baby that is on the way because her mother is all that she really owns. Simon obviously respects her, and his father I gather is very proud of her. I know nothing more.'

'Well let me fill in the picture for you. She is cow-like, submissive, sly, secretive, lazy, snobbish, a prude and anti-gentile.'

Simon looked angry. 'Cut it out Helen you're being silly. You've just developed a thing about her.'

Helen finished her drink quickly tilting her head right back so that her heavy blond hair fell back away from her face. She drained the last drop of drink and caught an undissolved lump of ice against her closed lips. She swayed slightly as she handed her glass to me to put on the bar.

'Be a pet dear, and get me another,' she said and held my arm for support. One of the girls in Simon's party, a redhead, was trying to persuade him to leave. When he caught my eye, he raised his eyebrows looked at the drooping Helen and indicated that he wanted to get away without her. I nodded assent and he left quietly. She hardly noticed that he had gone, but we could not get her interested in going back to the dining room for a meal. When she went off with Hetty to repair her make-up, Hall turned to me.

'Mate, you've lumbered yourself alright. I should get her home if I were you as soon as possible, but have a snack at the bar first. I'd better leave you to it. I'll give you a ring on Friday, will that be OK?'

I agreed, and when Hetty and Helen came back, we went our separate ways. Helen was in control again, and felt hungry so we ate a quick bar dish of spaghetti bolognese at a side table. I asked her where her car was, and she told me that she didn't have one. Simon had brought her. She seemed to have stopped worrying about him already.

'Would you like me to drive you home?' I asked her.

Without answering she stood up, and expressionless as a display model in a shop window walked purposefully towards the apparently evasive cloakroom door.

I paid the bill and waited for her to reappear. More out of habit than through any desires to know the time, I looked at my watch. It was 11pm. I remembered Gwen with a resented awakening of conscience. I turned to ask the barmaid where the telephone was, but she was serving another customer. The man on the next bar stool lazily spun round to face me.

'Good luck my friend,' he raised his half empty glass in a mock toast and drained it before putting it down on the counter with the imprecise accuracy of the practised drunk.

'What do you mean?' I asked him.

He turned back to face the bar without answering. It made me feel as if I had been caught with my hand in a church offering box. He called to the barmaid who came as if pulled by invisible wires, continuing her conversation with the more favoured customers at the other end of the bar, and ordered two whiskies.

When they arrived, he looked at me expectantly, and although conscious of the fact that I was behaving like a fool, I paid for them. We drank, and he asked me if I was too old to accept advice. I said yes, but I was prepared to listen out of morbid interest.

'My God, you are a genuine dyed in the wool nit,' he said. 'For two reasons,' and held up his hand to stop me speaking. 'Firstly because you are honest and say what you mean, and secondly because – ' he was interrupted by Helen's return. I moved to stand up, but she leaned against my side and put her arm through mine.

'Stay where you are Peter, Sammy's going to buy us a drink. Doubtless he has been advising you to keep away from me. He's rather bitter and twisted aren't you Sammy?'

Sammy looked embarrassed and asked what she would have. There was a silence between them and a rapid exchange of eye talk which left Sammy in no doubt that he ought to know what she drank. The picture began to fill in.

'Helen,' I asked, 'would you prefer to be taken home by Sammy.'

The crowd of shouting jostling people was pressing in on us from all sides. She insinuated herself against me, her right breast pressed against my left arm, her heavy straight blond hair tickled my face.

'What's the matter, are you afraid I might bite you?'

'If you go with her,' Sammy said, 'you'll spend the whole bloody evening listening to a hate against the woman her boyfriend really goes for.' I could feel the girl's body shivering.

'Alright Sammy whatever you are cut it out, you've obviously got one hell of a chip on your shoulder anyway. As far as I'm concerned I'm just an outsider, none of this has anything to do with me. Don't drag me into your problems.'

Sammy slid down off his stool, until his portly belly pressed against my knees, and he was breathing beerily in my face.

'You're anti-social mate,' he said and nodded sagely. 'Do you realise I could give this kid a secure comfortable future, and she wastes her time – her youth, on a young fool who can get whatever and whoever he wants.'

Helen laughed bitterly, 'Almost everyone.'

It was Sammy's turn to laugh.

'A fat lot of hope he has of getting her, she's dead from the neck down. She doesn't even know what it's for yet.'

I seemed to be the only one not in the joke. The barmaid was listening in, and wiping the tears from her eyes.

'Oh Mr Eccles, you are awful, and how do you know anyway.'

He wagged his finger accusingly in her general direction. 'You can't catch me that way, what do you know about her anyway?'

'Oh I knew her before she found her gold mine. We used to share a flat in Upper Parliament Street and lived on chips and gin. Now of course it's got to be Kosher while her old man's around, and she never comes to see her old friends. I believe she's closed up like a clam since her first husband died. She came in here once to see old Geoff who used to teach her, and she was told that he was dead. She looked grey and only half with us until the boss asked her what it was like in Palestine then she let him have it. I've only heard about it but I believe she gave him Hell. He used to be in the Army out there during the First World War and he only wanted to know. Here he is, he'll tell you.'

A dapper little man who, although he must have been close to 65 was still as spry as a terrier pup, came in through the side door behind the bar. He nodded at Sammy and Helen, and looked at me in a way that called for an introduction. Sammy waved a limp hand in greeting. 'Lo Mac, Audrey was just telling us about the time the great Mrs Aaronsen came back from the Promised Land and tore you off a strip. What happened?'

He seemed reluctant to tell us but Helen persisted.

'I'll not say anything against her Helen, much as you'd like me to. She's a damned fine woman and she's had a rough time. Apart from her own kid, and the other one that's on the way now, she has no family of her own, and that was the only occasion when anyone has heard a bitter word from her.'

Sammy continued, 'Geoff was like a second father to her while she was a student as you ought to know Helen, and when she heard that he was dead that took away her last prop. I don't know the whole story but I've heard from Aaronsen that her first husband was one of the Terrorists, and he was shot in cold blood by one of our special branch people. The fellow who did it was cashiered or died or something afterwards, but I think the bastard should have been hanged. I believe it was a simple case of vindictive killing. No wonder our name stank there. Old Aaronsen's been very good to her, nothing too much trouble or expense, and all that he wants from her is a family. I've not much time for Jews as a crowd, but at least they stick together and don't go for each other's throats as we do.'

I pushed my untouched drink away from me.

'Perhaps Mr Mac whatever your name is, you ought to emulate the Jews, support your own people and try to imagine what it was to be a soldier out there. Get some facts from both sides.'

He looked at me embarrassed, 'I'm sorry if I've offended you but –'

I walked out, conscious again of a chill in the air and the growing silence which spread like a cold draught through the closely packed room.

Sammy's drunken slurred voice was calling something after me but I ran up the steps to the street two at a time. The fresh air outside was cool and clean and the star sprinkled velvet dome of sky steadied my reeling thoughts. The solid black mountain of sandstone which was the Anglican Cathedral grew up into the limitless sky, its feet in the sooty necropolis which occupied the half-mooned shaped pit round its north and east sides. The lights of the city feebly echoed the universe.

Casual groups of loiterers hung about the street corners, aimless, bored and hoping for the unlikely. Two Chinese youths in black jeans and leather jackets swaggered past talking about the crocodile of cars parked against the curb, in sing song, nasal, Liverpool voices, the Dublin-Lancashire noise sounded wildly incongruous. The door behind me opened letting out a stream of yellow light which threw my shadow out across the pavement, over the car roof and into the road. It was joined by two more shadows. The door closed.

'Helen and Mac stood on either side of me.

'I can't let you go without apologising properly, you see I had no idea that you had been out there, and I as only repeating what I had heard. I really am very sorry.'

'That's alright, Mac, how were you to know that it was my weak spot. You see I was there, and something very similar happened to me. Occasionally just when I have kept it in the background of my mind for something, I pick up a book or read a paper, or hear someone say something as you did, which remind me that although what I did was inevitable and I was just an instrument, I am a murderer. I killed a man who didn't have a cat in hell's chance of even defending himself. I didn't know them, but I have known for the last thirteen years.

'If I had the guts, I'd have shot myself there and then, and I would have saved myself and a lot of other people a lot of misery, I hesitated though and once you hesitate it's too late. I was committed to trying to live an ordinary life, without the proper mental equipment. No you needn't really apologise, you're quite right, really – we're all right, that's just the lunatic thing about the whole situation.'

Helen took my arm. 'I think you've got everything out of perspective, and you're probably a bit tight. Are you going to take me home, or will it give you another guilt complex?'

'There's not much room for any more and it's too cold out here for the story of my wasted life, come on.'

Mac leaned in through the car window. He looked troubled. 'I suppose by some queer chance you're not the same man are you?'

I was afraid to pursue the subject but I had to know, 'What was her husband's name?'

'I'm not sure,' he said and his mouth began to silently form a first letter as he thought. I watched his lips, afraid, with the same sick, empty-belly feeling that precedes the announcement of examination results. Before he could remember, Helen said.

'She had a photograph which she carried about with her, signed 'Jacov'.' And I knew.

'That's it, Helen, Jacov Bernstein,' he looked at me. 'My God boy are you alright?'

There was no escape I had run away only to find that I had gone in a circle.

Helen turned to Mac. 'He'll be OK just leave him to me, Mac, and you keep your trap shut tight. This particular situation is hotter than you'd ever realise. You ring his wife, tell her he's not very well and he'll be back later. Tell her he's gone to a friend's home for a while.'

'No for heavens' sake don't do that Mac, just say I'm giving a friend a lift home. I've only got one kidney, and there are a few other complications, so she'd throw a fit if you told her that. Here's my number and my name is Peter Wade.'

He wrote it down in his diary and we left. Helen was silent and very sober. I felt her looking at me, and I asked her where she wanted to go. I was surprised when she directed me to a street of mouldering ruinous big houses in Kensington which had all been turned into flats and bed-sitting rooms.

She had her own key and held the door open for me. The narrow lofty hall smelt stuffily of cooking, damp and sewage. A single 40-watt electric light bulb hung at the end of a long dusty flex and gave barely enough light to throw the shadows of its own cobweb stays onto the walls.

She took some letters out of a tape and drawing-pin rack, picked up a bottle of milk from the window sill and nodding her head to indicate that I should follow went up the stairs. We clumped up two flights, the footworn stair carpet giving way to worn linoleum after the first. Her flat was a further half flight.

She turned round and smiled. 'This exercise is very good for my calf muscles, as I see you've noticed.' I had.

She put her fingers to her lips as she opened the door. 'Don't make too much noise, Rachel is sleeping just across the corridor in what my old bitch of a landlady is pleased to call the 'Sitting Room'.'

She switched on a table light and pulled the curtains closed. We were in her bedroom, which had a small cooker and a sink and some cupboards in one corner. She groped in her handbag for a shilling to put in the gas meter, but I found one in my pocket and lit the gas fire. She kicked her shoes off under the bed and stepped into a pair of straw sandals, but kept her coat on. The room was cold and felt damp.

'Be a love and fill a water bottle from the tap,' she said and when I asked where it was she said 'in the bed probably.'

Feeling slightly foolish and more than a little out of my usual role, I did as I was told and she made a pot of tea in a very battered little aluminium teapot with a handle which had been bound with insulating tape. She was bubbling with apparent good humour and kept a ceaseless flow of chatter while she poured the tea. I asked her what she did for a living, and suddenly wondered whether I should have done.

She laughed, 'I don't work for a living, I work for an existence – part-time temping, proof-reading, waiting at bars, you know the sort of thing. What living there is is provided by Simon when I'm on his 'in' list and that's not very often these days. He's had what he wanted and of course he's bored now, so I'm just useful. I look after his little sister and my so called flat is useful for the occasional booze up when he doesn't want to drive home afterwards.'

She didn't seem to be very worried about it. I said so, and she shrugged her shoulders.

'It had to be I suppose, it was inevitable like your story, it happens to us all. We just happen to be somewhere when someone comes along, or something happens and if we're not moving in the right direction or we fail to recognise what is happening, your life goes shooting off down the wrong road. We've got a lot in common really, we're both the sort of people who are the fodder of the gas ovens, the wardens for the concentration camps and the targets for the God-damned bomb. There are times when I could kill someone out of sheer futile frustration. I'm useless, I don't do anything, make anything, I've never been loved by a man worth loving and look at this bloody hole, where I live. No-one seems to understand or even wants to, they just run around like a crowd of blethering bleating sheep in blinkers. They only see their own way ahead as far as their bloodshot myopic little eyes will let them.'

Her hands were restless, playing with her necklace. She had suddenly become herself, and had dropped the daytime affected air of success and self-confidence, too much eye-shadow and the too short skirt which had slid unnoticed half way up her thighs.

She smiled wryly, looked down at her knees at me and said, 'Yes I'm just a bag, a 22-year-old bag, and I just don't give a damn. Even though you are in a better position to understand me, you won't. You've got your own problems, so you say to yourself this one's a whore, short term investment, a second class woman to be kept in the background. Never mind, have some tea, you're several degrees better than most. Cold or not, most men of your generation would have been making claims to their pound of flesh by now and had me stripped to the chassis. That's a Simon joke,' she explained unnecessarily.

'As a matter of fact, Helen, I was just wondering what the Hell I was doing here. I've lost today somewhere and I was just thinking that somewhere along the line I've missed a lot of life, probably in the same way that I've wasted all the hours of today. Working on Hall's car has done absolutely nothing to further my future, it will only make it go a little better for John Kenning while, if I'm lucky, I'll get the hack car. Now without an intention of doing anything but drive you home, I'm sitting here with you in your bedroom, the daughter of the man I killed is asleep across the corridor, and you have decided that because you sit in your skirt three quarters of the way up to your backside, that I'm mentally in bed with you.'

She took her coat off, and bringing the two glasses and a bottle of wine, came and sat on my knee.

'Does this disturb your delicate conscience?' she asked. It was not my conscience that was being disturbed.

'What's the celebration for?' I asked. She put her right arm round my shoulder and settled herself down comfortably before trying her drink.

'Cheers' she said and kissed me warmly and at length behind my left ear. I tried to look at my wrist watch, behind her back but she put down her drink, took my watch, dropped it down the front of her dress, and looked at me defiantly.

'What will it prove to you if I recover my watch?' I asked.

'That you're just another dirty old man like the rest of them.' She was laughing at me, and sitting back at arms length linked her hands behind my neck

'But I want to know the time.'

'You don't you fibber, you just pretended you did because you thought the situation was getting out of hand. You were thinking: What the devil have I let myself in for, doing Simon a good turn getting her off his hands and now getting stuck with her like this.'

'What gives you the idea I got you off his hands?' I asked but it was obvious that she knew. She didn't even bother to answer but finished her drink and getting the bottle, gave me another in spite of my protests.

'It'll do you good my friend in adversity. I'm going to have a bath and I'll run one for you. It will sober you up nicely before you go home to the little woman.'

She gathered her nightclothes from under the pillow and her housecoat from behind the door and went out. The noise the plumbing made must surely have woken the whole household with roarings, rumbles, glugs and hammering like a dozen mad do-it-yourself tinsmiths in a regular orgy of creation.

I looked at the room. A large Bracque print hung over the fireplace and two oils of a Welsh mountain landscape hung either side of the bed. A photograph of Simon stood on a light oak bedside table and several small framed snapshots stood on the heavy wooden mantelpiece.

The yellow cracked ceiling had a moulding which ran round three of its sides, and disappeared into the wall behind the bed, which had obviously been added to make two small rooms out of the original big one. The remains of a moulding in the ceiling at the head of the bed wall must have been where the chandelier had hung.

Rough plastering on either side of the fireside wall showed the run of the gas piping and the position of the old gas brackets. On a well-worn rug, one side of the bed lay a child's teddy-bear, with its waistcoat button eyes staring up sightlessly at the ceiling. A sad little bear worn furless by too much loving. I picked him up and sat him on the pillow, but he had no stability. I was still trying to make him sit upright when the door behind me opened and Helen came back in.

'Oh I forgot to introduce you Peter, that's Ignatius, we've been together since I was three. He's the one stable feature of my life. He's always around. I know this sounds idiotic, but I'm scared stiff of the dark. Simon found this out not long ago and took Iggy away with him one night. It nearly drove me round the bend. I looked everywhere for him, in the craziest places.'

She sat down on the bed, tucking her bare feet under her, the bear on her lap.

'You think I'm crazy don't you?' She was not smiling, and her face told me that my reply would be remembered.

'Not at all, I'm scared by heights and crowds of people, and sitting in a room with the lights on and the curtains open.'

She laughed, 'You're as nutty as a fruitcake. I am not at all sure we are safe together, but what am I babbling about I've run the bath for you. Here keep still, let me take your tie off.'

The idea suddenly seemed very pleasant, to relax in a hot bath. I would never be bothered if I left it until I reached home, so I relaxed and enjoyed the sensation of having my collar and tie and jacket removed. The weariness of my body gave me a sharp reminder that unless I took care, it would not do what was required of it driving in the race on Saturday. That was its only function from now on, an elaborate servo-control system. It had been its only function, but now there was Jacob's widow and her child. What should I do?

Helen slid to her knees in front of me, and taking one of my feet into her lap, began to undo my shoelaces. Her hair was as fine as silk, and thick. The front of her housecoat fell open revealing the soft gleaming white curves of her bare breasts. The pale blue blood vessels shone through her fair skin. She made no attempt to re-arrange her dress, but looked up and tossing her head to throw the long hair out of her eyes, smiled.

She stood up and walked over to the stool in front of the dressing table and began to brush her hair. I went to my bath, and half dreaming, half thinking tried to consider Jacob's child and her mother and wondered what Deborah would want me to do. Obviously they wanted for nothing that money could buy, but I felt that my life no longer belonged to me and that I had to do something for them. I tried to remember that night on the hillside and what Jacob and I had said to each other, whether he had mentioned a wife but very little remained of the words, only the feelings and they were becoming blunt with time. I dressed, and went back into the bedroom.

Helen was in bed, the bedclothes tucked under her chin. I asked her for my watch, and she nodded towards the bedside table. I put it on, and saw that it was twelve o'clock. A car drew up in the street outside and its door slammed. Drunken voices, talking altogether accompanied stumbling slithering footsteps over the pavement. A clock in the distance rang midnight tinnily and the traffic on the main road to Prescott was still a steady murmur.

She was looking at me, no longer teasing – 'Peter can't you stay a little longer? I'll never ask you again, not even now, but I won't be able to go to sleep without you. You've listened to me talk about myself all evening. You've been so gentle and asked for nothing, now I'm asking something more, stay with me for a few hours. Make me feel as if you are just a little bit fond of me. You don't have to make love to me if you don't want to. I don't really, that's why I'm not going to make you want to. I could you know.'

'I assure you Helen, you could quite easily, but what is the matter? How can I help? You don't even know anything about me.'

She reached out of bed, and took the alarm clock and began to wind it.

'I'll set this for 3am then you can go free and forget that I ever existed. Now take your clothes off and get into bed like a good boy.' I had always tried to find reasons and conclusions before doing anything, but this time reason went by the board. As I was getting into bed, she put out her hand to stop me.

'You poor old wreck' she said. 'Whatever did they do to you? Was it the Jews?' When I said yes, she snorted angrily.

'You really are a prize idiot aren't you?' She did not wait for an answer but went on to tell me what she thought of a wreck like me worrying about what I had done to the man who would make such a mangled mess of my body. I explained that our own surgeons had been responsible for several of the more spectacular scars but she was unappeased.

Her warm arms enfolded my body, and her knee slid between mine. Her breath was warm on my cheek as I rested my head on the pillow.

She laughed quietly. 'This is only a single bed you know. Friendly isn't it?'

'Aye verra sociable.' I replied and thought that if ever I would have to quote a typical bit of British understatement that would do very well. The only trouble would be that no-one who knew me would believe it, so it would have to remain a private joke.

She began to ask about Gwen, how long I had known her, how we met and what sort of woman she was. As a subject for conversation it hardly seemed suitable, so I evaded the questions whenever I could. To my astonishment she asked me why I had stayed with her and when I told her that it was because she had asked me to, she laughed. I tried to raise myself on one elbow but she pulled me down, her lips finding mine in the dark. Her hands were hot, and her parted lips were warm and moist. My heart was thudding and the blood roared in my ears.

Tomorrow and tomorrow and tomorrow were aeons away beyond the intense awareness of the moment, uncomplicated and simple.

A car door was opened in the street and closed after the second attempt, shaking my mind into realisation of who and where I was.

'For heavens' sake Helen, this is impossible. I didn't come prepared for this to happen.' I said but she put her finger against my lips and told me that I talked too much.

'Relax stop all these modest protestations and just make love to me. I was in the Girl Guides and I'm prepared, life's too short, and I'm getting older, every minute.'

Later we were lying watching the moon throwing the patterns of the leaves and branches of a tree in the street outside on the curtains and talking sleepily about the long summer days of child-hood, when the alarm clock rang.

The cheap stove enamelled pressed tin, jangling, lifeless box of meshing teeth and fragile coil spring, rang the death knell of my youth and left me with the prospect of an endless cold dawn and empty wet street. Wet streets, drawn curtains and prowling ill-fed homeless cats picking over the discarded garbage before the steep cobbled streets were dragged back to existence.

Her body and arms and lips tried to hold me in her fantasy world but my own cold road was waiting for me. Cold clothes, stubborn shoelaces and the coming dawn were the realities.

I heard her sigh, she knelt behind me as I sat on the edge of the bed dressing, and kissed the back of my neck.

'Thank you for being so gentle honey, don't just forget me will you? I don't know how this happened but I'm glad it did.' She sounded surprisingly defiant, almost apologetic. My feelings were a confusing mixture of anger with myself and either gratitude or affection towards her, so I kissed her, tucked her back into bed like a small child and left.

I was too wide awake to sleep by the time I arrived home in Bebington, so I crept quietly into the house and left a note on the kitchen table to say that I would be at the garage, working until 9am then I would come back for breakfast. To my surprise the lights were on in the workshop and the sound of Ron's tuneless whistle crept under the ill-fitting corrugated iron doors.

He looked up quickly as I went in. 'Hello gov'ner where've you bin? Mr Crompton and me have been lookin' everywhere for you. Things have bin' happenin'.'

'What's the matter then?'

'Cripes, what hasn't been happenin'. D'you know them con' rods you sent off for crack detection? Well they've all got hairline cracks beginning at the little end bosses, so that only leaves the spare engine's rods. I've spent the night takin' them out ready for checking and assembling in the new motor. Is that alright?'

'I reckon so Ron, but I'd better get the crankshaft and fly-wheel out of the new motor so we can balance the lot together. What else has been going on?'

'Oh hell yes, I forgot, that Mr Hall wants you to drive for them on Saturday, apparently Mr Kenning had a pile-up on the East Lancs last night when the bloke who was driving them back from a party tried to crash the lights at Queen's Drive, and thumped a lorry. The driver's got a fractured pelvis, and Kenning's badly bruised so they want you to drive the Formula Libre car. Mr Crompton spoke to him, and then rang your home. Apparently your missus was not expecting you home at all last night because a bloke from some club in the 'Pool rang to say you would most likely be staying with some friends.'

'I did Ron, so let's get on with this job.' He was looking at me with an expression halfway between admiration and reproof.

'What's the matter?'

'Nothing gov'ner, except Mr Crompton rang young Mr Simon

Aaronsen to tell him that he would be driving the Pig against you on Saturday, but that we hadn't been able to find you to tell you about the trouble we were in with the car, and he said he knew where you were, but it wasn't on the phone. He laughed, and wouldn't tell Mr Crompton where it was.'

'You're like a lot of bloody old women.' I told him and got into a set of overalls to begin work.

By eight o'clock when the men arrived we had both worked ourselves to a standstill, so I sent him home for breakfast, and a sleep and left a message that I would be back at 10 o'clock to see how the job was going.

As I had said that I would take Rachel to the Lakes, it meant that I would have to leave the supervision of the rest of the work to Crompton. I was tapping out a list of jobs with one finger on our old rheumaticky typewriter when he came in. He looked at me as if I was a God-sent gift to relieve him of all his personal worries.

'Good morning Patrick' I greeted him, and carried on with my typing.

'I won't ask where you've been or why, but by all that's holy, I'm glad to see you. Have you heard the news?'

'I don't know,' I said. 'What's your version?' I looked up.

He was sitting his hands on the edge of the desk, swinging his legs. 'I often wonder whether you are pulling my leg or you really don't care what goes on. You despise me really, don't you? You still think I'm just a troop sergeant.'

'What the devil are you rambling about Patrick? What have I done to upset you now? I don't know why you worry, you virtually own me. If you wanted to you could get rid of me almost as easily as you do with the blokes on the shop floor. You certainly don't consult me before you start talking business with other people.'

'That's the whole point, Peter, you're just not interested enough, so I have to do all the worrying you just sit back in your little dinghy and let events carry you along. You used to be a hell of a fine troop leader, the best I've ever served with, but look at you now.'

'For God's sake shut-up, we're not in the army now. Do you

know what I discovered last night? As the result of your big business deals, we are just about to get involved with the man who is married to Jacob Bernstein's wife. Now what do you have to say?'

He was thinking – mouthing the name Bernstein.

'You don't mean one of those characters you shot in Palestine do you?'

'Yes.'

'Oh come off it. I know the world is supposed to be a small place, but that is impossible. How do you know anyway?

I went over to the office safe and unlocking it took out Jacob's pistol which, without its breech mechanism, was locked in a small cash box.

'I don't know Patrick, but whatever else happens, I want you to chuck this into the Mersey if I should come unstuck during this race on Saturday. I would like to see her myself, but I don't know if I could put what I have felt all these years into words, or even if she would understand.'

I gave him the box. He felt its weight and looked at me puzzled. 'What is it?'

'Never mind, but when I die and if ever you considered yourself a friend of mine, please do what I ask. Will you?

He looked very doubtful but agreed, and locked the box away again.

'There's no reason why you need ever meet her you know,' he said, 'because the deal as you heard about it last, is off. Aaronsen has offered to put ten thousand quid into Crompton and Wade so that young Simon can join as a junior director, and, offered to pay for the development of a Formula One car, if you will supervise the design and construction of three cars for next year. He has also offered to buy your three-wheeler design and pay you a retainer of £500 a year to act as a consultant, plus fees and expenses. There's only one condition on the debit side, he insists that you don't do any more competition driving and the team should be known as the Aaronsen stable. Oh yes, and he doesn't want to see you again. He says you're anti-Semitic.'

'The devil he does, well I'm driving on Saturday and I'll be competing against his son and heir, what will he think of that?'

'Well as it happens, he's not keen on Simon driving, and wanted to know why you weren't taking the Pig. Incidentally you've given me a hell of a lot of work to do today, juggling with entries, and trying to convince the RAC and the secretary that it's in the interest of the meeting that we should shuffle you and Aaronsen around. Oh, and another point, Aaronsen would like you to enter the GT car event. I told him we have a provisional entry.'

'And what the devil are we going to enter, now that the Modena crowd have let us down with the Maser, there's only the demonstration car, and with the E-types and Ferraris entered we'd look stupid.'

'Would you like a decent entry?'

'Are you joking,' I asked, but there was something about his expression which hinted at a reluctantly maintained secret.

He looked out of the office window and smiled. I stood up to see what he found so amusing. A car stood on the garage forecourt, and was almost entirely surrounded by small boys and mechanics who gazed at it in bemused admiration. I could feel Crompton's eyes on me.

'Well?' he asked.

'Whose car is it?' I asked. It was not every day that a 250 Gran Turismo Ferrari visited us.

'It's Mrs Aaronsen's wedding anniversary present from the old man, and you're to drive it on Saturday in the GT event. He isn't going to tell her until you're due to go to the start. It's his idea of a surprise.'

I looked at him to see if he was joking.

'Holy smoke, this man Aaronsen must have a grotesque sense of humour. What would your reaction be if someone gave you the latest gleaming Maranello creation, and then told you that some joker you'd never seen before was going to race it before your backside had even warmed its seat? The man's psychopathic.'

'He's deadly serious Peter, and presumably he knows his own wife. Come and see it.'

The telephonist came in with two cups of coffee and reminded me that time was passing. It was half past nine. I explained to

Crompton that I had promised to take young Rachel up to the Lakes and would be staying overnight in Coniston so would meet him at Aintree for practice on Friday morning at 10am. He looked annoyed, but grudgingly agreed to see that the work on my list was carried out. He apparently had been promised the help of the two spare Ferrari mechanics who were being brought over for the private entrants benefit.

I took one of the Zephyr hire cars, and was just on the point of leaving, when he came over to the window of the car and signalled for me to open it.

'By the way, I promised the old man that I would drop a hint to you about your racing overalls, he wants us all to be property turned out. He thinks yours have had it, and wants you to get a new pair. I've got to go over to town, shall I get you another pair?'

'No certainly not, I'll wear the ones I have. I wouldn't feel comfortable in new ones.'

The idea filled me with a strange feeling of disquiet as if it had been suggested that I should have a new face fitted. Surely it couldn't be just superstition, but there was no time for debate. The feeling stayed with me though until I arrived home.

The sun was becoming warm enough to make a jacket uncomfortable as I walked up the path. Ian had his nose pressed against the glass of the front door, his hands spread out either side of his face. I pressed my nose against the glass opposite him, and crossed my eyes.

His husky laugh was chopped into fat sausages of sound by his yelps of pleasure as he tried to grasp my nose through the baffling glass. Gwen swept him up into her arms and opened the door, while he wriggled lustily. She looked tired.

'How long will it take you to dress his lordship, throw some nightclothes into a case and get into the car Gwen?'

'Why where are we going?'

'Coniston, leaving in half an hour.'

'For heavens sake why? Where have you been anyway, I've been worried stiff. Some strange man rang last night with a garbled story about you taking friends home, and having had a bit of a shock. What on earth is going on?'

'It's a long story, but I'll tell you as we go. I'll shave and dress monster son, while you get the rest organised. OK?'

Half an hour later, Ian was sitting between us in the front of the Zephyr and we were pulling into the street where Helen lived. Gwen knew part of the night's events, and for the first time since I had known her I had told her a deliberate lie.

She stayed in the car with Ian while I rang Helen's doorbell. Curious faces floated behind lace curtains on all sides. A cat arched its back and rubbed its flanks against my legs. Footsteps, carpet slippered, slithered and slapped down the hall. An old man in shirt sleeves and braces opened the door his bony, bald skull thrust forward like a vulture's head. I started to say that I had rung Miss... then realised that I didn't know her surname, so instead of Helen asked for Rachel. As I started to shout the question a second time, Rachel appeared at the top of the stairs with a small suitcase. She called good morning and ran down the stairs two at a time, looking quickly past me into the car to see Gwen.

As we walked to the car together down the short path Gwen watched us and her expression was almost one of recognition. I introduced them, and Gwen joined her in the back seat leaving Ian to his favourite role of funny driver's mate and critic extraordinary. The miles rolled away easily, and soon we were driving along the western shore of Coniston looking for a picnic place. A heat haze hung over the glass smooth surface of the lake, and Peel Island seemed miles away.

When we stopped, Gwen unpacked the picnic hamper while Rachel played with Ian in the smooth sheep-cropped turf on a small promontory above the lake. I went to help Gwen to light the oil stove, and noticed that she was still looking slightly puzzled. She saw me watching her.

'Peter, where have I seen this girl before. I've never met her with old Mr Aaronsen, but there is something very familiar about her. It's a bit crazy really, do you know what I mean?'

I had not told her about her relationship to Jacob and who Aaronsen's wife was. In spite of the warm sunshine I shivered.

'You do know what I mean don't you?' She knew there was something wrong, but I could not define it.

'Peter we've got to talk, something is happening between us and I'm helpless. Patrick tells me that you are going to race on Saturday. I had hoped that you would give it up finally now that we have Ian. You have been very lucky until now, and it can't go on for ever. I just can't stand the thought of one more race. I didn't sleep at all last night. Please, please stop before it's too late. I have a terrible feeling about Saturday.'

'Gwen stop being so murkily Welsh, you have a 'terrible feeling' about every race I ever enter, of course I can't go on for ever, but I must while I still can, the years are running out. It's the only thing that matters now.'

I had said it before I could think of the consequences or what it meant. She flinched as if I had struck her. I put my hand out to touch her shoulder, but she shrugged it away and bent over the cloth she was spreading on the grass.

Rachel walked towards us carrying Ian on her shoulders, she was bouncing him up and down and he was laughing, delighted by being entertained so exclusively. During lunch, Rachel fed him, keeping up such a flow of uninhibited, good humoured anecdotes about school life, her friends and family, that soon the strained atmosphere was relieved.

As Gwen tidied the basket and car, Rachel whispered to me 'You seem to be in the doghouse, is it because of me?'

I shook my head, 'No – racing. Simple issue, car racing or marriage, oil and water.'

She sighed, 'The trouble with you is that you just don't care, you don't understand how she feels, you probably don't understand what love means, or hate. My mother's a bit like you. She's a cabbage, never moved by anything, or worried or frightened. She behaves as if everything in the world has happened to her, so ordinary little people's feelings don't matter a damn. I love her to bits, but she makes me mad. Gwen's so different, but you just don't understand. Men! You're just like children.'

I took her rebuke in silence and with a certain amount of admiration. Her dark brown eyes glittered with rage and intensity and her black hair tumbled over her forehead as she threw back her head to look at me squarely.

'Why does it worry you?' I asked.

'I suppose it worries me because I like you, and Gwen and Ian, and it seems such a pity to risk so much just because you enjoy the thrill of driving fast cars. It seems immoral to me, and much worse than if you were permanently drunk, because you could die or be maimed. I suppose you think that it's your life that you're risking but it isn't. What will those two people do without you? If you die, you will be stealing part of their lives.'

'Rachel you are making the mistake that we all make when we are young, there are no rights and wrongs, blacks and whites, it would be much better for Ian to have a good living mother and a dead father whom he could remember as a hero, than the reality of creeping into a foggy-minded mumbling failure of senility who looked after his carcase so that he could become a millstone to his children when he could no longer work.'

'For myself,' she said, 'I would prefer a living failure to a dead hero, and I never had the choice.' She stood up and walked to the edge of the lake where Gwen was washing Ian's face. Her words scourged me, and I tried to stand, to walk away. I could feel a nerve at the corner of my left eye twitching. I wondered if she could know who I was, and if she really knew how she was inflicting punishment. Could her mother have told her who killed Jacob? Perhaps Simon knew as well, after all he had spent a lot of time with Crompton and he might know enough about the incident to suspect that I was involved. They were certain to discover eventually. Saturday would have to be the end of the association and might, in itself provide a solution.

A lone heron beat its way through the heat haze over the glass smooth water, its reflection keeping pace in inverted mockery among the shimmering reflected hills. Reality and its image seeming equally tangible until a breeze trailed its skirts across the liquid world and splintered the reflected image into a million glittering fragments. The vision had gone, the moment passed and left only a half remembered sequence of images. Tomorrow the memory would have been wiped away, by another little pleasure or pain to make way in the blood-fed and time-guarded pulsing brain that is me.

This brain and carcase and awareness had bought itself another generation of existence, growing and learning, feeling the power of life preparing for his role as man the reasoning, killing animal. Man, the only immoral animal, who always justifies his murders, but despises the animals because they kill to survive. Would this little man child of mine, growing into man's height in the generation of the Bomb, learning more sophisticated ways of making widows and orphans, or would he learn in time? If I were to die now, he would be brought up to think that violent death was a form of virtue, not by the women around him, but by the morbid admiration and respect of his schoolfriends.

Gwen and Rachel were walking back from the lake Ian between them, rejecting help with his stumbling progress. The bright sun cruelly threw into relief the long hard years between Gwen and Rachel, and caught my conscience by the sleeve. Pity is not an acceptable substitute for love, and Gwen may have read it in my quick unguarded look.

I finished packing the car and we took Rachel to the hostel where her course was based. I carried her case up the path to the house, and just as we were saying goodbye, she surprised me by apologising for being rude. I said that it didn't matter but wondered why she felt so strongly about someone else's slight domestic difference.

'I suppose it's because I never had a father, and I don't see why you have such a blindspot about your importance to Gwen. She loves you you know. I know that you have to drive on Saturday but will you please think about giving it up?'

'Rachel I can only presume that you know very little about me, otherwise you might not ask me to take such care of myself. I'll remember what you have said though. Will we see you again?'

She smiled. 'I know I am an insufferable brat and I talk too much, but if you let me come and see you during the summer holidays, I'll promise to be good, quiet and unargumentative, and I can babysit so you can take Gwen out occasionally. As a matter of fact, she has already asked me to come if you agree.'

Two of her friends came running leggily out of a side passage, and the conversation was interrupted for introductions. The three girls together immediately became schoolgirls in a secret jargon-shrouded freemasonry which made me feel like a very old man.

They hardly noticed my leaving, and a little of the sense of age came with me to the car. We drove back to the cottage at Torver and were soon busy unpacking the car, making beds and getting out the deck chairs to spend the rest of the afternoon in unaccustomed sloth. Ian was playing in the sandpit, discovering toys left from the previous summer when Gwen turned to me and said, 'I like that child.'

'Well I suppose that is quite natural Mrs Wade, don't worry about it too much, after all he is yours.'

'No you clown, I mean Rachel. I would like a daughter like her. One hears people criticising this generation, but if they are anything like her, they make us look silly. She talks more sense than all of our friends put together. What had she said to you just before you came down to the lake? I saw your face, and it looked as if you had seen a ghost.'

Sooner or later she would have to know so I told her what I had heard at the club the night before and what Rachel had told me about her father's death and her remark about not having any choice.

'Oh Peter, what a dreadful thing to happen, and I've asked her to come and stay with us this summer. You don't think she knows already do you?'

'I don't think so, and I have asked her to come and see us as well. I don't know what the answer is but one thing is certain we must get out of this Aaronsen set up before someone else realises. It would be a terrible thing for Rachel to discover. This is my main reason now for joining Hall's organisation. There is nothing else I can do. Nothing is very clear at the moment, and I can only really think as far ahead as Saturday.' She reached over and squeezed my hand and we dropped the subject.

Next morning after breakfast we left for Aintree and practicing. Gwen carried on in the Zephyr to Bebington.

CHAPTER 6

Aintree

THE circuit was alive with movement and sound, the pits and paddock full of urgent mechanics and shining machinery. There was a dress rehearsal air about the full stage and empty grandstands. A light breeze stirred the flags over the pits into gentle fluttering life. The loudspeaker was playing an old Glen Miller record in between testing, the smooth strings and clear trumpet notes occasionally submerged under a deluge of savage exhaust noise as a car swept past the pits, changing down to enter the first corner and Gran Tourism cars were filtering out to the exit from the paddock to begin practice. I sprinted across the circuit to the pits, looking for Hall and his cars as I went.

Crompton came running to meet me. 'Come on Peter, hurry up, you're just in time. I've warmed up the Ferrari, and Simon is with it at the Scrutineers tent.'

I told him that I ought to see Hall first , and he started to protest, but changed his mind and pointed out the Hall Equipe. The three FI cars were parked side by side, engine covers on, and polythene covers over the cockpits, indicating that they were completely ready and confident or else they had given up.

Mrs Hall, John Kenning and the chief mechanic were talking and drinking coffee by the tailboard of the transporter. Three more mechanics, Hall and another man whom I presumed to be the other driver were sitting inside the vehicle listening intently to Hall.

He stopped talking when he saw me.

'Morning Peter. We were talking just about you. Let me introduce you to Peter Hemingway, our No. 1 pilot. Don't think you have met have you?'

Hemingway seemed to be about twenty-five or six, stockily built with thick straight hair cut short at the sides, and his muscular forearms were covered with a haze of fine blonde hair.

Both he and Kenning were wearing pale grey racing overalls.

Hall waved his hands towards the three cars. 'I've decided to put all three in this meeting now that the Vanwall team has not turned up, it left a spare entry so Kenning says that he's fit so he will drive it. Peter I want you to support Hemingway, and both be ready to have a go as soon as the Maserati and Ferrari teams have sorted each other out. When we're ready I'll give you the 'flat-out' signal, and Hemingway will drive for a win and you Wade will try and keep the opposition off his tail or entice them out of his way. Until you're near the head of the field at about eight tenths of the distance, Wade will lead and Hemingway will slip-stream him. Then when you're clear of the rest of the field Hemingway will go to the front and win. Is that clear?'

'Yes,' I said, 'and now if you'll excuse me I must get out and practice in the Ferrari. What time is the Formula One session?'

Hall looked at his watch. 'You be back here at 12.30 pm at the end of the odds and sods practising, and have some lunch with us, then we go out at 1.30 after reporting to the clerk of the course.'

I found the Ferrari waiting at the exit from the paddock Simon sitting in the driving seat drumming his fingers on the wheel, while the other cars were lining up at the grid. He saw me coming, got out quickly to make room, and handed me the helmet which had been resting on the bonnet.

'Holy smoke Peter, I thought you'd never come. I've had this thing out once already, and it's going like a bomb. What's the matter? Why are you looking at me like that?'

I had not been listening to what he had been saying, my mind was occupied with the thought that this car belonged to Jacob's widow, and that she would be watching me drive it tomorrow. Before I had thought of a suitable reply, his puzzled expression gave way to a broad grin.

'Oh is it because of Helen? Don't worry about that, she was becoming a bit of an embarrassment, so you did me a good turn last night. Did you stay with her?'

A marshal bustled over, clucking like an anxious hen, his red veined face mocked by an incongruous knitted bobble hat that would have looked more at home on a schoolgirl.

'Come on 23 if you're coming, at all. You're the last one.'

I got into the car, and re-acquainted myself with controls that I had not seen for almost a year. The car had several special features, but was a fundamentally standard 250 GT Coupe.

My stomach fluttered in its now familiar way, and as always I had the feeling that it would not happen if I did not feel so hungrily alone on these occasions. I drove out onto the grid and was directed into a place in the back row between an identical Ferrari and a 3.8 Jaguar saloon.

Puffs of blue haze were pulsing out of the twin tail pipes of a Porsche in front of me. The starter's flag was raised for the next row of Elites and Porsches and two TVRs.

A quick check, oil pressure, water temperature before the row in front went into bottom gear, clutch dis-engaged, handbrake off, while the flag raised for us.

The road in front was empty now, and the flag was up, I watched the starter's face as the flag moved, the revs built up and the clutch bit home. Not too much power, keeping it down to 5500rpm in first, second and third as the corners streamed by.

The road was full of cars as Tatts corner came up for the first time, red cars, green cars, silver cars and all trying to find the quickest way round the flat corners, devoid of any features, but straw bales and advertising banners. The pure sensual pleasure of becoming an integral part of this beautifully elegant motor car with its smooth twelve cylinder engine emptied my mind of every other thought.

Following the 3.8 through Melling crossing, I watched with horror the frantic performance of its rear suspension as the driver went from one lock to another. It looked near to the limit, and I decided that if possible I would keep out of his way during the race.

The other Ferrari was filling my rear view mirror and he passed me as we came out of Tatts. He had apparently decided to do a couple of fast laps before practice finished, as I had. I decided to let him go before trying to get a little nearer to my time for the circuit, and as he went into the first corner after the grandstand, straight I was passing the pits. A quick check on oil and water again, before I arrived at Waterways and accelerated out of it up to 7200rpm. Two hundred and fifty odd horsepower hurled the car into the Country Loop bends like a rocket, through flocks of slower cars travelling nose to tail like tourists.

Feeling for the limit of adhesion between tyres and road, and keeping the tachometer needle floating between six thousand five hundred and seven thousand, the laps flew past and all my being was concentrated on the one task – the rest of the world ceased to exist. The flag signifying the end of practising was showing so I completed a slow lap and drove back into the paddock. Crompton ran to meet me.

'Holy mackerel, it's your day today Peter, its going like a dingbat. Are you happy with it?'

I switched off and removed my helmet. I felt both tired and elated. An almost forgotten feeling of confidence was flowing back into me.

The nearside door opened, and Helen got in, the low seat forcing her to fall into the seat rather than sit. She struggled ineffectively to pull her skirt over expensively nyloned legs.

I wondered at this new found modesty and asked her how she had managed to find the time to watch motor racing when she should have been working. She looked at me out of the corner of her eyes, and without smiling raised her eyebrows.

'I just happened to want to watch you driving. Rachel rang me last night and told me that she is very worried about you. She thinks you're past it you know, and that you don't really care whether you stay alive or not. Believe it or not, and you probably won't, but I also think you ought to stay alive a little longer, so I came along to keep an eye on you.'

She looked embarrassed by her own words and before I could think of a reply, she started to ask me questions about the car.

Ron, the mechanic and his two assistants came to take over the car to prepare it for the next practice, so there was no further opportunity to talk to her. After discussing what work had to be done to the car with Ron and Patrick, I joined the GMT team for lunch.

I could see Helen standing by Simon Aaronsen's Elite talking to him through its window, and was wondering about this and saw the world in which we both lived and had met, when Hall nudged me in the ribs with his elbow.

'I'll bet a large brass clock to a fly button that your mind wasn't on cars then.'

'Well, I suppose a change is as good as a rest,' Mrs. Hall said. 'I'd rather have my husband thinking about a woman once in a blue moon, as a change from cars, but that's too much to hope for.'

A stir of excitement at the entrance to the pits provided diversion, and proved to be caused by the arrival of the Ferrari works team.

The travel-stained transporter with its prancing horse added spice to the predominantly green mixture of cars and as picnic meals were tidied away and the Grand Prix cars warmed up for the second practice of the day, it discharged its scarlet cargo. Almost as soon as the Ferraris were out of the transporter, they were submerged in a seething crowd of people trying to see the favourites for the main event.

I took the opportunity to try my car for size and meet the mechanic who was in charge of it. I was surprised to find that I had been given the experimental GMT which had a chassis frame built up from a mass of small diameter light alloy tubes. The rear, flat-eight engine was very similar to the Ferrari unit in layout, but was fitted with a special six speed gearbox and inboard disc brakes. The brakes had a relay valve supplied by an engine driven pump, and an electrical anti-skid system which opened a solenoid valve in each brake line. It seemed heavy and rather complex but Harry, the mechanic assured me it worked well.

The fibreglass seat fitted closely round the hips and under the thighs and promised to be comfortable even for a 200 mile GP.

The fact that a six speed gearbox was fitted to this car seemed to indicate that the power unit lacked torque at low engine speeds, and this fundamental difference between the Pig and the GMT suggested that I was not going to find this car easy.

Harry and Kenning looked at each other quickly when I asked them about this characteristic, and Kenning told me that this was in fact the reason why I had been allocated to it. It appeared that

Hall considered my experience driving a variety of cars made me the most suitable driver although I had far fewer successes to my credit.

I felt ill at ease in this unfamiliar cockpit, and wished that I had been driving my own car in the Formula Libre race but it was too late for regrets. The marshals were checking starters, and the loud speakers announced the practice period for Formula One and Formula Libre cars.

Kenning and Hemmingway were putting on their overalls and helmets when Hall called them over to my car to give his final instructions, before we started and drove onto the circuit. The three of us were among the first twelve to arrive at the pit exit ready to practice and we were waved straight onto the circuit in front of the track marshal's car.

It was a relief to get away on my own, and find my way round in yet another new car. The car felt very low and taut after the Pig, and the Ferrari, with very quick steering, although the engine sounded and felt both erratic and lumpy.

I allowed the other eleven cars to get away into the first corner before getting up into a second gear and turning on the power. As the rev-counter needle slid round to 8,000rpm the exhaust note cleared to a resonant blare, and the car leaped away like an unleashed greyhound. Somewhat startled as Waterways corner was approaching rapidly. I eased off the throttle and heeled the brake. My toe scraped the side of the cockpit and the car twitched its way round the corner. I began to feel hot and uncomfortable with self consciousness and the heat from the engine which was soaking through the bulkhead behind me. I would have to do a lot better than this.

For lap after lap, I persisted, trying to master the temperamental little fiend of a car, which persisted in misfiring and slithering coming out of corners as well as lifting the inside front wheel. As I reduced my lap times the heat from the engine bay became less troublesome. Fewer cars passed me, and the corners became single-radius drifts instead of a series of heart stopping slides and twitches.

Coming round Beechers Bend, two works Porsches were in

front and a quick glance in the offside mirror showed the yellow nose of Hemingway's GMT approaching rapidly. This seemed to be the moment to compare performance, so I took the rev-counter round to the yellow mark at 8,500rpm before changing up into each gear, passing both Porsches in fourth gear by the brook. A quick look in the mirror showed me that Hemingway was falling back although he was between the two slower cars.

The wind roared over the top of the screen in waves of pressure that hurt my ears as I changed into top and took the speed up to 8,700rpm. Almost at once it was time to brake and change down for the tricky Melling Crossing where the road circuit crosses the Melling road. A short straight up into fifth down again for the kink before the straight into Tatts. A gaggle of Coopers, Porsches and a BRM were going round Tatts in a company.

A gap presented itself between two cars at the run into the corner and the GMT sprinted through onto the line for the corner. I had begun to discover that the flirtatious inside front wheel meant little and could safely be ignored so I pressed the car round close to my limit and carved my way through the pack to the open road past the pits. I saw Hall sitting on the counter, and raised a hand to him before snatching top gear.

Two more laps at the same pace showed me that the car although not easy to drive could win races in the right hands. I pulled into the pits to have the fuel system checked because it still showed the same tendency to misfire when accelerating after a corner. Hall's face gave nothing away, as he walked over to ask how it was going. Harry and his mate took the engine cover off while two more mechanics changed the tyres.

The greater brake efficiency was wearing the tyres more rapidly. The fact that I could brake without fear of locking a wheel, was inducing me to use them more liberally. Mrs Hall came out of the transporter with a cup of tea for me.

'When you have finished practice Mr Wade, can you give Helen a lift home? She's helping me to make tea at the moment.'

Hall turned to her before I could answer.

'Yes, yes, dear, of course he will, but he has to get in a good lap time and we don't know what the Ferrari times are going to be like yet, or for that matter the Coopers. Just let us get on with the job before we worry about our social lives.'

Hetty shrugged her shoulders and looked at me pityingly.

'Tell her I'll be over to see her in a minute, the Ferraris are going out now, and I want to see how they are going to go. I'll be back and have a crack at their time before practicing ends at about half past three.'

I asked Hall if we could get my last two lap times from the timekeepers and he sent one of the boys to find out. He came back with the news that the fastest lap to date was set by the Walker Lotus fractionally faster than the lone BRM, although they thought that the No. 1 Porsche had almost exactly equalled it. I had the fourth fastest time at one minute, fifty nine point eight seconds. Hemingway was still trying to get down to the two minute mark, and Kenning's car could not get below two minutes fifteen. On present form, I would be on the second row of the grid but it was too early to count chickens.

Both Kenning and Hemingway came in together, looking irritated and hot. I went to see Helen. She was sitting in the passenger seat of the transporter and looked pleased to see me. We talked for a while, but I could not keep my mind on any subject other than the car.

After a while she gave up the struggle of trying to make conversation and with a rueful smile, she was silent. I could hear the scream of the Ferraris through the flat burble of the Porsches and the hard clamour of the assorted Climax-engined car, and it was like a challenge. I could stand it no longer.

'Come on Helen, let's have a look at the opposition,' I said, and we went to the inside of Tatts corner to watch.

The three low red cars with their strange bifurcated intakes were fast, steady and consistent at Tatts and showed far more discipline than one had been accustomed to expect from an Italian team. Times had changed since the hair raising battles that went on in the team when Castellotti and Musso were fighting like alley cats for the Italian championship.

Helen checked them with a stop watch that Mrs Hall had loaned her. They were lapping under two minutes consistently. Three minutes later they came in for a tyre change and re-fuel, so we went to look at them. Simon was already there talking to the motoring correspondent of one of the daily papers, apparently discussing the Pig because when I approached he waved his hand towards me and said, 'Here's the man you should ask, he built it.' I soon became involved in a discussion about the design of the car, and my reasons for building it. Simon in the meanwhile had taken Helen on one side and was talking earnestly to her. Crompton joined us, so I introduced him to the journalist, and made an excuse to leave.

I had seen the Ferrari team leader coming out to get into his car. Only fifteen minutes of practice were left, and the Walker Lotus had, it appeared, just gone round in one minute fifty nine point one seconds.

Our pit was a hive of activity. The engine cover was back on my car, and the mechanics were looking happy. Hall was wiping the windscreen and one of the mechanics was cleaning the steering wheel. Hall saw me.

'Come on laddie, you're our only front-row prospect. Hemingway reckons he's reached his best time and Kenning is suffering from the effects of a leaking exhaust system.'

I got into the car and put on my helmet and gloves.

'Just let me know their best times, as they do them, and I'll tool around until they think they're best. Then I'll have a real crack at it. OK?'

Hall grinned, 'OK' he said, 'Ready to go?' I nodded and as soon as the road was clear, we started.

The difference in the engine was immediately noticeable. Although the band of useable power was still very narrow, it was clear and consistent, without stuttering or misfiring.

The Ferrari swept past me in the Country Loop a works Cooper on its tail. I let them go and continued my steady progress at about two minutes three seconds per lap. I took a quick look at my watch, as I came past the pits. There were six more minutes to go. The Ferrari was at the far end of the straight braking for Waterways. The Cooper had passed him and was obviously trying hard. Now was the time. I saw one of our other two cars accelerate away from the pits, and as I passed him I saw that it was Kenning.

He kept looking at me in his mirror, obviously annoyed that his superior engine was helping me because of his lack of vigilance. He swept past the Cooper who was unable to tuck in behind us because we were on a different line through Melling.

At Tatts, the Ferrari got over into the left gutter. The nose of the car dipping under fierce braking, so I stayed to his right and did not start to brake until I had passed him. I came out of Tatts with the nearside wheels in the dirty Merseyside grass, but three lengths ahead and an open road in front of me.

He was on my tail through Waterways and trying to get past all the way up to Beechers. There was no sign of the Cooper.

He came alongside down the long straight, and my mouth was dry with the suppressed excitement of the chase. This was obviously going to be a game of 'chicken', to see who would shut off first for Melling. I was on the right line for the first kink and he saw this, he shut off and fell in behind me.

Kenning in the other GMT was going past a private Cooper through the crossing when he suddenly swerved to the right with his rear wheel behind the front nearside wheel of the Cooper. Suddenly the road in front of us seemed to be filled with spinning green cars. In the middle of a drift, I dare not brake, but looked for a gap to go through between the cloud of dust and earth on the right of the road and the sliding inverted Cooper in the centre and the inert form of its driver. Instead of being on a chosen line, I had to swerve and the car spun. Hedges, brick buildings, running marshalls and a cloud of flame-flickering black smoke rushed past my eyes, until suddenly it slowed down and I was pointing up into Tatts corner on my own. The engine was running so I dropped into bottom gear and motored back to the pits.

Hall and the mechanics thumped my back, and yelled to me, their faces showing that I must have established a reasonable time. I felt sick, and got out of the car with difficulty.

'For God's sake Hall get over to Tatts quickly, Kenning shunted a Cooper, someone's burning. I think it's Kenning.'

His face went white, and he ran off with two of the mechanics just as Helen reached the pit counter. She instantly realised that something was wrong and asked me what had happened. I told her as much as I knew while I had a glass of water.

The loud speaker coughed into life, and announced that practice was at an end. It went on to say that there had been an accident and as it spoke the din of engines and conversation died away until only the noise of the traffic on the main road could be heard. A few moments later an ambulance left the circuit, bell ringing and sign flashing, followed by a second one in no particular hurry. A marshall turned to us.

'It looks as if one of them's bought it.'

No-one answered him, but got on with tidying the pit areas, stowing tyres and wheeling cars off to the transporters.

Crompton looking through the door at the back of our pit saw Helen but not me.

'Where's Hall,' he asked, and before she could answer he said. 'Peter's wife just turned up to watch practising and got to Melling just in time to see him crash. Where have they taken him to?'

I stood up so that he could see me over the counter.

His expression might have been comical at any other time. 'Where is she Patrick?' I asked.

Thank the Lord you're OK. She's in my car now. She passed out like a light when she saw the body.

'What the hell are you talking about?' I asked.

'Well she thought it was you, and she could see him trapped under the car burning and no-one could get at him.'

Helen was pale, 'For God's sake shut up, go to her Peter.'

Gwen was being attended by a doctor when I arrived and Ian was playing happily with Mrs Hall. Crompton told her before she saw me, over and over again, 'He's alright Gwen, really.'

She would not let me touch her or try to comfort her but asked Crompton to take her home. He looked at me appealing for help, but she would not speak to me. The doctor prescribed a sedative and Crompton drove her away with Ian and Mrs Hall.

Simon was standing beside me. He shook his head. 'Women are a complete mystery to me. If the thought of you dying worried her so much, why isn't she pleased to discover you're still alive?'

I should have felt sympathy for her, but the faint sense of guilt and a much stronger sense of encumbrance and irritation filled my mind. We watched, Crompton's car making its way through the aimless, curious crowds of hangers-on who filled the paddock.

'I don't know Simon, but I suppose it must be shock. Things like this make very little impression on my mind now, but Gwen has no shell.'

Groups of unoccupied competitors, mechanics and friends drifted in and out of the team areas, loosely knit cells of corporate bodies connected by invisible elastic threads of association and common interests. A chance gap in the crowd, the movement of a car, an engine cover being taken off, initiates the movement in new directions. One goes, the next two follow without knowing why, and the last one feeling insecure and the faint tugging of the common mind follows, filled with vague woolly curiosity. From above, they lurch and seeth about like living cells seen through a microscope. Caps, berets, bald heads, knitted caps and deerstalkers, headscarves and hair.

Someone was pushing his way through the crowd towards the GMT transporter, propelled by official purpose. The authority of his marshall's armband raised him above the crowd.

'Has anyone seen Mr Wade?' he asked, and Hall, who was supervising the loading of the two remaining cars, pointed towards where I was standing.

'I suppose the stewards have called a meeting to try and find out what happened to Kenning,' I said to Simon.

When it's over, I'd like to talk to you about the Pig and one or two other things. Have you any plans for this evening?'

'As a matter of fact, I wanted to discuss the future with you as well, and asking you one or two things about the car. I'm having dinner with the family tonight, but I should be free by nine. Where shall we meet?'

The marshall interrupted to ask me to go with him to the Chief Marshall's office, and Simon quickly suggested that we should meet at the Twenty Club at 9 pm. I agreed and followed my guide to the enquiry.

It proved to be a formality, the only complication being

provided by an argument between the Italian driver of the Ferrari who had followed me, and the interpreter. Just as I was about to leave, having given evidence, the chief scrutineer came in, and asked me to stay.

He turned to the chairman of the meeting. 'Could we call Mr Hall in? What we have just found has some bearing on his team, and their entry tomorrow, that is if they are still intending to run.'

I said that I had not heard anything to the contrary, and asked him what he had discovered.

The chairman rapped on his table with a paperweight and reproved me for interrupting a witness. He sent a marshal to bring Hall and Hemingway while we waited in silence.

The tension was eased by Hall and Hemingway's arrival and so that they would know the background to what was about to be said the RAC steward read out the witnesses statements. As he finished a marshall came in and handed a handwritten note to the chairman.

The chairman read it and looked up.

'Gentlemen, I am very sorry to have to tell you, that John Kenning died in the admission room at Walton Hospital shortly after reaching the hospital. Harrison who was in the Cooper was apparently only concussed and suffering from shock. He has pretty extensive bruising but they don't think he has broken any bones. Now we had better hear what Mr Jones has to say.

The scrutineer stood up.

'Mr Chairman, gentlemen, we have just finished our preliminary examination of the two cars involved in this unfortunate incident. The Cooper is not irreparably damaged, but of course the GMT I am sorry to say is a complete write-off. One of the flag marshals and Mr Wade both spoke of the sudden swerve to the left which the GMT made. This caused me to look at the nearside suspension of the wrecked car, which had been badly damaged. When I first saw the wreck I assumed, as did my assistant, that this must have happened during the contact with the Cooper. When we examined it more closely we saw, however, that where the upper leading arm of the wishbone had been sheared off the bearing boss, only half the exposed surface of the casting was bright and clean. The remaining surface of the casting was discoloured and fretted on the high spots. This indicates that the casting had been cracked prior to this accident and caused the top nearside wishbone to fracture allowing the suspension that side to collapse. I would suggest that Mr Hall's team cars should be re-submitted for examination, and dye penetrant crack detection of their wishbones should be carried out.

I looked towards Hall. He was standing with Hemingway at the back of the room, his eyes on Mr Jones.

'Where do you propose that this investigation should be carried out Mr Jones and when?' he asked.

'I will let you know later Mr Hall, but we will have to do it as soon as possible to give you as much time as possible to re-build the suspension units.'

Hall jumped to his feet, and the chairman anticipated a protest and asked for silence. Several people were talking at once. The chairman hit the table with the paperweight, the pens and paper hopped about as if they found the noise irksome. Eventually there was silence.

'Mr Jones I would be grateful if you would state your findings in a report to me, bearing in mind that this evidence is liable to be used in the inquest on this unfortunate young man. Before this however, I would like you to let us know what is involved in these tests, and what you need Mr Hall to do. In the meanwhile I think we can allow the rest of these good people to get on with their work.

Jones described what he wanted doing, and it seemed apparent that Hall and his mechanics were going to have a busy night. It seemed that each wishbone casting had to be removed, stripped down to the bare metal and painted over with a penetrating dye. The dye would fill any cracks invisible to the naked eye, remaining there when the surface was wiped clean. Covering all the surface with an absorbent film would reveal where the dye was lying in any cracks. It seemed simple enough, but it meant a loss of time doing it to sixteen fittings.

Until this discussion, I had not considered the detailed design of the GMT, but the use of this particular type of casting for these highly stressed components, did nothing to reassure me.

I slipped quietly out of the meeting and went to have a look at the wrecked car where it lay on the inside of the circuit. A crowd of amateur photographers and a couple of professionals were taking pictures.

I tried to ignore the smell and the tangled mass of tubes and blistered paintwork, and keep my mind on what I was looking for. The nearside rear wishbones should have taken more punishment on this circuit during practice as the car was rear engine, and only a small quantity of fuel had been put in. Nearly all the corners are right-handed, and most of the weight is at the back. The nearside rear suspension was missing completely, the half shaft with its wheel-end universal joint resting in the torn earth.

I looked round, and saw the missing wheel lying with a split and flame-blackened crash helmet and an odd glove against the straw bales. The scene looked strangely like the aftermath of an aircraft crash.

Kneeling by the wheel with its buckled rim but still inflated tyre, I was almost afraid to look for what I knew I was going to see. The lower wishbone showed the beginning of a crack at its outboard end, starting at the junction of two machined radii which had caused a sharp change in section. I walked quickly back to the pits, and up the tail ramp of the GMT transporter.

'Ron,' I called, and he looked in from the driving seat.

'What is it guv'nor?'

'Bring me a torch and a magnifying glass if you've got one.' I heard someone ask him a question and his muffled, 'Christ knows' in reply.

The thought of what I had been risking that afternoon made the dark inside of the trailer feel like a coffin.

'You'll soon bloody well know too if you don't get a move on.' My voice sounded shrill and cracked.

He came quickly and switched on the internal light.

'Sorry Mr Wade,' he said 'what's up?'

'That's just what we are about to find out.' I said and focussed the light and magnifying glass on the wishbone. The polished surface threw back glittering reflections which confused my tired eyes. I rubbed them with the back of my hand. The surface had been finished much more efficiently than on Kenning's car, but a series of faint scores ran away across the surface from the sharp corner. They could have been emery cloth scratches. I looked at the nearside rear unit, and there it was, a crack two or three inches long along the radius between the bearing boss and the web. I gave the glass to Ron without comment, and stood shakily. Hall was standing beside me, and sober-faced Hemingway.

'Well?' he asked.

'We've got troubles,' I answered and applied my numb brain to finding an answer which could get us onto the starting grid tomorrow while Hall went on to examine Hemingway's car.

'God almighty, this one's on its way as well,' he said. 'They can save themselves the trouble of crack-detecting this lot. Have we any spares Ron?'

Ron shrugged. 'Just two,' he said 'but there's the old ones. I could send two of the boys off to Towcester to get 'em, and they could be back before midnight if they left now. That would get one car mobile.'

'What about it?' I suggested. 'We could take the offside wishbones off these two cars, crack detect them, then if we can get a complete set blend out this corner and fit them. We might get away with it, because they're not handed.'

Everyone brightened visibly, except Hemingway, who looked at me wryly. 'That seems to fix everything pretty neatly, except for one thing, who's going to get the cast wishbones on his car?'

'If they get a clean bill of health when tested, and I modify one which Hall's boys can use as a pattern, I'll have them.'

He laughed, 'I hope for your sake that you know what you're talking about. As far as I'm concerned that's OK so let's get cracking.'

'While you start dismantling, I'm going to ring Gwen to see if she's alright,' I said to Hall. 'I'll see you in about half an hour.'

He nodded to me, and followed me out of the transporter. 'Did I detect some implied criticism of my engineering in your insistence on modifying these castings to conform to your ideas?' he asked.

I stopped walking and turned to face him.

'I'll answer that with another question, Mr Hall, do you think that their design is right?'

'Perhaps not, but I'm damned if I'll be criticised in front of my own staff.' He was trying to control his anger.

'If that Cooper driver, or any of Kenning's relatives, decide to sue you, you'll hear a great many harder things than I'll ever say to you, apart from which my life is going to depend on this damned car tomorrow. This is just one thing we have found, how many more unknown faults are there? You forget last Wednesday's nonsense when we had a similar failure on another component your mechanical butcher had been playing with. You try looking at it from my point of view. I intend to stay alive a little longer and I will do it by eliminating all the unnecessary risks.'

I turned and went to look for a telephone, conscious that I had been too hard, and had probably not helped anyone by putting his fears into words. I had also helped to destroy the team's confidence in their leader, something no more words could restore.

A steady stream of cars, transporters and people were leaving the circuit as I made my way to a call box.

The inside of the telephone box was dirty and littered with cigarette ends. The air smelt of stale cigarette smoke and perspiration. The mirror was cracked and the silver tarnished. The electric light bulb was missing.

I held the door open to let in a little fresh air while the number was ringing. There was no reply.

I rang Crompton's house and his wife answered the phone. Her English was still imperfect, and difficult to understand unless one could see her lips, but I gathered that Patrick was at the garage changing back-axle ratios on the Pig.

I rang the garage and Patrick answered. The nasal Liverpool accent was accentuated by the telephone. He had taken Gwen home and rung Pam who came over to put Ian to bed. As far as he knew Gwen was still at home.

I told him that I had been unable to get an answer, and he suggested that she might have gone to spend the night with Pam and Charles. I thanked him and rang off. I had run out of pennies and the only other money I had was in my jacket pocket.

The slowly moving tide of transporters and cars pumping petrol rich exhaust fumes into the grey evening as it poured slowly out of the gate, clogged the road out of the car park. The swelling banks of storm cloud were advancing like an irresistible army from behind the ramparts of roofs and chimneys. Already the low evening sun was hidden behind the iron grey curtain of cloud and smoke from the city, and the cool wind found the open neck of my overalls and breathed icily on my throat and shoulders. I shivered.

* * *

The lack of four pennies stood like an unknown ocean between me and my world. Four pennies were stealing time from me. Valuable minutes and perhaps hours when I could ill afford them. The experience of the afternoon, those fragmentary images of the world spinning around me, of flame and the smell of the wrecked car, carried into my mind the lust to live. Life had become too easy, too vegetable and devoid of feeling. Tomorrow it might be my turn, and now I had no idea how Gwen was. I would have to find her as soon as I had finished what I had to do at Aintree.

The paddock was almost empty when I returned, Simon and our own team had left taking the Ferrari and the Pig.

The GMT team had almost finished removing the wishbones. The tramped grass round the cars and the transporter was littered with sections of the car's bodywork and wheels and tyres. Each chassis was supported on wooden blocks, and looking like re-constructed skeletons of prehistoric animals on display. Ron seemed to be running the operation with Hetty Hall and Helen cleaning the castings at the bench inside the transporter. Hall and his Elite had gone from the scene. So had Hemingway.

Hetty turned to see who was blocking the light that was coming through the double rear doors.

'Oh hello Peter,' she said. 'Jack has gone down to Towcester for the spare wishbones, and Hemingway has gone to see young Kenning's family. Jack suggests that you should go and get a good night's rest. We can cope here.'

'Well I would like to get away and see how Gwen is. I've no idea where she is, but where is this crack detection going to be done?'

She carried on working as she told me that the chief scrutineer had arranged to take them to Napier's inspection department to have them examined and would return them by 10pm at the latest with a report.

There seemed to be little point in hanging about, as there would be nothing to do until the parts were returned and Hall came back with the spares. I said that I would return later, but Hetty said that she would ring and let me know what the situation was before 9 p.m. and asked me to take Helen home on the way back into town.

Gwen had left the Anglia unlocked, and the keys in the glove box. I re-adjusted the seat, and as I pushed it backwards it crushed something in the rail. I groped behind the seat with my right hand and found the splintered remains of a bright yellow plastic rabbit. It joined the graveyard of lost toys, sweet papers and lolly ice sticks in a polythene bag in the glove box. I wondered what conclusions an archaeologist would arrive at if he examined the contents of this indestructible bag some centuries ahead if a nuclear war destroyed our civilisation.

Would he assume that its contents must be precious because of the care we had taken to preserve them? Would he assume that we took more care of possessions than people? Some of us anyway. My own car, like the traditional decorator's house, was a monument of neglect. Although it was mechanically sound, the radio did not work, the heater selector switch was without a knob and it had not been washed for at least a month.

Helen came towards me putting on her coat as she walked, and smiled, almost shyly as her eyes met mine. She got in, and turned to me.

'I know I'm a bit in the way at the moment because you've got enough to think about, just drop me at Queens Drive and I can catch a bus home.'

'That's alright Helen, another few minutes can't make much difference. I'll take you all the way. I can't get an answer from home, so I think Gwen is probably with some friends of hers. The only puzzling feature is that it's Ian's bedtime, and she insists on that being rigidly adhered to.'

The traffic was dense, and slow moving, with reckless

pedestrians and cyclists weaving in and out of the streams. I looked at my watch, it was ten past six.

Helen sighed, 'You had better put me off at Queens Drive, it will take ages going round by Prescott.

I was feeling stubborn and frustrated by her presence but insisted on taking her home. By the time we reached her road, it would only have needed one ill-considered word to have provoked a quarrel. Rain was beginning to fall in widely spaced fat drops which exploded on the windscreen and bonnet.

As I stopped the car outside her home, she put her hand lightly on my arm. 'If there is anything I can do to help, please give me a ring, my number is in the directory.'

I was just about to say thank you and open the door for her to get out, when it occurred to me that I would not be able to find her number even if I wanted to, because I still did not know her surname. The lunacy of the situation nudged me like a jocular elbow, and made me smile in spite of my ill humour. Less than a week ago we had met, and without any of the fairy tale preliminaries, grand emotions and protestations of endless duration, had made love and gone our separate ways. It had not even occurred to me to ask her name. It seemed to be no more than the random rushes and aimless brainless hovering of minnows in a pool, or drops of rain on a window pane.

My feelings of guilt about Gwen were added to by the realisation of the way I had neglected to even consider Helen as a being like myself. Perhaps insensitivity to the feelings of is the result of the mind becoming covered with unfeeling scar tissue, the relics of old wounds. Perhaps there was still some hope, at least I knew and as I knew I must feel.

'Why did you smile?' she asked.

I explained and she told me that her name was Pailton. I wrote it in my diary together with her phone number because I knew that I had already begun to forget.

As I drove away she stood on the pavement her hands thrust into the pockets of her blond leather belted raincoat while the rain smoothed her hair into a heavy shining cascade closely round her head and shoulders. She was still standing watching as I turned into the main road which led to the tunnel and home.

I parked the car in the short drive which just allowed the gates to close behind the rear bumper if the front one was within two inches of the garage door. The house looked dead, with its curtains open, no light and no smoke from the chimney. The evening paper lay in the hall behind the door together with some circulars and a letter from the Inland Revenue. As I wiped my shoes on the doormat and closed the door, I called 'Gwen' but the house was silent and cold.

I went from room to room, turning on lights and closing the curtains, looking for some indication of where she was. Ian's cot was empty, mattress and blankets were missing, and his toy box had gone. I went to our room, some of Gwen's meagre wardrobe and her make up was missing from the dressing table. Both of our old suitcases had gone from the top of the wardrobe only the pattern of dust showed where they had lain.

I looked for a letter or a note, but there was nothing, only a cold and empty house which had already begun to feel like a prison cell. If in the first few moments of bewildering realisation of what was happening to me, I had any doubts about Gwen's reason for leaving in this way, the neglected paintwork, threadbare carpets and the wad of unpaid bills behind the kitchen clock were silent but eloquent evidence. Neglect.

Following an instinct which probably was indicating a way to re-establish a sense of security, I filled the electric kettle to make a cup of tea. The frayed insulation of the electric lead to the kettle turned the knife in my conscience, and made me wonder how many times in the years since we had been married, Gwen had felt my lack of consideration for her reminded by these signs of neglect.

I sat down in the kitchen while the kettle boiled and thought about the situation, wondering vaguely why a feeling of relief so easily came to the top of the jumbled heap of emotions. Resentment, self pity, even a sense of loss, were only lightly felt compared with the lightening of an unseen and immeasurable load which I would never have been quite brutal enough to have shed deliberately.

I watched the rain running down, the un-curtained kitchen

window. First the raindrops ran in parallel paths, then meeting some unseen resistance, taking an easier path till they joined a well trodden route which allowed them to run more easily and perhaps join another. Together they ran faster, growing in size as they collected other drops, until they collided with others their own size and merged. As they grew bigger and heavier, rushing down to the bottom of the pane, they turned aside for nothing: blind, senseless but with a common direction.

The empty silence of the house closed in on my head like a light but dense ball of cotton wool that filled all the space inside the walls, robbing my mind of the ability to think. The suddenness of the emptiness and enveloping silence after the noise and tension of the day was like the stupefying shock of jumping into a deep mountain pool on a hot day.

I switched on the radio to fill the dead air with life and movement, and restlessly collected cups and saucers, milk and sugar, and then warmed the teapot. The tray I had laid with crockery, held two cups and two saucers.

I decided to ring Pam and Charles' home. Charles answered the 'phone, and obviously reluctant to discuss something for which he did not want to accept responsibility, called for Pam. I heard him mutter to her as he handed over the receiver. 'It's him.'

'Hello Pam, is Gwen with you?'

'Yes,' she said, 'she's in bed and fast asleep. She has had a bad shock you know.'

'Well as it happens Pam, so have I, but why didn't you bring her home?'

'Quite simply Peter, because she didn't want to go home. She said she would rather go anywhere than there tonight, and she asked Charles to take her to her mother's home tomorrow. She asked me to tell you if you remembered to ring, that she can't stand her present existence any longer.

'She really is in a terrible state Peter, the doctor says that unless she has a holiday now, with complete rest, she will have a break-down. I knew that if you missed this meeting tomorrow and took her away for a holiday everything would sort itself out in time, but if you race, I wouldn't like to predict the future.'

The irritating blare of the radio in the kitchen thumping out the Khachaturian *Sabre Dance* kept part of my mind tethered, while Pam's tone of righteous but peevish complaint stung me into defence when I should have felt remorse, regret, perhaps even love.

'For God's sake why don't you learn to attend to your own affairs Pam. You seem to have appointed yourselves as a two-person commission to manage our lives for us, and so far you have only managed to get us in a hell of a mess, and involve Gwen in business intrigues behind my back.'

She tried to protest but I cut her short. 'No, let me finish. For the first time in the last ten years, I have a real chance to do what I have always known I could do well, and with time I am going to take that chance, and nothing is going to stop me. It's no use trying not to hurt people all the time, you just get hurt yourself and everyone despises you. In 1948 I took the easy way out of a situation because quite honestly I hadn't the guts to go through with it. I had been anti-authority just too long, they had ground me down, so I took the easy way out and walked out of the only chance of real happiness I ever had. What has been the result? Everyone else assumes that I can be pushed around and organised. Well from now onwards I have changed.

'It's no use Pam, I'm sure that you think you are doing the right thing, but it would be better if you didn't get involved. There are no real rights and wrongs; we can't really help the effects we have on other people and the effects they have on us. It just happens that we have both become different people during our separate contacts with different people. Tell her that I will pick her up tomorrow night after the race and bring her home. If all goes well I should have enough money tomorrow night for a short holiday.'

'It's no use, Peter, she wouldn't listen to me if I tried to tell her unless you give up the idea of racing. Come around tomorrow morning and take her away.'

'I have already told you Pam, I am going to race tomorrow providing the car is ready, and that is final.' She sighed.

'You are very foolish, and very selfish, and I think Gwen has done the right thing in leaving you.' She put down the receiver.

The silence that followed, before the operator asked if we had finished with the line, cut me off from Gwen completely. It would be impossible for me to go to Pam and Charles' house and ask to see her, because it would force Pam into the role of protector making her feel justified in denying me entry. Inevitably this could only lead to an argument, and would not be any help to Gwen.

Tomorrow would provide an answer, and show which way I should go. If I could manage to get a place in the Formula One event, then it would almost certainly mean that I would have a future in professional racing for as long as I could keep a car up with the leaders. When failing sight and slowing reactions began to make themselves apparent, by slower lap times, I could go back to engineering. The aimless years since I left Jerusalem must not be repeated because time was running out.

Whatever the result tomorrow, I must leave the Aaronsen organisation before they discovered who I was. I became aware of the kettle's whistle, and found the kitchen full of steam.

Sitting on the edge of the kitchen table, while I drank a cup of tea, I wondered if the Aaronsens knew what had happened to Deborah and where she was. Would it be possible to discover where she was living without letting them know who I was?'

It seemed impossible but I applied my mind to it with a re-awakening awareness of the feeling of isolation which had become part of my life. Instead of a carefully nurtured defensive hedge it began to feel like a prison as the idea of seeing Deborah again began to take form. Just to see her again, would be worthwhile, and perhaps to speak to her. I tried to remember her face, and her voice but only half formed shapes and imperfect memories of sounds came to mind. It seemed wrong that this girl who had thrown my life out of the well defined track in which it was running, during the course of that one brief summer, should now be so hard to remember. Probably by now she would have a large family, and have even forgotten my name.

I remembered that I had arranged to meet Simon Aaronsen at the Twenty Club at 9 p.m. With a faint feeling of annoyance at the idea of having to drive all the way back to Liverpool. I looked in my wallet and discovered that it only held a single crumpled one pound note apart from a muddle of papers, letters and licences. An exploration of my pockets only revealed half pennies, one penny and a florin. I searched through the pockets of my other clothes and the old teapot in the pantry where we sometimes kept the odd banknote for emergencies, but it proved fruitless.

It had not occurred to me to ask Hall about money, and I had not been to the bank since the previous Friday. I hoped that Simon would be on his own, and that he would not get us involved with a party. We certainly had a ready-made excuse for keeping away from the bottle on this occasion, so perhaps the situation was not too bad.

I decided to look for something to eat, a search of the pantry yielded four eggs, some bacon, two tins of beans in tomato sauce, and half a loaf. Two boiled eggs and toast provided the easiest solution, and I was just taking the eggs out of the pan when the doorbell rang.

It was Crompton, and he stepped into the hall to get out of the deluge as soon as I opened the door.

'By God, it's bucketing down,' he said. 'I'm damned glad that I'm not going to drive tomorrow.'

'Why, what's the forecast?' I asked.

'Rain and strong westerly winds,' he replied, 'probably clearing from the west coast later in the evening.'

'A fat lot of good that will be to me. I hate driving in the rain at the best of times, and this GMT will be an absolute bastard in the wet. It has a torque band half the width of a gnat's whatnot.'

He smiled grudgingly as if ashamed of his weakness in smiling at one of my jokes.

'Come into the kitchen, I was just about to have something to eat. Would you like a cup of tea, I've just made a brew?'

'Have you ever known me to refuse?' he asked, and followed me. We sat in silence while I took the top off an egg to begin to eat, but quite suddenly the idea of food made me feel sick so I put the spoon down. I felt Crompton looking at me.

'What's up Peter?' he asked.

'Nothing really, I think I must be too tired.' But I felt cold and began to shiver so that I could not keep my hands still.

'Nothing Hell, you're shivering from delayed shock. The best place for you is bed. I'll give Carla a ring and tell her to get the spare bed made. You can spend the night with us.'

'Stop fussing I've got to go out again because I promised to meet Simon Aaronsen. I appreciate the gesture, but I'm all right really.'

'From where I'm standing you look anything but alright, but I have known you long enough to know that it's a waste of time to try and make you change your mind. Where are you meeting Simon?'

'At a club in Liverpool' I told him, 'at nine o'clock.'

He looked genuinely concerned. 'Can I drive you there, or would I be in the way?'

The idea had not occurred to me, but it was a very welcome suggestion. 'Are you sure that you wouldn't rather stay by a warm fire tonight, although when I think about it, it would be better if you did come, because he said that he wants to discuss the future. After tomorrow I don't expect to have any future in this company, so it'll be of more interest to you.'

He looked puzzled, 'What d'you mean, no future?'

I poured a cup of tea for him.

'It's quite on the cards that the Aaronsens know by now who I am, and I can't really see them wanting to continue the association any longer than they have to. At the end of the Grand Turismo car race tomorrow, I intend to resign from the board.'

Crompton was looking at me with an expression which was a mixture of amusement and irritation.

'D'you know Peter, one can always rely on you to go off at half cock. Which board are you going to resign from? You can only resign from ours you know. We are not tied to Aaronsen's organisation yet, and if you don't want us to be, then there's nothing I can do to alter the situation.'

'Well, it seemed to me that I had done enough harm already without making matters worse, so I thought I would get out of your way now that you have a real chance. You need more capital and we haven't got it but Aaronsen has.'

'Peter you're a bloody nit, we started off as partners and that's the way it's going to stay. We can manage pretty well as we are.

If only you'd give up your schoolboyish enthusiasm for racing and taken a bit more interest in the business, we could do very well.'

Surprised by his unselfish attitude, knowing as I did how much he wanted to make a success of the garage, I could not think what to say. The prospect of a working life without the excitement and stimulation of racing, seemed grey and featureless, and it was difficult to be grateful for his act of friendship and real sacrifice.

'Thank you Patrick I appreciate what you have just said, and what it means to you, but let's not make any decisions until after tomorrow, it could be the next turning point in my life – what about the Pig? Is it going properly?'

He shrugged. 'Oh yes I suppose so, but I'll be surprised if it lasts the distance with Simon at the wheel, he's a bit insensitive to machinery. This afternoon for example, he went out and did three laps with the rear brakes binding, and complained about being five hundred revs down in top gear when he came in. He gets through clutch linings and tyres like nobody's business.' He sighed, 'But I suppose that it's just lack of experience. He is very keen for you to stay with us you know, and so is young Rachel, you seem to have made quite a conquest there.'

'I didn't know you had met her Patrick.'

'Oh yes, she came with Simon and the old man when they first came to look over the garage.'

'When was that?'

'November, you were at Modena at the time.'

'You might as well tell me now Patrick, why didn't anyone tell me just what was going on? Did you think I would try to wreck it?' He finished his tea and slid the empty cup across the table for it to be refilled, but the pot was empty and the water in the kettle cold. He laughed.

'There's your answer Peter. I take my hat off to you, as an engineer, and you're not a bad driver, but by the Lord Harry you're out of touch with everything else. When you were a young Cornet I remember I was shit-scared of you, you were so much on top of your job. You made me feel like a young incompetent lance-jack with his first job. I'll never forget our first meeting but since you got involved with that shifty police job, you've been a changed man. I honestly daren't tell you about Aaronsen's interest in case you loused the thing up.'

I began to form an ever more depressing view of my own character from the image reflected by Pam and Patrick, to hear already suspected failings put into words that stripped my remaining illusions away, increased my already deepening mood of depression.

'Oh for God's sake Peter, stop looking so bloody miserable. I don't know what's the matter with you. Try looking at other people for a change. You spend far too much time thinking about yourself, and worrying about your conscience. It's a pity you're driving tomorrow, otherwise we could go out for a class one piss-up tonight. It would do us both a power of good. Never mind, we can do it tomorrow.'

The idea appealed to me as being a sharp clean cut way, for at least a few hours, of forgetting the sense of futility which was reducing my mind to cold suet pudding.

'You're on Patrick, tomorrow night after the meeting, we'll go and raise a small amount of hell, whether we've won or lost. You'd better tell Carla that you won't be back until very late.'

He smiled and stood up to leave.

'Well I don't know what's got into you Peter, but at least it's an improvement. I'll pick you up at 8.45 OK?'

I saw him to the door, then turned on the immersion heater to prepare the water for a bath. I could not stop shivering, and wished that I could just throw off my clothes, step into a warm bed and sleep.

At ten to nine Crompton called and we went to the 20 Club. It was so crowded that it was almost impossible to get inside, but by persevering we managed to reach the bar. The place seemed to be full of drivers and their usual circle of hangers-on. Snatches of car racing conversation in English, American and Italian soared out of the general 'Rhubarb-Rhubarb' of conversation in disjointed fragments.

Simon and Aaronsen were leaning on the bar, talking earnestly. Simon was illustrating a point by drawing a diagram on the bar counter with a lump of ice. They were too absorbed to notice our presence and were discussing the accident which had caused Kenning's death. Crompton coughed and Simon looked round. I apologised for being late and Simon ordered drinks. Aaronsen senior explained that he wanted to see me and had used Simon as a stalking horse because he was afraid that I would not come otherwise. I felt obliged to deny this, but he smiled and said that it did not matter, continuing, 'I have just been hearing about this afternoon's incident and I am more than ever determined to have you in our organisation.'

'Why Mr Aaronsen?' I asked, frankly puzzled, because although it had been a quick decision made in an emergency, my action in driving on and finishing the lap when I knew that one of my team had crashed badly was not calculated to inspire faith in my integrity. No-one else could be expected to know what putting up the fastest practice time in a Grand Prix meeting meant to me given this first real opportunity. If I had been younger, there might have been other chances, but this would be my last, and I had to take it. If I had stopped it could only have been a gesture as there were plenty of marshals about, and the Ferrari was hot on my heels so might have run into me. The fact that he had stopped to pull Kennedy out, made my action appear more discreditable, but he was secure, with a regular team car and a place on the front row of the grid assured.

I wondered how many of the other drivers would have stopped in the same situation and tried to suppress the unwelcome answer that most of them would have done, instinctively, the only other exception being a driver with a reputation for selfish big-headedness that made him the odd man out in any gathering of professional Grand Prix formula drivers. I would probably be classed with him, and not without a certain amount of justification. The thought gave me no pleasure, but I had made the decisions, and it was too late to ask for another change. Aaronsen was smiling.

'I would have thought the reason obvious Mr Wade, I like your independence and your single-mindedness and you can make a decision. That incident was a real test of character. A smaller man would have dithered, and caused a worse accident or else scraped through by the skin of his teeth, then stopped with typical English muddle headed sentimentality and gone through the motions of rescuing the injured. You might have been able to get him out quicker because there weren't enough marshals to lift the car, but there's an element of doubt so you quite rightly did the certain thing and finished.'

I wondered with horror what it had been like for Kenning watching the struggling marshals trying to roll the car off him while he burned, only to see them give up, beaten by the weight and the heat. I looked at Simon who was examining the whisky in his glass and Crompton who was smiling broadly.

'Don't read too much into my actions Mr Aaronsen, at that speed within half a mile of the finishing line, with a works Ferrari snapping at my heels, I was a hunted animal running for its life. When pushed to my limit I'm inclined to become a bit primitive. My father didn't believe in public schools so I'm a bit short of some built-in inhibitions.'

Aaronsen laughed. 'Didn't he? Perhaps he had a bit more sense than I had, because I wasted a great deal of hard earned money sending Simon to what is supposed to be one of the better Empire Builder faculties and look at him, he hasn't an inhibition to his name.'

The barmaid who had come in answer to Patrick's signal smiled wryly. 'That is the understatement of the year, Mr Aaronsen.'

He turned slowly to face her without expression, until she began to look uncomfortable, then pointing to Patrick and without removing his gaze from her face asked her if she would be kind enough to take Mr Crompton's order. She blushed violently, and turned to Patrick to ask him what he wanted. Simon's mouth was curved into the shape of a smile but it did not hide the murderous way which he looked at the back of his father's head.

The new round of drinks arrived and Aaronsen asked me what I thought of the Ferrari, breaking the tension which he had created.

The conversation went on about cars, and my fee for driving the Ferrari until I was able to get Simon's attention and asked him what he wanted to talk to me about. He seemed reluctant to talk freely and evaded the question making it clear that he did not intend to talk in front of his father. Instead he suggested that I might like to see a new car which he had only just acquired, so we went out of the hot smoky atmosphere of the club and walked round the corner to where it was parked. It was an E-type Jaguar in fixed head coupé form, painted metallic bronze. He got into the driving seat, and opened the passenger side door for me to get in.

'I had to have a word with you Peter before the old man gets everyone's hackles up in his usual way. He is going to ask you to stay and build up a small Grand Prix stable, which he wants to be the best in the world. Don't think he doesn't know what he wants or for that matter, what he is talking about. He simply wants the publicity, but to get it, the team will have to win. For this sort of result he is going to have to pay real gold, so be fore-warned and when you think of a salary, double it before you start talking terms.'

I wondered why Simon should take this standpoint and was about to ask him.

'Let me finish before you ask any questions. You would probably rather race, but we're not talking about sport now, this is hard business. Neither you nor I are top class drivers and the best will be needed for this, but we will need you to run the show. You are a driver and an engineer and Patrick tells us that you have some shrewd ideas about the trend of developments in the next few years. Two years ahead, we want the manufacturer's championship and have the world champion driver in one of our cars. Whatever you think of the old man, he's an excellent judge of character and he has you neatly ticketed as the man for the job. I want you to take it for two reasons, one my own and the other Rachel's. If you don't take the job he will expect me to act as your stooge and help to run your business for you, but I don't want to be tied to this project entirely, or spend half my life running round the Continent.'

'What is this about Rachel?' I asked.

'I don't really know,' he said, 'but she rang me this evening after practice to ask how I got on, but very soon switched the conversation to you. She's not exactly the emotional type, rather cold and a bit bitchy for her age in fact, but she got into the hell of a tizzy when I teased her about having a crush on you. When I told her what a narrow squeak you had, she begged me to see you and tell you that whatever else happened you must look after yourself tomorrow and that I was to try and talk you out of driving again. She apparently tried to ring the old man later and get him to cancel your entry in the GT race, but he was on his way here with us and we only heard when his secretary rang here to pass on the message. He'd do anything for that kid but she still resents him, so don't be surprised if he asks you to forget tomorrow's race later.'

'I don't understand why she should be so upset about me racing unless she has somehow found out that Gwen left me because of it, and I don't see how she could have heard about that. Did you tell her?'

'No, how could I? This is the first I've heard of it.'

'Well I suppose it's not unheard of for thirteen-year-old girls to get a crush on a middle aged man. It should wear off in a week or two.' I treated it as a joke, but the thought of the mental suffering which the child would be subjected to if she were to discover who I was was anything but funny. I wondered whether to tell Simon the whole story, but I could not find the right words to break the silence. He put his hand on the door handle, it would soon be too late.

'Shall we go back? The old man will begin to think I'm plotting behind his back.'

'OK Simon but I think you ought to know that I was once on the Irgun Zwei Leumi execution list, and that I have an idea that Rachel is the daughter of one of the men I killed.'

'Oh yes Peter, and I have a confession to make. I'm a member of the family that made the nails that crucified Jesus Christ.' We had got out of the car and he was locking his door.

'For God's sake stop playing the fool Simon, it's true.'

'OK so what the hell is the, whatever you said?' I explained briefly as we walked back to the club.

'Well what's the problem?' he asked. 'This is something that happened donkey's ages ago and it might equally well have been you. Forget it, that's the sensible thing to do. It certainly doesn't mean a thing to me. It would be a terrible thing for Rachel to learn, particularly as you seem to be her pin-up boy at the moment.'

As we made our way back through the crowded bar we could see Patrick and Aaronsen laughing uproariously at some private joke. Helen stood between them, her elbows on the bar behind her. She was wearing her raincoat unbuttoned over a white mohair sweater and slim black skirt.

The cigarette smoke made my already tired eyes sting, and I was beginning to feel drained of the ability to make small talk. I hoped that she would not want to ask me about Gwen, but it was Patrick who spoke first, reminding me that it was my turn to buy a round, while Helen watched me steadily with unblinking grey eyes.

As I handed her a drink, she reminded me that Hetty Hall was going to ring me at nine o'clock and asked if I had heard from her. We had been on our way to Liverpool at the time, and I had forgotten about the GMT temporarily. She looked in her handbag found four pennies and gave them to me.

'Do you know where the phone is Peter?' she asked and when I said that I didn't she took my left hand in hers and said, 'Come on, I'll show you.'

The telephone was in the passage leading to the back yard; a passage that was used for storing crates and empty bottles, and was illuminated by a single cleaner's light. It was cold and draughty, and while I waited for the operator to answer, Helen rested her shoulders against the bare brick wall, her hands thrust into her raincoat pockets. Her face was a cool young mask with downcast eyes. I felt the need to touch her, to stroke the gleaming blonde head and bring the lifeless statue back from its detached existence into   contact with me. But I was afraid. Afraid of the thaw, of the eyes that would meet mine, the conditional response that would follow of her lips and arms and body. I held the telephone receiver in both hands and read the names and telephone numbers scribbled on the back of the directory. I could feel her looking at me and could not reasonably avoid her gaze any longer.

She was smiling, but it was with amusement and not doting admiration. I found myself smiling reluctantly, then we were both laughing.

'You're an idiot Peter, what are you frightened of, me, or just the thought of falling in love?'

I was saved from answering by Hetty's voice at the other end of the 'phone. She told me that they had just finished work on both cars and would take them back to the circuit in the morning, meeting me there at ten. She suggested that I should get some sleep, but did not mention Gwen.

My mind was only half on the conversation, as Helen had unbuttoned my jacket while I was talking, slid her arms round me and was running her warm hands up and down my back. Her lips were pressed gently against my throat so that her breath was tickling me so that I found it difficult to maintain a steady voice while talking to Hetty. I replaced the receiver and holding Helen's shoulders, pushed her gently away from me.

She shrugged her shoulders, and turned to walk quickly back along the corridor. She reached the door first, and tried impatiently but ineffectually to open it, avoiding my eyes and not speaking. I placed my hand over hers on the handle and as I turned it, pushed both hand and handle forward; the door swung open easily. I held onto her hand and by taking the other in mine, turned her to face me.

'Don't be cross with me Helen. It will do your life less harm if we stay uninvolved. We only find each other attractive now, later we may get around to needing each other. It wouldn't be fair to you the way I feel tonight. The very idea of love and sympathy is enough to make me dissolve in an orgy of self pity.'

She pulled her hands away from me, put them on her hips and looked at me with her head on one side. 'Aren't you taking rather a lot for granted?' she asked.

I found myself stammering, not really knowing whether to apologise or protest, and she began to laugh. I caught hold of both her ears and held her face still while I kissed her. The door behind her opened suddenly, hitting her back and pushing her against me. It was Simon, the bright light behind him throwing his face into shadow, concealed his expression but did nothing to conceal the iron in his voice.

'Well, well, what have we here, an opportunist in operation?

I'd better warn father to lock up Deborah tomorrow, although I doubt whether she would appreciate having her ears pinned back while she is kissed!'

'It's an old Welsh custom' I said, and trying to control a feeling of rising panic. 'But as a matter of interest, who is Deborah?' I had not spoken the name for years, and my question, which had been intended to sound inconsequential, emerged like a roar from an overwrought mouse.

'His wife of course, who else?' He peered at me closely. 'Well what have I said?'

I found it difficult to form a reasonable answer, and in any case would not have trusted my voice to say anything. He looked from me to Helen.

'For God's sake, I was only joking!' She shivered, folded her arms and smiled wanly.

She continued, 'I don't know, but I have a feeling that he was pleased to see you then, you really have a lousy sense of timing Simon. Come on you two, you're both tired and jumpy, you ought to be at home in bed getting some sleep before tomorrow.'

Simon looked at me, shrugged, and went back into the club.

'Peter, for heaven's sake, what is the matter?' she asked, genuine concern in her expression. 'It isn't the same man's widow is it, what was his name, Jacob, or something like that?'

I didn't know, but there was a feeling of the inevitable in the air. For years I had kept the faint hope that I might meet her again, imagining the meeting, how she would look, what we would say to each other and ignoring the practical considerations. I tried to forget that in all probability she had been using me as a stalking horse so that they could kill Warrender. I had only remembered the good days when we were happy.

'I just don't know Helen, but suddenly I've caught a little of your fear of the dark, and loneliness. It's going to be a damned long night. Let's go back into the madhouse.' I opened the door and held it for her. She looked at me anxiously.

'Would you like to stay at my place tonight – I've a feeling there's more to this than you've told me.' I explained that I would be spending the night with Patrick and his wife.

'Well, that's tonight, but I gather Gwen's not at home and you'll be fending for yourself tomorrow. Would you like to come and stay until you get yourself sorted out? – no strings attached, I'm not trying to sell you anything.'

I told her that I had not been able to see Gwen and therefore had no idea if she intended to stay away permanently, or what she intended to do about Ian. As we reached the table where Simon, Aaronsen and Patrick were sitting, Simon stood.

Patrick asked, 'Well Peter, are you on tomorrow?'

Simon laughed, 'I reckon he's on tonight!' I ignored him and told Patrick about the arrangement we had made to ensure two cars starting the next day.

Aaronsen pursed his lips. 'You must be a very hard or unimaginative man Mr Wade, to be able to drive tomorrow after one of your colleagues has died so unpleasantly in a similar car. Have you no feelings about it?'

'Of course I have, the way I acted today was as I said, instinctive and not particularly laudable. Now we know what happened, and therefore at least half the reason for being scared has gone. Besides, there are too many other things to think about. As far as young Kenning is concerned, it was better for him to have died on the way up the ladder – well, no, perhaps I don't really believe that – you seem to have the knack of forcing me into situations where I feel the need to adopt attitudes. At least Kenning's name will mean something to people when they read about his death. Now if I come unstuck tomorrow, unless I take half a dozen spectators including Mrs Topham with me, no-one will notice. But as I have quite suddenly developed a curiosity about the future, I'm going to get a good night's sleep.'

'Oh for goodness sake Peter, stop being so morbid!' Helen said, and turning to Patrick. 'Will you be a pet and give me a lift home?'

Aaronsen looked quickly at Simon. 'You should take the lady Simon, you are becoming very neglectful.'

'I would, but you are forgetting that I said I would pick up Deborah at Speke,' he said and stood up to leave. The old man shook his head.

'Oh yes of course, you've not left yourself much time. Go, and don't drive too quickly. You're probably a good driver, but I don't think you would be a good midwife, and the baby's only two months away!'

I found myself staring at Aaronsen, wondering how the girl Deborah could have become the woman who could tolerate those too fat white hands with their bitten nails and gleaming beads of perspiration clinging to a tangle of grey hairs on the backs, holding and caressing her. As he laughed at a joke, which I had not been listening to, a spray of saliva formed a random pattern in front of him on the polished table top.

The others were laughing in different ways, Helen noisily like a horse showing all her teeth, Simon with one side of his face as if he were reluctant to admit that he found it amusing, while Patrick was simply demonstrating his loyalty.

The room was hot, airless, full of smoke and noise so intense that it battered the mind into a tangle of spikes like a ball of barbed wire. It was eleven o'clock, and as Simon stood to leave, I caught Patrick's eye and pointed to my watch.

Simon smiled, 'You've got something there Peter, we could do with some sleep even if these people want to stay up all night.'

Aaronsen laughed, 'It must be Mr Wade's round again, first the telephone, now his bed calls. I'm beginning to suspect he's not a Goy after all.'

I called the waiter over, ordered drinks for Aaronsen, Helen and Patrick and asked Simon if he could give me a lift to Central Station so that I could catch a train to Birkenhead. He said that he would and Patrick only protested feebly, so we left them to continue drinking after arranging to meet at Aintree in the morning.

It was still raining and the sky was obscured by a thick blanket of cloud and smoke from Merseyside's chimneys. The thought of the clean air and open spaces of Wales, with few people at this time of year, made me decide to take a few days of holiday before the serious racing began.

I went to sleep to the sound of the rain lashing against the window and my mind full of shifting images and ideas; of mountains and lakes, of sunshine and fast moving cloud shadows, but my dreams were full of un-named anxieties.

CHAPTER 7

Race Day

WE had an early, silent breakfast, and arrived at the already busy circuit at eight o'clock. The racing tender had arrived and had been unlocked. One of the apprentices was filling the Pig's tanks, and the other was polishing the Ferrari. I signed in at the secretary's tent and not without my usual misgivings, had my competition licence and medical certificate checked. Although the doctor who examined me was an old friend of my father's and did not actually need to perjure himself on my behalf, the fact that I only had one kidney and reduced movement of my left leg, did very little for his peace of mind. I always hoped at this juncture, that someone would question my fitness to drive, but no-one ever did and I had to go through the ordeal of waiting until the starter's flag would drop and my self-confidence would return.

Several laps in the Ferrari while the track dried out under the emerging sun, and I settled down to the rhythm of the circuit. Simon took the Pig, or as the programme now called it the 'Integrity Finance Special', out onto the circuit for practice with the other cars entered in this class. If the new Formula proved successful, it would help to develop the standard engine instead of forcing the design of grossly overstressed and very expensive small capacity Grand Prix engines which had no practical application.

Checking some of the lap times showed that the two Jaguar engine specials which used modified Lotus frames, were going to be hard to stay with, let alone beat. I began to wish that I had been able to put a little more money into the car and place the engine behind the driver. The need to keep the cost down had forced us to use as many of the existing transmission components as possible and prevented us from having a special gearbox-differential unit built. Our wide, low engine and offset transmission line, made the chassis frame and therefore the body, oval in section and low.

When viewed from the front, the driver and the high faired tail, were offset to the right. Its distinctive shape and burbling V-eight engine made the car easy to recognise among the more orthodox Lotus and Cooper derivations. Simon seemed happy with it and gave me a thumbs-up sign as he went past the pits, so I went to check the Ferrari before the first race at one o'clock.

Hall was standing by the car talking to Patrick. He looked tired and was still unshaven.

'Hello Peter, are you fit?' he asked.

'As fit as I'm ever likely to be. How are the cars?'

He shrugged slightly and forced a smile.

'I reckon they'll hold together, and providing you and Hemingway stick to the plan, we might even get one of them into the first three. You tow Hemingway until I give the Flat-Out signal, keeping within striking distance of the leaders, then you'll let him past and keep the opposition off his tail. The situation may well change during the race, but that's the way we'll start. By the way, we were going to enter a car in the new monoposto-production formula but it's not ready yet. Would you like to drive it at Goodwood?'

I would drive almost anything given the chance, but I had decided to have that one week's holiday before becoming too involved. I told him that there was some doubt, but would let him know by Sunday night. He seemed satisfied.

The Pig came in at the end of the practice, and Simon said that it was going very well but understeering a little more than he liked. Checking the tyre pressures revealed that the front and rear pressures were out of balance. The rest of the car seemed to be in order with no oil leaks or rattles and the oil pressure was steady.

Practice with the GMT passed without incident, although the circuit was crowded with fast moving cars and the tar on the road surface in the Picnic Loop was beginning to melt as the sun grew hotter.

At twelve o'clock the sound of racing engines began to die away, until only two desperate teams of mechanics were working like beavers to complete some work on their sick cars, while everyone else ate a quick luncheon before the Gran-Turismo race.

I hoped that we would not be bothered by Aaronsen and his friends before the race, particularly if he had Deborah with him. My heart thumped against my ribs at the thought of seeing her again, so that I thought Patrick and Ron would be able to hear it. My mouth was too dry to eat the sandwiches that Carla had cut for us and my stomach seemed to be full of bats which were flying about looking for the exit. I looked at my watch for the tenth time in five minutes. Ten minutes to go.

I got into Patrick's Zephyr and switched on the radio. The Light had a programme called *Any Questions* which I could never find entertaining or instructive and the Home Service had a journalist talking about his half-century of motoring experience. It seemed relevant, but hardly a distraction. A search along the medium wave band revealed Walton's violin concerto, the soloist pouring out streams of pure notes some flashing and darting like silver flanked minnows, others warm, glowing thick and slightly husky, so that the steadily creeping fingers of my watch were robbed of their ability to inspire fear.

Someone started the E-type Jaguar in the next pit, the blast of its exhaust rocking the Zephyr and drowning the orchestra. I switched off the radio and went to my own car to put on my helmet and gloves. At variance with my usual practice, I put my gloves on first and was struggling with my helmet strap, when someone took hold of my elbow and turned me round. It was Rachel.

'Let me do that Peter,' she said, and standing on tip-toe, completed the job neatly and quickly.

'Thank you, you've just come in time for the start. Where are your mother and father?'

'I don't know,' she said. 'We arrived here about an hour ago, had lunch at the car and everything was fine. Then I bought a couple of programmes and pointed out Simon's name and yours and suggested that she should come over to meet you.'

'What happened?'

'What should have happened?' she riposted.

'How should I know? But the implication is that something did.' It sounded like the feeble evasion that it was.

'Well, I thought she was going to faint and when she saw Simon looking at her in, well a sort of knowing way, she looked away quickly and said that it didn't seem a very good idea as she wasn't looking at her best and in any case she didn't feel very well at the moment.' She told the old man that she thought she would like to go home, but he insisted that she should stay as he had a surprise for her which I had nearly spoilt. What on earth is going on Peter, won't you tell me? You know something don't you? Just look at your hands, they give you away.'

What could I tell her, I could only guess although the answer now seemed certain.

'Quite simply Rachel, I think that your mother and I met while I was in Palestine during some very unhappy times and it must be very painful for her to be reminded of them.'

'When?'

'What d'you mean, when?'

'When did you meet her?' Her eyes were glistening and her fists were clenching and opening with half-controlled excitement.

'In the summer of 1947.' I watched her anxiously as her mind absorbed this information and she did the inevitable sums, arriving at a conclusion that I had begun to consider.

'But you're not a Jew.'

'No, why did you think I should be?' I was thrown off balance by the unexpected question.

'Well, Grandpa Bernstein always said that my father was in the Irgun and died fighting the British.' She smiled wryly. 'But it would seem that his wishes were in conflict with the facts – poor silly old man.'

Her eyes were full of tears and she suddenly looked like the lost little child which she had been, thin, awkward and more than a little afraid of the world. She was only an arms length away from me across an impassable void, and in another long, long wordless second, it would be too late to reach her. I held out my hands to her, but could not trust my voice to speak. Her great dark eyes and pale face filled my conscious world, but she made no movement to meet me. I touched her arms, hanging limply at her sides, but still she just stared at me.

Patrick was at my elbow.

'Rachel,' I said, and she flung herself into my arms, hands covering her face and sobbing convulsively. She was trying to say something but I could not understand and led her gently to the car. Curious bystanders, in typically English fashion, pretended not to look, but waited until we had passed before staring to their heart's content.

In the car I tried to persuade her, as I had tried to convince myself, that she was jumping to conclusions, but she insisted that she knew and begged me not to leave her.

'For God's sake Peter, for the last time, the other cars are on the grid, and you should be on the second row. Come on, they can't wait any longer, I'll look after Rachel.'

She let me go reluctantly and I sprinted for the Ferrari which Ron was warming up for me. As I was about the close the door, Simon leaned in.

'I gather you have problems – just forget them for the next half an hour or so, I don't want to be faced with the job of sorting this mess out if you bend yourself through not concentrating!' Without waiting for an answer, he slammed the door closed and waved me on.

'Hell, what a way to start a race!' I thought as I pressed the car through the crowded paddock and onto the circuit.

The one-minute hooter sounded as I settled into position on the grid. The starter's flag rose and the engine sounds all around rose in volume and frequency. As the flag reached the top of its travel, the cars around me began to creep forward. I built up the engine speed, the white tacho needle swinging freely round the dial, and began to ease in the clutch.

*   *   *

Down went the flag and the clutch bit home. Flicking over to the left to clear the car in front, I unleashed the Ferrari down the clear road ahead. Out of the corner of my right eye I could see the dark green snout of the E-type, and in my left mirror, another Ferrari.

I held second for as long as I dared and snatched third for the brief dash to the first corner. Easing over to the left I cut out the Ferrari and got onto line for Waterways, while the E-type tried to force his way through on the inside. At the eleventh hour, my car's nose was still ahead and on the right line so he gave way and followed closely through Picnic Loop. After three laps, during which we had each held the lead, we were both passed between Tatts and the pits by a grey E-type carrying the number seven. The only thing which surprised me, was that he had taken so long to catch up and assumed that he had been baulked at the start.

The next five laps were as good as a driving lesson, as I tried to stay with the leader, watching and following his line on each corner as far as the different characteristics of the two cars would allow. Each time we came to Melling Crossing however, he pulled away from me by a few more yards by a combination of sheer artistry and nerve which I knew I could never match. What proved to be even more annoying, was the realisation that he lacked the real threat behind him which would induce him to drive nearer to his personal limit!

I pushed the Ferrari as hard as I dared along the pit straight. Railway straight and round the slower bends of the Picnic Loop but however I punished the car, the driver of the E-type remained unruffled. For one brief moment I managed to get alongside while running into Village Corner after lapping a Porsche and a Giulietta, but we were back in the old routine on the way out.

As we came out of Tatts I was a comfortable 25 yards behind him and to my surprise saw the chequered flag come down for us. I had been so completely absorbed that the race hardly seemed to have begun! Looking in the rear view mirrors I saw that we were on our own and it was not until we were motoring slowly round Waterways on our lap of honour that the next car finished. Everything but driving and learning by following a master, had been driven from my mind, even Deborah and Rachel! I was bathed in perspiration and noticed for the first time that I had been driving with the windows and the cool air intakes closed.

As I drove back into the Paddock Simon, Patrick and Rachel came running to meet me. I tried to look past them for Deborah but as soon as the car stopped Patrick flung open my door and began shaking my hand and thumping me on the back while Rachel got in through the other door and hugged me so that it was impossible to get out of the safety harness. As I finally managed to get out of the car, Aaronsen walked over to join us in the middle of the milling crowd of small boys, marshals and general hangers-on. He was wearing a startling beach shirt which might have looked better on a Gaugin model, Bermuda shorts and Panama hat and was obviously enjoying his triumph. I wondered how much of the day's developments had filtered through to him, but I no longer cared. I was beginning to recover my almost forgotten self-confidence.

Rachel took my helmet off, fussing around me like a hen with one chicken. Patrick laughed.

'Do you know Simon, it always astonishes me the way Peter has a knack of bringing out the maternal instincts of women. It must be a Hell of a handicap!'

Aaronsen joined in the joke.

'He should be safe enough to meet my wife then, although her motherly instincts are just about fully occupied at the moment.'

His face gave no indication of anything other than simple amusement.

'Come along Mr Wade, you're going to have the job of teaching her to drive this monster – you can meet her over a glass of Champagne.'

'I could do with a wash first if you don't mind. I've been pot-roasting in this car for the last half hour and I've no best friends! Tell me where your car is and I'll meet you in five minutes.'

'OK, OK. I'll get some bottles opened, we'll have a small celebration when you come.'

As it was Simon's race next, he and Patrick went to get the Pig out onto the grid. Aaronsen put his hand onto Rachel's shoulder.

'Are you coming with me chicken?' She looked at me.

'Yes you run along, I need a good scrub. I'll see you in figures five.' I watched them make their way through the crowd, before going back to the transport to wash.

It was not difficult to find Aaronsen's immaculate bronze Rolls Royce even in such an expensive collection of cars because Rachel was standing on tip-toe looking round her and ran to meet me through the crowd making its way to the rails for the start of the next race. She linked her arm through mine and skipped beside me until we were in step.

'I've told her!' she said.

'What have you told her?'

'That you were who she thought you were, and that you are my father – and that I'm a little bastard' She laughed uncertainly.

'And how did she react to this extraordinary announcement?'

'She asked me how many people I had revealed my innermost thoughts to – but she really wasn't amused. I think she's frightened, but you can't be sure. She's like one of those dark green bottles. You think you know what's in them but when you pour them out it's not wine, but water or ink or blood or something.'

'In my experience – it's usually something,' I said to keep the thing in a lighter vein, but she looked reproachful as if I had scratched myself or belched at an investiture. It was difficult to see this ridiculous situation as high drama, but from the child's point of view, it must have looked very different. Now that it had finally happened, it did seem ludicrous, and I only wanted to laugh, to walk past her and her husband. Damn the whole pack of terrorists, freedom fighters, Arabs, Jews and politicians of all shades and above all the grey shadowy men who manipulated us all.

There she was, there was no doubt and no room or time for escape. She was still beautiful. The eyes which remained as a visual image long after the face had faded, were the same, but they were guarded and told me nothing. Rachel's hot little hand slid into mine and gripped it tightly.

'Mummy, this is Peter.'

'Ah Mr Wade,' said Aaronsen, 'I don't believe you've met my wife, Deborah this is Mr Wade.' He apparently thought Rachel's introduction unsuitable.

'I am delighted to meet you Mr Wade. I have heard a great deal about you in the last few hours from Rachel and my husband, and my curiosity was aroused. Theo was just about to open a bottle of Champagne. Will you have some?'

She knew perfectly well that I hated the stuff, or at least she used to know. Aaronsen opened a camp chair for me and asked what I would like to drink.

I told him that I did not want to be difficult but would prefer beer or water to Champagne. He seemed a little surprised but went to the boot of the car to get bottles and glasses. Rachel followed him leaving me alone with Deborah. She avoided my eyes and there was an awkward silence, broken when we both began to speak together.

'I believe you are married Mr Wade and have a little boy.' she said when we had sorted ourselves out.

'Yes, at least I was until I came here to race today. Heaven knows what the situation is now though. But Deborah I must speak to you alone, please.'

She looked round nervously, but still wearing a polite conversational smile asked, 'Have you a photograph of your wife Peter?'

I took the wallet out of the breast pocket of my overalls and handed her the faded photograph of herself at Giniefa. She swallowed nervously and handed it back to me quietly.

I pointed out the faded writing on the back.

'You missed this, can you remember what it said?'

'Please Peter, stop it. He's terribly jealous and is sure to notice something. I don't want to hurt him. What do you want of me anyway?'

'My God! How can you just sit there and ask a question like that? Do you know that I still don't know whether you really did once love me, or whether you were just doing a job for the I.Z.L.' She looked stunned, her hand went to her throat where a vein was pulsing slowly.

'Oh surely you didn't think that? Then – you must have thought that I led you into a deliberate trap in Jerusalem that day.' She looked tired. 'And you've lived with that all these years. God, no wonder you – is that why you left me?'

It was my turn to be perplexed, but there was no time for further discussion as Aaronsen came back.

We drank to success and the atmosphere was beginning to ease a little when Hall and Patrick came walking between the rows of parked cars apparently seeking someone. Aaronsen called to them and when they saw me Hall said, 'Oh there you are. There's been a change in plan. You seem to have got yourself on the front row of the grid between the Walker Lotus and the number one Ferrari, so you're going to have to mix it with the big boys for a few laps until Hemingway works his way up to you. We'll just have to play it off the cuff now so it's up to you not to overdo it.'

'That suits me very well. Providing the rain holds off I think I can stay on the same lap as the Lotus, but I make no promises about the red one. I'll do my best though.'

He looked a little unhappy, but only he and I knew the real source of his concern, the suspect wishbones. The one minute hooter sounded for the start of the monoposto production race and Aaronsen finished his drink quickly.

'Come on Deborah, this is Simon's race and he's driving Mr Wade's car. Will we see you at the party tonight Mr Wade?'

'Party? I'm afraid I...'

'Didn't Mr Crompton tell you?' He turned to Patrick who was starting at Deborah as if he had seen a ghost. He heard his name, and jumped noticeably.

'Oh, I'm forgetting my manners Mr Crompton, of course you haven't met my wife have you. This is Mr Crompton dear, Mr Wade's partner.'

Deborah maintained her polite mask and smiling, shook his hand. He still looked puzzled. 'Have we met somewhere before?'

'Well we are all going to meet tonight,' interrupted Aaronsen to my relief, 'at the Victoria at Heswall, somewhere round nine o'clock, alright?'

I looked at Patrick quickly and accepted on his behalf as well as my own. 'Bye,' said Rachel and the three left to go to the grandstand to watch the race. They had only gone a few yards when Rachel ran back.

'Do you mind me calling you Peter?' she asked.

'No of course not you clown. Come and see me after the main event – Shalom.' She put her tongue out at me.

'Only semi-Shalom,' she retorted, and ran off, legs and arms flapping in all directions like a young foal.

'Are you coming back to the pits?' Hall asked, and looked at the pensive figure of Patrick.

Aaronsen's chauffeur was re-packing the picnic hamper and chairs and started violently when Patrick slapped his hand against his thigh with a crack like a pistol shot.

'Christ! I've got it.'

'Well keep it to yourself for the moment and don't give it to everyone,' I told him.

'No you nut case, I mean I know who she is!'

'Yes, that's what I mean. Belt up will you – I've got enough troubles as it is.' He caught hold of my arm and walking sideways, pulled me out of earshot.

'She's your friend from Giniefa!'

'Give the gent a coconut,' I said, and waited for the other penny to drop. His brows were furrowed with the effort of thought. A sly grin spread slowly over his face.

'How old is Rachel?'

'If I tell you, you'll have to take your shoes off to check, the answer's over ten and under twenty.' Hall was becoming impatient.

'Aren't you interested in your entry Mr Crompton?'

Crompton's grin spread from ear to ear.

'The human race interests me much more. You never know what to expect next whereas cars and drivers run more or less to form. Motor racing bores me to hell, but people never do. I suppose I must at least look interested – but tonight's party – I would not miss for all the tea in China. Tell me, are we still going to have that beer we talked about last night?'

'Yes,' I said, 'I feel as if I need it.' And we went our separate ways.

The blaring loudspeakers in the paddock were calling for drivers in the Grand Prix event to report to the secretary's tent in five minutes time, for the parade. The purpose of this parade was to allow the money-paying public to see the drivers who would be carried round the circuit in a fleet of open E-type Jaguars. I began to wish that my overalls were not quite so faded and ragged, but as no-one had probably heard of me, it did not really matter. It would be interesting to see if the commentator got my name right because they usually contrived to confuse me with a driver called Ward and a programme in Belgium had once listed me as Pieter Wod.

The monoposto-production race had ended with Simon in a very creditable fifth place, with the car intact and firing lustily on all eight cylinders.

The gruesome farce of a parade got under way just as the first clouds obscured the sun and before half the lap had been completed, it had begun to rain steadily and maliciously from a leaden sky. The crowds round the circuit blossomed like flowers in a herbaceous border as they donned plastic raincoats, cycling capes and headscarves and put up umbrellas, while the miserable drivers were conducted at funeral pace through the downpour.

The procession stopped behind the grid and we walked to our cars. The number one Ferrari driver rolled his eyes skywards and shrugged.

'Bloody Aintree – Raintree,' he said and apparently ran out of English, but he had made his point with an impressive economy of words.

Hall's mechanic had thoughtfully put an umbrella over the cockpit, so I did not have to start the race by sitting in a puddle. Behind the wheel I felt happier but a little overawed by my position on the front row of the grid. The two minute hooter sounded, starters were engaged and engines run up.

The GMT did not start at once and a slight feeling of panic began to rise in me, but it picked up on one cylinder, then two and quickly roared into life. I looked over my shoulder at the ranks of cars behind me, with their grim-faced visored drivers and swallowed. From where I was sitting they looked like a pack of wolves, but I tried to reassure myself by remembering that they were there because they had been slower in practice. One minute, and the marshals chivvied the crowd of photographers and mechanics off the start area. We were on our own.

The starter climbed into his pulpit, rain dripping off the peak of his deer-stalker. My visor was misting over and I wiped it quickly as the flag was raised. I made a poor start and was fourth into Waterways in the midst of a howling sliding pack of gleaming machines spraying Catherine wheels of water from their tyres and steam from their hot exhaust pipes. I had to get up to the front again otherwise I would not be able to see through the waterstorm which trailed behind the leaders. Closing on the tail of the Walker Lotus I tried to maintain the distance by driving right on my personal limit, while he closed the gap between himself and the two Ferraris in the lead. Melling was treacherous and I cleared Tatts for the first time with a sense of real relief. The road looked like a river and a great deal of the water was finding its way into the cockpit from somewhere.

Someone had spun off at County and gone through an advertisement hoarding through not being sufficiently relaxed. I nearly did the same at Village Corner. A Porsche occasionally appeared in my rear view mirrors, but he made no serious bid to force his way through the plume of spray in my wake.

After ten laps, having found the comfortable limit of adhesion between road and tyres and having become so wet that it no longer mattered, I settled down to enjoy at least the first 50 of the 90 laps. The engine was now producing a clean surge of power all the way round the rev counter from 3,700 to the normal maximum of 9,000 and the effect on the car's handling was remarkable; I began to feel that it was capable of winning races.

As we came past the pits on the 31st lap, the signal board showed that I was lying third – one of the Ferraris must be out of the race. The rain was blowing in swirling clouds across the track and the pools which formed between Melling and Tatts acted like brakes as they became deeper. The rain driven by the airflow over the body, climbed in waves up the curved perspex windscreen and curled round its sides. My attention was diverted for a moment by the wind-combed patterns of water and the Porsche hustled past, obscuring the road ahead with its trailing veils of spray.

'Blast, blast, blast!' I cursed futilely and cut over into his slipstream almost blinded by water and steam and irritated by my own stupidity and lack of concentration. The Walker Lotus was out of sight now and a second Porsche was snapping at my heels. I was completely boxed in between them but at least the front one was giving me an aerodynamic tow and saving me some fuel. I decided to curb myself and stay with them for a while providing my lap times did not suffer too much. After 50 laps, the car was still going like an express train, but my time had gone up to two minutes four.

Hall gave me the 'heavy-foot' sign, so when an opportunity presented itself while we were passing one of the Belgian Coopers, I scrabbled past the Porsche on the inside. It was untidy and left me committed to Village Corner slightly off my usual line. I found my heart thumping wildly as the car flirted across the road and rear wheel into the mud and water on the outside of the bend. Another few inches and Mrs Topham would have had me on the carpet, but at least I had gained a few yards on the Porsches.

I used maximum acceleration through the gears along Valentine's Way, going over to the left of the road, braking and changing down for Beechers. The Lotus was on the exit from the corner, streaking away down Railway Straight. Under acceleration along the long straight, my fuel gauge needle bounced back against the empty stop, so I switched quickly onto the second tank which would give me another twenty laps. I made a mental note to let Hall know so that he could make the decision when to call me in for a pit stop.

When I passed the pits, Hemingway's car was in and he was climbing out of it. The mechanics were peering underneath its rear end. Hall acknowledged my signal and on the next lap gave me the signal to come in for fuel. It seemed early to me but he was the boss, so on the next lap I stayed on the inside of the corner and pulled in to the pits.

Almost before the wheels had stopped rolling, the jacks were under the car and the wheels were being changed. As I climbed out of the cockpit, the fuel began to go into the tanks as an asbestos blanket was put over the hot exhaust system and a fireman stood by with a foam extinguisher. Hetty Hall wiped my visor and gave me a glass of lime juice. Hall told me that Hemingway's car had lost its engine undershield and had shipped a great deal of water, some of it getting into the electrics, the car was mis-firing badly, but there was little remedy apart from mopping the surplus out of the plug wells and sending him out again.

As the last of the fuel went in, the filler cap was slammed shut, the jacks were removed and I got behind the wheel. The engine refused to fire, the starter motor simply turning it over and pumping fuel-rich vapour out of the exhaust pipes. The engine cover was removed and the plugs were changed while valuable seconds ticked away and the leaders put more miles between us. I tried hard to remain calm and not drive the mechanics into making a silly mistake by urging them to hurry. A Ferrari pulled into the pits in front of us, with oil pouring out of its undertray. Its driver climbed out wearily with an air of defeat.

Hall leaned over and yelled in my ear, 'That's Carlotti, he was in the lead! That puts Hemingway in sixth spot and you in second when the two Porsches come in to refuel.' I nodded in acknowledgement, and one of the mechanics slapped me on the shoulder to tell me to try again. It fired at once, so the cover was refitted and I was ready to go. The pit area in front was crowded with excited Italians milling around the Ferrari in front of my car, so the marshal who had been observing our pit stop ran to drag them out of the way.

Before the road was clear however, I looked in the nearside mirror and saw a yellow Cooper sliding wildly with its four wheels locked along the front of the pit counter, scattering mechanics, marshals, tyres and jacks in all directions. It slammed into the rear of the GMT and shunted it forward for three or four feet, cracking my head back against the roll-over bar. I could hear Hall swearing at the unfortunate driver from his refuge on the pit counter, even above the engine noise.

I twisted round in the seat, and with sinking heart, saw the mass of crumpled light alloy. The mechanics, working like men possessed, tore off the damaged engine cover and after a brief glance at the rear end of the transmission, gave me a thumbs-up sign.

The road behind was clear, so I went back into the race and at the end of the next lap, I saw the two Porsches in the pit for re-fuelling. I was lying second. The increased drag without the engine cover was most noticeable and I had a feeling that there was something amiss with the transmission. Putting my misgivings down to natural pessimism, I pressed on as hard as possible to try and reduce the lead which the flying Lotus had established.

As I went through the pit area again, Hemingway was pulling in, and although my time was down to two minutes two again, and the rain had stopped. I was definitely short of five hundred revs!

On the eighth lap after the refuelling stop with only ten to go, I was called in by Hall and told to hand my car over to Hemingway for a last chance to catch the Lotus which was now slowing down. We changed cars and Hemingway tore out of the pits in a fury of sound and spray. As I got into his lame car to nurse it home if possible, a watery sun appeared briefly from behind the inky clouds. I waited for a gap after a fast moving group of cars had passed and stuttered out onto the circuit, the V8 Coventry-Climax firing erratically. The haze of blue smoke in my wake indicated a more serious malady than wet plugs and the oil pressure was ominously low. I concentrated on driving with a more or less constant throttle opening, then found to my despair that the brakes were unpredictable and spongy.

Coming down the railway straight, Hemingway went past trying very hard, but when I passed the pits he was just rolling to a halt, a trail of oil leading from his car all the way back to the exit from Tatts.

With only two laps to go, the oil pressure went completely, the water temperature gauge needle shot off the scale and I coasted to a halt just past the Melling Crossing almost where Kenning had crashed.

As the car stopped, waves of heat soaked up through the cover in a shimmering mirage. Two marshals ran over to see if they could help and when a gap presented itself, we pushed the car over to the inside of the track so that I could conduct it back to the pits on foot. It only seemed a short way in a car, but pushing one made it feel like a hundred miles. I waited a few yards short of the line so that I could push it over at the end and qualify as a finisher. The bitterness of the anti-climax made me want to strike out at something, but I had run out of energy.

As soon as the Lotus took the chequered flag, I rolled the GMT over the finishing line and gratefully accepted the help of Hall and the mechanics to get it into the paddock. I felt like crawling away into a dark corner and crying like a baby, but decided to get myself a generous whisky from Patrick's always-to-be-relied-upon, private supply.

He offered me a full hip flask before I had time to ask and I took a long appreciative draught and returned it to him. It was no time for idle conversation so I returned, alone, to the Anglia.

The loudspeaker system was announcing the results, but I had lost interest and lay back in the rear seat of the Anglia with my eyes closed, wondering what there was about this sport that could make me want to go on driving when I was in such poor physical condition. Although the car was motionless, my body and my mind were still driving it. I could feel the pressure of the left side of the seat against my hip on Waterways, the pressure against my back during the acceleration up to the Picnic Loop and the noise of the engine and wind in my ears. My neck and shoulder muscles were tired and I began to feel cold.

The car door opened, it was Rachel.

'Hello, may I come in?'

She seemed unsure of herself and hesitated, with the door half open, uncertain about the mud on her shoes and wondering whether my already dirty car could be made any worse. She was wearing a flowered silk head-scarf over her hair and a shapeless blue school coat that was already too small for her. Her bony wrists sprouted out of the too-short sleeves in a way that somehow irritated me.

'Of course Rachel, push my kit over into the back here and make some room for yourself.'

She handed my helmet and gloves over the back of the seat and thinking that I had taken hold of them, let them go and the helmet slipped to the floor, breaking the perspex visor.

'Oh dear! I'm sorry, I'll buy you another one.'

'Not to worry!' I bent to pick up the pieces, but instantly felt sick and dizzy, so left them where they had fallen. She looked alarmed.

'Are you alright?'

I felt distinctly second-hand, but told her that I was an old man now and tired by the effort of pushing the car home. Meaning it to sound like a joke, I was amused by the way she accepted the explanation as perfectly reasonable, but it made me take stock of my years. I tried to remember how life had looked as a teenager but, at that age, I had been in a tearing hurry for life to start and had seldom paused to look around me.

I had very little memory of relative ages, seeming to be as old and adult as my young aunts and uncles, although still agonisingly self-conscious about my first long trousers. They seemed to be made from horse-blankets they were so stiff, rough and baggy. Only the half-memory of days as long as seasons served to show how the curve of mounting years had begun to decay before I had really reached middle-age.

She took off the headscarf, shook her hair free and took a slightly crumpled envelope from her pocket. She handed it to me without comment. It was a brief note from Deborah asking me not to go to Aaronsen's party that evening, but to wait at home and she would ring me.

I tore the letter into small pieces, carefully and slowly as I thought about its contents. Why had she done this? Was she trying to keep me at a distance because I was an embarrassment to her, or was it because she thought it would be easier to tell me to stay away over the telephone? Perhaps she was still in love with me and this was the only way that she would be able to speak freely?

Rachel was watching my face anxiously. 'What on earth are we going to do?'

I shrugged, 'I'm darned if I know, but right now I'm going home to have a hot bath and to change my clothes. After that, I may be able to think more clearly. What do you think I ought to do?'

Her fingers were interlocked in her lap, knuckles white. Her face had the defenceless, vulnerable look of a lost child, when either a harsh or a kind word would provoke a flood of tears. The public address system was pouring out a brassy twist record, the sound from the more distant loudspeakers lagging behind that from the speakers beside the car, resulting in a crazy out-of-phase jangle of flat sound. It seemed to be an unfair question to ask her.

I said, 'Well, whatever you think, I don't know what the answer is... the right answer anyway. One thing's certain though, having found you both I don't intend to lose you again if I can possibly help it. That's probably selfish, perhaps I'm just a complication.'

I was terrified that she would say nothing, or worse, begin with the 'well' that would precede an attempt at gentle dissuasion from upsetting her ordered existence. She caught my right hand and pressed its palm against her cheek with both of hers. She blinked, trying to hold back the tears that rolled down her face and shook her head, trying to say something, but the words failed to take form.

I pulled her ear gently with my free hand and told her to stop worrying before she became eligible for the Golden Ulcer Club. The sound of someone beating a tattoo on the roof of the Anglia with the flat of his hands made me jump. It was Patrick.

Rachel turned away so that he would not see her tear stained face and red eyes and furtively brushed away the tears with the corner of her headscarf. He got into the driving seat and pretending not to notice Rachel, turned to face me.

'Well, I reckon you deserve a night out after the way you've driven today, but how're we going to fit it in? Aaronsen is expecting us for drinks at nine o'clock at the Vic.'

I explained that I would probably not be going because I was not feeling very well. Rachel turned quickly to look at me.

'D'you mean you don't even feel like having the odd jug?' he looked anxious, but I had little doubt about the real reason for his concern.

'Relax Patrick, I'll pick you up as soon as I've had a bath and changed, then you can go on to the Vic later and make an excuse for my absence. I just feel that Aaronsen and I will get along, providing we don't have to see each other any more than necessary.'

He looked reassured and turning to Rachel, with an unaccustomed shyness, patted the back of her hand.

'You see, he didn't kill himself. He's one of the careful kind who values his skin too highly to take un-calculated risks. I know him better than his own mother does, you can believe me, he'll live to see your grandchildren. Watch him though, he's a bit inclined to go off like a penny rocket in several directions at once.'

'Oh belt up Patrick, keep the sermon for tomorrow, it's Sunday. Who's doing the work while you're sitting around nattering?'

'Well you're not for sure' he retorted as he got out of the car, 'I'll deal with you later when you don't have your watch-dog with you.'

As he picked his way through the churned mud of the Paddock to the Pits, I noticed for the first time, how grey his hair had become.

'Are you really not coming tonight?' she asked.

'No, I don't think it would be very wise, and I don't suppose there will be much opportunity to talk to you or Deborah.'

'But you are going away tomorrow, aren't you?'

'No, I'll probably go later tonight. I must get some time on my own, and I must find out what Gwen intends to do.'

She looked at me angrily. 'I suppose you mean that if Gwen starts weeping on your shoulder, you'll go running back to her and leave us. I mean, well, she left you!'

I tried to interrupt her, but she would not let me. 'You'll leave us and spend the rest of your life tied to her apron strings, just because you hadn't the guts to tell her the truth. You don't love her do you?'

I had realised long before, that I had probably never been 'in love' with her in the commonly accepted sense, but a sentimental hangover from our childhood together with a need for companionship and a reasonable degree of compatibility, seemed to be an acceptable substitute for something which I had tried to write out of my life at Ciampino airport. But whether I loved her or not was no-one's concern but mine, not even Rachel's.

'Just let me handle this part my way Rachel, but I promise you I'll do no more running away.'

'Will you ring?'

I was not sure what she meant. 'Who am I to ring?'

She shrugged, but avoided my eyes, 'Mother I suppose.'

'When, tonight?'

'Before we leave tomorrow. They're going to pack me off to stay as an aupair with some relations of the old man in France. I'll be leaving Speke at three o'clock tomorrow afternoon.'

'Do you want to go?' I asked.

'What do you think?'

I wondered what I could do to prevent her being treated like a poor relation and keep her with me, but first we would have to admit that she was my child and that would lead to obvious complications – had she thought about this.

'What are you thinking about?' she asked.

'Are you really very unhappy with Aaronsen and your mother?'

'Wouldn't you be if you were pushed around from pillar to post, packed off to school as soon as you can blow your own nose, sent off to holiday-courses or relatives or school friends every holiday, anywhere but home. I hardly ever see Mother and when I do, she's never on her own, there's always Aaronsen or Simon or his grandmother, or business guests or political cronies. I hate being home almost as much as I hate school, but more than anything else, I hate staying at hotels with them.

'We have endless parties – cocktail parties, dinner parties, luncheon parties. If it were fashionable to have parties in the bath, Aaronsen would have parties in the bath. He loves to feel popular but they're all too afraid of him to really enjoy themselves. I was going to run away from school when I was sixteen and get a job in London, but Helen talked me out of it. She asked me to go and stay with her for a while. I think she wanted me to see what I was letting myself in for. She says that I don't know what it's like to be without money, but anything would be better than going on like this. I never meet any real people you know. They're all acting in a queer twisted sort of play and what makes it all madder is that most of them are badly mis-cast.'

I laughed in spite of the intense seriousness of her expression.

'It's obviously time we got together for a serious chat' I said, 'but right now I have an appointment with a hot bath. I might just come along to that party after all and in the meanwhile, I'll give some thought to the problem of getting you out of this trip to France.'

'Am I allowed to kiss you goodbye?' she asked.

'Of course, providing you don't mind starting a rumour that you are having an affair with a man old enough to be your father.'

'Good heavens, do you think...?'

'What's the alternative?' I countered.

She shrugged and leaning forward, kissed my cheek.

'See you later,' she said and left.

I climbed into the front seat, stiffly and painfully and drove out of the circuit through the crowds which were still leaving. It occurred to me that I must go and see Aaronsen even if only to collect my prize and starting money. While waiting for some traffic lights to change, I wondered how much would be due to me and groped in my jacket pocket for my distressingly thin wallet.

Among the assorted pieces of paper and old bills, lurked a crumpled pound note, one ten shilling note and the remains of a cheque book containing two cheques. Perhaps Patrick could cash one out of the office petty-cash box?

As I parked the car outside the house, my neighbours watched me slyly as they pretended to be gardening. But their stares no longer worried me. It would not be for much longer. I would sell the house, get out of the district and maybe find a village garage somewhere in the Lake District or on the west coast of Scotland. I felt tired and ill. The thought of even one full season of Grant Prix driving, with all the travel involved, living out of suitcases and with the bogey of increasing age and slowing reactions, made me aware of the fact that my opportunity had come too late. Perhaps I should have felt bitter, but instead, I felt an unexpected sense of relief as if I had been forcing myself to take an unpleasant medicine only to find that I was cured and needed it no more.

I had left the immersion heater on before leaving for Aintree so I was able to relax in a deep hot bath, while listening to the portable radio pouring out a vigorous Mozart quartet. I recalled with amusement, how I had once tried to convince a sceptical Gwen, that driving a modern Grand Prix car on a difficult circuit, was a satisfying artistic accomplishment on a par with playing in a Mozart quartet. Her comment had been that chamber music hardly exacted the same penalty for lack of concentration!

The strident jangle of the telephone tore through the intricate web being woven by the strings. I got out of the bath and dried myself as quickly as possible. By the time I had found my dressing gown and put it on, the 'phone had stopped ringing.

Going into the bedroom to get a clean shirt, I noticed an

envelope lying on my pillow. It carried the name 'Peter' in Gwen's handwriting.There was a single sheet of notepaper inside. I sat down on the bed to read it, knowing before I started, what it would say and that it would give me no pleasure.

Perhaps it was just wounded pride because I had failed as a husband that filled me with a feeling of defeat and loneliness, when logically I should have experienced relief, but whatever the reason, I could not have felt more depressed if it had been a suicide note. 'My Dear,' it began:

> Because you are too soft-hearted to administer the coup-de-grace by telling me that you no longer love me, if ever you did in the past, but would rather neglect me to the point where I must make the move, I am forced to leave you. If I stay, we will soon begin to hate each other and Ian will grow up in the poisonous atmosphere of a home only held together by a distorted sense of duty. Apart from anything else, it is only since taking an objective view of you, that if you had not met Deborah and introduced me to jealousy, I would probably have got you into perspective by meeting other boys of your age. If I had not thought that you were being taken away from me, I would probably not have rated you so highly.

> What you did yesterday, showed everyone else what I had known for a long time, that you are completely selfish and consider no-one but yourself.

> I can't stand it any longer and can't bear the thought of Ian growing up like you. I don't think I will be able to stay at home any longer than it takes me to find a job, because I am already tired of hearing people say 'I told you so'.

> As you know, I don't believe in divorce, so please don't make us enemies by bringing lawyers between us. You know that I will do nothing to prejudice Ian against you and if you want it, he will be able to come to you for holidays

> There is no going back and nothing more for us to say to each other.

> Take care of yourself,
>
> Gwen.

My first reaction was to crush the letter into a ball and throw it away, but stopped myself, smoothed it out and put it on the dressing table.

The dressing table mirror was gone, as had the wardrobe. My clothes were neatly piled on the bed, which only had one pillow. I walked into the front bedroom. Everything, even the threadbare carpet, had gone. Ian's room was the same, only the faded wallpaper revealed where his cot had stood.

I sat down on the top stair and noticed that she had left the carpet. I wondered how she would find a job which would support herself and Ian, who would look after him while she was working. The perspective and relative proportions of the moment's problems, were very different to those of a few minutes earlier.

I had begun the day believing that it would resolve my problems by giving me the opportunity to drive a car with a reasonable chance of success but although there were compensating features, most of my progress had been backwards

Beginning to feel cold reminded me that I was only wearing a dressing gown and wasting valuable living time on self-pity. I began to dress and vented my ill-temper on the malevolent idiot who invented collar studs and cuff-links, as well as the manufacturers who contrived to make them with built-in destructor units which permits them to disintegrate instantaneously, silently and without leaving any recognisable fragments, the moment they are removed from a shirt.

An inordinate amount of my waking seemed to be spent hunting for studs, or buying the cheapest possible replacements. At last, after searching in all the old sweet tins full of odd buttons, face cream jars and the bathroom shelves, I found two in a dirty shirt in the kitchen. Having dressed and laid the kitchen table for breakfast in the morning, I went to pick up Patrick.

He had anticipated my usual shortage of ready cash and had collected my fee as well as my share of the starting and prize money, before leaving the circuit. My wallet lost its lean and hungry look for the first time in many months.

We went, at Patrick's insistence to a pub at the Mersey end of the ship canal, which was the size of a Victorian castle in mill owner's

Gothic style, built of yellow and red Ruabon brick, with stained glass windows and acres of darkly varnished bar counters and furniture.

The walls were manfully withstanding the pressure of human bodies. Hard Merseyside voices, as raucous as caulking hammers on a steel hull provided the almost tangible bulk of the sound, while the sing-song lilt of Norwegian indicated the sources of the background smell of whale oil. Blue serge suits, jeans and leather jackets, winkle-picker shoes, sea boots, narrow Italian style jackets and colourful Scandinavian sweaters, were packed as closely as clothes in a wardrobe, the only difference being that these clothes were occupied.

Patrick ploughed his way through the crowd to a corner where Ron the mechanic, his right-hand man Henry, and our graduate apprentice, were sitting.

Henry seemed to regard racing cars, drivers, other mechanics and the government, as crosses to be borne until his rabbit farm began to show enough profit to allow him to leave us. The new boy, a recently graduated product of Imperial College, had joined us, 'for the experience', was renamed 'chopper' within the first day and had already been diverted from his plans for fame and early wealth, by the sound and smell of racing machinery. He had the look of a fanatic and was clearly doomed.

Judging by his shining red face, glazed eyes and effusive greeting he seemed to be doubly doomed. A table full of empty glasses stood in front of them, and within ten minutes the time-established ritual of beer drinking and beer talk was under way, brimming pots and wet tables, the same old jokes around the same few subjects.

Patrick launched himself thirstily into the bachelor party spirit, but I was only partly with them, my body still un-relaxed and keyed to racing concentration. I could listen, watch and drink, but with only half my attention and only the fear of spoiling their enjoyment prevented me from looking at my watch every few minutes. I wondered whether I should ring Deborah before going to Aaronsen's party or if it would be better just to arrive and let events take their course.

Time was slipping away quickly, with Deborah only eight miles away at Heswall while I sat listening to Patrick and Ron both trying to find the end of a long rambling story that they had both forgotten.

It was half past eight, and Patrick, seeing me glance at my watch, drained his glass and stood up to leave. We supported each other by protracted hand-shaking during the long farewells which would have been more appropriate for the beginning of an Antarctic expedition, and I learned to my surprise, that the day's racing was considered to have been a great triumph for me.

I was at first amused, then curious and when I asked Patrick what he had thought about my drive, he told me that it had surprised everyone who knew me. For Patrick, this was pretty close to a compliment!

When we got into the car, I pulled the starter knob and the pinion jammed in the starter ring as it had begun to do regularly. I got out and with the car in gear, rocked it backwards and forwards until it freed. Upon trying the starter, it jammed again. After several attempts it worked. Patrick sat silently throughout the whole operation, which took some five minutes.

'How long has this been going on?' he asked.

'Oh, I'm not sure, probably about a month I suppose.'

'I don't know about you at all,' he grinned and slowly shook his head.

'Why the hell don't you chuck the thing into the garage, get it sorted out and sold so that you can get a new one? It's bad for business for you to be seen driving a clapped-out wreck like this!'

'I wish you'd make your blasted mind up about me. It's only a week ago that you told me that I was a luxury the business couldn't afford, that I was wasting money and was less use than the pump boy!'

'Oh for christsake!' he moaned, 'you take it all so seriously, you ought to know by now, I'm a bit inclined to go off at half cock at times. Is that why you've been sulking all evening?'

'No, I'm just a bit off-net, just give me time.'

We were passing through Barnston.

'Hold it!' he yelled in my left ear, 'I'm thirsty and it's your round.'

236

We settled down at the bar of the Coach and Horses and attained a pleasant degree of convivial comradeship which had begun to wear a little threadbare during the previous two years.

'What are you going to do about Mrs. A?' he asked, examining the contents of his glass against the light with woolly concentration.

I could only shrug and silently wish that I knew

'You know what you ought to do, don't you?' he asked.

'Yes, pick up Gwen and Ian, take them away for a holiday, forget racing, forget Deborah and forget that Rachel ever existed, teaching her a useful lesson at the same time. You can trust no-one and rely on no-one.'

'Well, you're learning sense at last,' he said and rested his hand on my shoulder. 'Now let's take this heap of a car back to the garage and you can borrow the MG coupé until you decide what you want. After that, we'll mosey off to the 'pool by taxi and get pleasantly pissed, conveniently forgetting the Aaronsen party.'

'Sorry, I'm going to that party if it's the last thing I ever do.'

'It might well be you fool.'

'No, seriously, I must see her, there are things I must know, about Rachel, about the attempt on Warrender's life.'

He sighed noisily, 'You're as daft as a brush! You'd be well advised to stay away, particularly now you have a drive with a works team, you're on the way up. But if you've made up your mind, I'd better come along and keep you out of trouble. Poor little Gwen, what the hell did she ever do to get lumbered with you.'

It seemed to be a rhetorical question, so I did not answer, but it was a question I had sometimes asked myself. From the purely practical point of view she had everything to gain from leaving me. Instead of irritation and resentment, I had begun to feel re-newed affection for her.

'Here's to her, may she find herself a better man than me.'

We drank to it, and noticed, without concern, that the fingers of the clock were pointing to ten o'clock. Several rounds later, Patrick was telling the landlord how the Dragoons were paragons of all the military virtues, and he knew better than to disagree.

Wisely, he suggested that he should call a taxi for us and we agreed. Leaving the Anglia in the car park, we set out for the Victoria, and almost came to blows over who should pay for the taxi. No-one seemed surprised by our late arrival, in fact it almost went unnoticed.

My eyes were reluctant to focus on anyone in particular and Deborah was nowhere in sight. Charles and Pam were standing by the door, but I pretended not to see them and made my way over to where Simon was talking to two girls who were strangers to me. He introduced me, but their names did not even roost for a moment on the perches of my memory, but flew, like alcoholic hens, out of the other ear. They were equally un-memorable, fluffy, meringue complexioned debutantes, with voices like swans.

Aaronsen materialised at my elbow.

'Ah, Mr Wade, your glass is empty and that is wrong today of all days.'

'What's so special about today?'

'Don't you feel that's playing the modesty angle a little too... I mean, you do happen to have caused a bit of a sensation with the GMT. It's been on all the news bulletins and TV and now everyone's speculating about Zandvoort, wondering how you will perform if the car holds together.'

It had not occurred to me that anyone else could view the day's results as anything but a complete fiasco, even though I had enjoyed most of it. Other people joined the group and the conversation flowed like fun-fair music.

Patrick was sitting on the arm of a chair in which Hetty Hall was reclining, shoes kicked off and nylon toes wiggling. She looked almost un-dressed without her usual belted raincoat and headscarf.

'Hello Peter!' She beckoned imperiously. 'And where d'you think you've been hiding? We looked all over the shop for you. I suppose you know you were disqualified for pushing the car back to the pits?' I sat on the free arm of her chair.

'Hetty, you look like the collected works of Emile Zola between two rather old-fashioned book ends.'

'And you're as tight as a perishin' tick... but never mind it'll do you some good. You're too damned inhibited to be true!'

Patrick choked while trying to drink and laugh at the same time.

'No, I mean it Patrick. He's not living in the same world as the rest of us... you must see it better than us. We've only known him for a week, but it strikes me that he's opted out of our world and is living in a one man monastery with no religion.'

'Amen' said Helen, who had just joined the group, in search of her host. 'I've no need to ask who you're talking about!' She wrinkled her nose at me amiably.

'I've been asked by a certain young lady, who has not been allowed by her stern father to come to the ball, if Peter will slide away subtly and say goodnight to her.'

'I'd better stick my head under a cold water tap before I do! I'm not used to all this alcohol.'

Helen laughed, 'Whether you're used to it or not, it certainly suits you. Who's taking you home tonight?'

Hetty and Patrick joined in the general hilarity which followed and I found myself blushing again.

CHAPTER 8

Meeting

IT was a relief to get into the cool hall but the cold air hardly penetrated my numb and tingling senses. My brain was fizzing pleasantly like a bottle of pop on a summer's day. If someone had suggested that I could have flown up to the top floor with my feet six inches above the stairs, I might almost have tried it.

The landing was long and the carpet as thick as a spring meadow. The door numbers were designed to confuse, but rather than stop to think about it, I walked on around the corner as fast as I could.

Outside number 21, closing the door behind her, was Deborah. We almost cannoned into each other and I put out my hands to save her. Clumsily I tried to kiss her, but she caught my wrists in her hands and held them away from her at the same time twisting to avoid my lips.

'You idiot Peter, someone might come!'

'What the hell if they do.'

Her key was still in the lock and I put my hand on it to open the door. Her hand was there first. My reactions were obviously slow. She opened the door and gently propelled me inside, then followed and closed it quietly behind us.

Only the bright moon light illuminated the room. Brilliant sodium lights on the coast road over the river, strung along the dark blue hills, were duplicated light for light in the dark water of the Dee.

She was leaning against the closed door, her hands resting on my forearms. Her face was a pale mask in the dark. It was silent except for the sound of her breathing and the beating of my own heart.

She laughed quietly and rested her head against my chest.

'Just listen to your heart! Surely I don't have the same effect on you after all these years do I?'

I didn't answer, but kissed her on top of her head. She tilted her head back and offered her lips for a proper tribute.

'Well, you've certainly changed!' she said, trying to make a joke mask her shaking voice. 'The old Peter was not the sort of man to make love to another man's wife... a very pregnant wife to boot!'

'The old Peter died a long time ago! But this one seems to have the same old Achille's Heel... he's still in love with you. It's bloody ridiculous, but I am.'

'Peter...'

'No, let me finish... I wasn't sure of anything until I saw you again. Even now, I don't know whether you were using me as a stalking horse to kill Warrender or whether he was setting the trap. I tried to tell myself that's why I came here tonight. That's what I tried to tell myself... but it's you that I want... and Rachel. Suddenly it's all quite simple.'

She sighed and reaching past me, switched on the light.

'Do you still think it will look simple tomorrow morning at breakfast time? You are just a bit tight now and feeling a bit sentimental. If you'd really wanted me, you could have found me after all the fuss and fury of partition had died down. But what did you do? You crawled back to England with your tail between your legs, probably glad to get out of a difficult situation.'

'For God's sake Deborah, stop it... what the hell did you expect me to do? Sit around as a target for your trigger-happy friends? Sure, I was damned glad, and lucky, to get out, but what d'you think I felt when I realised who was trying to kill us? It was all a bit more than a coincidence wasn't it?'

'And you say you still love me?' she asked, as gently as if she were talking to a child. I could only nod assent.

'Well, God help us... I still love you.'

We could only stand and look at each other like a pair of drunken owls.

'Deborah... but why didn't you answer my letter?'

'What letter?'

'Well, I wrote to you from Cyprus at the same time that I wrote my letter of resignation, or did I ever post it? Oh God, it's all like a half remembered nightmare, but you must have wondered when

I was posted 'died of wounds and complications following surgery.' It was all supposed to have happened in an Italian military hospital in Rome. Only my parents were told the half truth and they were forbidden to tell anyone else, even Gwen.'

She was shaking her head slowly, 'I have no idea what you are talking about – you were supposed to have died?'

'Yes, and no one told you?' She looked totally confused

'Yes, I was reported dead and became someone else, working in our Consulates and Embassies for almost three years, unable to even write or 'phone my family, didn't your friends in Irgun or Mossad keep you informed?' She looked at me with pity. 'Even your husband seems to have discovered more than enough to make me feel very uncomfortable.'

'Why has he been probing into your past? That really worries me.' I explained that it was all to do with possible business relationships in the future, but even though any normal person would have been very puzzled by someone's 'death' and return to life, he must have penetrated the deception and decided that it had no bearing on his future plans. It worried me however because it gave him knowledge which could become a weapon.

'I too was an embarrassment. They all thought that I was or had been sleeping with the enemy and was carrying an Englishman's child, so I was spirited out of sight, to a Kibbutz close to the Syrian border to have my baby out of sight when the time came.'

The silence between us seemed to last forever.

'How completely bloody stupid can we all be, all that killing and hatred and we have been kept apart by – what? By being kept in the dark?' There were footsteps in the corridor and we were silent, holding our breath and overcome by a fear of discovery, death or just shame. As they went on past the room, we both laughed quietly with a feeling of guilt and some fear.

'Deborah, you are the mother of our daughter and I already love her dearly, I just don't know where we are going to from here.'

'Neither do I, although my instincts are shouting loudly and clearly, just pack up and run – but we both know that if we do, lots of other lives are going to come tumbling down in catastrophic heaps. I just think that a little thinking time is called for – yes?'

I was forced to concede that to do anything on impulse now would do too much damage even though it seemed so simple on the surface. I told her that as a last resort if we could find no tidy way out of the impasse which faced us, I would have some bags packed ready to take her and Rachel to some secret hideaway any time as from now.

'You really are out of touch with the real world, even if you have come back from the dead. What was your reward for all that, lots of financial rewards or public affirmation?'

'No my love, a CMG and a micro-pension and a suggestion that it would be best for me and the Empire, if I disappeared from public life. So I did and as a result, have a huge gap in my career which has not helped very much and lost me the love of my life and my daughter.'

'Well, I will pack a bag, but at the moment I can see no easy way out of this, but what is certain is that we can't stay here any longer without creating new problems. Rachel knows a great deal and doesn't want to lose you, so let's keep in touch and see what we can work out, if anything.'

I told her that I had been on the way to say goodnight to Rachel, and she stood to let me out of the room, switching the light off first. As I was closing the door, Patrick turned the corner and came face to face with Deborah. His expression as he looked from her to me, was one of blank astonishment. He hurried to me.

'You stupid bloody clot,' he whispered hoarsely, 'the whole pub's crawling with Aaronsens and here you are snogging with the old man's wife in her bedroom. You must be completely round the twist! This is the last time I'll ever go drinking with you... you're a flaming menace!'

'Oh drop it Patrick, you only know half the story. Where's Rachel's room?'

'It's number thirteen. But just hold on for a minute... are you still tight or do you know what you're about?'

'For the second time in my life... yes, I almost know. I've only been half alive for years... now I'm going to make up some lost time.'

He ran his hands over his face, 'Mmm, I hope you do, but before you go off into orbit, Hall has just arrived and says that he's had a row with Hemmingway over the GMT that you drove. He claims that you were given the faster car – says he didn't have a chance. One word led to several others, mostly about each other. Then Hall told him where to go and it looks as if he went. Anyway, Hall is downstairs now looking for you. He wants you to leave for Zandvoort next Friday and get to know the circuit – you're going to be number one, if you want it.'

'Does Aaronsen know about all this?'

'It's all over the place. He's getting a bit uppish because he says Hall's poaching. As a matter of fact the cheeky sod has just sent me to find you before you see Hall. He wants you to sign a contract a bit jildi!'

'He may not be so keen on that idea tomorrow. How much do we need him to keep the business going?'

'Well, we were really just going to have the 'no capital' problem removed, in return for which, we were going to provide a toy motor business for Simon to run... but we're not really stuck with it. Why?'

'Just that as I intend to start making a bit of an omelette... a few eggs may be about to be broken. In a funny sort of way, I am beginning to like the old man and I think Simon could improve with knowing, but from tonight onwards I may be on their out list. So you might as well tell the old man, fairly politely, that he can keep his contract.'

Patrick took it calmly. 'OK then we might as well forget the whole deal. I can't think how I let myself be talked into it... seemed quite a good idea at the time. Pity about Simon though, he would have been useful.'

'Well, try him with a partnership offer, it might be a good idea. Tell him I would like it.'

'Then I take it that you want to stay in the business?'

'If you'll still have me. After all I'm going to need money. I'd like to do a full season with Hall's team if I can, then perhaps we can scout around for a bread and butter agency for some suitable Continental cars. I've an idea at the back of my mind for an export sales set-up, and manufacture of the three-wheeler.'

I looked at him with some anxiety. 'What d'you think?' Judging by his grin, there was no need for worry.

'Now you're beginning to talk like your old self... you're on!' We were shaking hands, when Rachel looked round the corner

'Oh, I thought you'd got lost. Aren't you coming to say good-night to me?'

'Of course I am... we were just trying to make a few plans for the future. I'll be right along.'

Patrick put his hands on his hips and slowly shook his head.

'And what about her... does she know about you and Mrs A. yet?'

'Not the latest, but generally, yes. In fact she seems to know a lot of things that I'm not sure about yet, but not my part in the Bernstein affair. I haven't even had time to sort it out with Deborah yet. I had no idea what happened after I left. I've always had an idea that she was set up as bait so that the Irgun could get at Warrender, and I was just a stooge. Not very good for the old ego – but conversely, I suppose she might equally well believe we were trying to get at the Bernsteins through her. It's bothered me for years, but now it doesn't seem to matter very much. We've wasted so much time.'

We were outside Rachel's door. He spoke quietly and urgently.

'It's not too late yet Peter, just think, when you've lived together for a few years, if it lasts that long, it'll be just another marriage. You're just fooling yourself into thinking it's something special. Don't you think it's even more remarkable that Gwen married you after the way you treated her? You've got to remember that Mrs Aaronsen is married to a much older man. She probably has all sorts of romantic notions about you – and boy – they're going to take some living up to. She'll expect a great deal more of you than Gwen ever did, and the woman hardly knows you, for that matter, how much do you know about her?'

He was going over some pretty familiar ground, which I had already travelled.

'Everything is on hold at the moment, because there is potentially another major problem. Did you know that Aaronsen had done a major and very thorough search on my background ?'

'Jesus! Does he know what you were up to with the SIB?'

I could only shrug my shoulders. 'If he does, he's keeping it to himself for the moment and that really worries me. It might make a contract unavoidable on the one hand and playing tick with the tiger on the other to accept it, either way though we're wasting valuable drinking time. I'll see you downstairs in a few minutes.'

I went in to see Rachel. The door was ajar and the light on. She was in bed, raised on one elbow.

'Hello wenchlet.'

She smiled dutifully, but without amusement. I sat on the edge of the bed facing her and folded my arms, hoping that I didn't look drunk.

'Peter, what is the Bernstein affair?'

'Where did you hear...?'

'My door was open,' she replied with disarming frankness, 'and besides, I heard grandpa, he told me something, but I can't really remember. But what's it got to do with you?'

'How much did you hear?'

'Oh, Mr Crompton reading you the Riot Act, is he right?' She looked so anxious that I could not prevent myself smiling.

'Well, he's just a wee bit on the cynical side, and he doesn't know the whole story. Again he's quite sensible and according to the rule book, his advice is pretty sound, but when I stick to the rules, I get into as much trouble as when I don't, if you see what I mean.'

She was still looking at me solemnly and very silently.

'He's wasting his breath telling me though. The awful, dismal truth is that I've virtually no money, my health is decidedly dodgy, for at least the next half year, I'll be wandering around Europe from one circuit to another like a gypsy and worst of all there's only the slightest chance that Gwen would consider a divorce! It doesn't exactly add up to the picture of the most eligible bachelor on the market does it?'

She sat up, her arms wrapped around her knees, head tilted back with her eyes half closed and her thick, glossy black hair framing her pale oval face.

She was silently rocking from side to side to the rhythm of the dance band which had begun to play downstairs. A delicate tracery of blue veins showed through the translucent skin of her eyelids. Her thin arms and bony elbows and wrists, the childish pyjamas, expensive but arbitrarily bought for her, without particular thought, or love, made my throat ache. I longed to take her away. I stood up and looked out of the window.

'Don't you want me to come back to you Peter?'

I told her to lie down, and tucked her in like a child.

'You, my idiot child, you're going to learn what it's like to be smothered with paternal affection and general fussing. You'll probably wish we'd never met, but right now, you're going to look as if you're asleep. I'm going to try to have a few words with your mother.'

As I was turning out the light, she called me.

'I've got a case packed – just tell me and I'll come with or without my mother. I need a life of my own.'

I closed the door quietly, trying to control my confused emotions. A noisy dance was in progress when I went back. Aaronsen was lurching about like a drunken bear, doing the twist by himself and getting in the way of other dancers.

Patrick was standing by the temporary bar, looking very sober and thoughtful and listening to Helen who was talking urgently, emphasising some point by tapping his chest with her forefinger. I wondered, with some amusement, how he was enjoying it, because I had heard a story about a Sergeant's Mess guest night when a visiting Guard's sergeant had been foolish enough to try and drive home the point of his argument in the same way. Patrick had caught hold of his hand and bitten his finger between his nutcracker-worthy teeth. They had both been somewhat drunk at the time, but it had triggered off a memorable brawl which had in turn resulted in a surcharge of seven pounds per head on the month's mess bill, to pay for the damage.

Deborah was sitting beside Hetty, talking to two men I did not know. I was hungry and went in search of food. The manager and a receptionist were sitting in the kitchen drinking coffee and I persuaded them to make me some sandwiches and coffee.

Two rounds of ham sandwich and a small pot of coffee cost me eight and six, so even when I discovered that they tasted like dry blotting paper and inner tube I felt obliged to finish them. The coffee was good and hot, so I sat in the deserted hall and finished the whole pot. The occasional couple would slip unobtrusively out of the party looking for dark privacy in the hall, but on seeing me in the half light, would pass by.

Feeling fully in control of myself, I went back into the party. Patrick immediately left his dancing partner and came to join me.

'She's looking for you, where've you been?'

I told him.

'Well. I'll keep the old man busy while you do a couple of circuits with her. For Pete's sake though, don't get yourself committed to anything drastic tonight. We all need a bit of thinking time before you rob Deborah of a comfortable life and cause Gwen, Ian, Rachel and yourself to have to live on the cube root of bugger all income – remember that we are going to be struggling all over again even if you start making mega-bucks racing. You know that you're very soon going to be yesterday's man. You know as well as I do, that one day's racing without any real travel has left you totally shagged today. Right?' There was no argument, he was as usual completely right. I nodded silent assent.

I found Deborah and asked her for a dance. Although Aaronsen seemed about to suggest that she ought to rest, she stood up and followed me onto the still crowded floor. We danced for a while without saying anything and I could feel Aaronsen's eyes on us.

'Does he know anything?'

'I wouldn't begin to know,' she said. 'I don't know what he thinks, apart from business. He's not very interested in people. I think they bore him, but he's curious about you and I believe he's a bit worried. He told Simon that you're a fanatic without a cause.'

'What did Simon say?'

'He said you were probably anti-Semitic.'

'Does he love you?'

'It may seem odd, but that embarrasses me, perhaps because you are asking.'

'Well, does he?'

She shrugged and pursed her lips, but did not answer.

'Then what do you think he would do if I were to walk up to him now and tell him that we were leaving together tonight?'

She looked alarmed. 'Don't worry, I've no intention of starting a war that no one can win, or as Patrick would probably say 'pissing on everybody's chips'.' She looked very relieved.

'But really, what would he do?'

She did not answer immediately.

'He would be very offended, yes, offended would be the word. He'd certainly call you a few names but he'd keep pretty quiet about it, in fact I think he'd rather sell me than get a bad press!'

'What about you love? Have you really made up your mind?'

She smiled. 'I really don't know, partly because I am at the moment about to be a new mother again, and I have been overwhelmed by events. I was sure when you showed me that old photograph this afternoon but, do you mind if we sit down. It would need more than a little skill to dance with this particular symbol of motherhood at the moment. I am not in a condition to make such a decision at this moment, I mean for goodness sake just look at me.'

We sat down by the bar, a sudden hard-to-break silence between us. We both began to speak at once. She made a sign for me to carry on.

'I was just going to say this is where we came in.' She laughed and patted her belly.

'You could hardly say that. We've both been getting a little shop soiled since Jerusalem, funny, it doesn't seem so long ago now, and even tomorrow isn't such a problem any more. What about you?'

At the moment, my only problem is Rachel, 'What will Aaronsen do if she came with us?'

She laughed. 'He'd probably give you a big brass clock. They can't stand the sight of each other, but you're pushing things too fast. I really must have a little thinking time.'

Patrick came through the crowd carrying a tray full of empty glasses, which he put on the counter. He ordered some more from the barman, and without saying a word to us, put a ginger beer on the table in front of me and an orange juice by Deborah. After delivering the rest of his order, he came back to our table and sat down.

'Thanks for the drinks – why are you looking so worried?'

'You!' he said, 'you're sitting over here like a couple of moon-struck kids, and you didn't even have a drink in front of you.'

Deborah and I looked at each other, it struck us as being uncommonly funny.

'Oh hell! You're as bad as he is, what are you aiming to do?'

'When we've finished this drink, I'm going to pick up the car, pack some gear from the house, then it is just possible that we may be leaving some time in the near future, for somewhere or other.'

He turned to Deborah. 'Where, not tonight surely?'

She smiled and shrugged, 'God willing, but not tonight, maybe even not at all.'

'The old man would do his nut!' he wailed, with an expression of extreme anguish which nearly started us laughing again, 'but please in the name of commonsense let's get through the Zandvoort bit and make some acceptable plans. You at least owe me that before you totally destroy the business, such as it is. Please Please!'

She looked at me, clearly moved by Patrick's plea. 'He's making sense you know,' and it was impossible not to agree even though I could sense losing control of the future. I was worried about Rachel even more than myself.

'And Rachel, she doesn't want to be packed off again to God knows where.'

Patrick, who clearly saw an opportunity to deal with a more manageable element of the problem, looked brighter. 'Didn't you and Gwen invite her to stay with you?' Then remembering that Gwen had moved out, 'Peter, you're making a real bugger's muddle out of all our lives – why can't we put every damned thing on hold, at least until this baby arrives?'

Deborah looked at me and nodded in agreement. 'He's absolutely right, and we all know it. You and I are grown-ups and can take a few more knocks, but Rachel needs you Peter. She could not face losing you now.'

We all recognised that our choices were limited, but Rachel must come first so it was agreed that Deborah would arrange to cancel the French trip and tell her husband that Rachel would be going to stay with Gwen and me at Torver for a short break, as from the morning, about mid-day.

Patrick looked at me sideways, 'Good plan, but one player not on the field at the moment, no Gwen!'

'No car either Patrick.'

'Well, we can solve that part right away, while you apply yourself to getting your real life back on the rails for at least the next two months while nature takes its course and Rachel becomes our joint project, but yours particularly. After all the poor kid didn't choose to be born into all this high drama.'

'Now that's a bit more like the old Patrick! You can come and help to get that MG out of the show room, but right now, you could slip out and see if you can conjure up a taxi!'

'Hell... are you pulling rank on me?' he asked, but went all the same.

When he had gone I took Deborah over to meet Pam and Charles and left her with them while I discussed the immediate working plans with Hall. I told him that I was going to take a short holiday, but would meet him at Zandvoort in a week. He asked if he should book a room for me and I told him that I would probably want two singles.

I managed to get Charles Green on one side and having apologised for having involved him in our lives during the last few weeks, involved him even further. I asked him to draw up a deed of gift to convey the house and everything in it except my clothes, to Gwen. I told him that I would make the necessary arrangements for a regular allowance to Gwen after Zandvoort if she still wanted a separation. He made no comment other than to agree and wish me luck with the new job.

Someone called for silence and the band limped to a ragged halt. Aaronsen was on his feet... he was very drunk.

'Tnni's li'l party is to celerbra' the firs' of many sussesses in the fiel' of moror racin',' he paused and peered about him, 'Where's Simon? Com'on don' be so blurry bashful... an' you th' other feller.... Peter Wassisname... stan' up.... be toasted.'

We were duly toasted, then Hall felt obliged to make a mercifully short speech to thank Aaronsen for his hospitality. Aaronsen called for the press to take some pictures, but they had long since gone. Someone else produced a camera and wanted to take a picture of Hall and me together.

Aaronsen objected and claimed that I was on his staff. It was apparent that a chill had descended on the room so Hall invited Aaronsen and Patrick, who had just returned, to join the group for a picture. The photographer persuaded them to shake hands, so the incident was forgotten for the moment. Patrick and I, slipped quietly out of the room to the taxi. The last thing that I wanted at that moment was to be forced into agreeing to a contract with Aaronsen, even in principle.

The taxi driver did his best, but it seemed to take ages to get to the garage, then longer to shuffle the cars out of the way of the one we wanted. As always it was at the back of the showroom, behind a new Jensen whose prospective owner had suddenly found himself with more debts than assets. We had some sympathy for him, and had kept it for a while in the hope that he might find some hidden resources. I had suggested to Patrick that it might be more suitable than the MG and to my surprise he agreed. Perhaps he was too tired to argue. We talked about the business and of the sort of life which we would be leading during the rest of the season. All my doubts about my ability to withstand the rigours of Grand Prix racing had gone, at least for the moment.

It only took ten minutes to pack a couple of suitcases and throw them into the boot, and he finished the contents of his hip flask standing in the cold kitchen before beginning the short journey back. It had started to rain, but the inside of the car was warm.

'On the basis that for the sake of Rachel, you and Gwen must at least for the sake of appearances, get together for a few days and work out a plan, I've taken the liberty of talking to her and suggested you spend the next few days at Torver. Oh, and before you go any further, yes it is free, because that is where Gwen was going to go tomorrow night and yes, she will be expecting you there together with Rachel.'

'You really are the Eighth Wonder Patrick. I really couldn't think what the hell to do next. I'll remember you in my will.'

He grunted, 'A fat lot of good that will do me. I suppose you're fit and sober enough to drive to Torver are you?'

'Yes, I've been deliberately heel tapping latterly. Incidentally, I think I'm going to like this car.'

It was handling beautifully, with ample power available even at low engine speeds, and the brilliant white headlights made daylight in the dark winding country roads. We ran in between some tall trees, the road curving sharply down hill towards the bridge.

On the apex of the bend, we met another car, out of control, its offside scraping along the stone wall on my side of the road. I swung the wheel over and broadsided the car, but the road was greasy under the trees and I over-corrected the first slide. It flicked its tail round, across the narrow grass verge, and smashed through the low stone wall. The car hung for a moment, then dropped nose-first down the steep bank onto the slimy, wet grass of the steeply sloping field. Patrick, his hands braced against the scuttle, swore quietly to himself as we slid sideways down the steep slope towards the river.

'Get out,' I yelled. He flung the door open and rolled out, but I heard the thud as it hit him and flung him to the ground.

Suddenly the back of the Jensen dropped over a bank and it somersaulted backwards tearing off the swinging door on some obstruction. I was helpless, hurled around the inside of the jolting car, against the steering wheel, the roof, the floor and the instrument panel. Finally, it stopped and I was trapped, half in and half out of the open door, with the car resting upside down on the crushed-in corner of its roof.

Taking stock of the situation I saw that although I was lightly pinned down by the rim of the steering wheel, and suspended by my right leg which was wedged between the front seats, I did not seem to be badly hurt. Nothing seemed to be broken. There was no fire, although there was a strong smell of petrol, and although the car had come to rest in the stream, only my right shoulder was in it. I moved slightly to try and get a grip of something and the car rocked ominously. I tried to think how anyone could set about lifting if off me but the beginning of panic was driving out reason.

'Patrick', I called, 'are you alright?'

'Yes, where the hell are you?'

'For God's sake don't move anything. I've got the whole bloody motor car poised over me. See if you can get the fire brigade, they should have a few clues about recovery.'

I heard his feet as he came closer.

'Well, we can't do anything without lights,' he said, 'I'll go and get some help. Christ, what a stupid mess. Are you sure you're OK?' I reassured him and asked him to keep people away.

'You bet I will,' he said, 'don't go away now.'

As he turned to go, he swore. 'Here come those bloody morons from the other car.' Then in a parade ground voice which I had not heard for many years.

'Hey, you! Keep away from that car, there's a man under it, and put that bloody cigarette out, there's petrol all over the shop!'

'Sorry mate, I dunno whar 'appened. I couldn' 'elp it, it was the blurry road – '

'I don't give a monkey's what happened, not just now anyway, but if you go anywhere near that car, so help me I'll crucify you. Have you got any pennies for the phone?'

I could hear the jingle of coins and Patrick muttering impatiently. 'OK Peter, I'm going now. I won't be five minutes.'

It was raining heavily, straight through the shattered windscreen onto my upturned face, trickling up my nose, into my eyes and ears. I wondered how I had got into this silly position, when had it all begun. The two drunks were talking, arguing quietly and repetitiously together. One of them called.

'Hey, you, are y'alright?'

'Yes, but just keep out of the bloody way.'

'We're sorry mate, but it wasn' all my fault, you was goin' far too fast.'

'Oh for God's sake belt up and do something useful like going up to the road and seeing if you can wave down a car.'

'It's no good, there's nobody else out tonight.'

His companion was vomiting noisily and moaning softly to himself. I did not feel particularly sympathetic. 'What the hell's the matter with him?' I asked. I was not very interested in the answer when it came either, because I had pins and needles in my legs and was unable to move them. I tried wriggling my toes, but it only seemed to make them worse, and gave me cramp into the bargain.

'Blast!' My calves bunched themselves into anguished knots.

'Wha's a marra? Would ye like a fag?'

'No you bloody oaf, don't you dare light a match.' How long would Patrick be? It was difficult to remember how long he had been away. In a strange way my mind was beginning to confuse the situation, and Patrick going for help, with the previous time, only now there was the rain in my face to remind me where I was. I was also shivering uncontrollably. It must have been shock.

I could hear my unseen audience discussing something, then they made noises in agreement. They spoke to me, but the sound of the stream masked their words. One of them told the other to be quiet and tried again.

'I said can y' ear me?' I told him that I could.

'What d'you want?'

'Well, it could be bloody ages before ye' mate gets back, and it could be even longer before some real help comes, so I reckon we ought to be doin' somethin' instead of jus' sittin' 'ere on our arses gettin' wet.'

'I can wait,' I told them. 'Why don't you just wander back to the road and have a smoke.' I listened hopefully, but they didn't move.

'I know you're bloody mad with us, but honestly we're sorry about this, and we want to help.'

'OK, but please, please just keep away. I'm not very comfortable but I've not broken any bones, and providing nothing happens to topple this car on top of me, I should stay this way.'

'Well, you can't see from where you are mate, but we reckon it might slip any time unless we do somethin' about it. We're both bloody strong, an' if we both lif' together, it'll get the weight off ye an' ye'll be able to crawl out.'

'For Christ's sake, don't do anything so flaming stupid. You're both too drunk for a start, and help can't be far off now.' I tried hard to stifle the panic which made my heart thump like a trip hammer.

'It'll be bloody ages before 'e gets back, 'e must 'ave 'urt 'is leg, 'e was draggin' it.'

They began to move. A stone rolled down the bank, and hit the crumpled glass fibre with a dull clunk. I shouted as loudly as I could, 'Keep still can't you.' But they kept on coming.

'It's alright, don't worry, we'll 'ave you out in no time.'

At least they seemed to be getting more sober. Their feet slithered closer. I could hear them breathing above the noise of water.

The car rocked slightly. 'Take it easy for pity's sake.'

'The trouble with you, is that you worry too much. Just get ready to try and get out when we lift. I'll say, one, two, three, LIFT, then you have a go, OK?'

I was not in any position to argue any more, and agreed. The car began to rock slightly. I could hear their shoes sucking in the mud, and the sound of their hoarse, rasping breath as they struggled to lift the heavy, slippery car.

'Right mate, get ready to try and get out, I'll say ready, steady, GO.' The time for arguing had gone, so I braced my hands against the wet earth and my left foot against the steering column, and prepared to push.

'Right,' I called.

'OK now, one, two, three, GO!'

The car began to move slowly, and a suitcase, dislodged by its movement, fell and wedged itself across my hips. I struggled and pushed, but my right leg only became more securely gripped between the backs of the two bucket seats. I felt the lower side of the car slip, and cold water began to lap around the back of my neck and into my ears.

'For Christ sake, 'urry up, we can' 'old it much longer.'

Struggling with desperate, feverish energy, I succeeded in turning the top half of my body and grasping a tree root. I pulled on it with all my strength, pushing my foot against the steering column as I did so.

'Hey, what the hell's goin' on down there?' It was Patrick. There were lights all around me, and voices.

I expected pain, but there is only suffocating pressure on my chest. There is no air, only the water and mud and then the taste of blood. There is so much noise, that it hurts, and I can't think. I can no longer remember who or where, or even her face. The whole world rocked and swayed, and with the movement came the pain in hot screaming thrusts. Oh God, make them go away, I'm trying to remember and there's no time left. There's not enough time. There's not enough time!

Suddenly, I was tired. The water was higher, roaring in my ears, and something hard and heavy was pressing against my forehead. I tried to lift my head out of the water, and heard voices bubbling. I could feel the thud of running feet through the earth. The car slipped.

As it did so, it must have twisted and dropped back onto its wheels, because my head came out of the water and I could breathe air again, but my body twisted so that my weight was taken by my trapped leg. The sudden pain and audible crack let me know that my knee had taken the strain, but at least Patrick was firmly in charge and I was alive. By the time the heavy suitcase had been removed, the ambulance team had taken charge and had me out of the car, splinted and strapped onto a stretcher and I was ready for transporting to hospital.

The traffic police who had just arrived were mainly interested in collecting names, numbers and statements, but Patrick, having given them the basic facts and having no independent transport now, had different priorities. He came in the ambulance to Clatterbridge Hospital and stayed until he had also been attended to and we had been shown the X-rays of my fractured fibula, tibia, and assorted rib. While being washed free of mud, grass and some blood, a variety of cuts and abrasions were revealed, stitched and dressed. By the time I was tightly tucked into a bed in the reception ward, I almost looked as bad as I felt.

It was only then that Patrick allowed himself to be driven home and I was reminded what a long suffering and forgiving friend he had been to tolerate my self-absorbed neglect over so many years. Well dosed with pain-killers and tired however, I fell asleep knowing that I was a helpless parcel, at least until dawn.

The change of day and night staff probably woke me, but there were almost immediately pills to be swallowed, temperature and blood pressure recorded and at last, a cup of tea. Life was beginning to adopt a controlled pattern.

A tepid boiled egg and cold toast held little appeal and because my jaw and right cheek had taken some of the impact with the rocks in the stream, both talking and eating were painful, but at least they could be avoided. The same could not be said for bruised or broken ribs which made the act of breathing uncomfortable, but my circumstances suggested that I was not going to laugh very much for a while. My inventory of areas of pain was interrupted by the arrival of the young doctor from the emergency reception, together with the ward sister.

After more questions and note-taking, I was informed that my jaw and chest would have to be X-rayed as soon as the day shift took over and that he thought that I might find it possible to get into a wheel chair to go there. At which point I realised that it would be helpful to have a dressing gown, which would have been in the suitcase in the wrecked Jensen. The sister looked at her clipboard, 'Oh I have a note about that from the night staff nurse, it appears that your wife brought a suitcase with some replacement clothes for you when we told her that we had to cut yours off you when you came in.'

'Are you sure? How did she know?' I asked. She shrugged.

'There's just a brief note here that your friend who was with you in the car could not wait, because someone would have been waiting for you, so we found your home address from your driving licence. It took the police quite some time to locate her and she only got here about three hours ago.'

The doctor looked at his watch and asked to be called when the new X-rays were available. The sister was beginning to look worried, 'I wonder if she is still here? There's nothing about a contact phone number or address for her. I'll take a look in the waiting room.' It was probably not long, although like an age before she was back.

'The poor soul is fast asleep in an arm chair with a cold cup of tea beside her and a rather battered looking suitcase with your name on the label, but I hadn't the heart to wake her.'

I suggested that if someone could bring the suitcase out without disturbing her, I could at least get my dressing gown and slippers and get into a wheelchair. This might possibly make me look less of a wreck than if she were to see me as a horizontal body. She smiled and clearly agreed, so that one of the porters soon had the case at my bedside and after the curtains were closed around the bed, I eventually managed to get into the chair. After all the pain and grief which I had caused her of late, it seemed that a short sharp period of physical pain would be least that I could undergo to reduce her anxiety. With the sister's agreement, the porter wheeled me into the waiting room where Gwen was just beginning to wake up. She looked exhausted and in the harsh hospital lights, pale and frightened. The realisation that this was my responsibility filled me with a pain far worse than anything which my body had ever known.

She looked at me as if I were a ghost and knelt in front of the chair, with tears rolling down her cheeks and without any warning I found myself crying quietly, trying to suppress the sobs which demonstrated that I had broken ribs. Gradually we regained some measure of control, until she laughed at the spectacle which I must have presented and in joining her, found that this was even more painful. So, a sort of normality returned and she wiped my eyes as well as her own. This made her realise that I was virtually untouchable.

'Is there at least somewhere visible where I could kiss you without it hurting?'

I suggested my lips and felt no pain, but was reminded gently of the years which we had invested in life together. Payback time was long overdue, rather than what only the night before, seemed like a chance to reclaim my own life but was really only reinforcement of my single-minded pursuit of self-destruction. I had been within a hair's breadth of achieving it.

I was kept in hospital for ten days, on the first of which Patrick came to see me and arrived before any other visitors. He looked at me with an expression of theatrical pity and a certain overtone of envy, without speaking.

'That's a damned queer look Patrick, what's going on inside that skull of yours?'

'You,' he said 'are the wonder of the western world. You look as if you've spent the last week in a tumble drier, no woman with good taste and half a brain would look at you twice and even Gwen who should know you has moved back home – ' I was about to speak but he held up the palm of his hand in a clear stop sign and continued, 'Not only that, but she's taken in your new-found bastard daughter like one of her own. All this when you were only saved from running off with an old girlfriend from your murky past and nearly getting us both killed.'

'I'm really sorry about that last bit, but you were there, you know it wasn't my fault. I'm just glad that you weren't hurt and were able to stop those clowns from drowning me as well. Do you realise that this is the second time that you've saved my life? Therefore we're into pay back mode.'

'Mmm, well, I've not been keeping score and your turn may be coming one day, but in the meanwhile life has continued in your absence. I went on from here hot-foot to let Deborah know that her love life was on hold, to find that the bird had flown having gone into premature labour during a very public row with Aaronsen over her lack of involvement with his racing ambitions and lack of gratitude for the Ferrari birthday present. He had totally failed to notice her packed bags and 'dear john' letter on her pillow. But perhaps he doesn't go there any more. Luckily, Rachel was quick-witted enough to snaffle the letter and burn it as well as claiming credit for packing the overnight bag. She's a smart little cookie!'

'But, what about Deborah, how is she?'

'I'm not sure I know the answer to that one. Firstly, she had a rough 24 hours, but she produced a son for the old man, a month ahead of schedule, but he's healthy and Kosher and is probably enrolled for prep and public school by now. So, there is general rejoicing within the land and I am led to believe that you will in the fullness of time be receiving your own 'dear john' letter. I took her some flowers from us both this morning, which she received most graciously and said privately that she hoped Rachel would serve to remind you of her.

'I think, but can't be sure, that against all reason, she is at least very fond of you. Well, that's the impression she clearly wanted me to get, but then I always thought that she was a born actress. Be careful though, she is keeping you on one hook even though the line is silk! But as far as I'm concerned, that's it. Now it's up to you.'

It was no time for debate and there seemed nothing to be said or done immediately, beside which, silence and the absence of turmoil was all that I wanted at that point.

'Right?' he asked as he rose and turned towards the door.

'Absobloodylutely' I responded and made a genuine but painful effort to smile.

The absence of personal visitors, gave time for the mind to float in the space outside an overcrowded life, observing events and follies, racketing around my part of the stage, enacting an ill-directed melange of comedy and drama, culminating in a hospital bed yet again. The bodily pain was only a reminder that I was still alive and therefore able to realise how I seemed to be a lightning conductor for grief and misfortune for those who had the misfortune to be close to me, either physically or emotionally. Gwen's tears were like the misericorde dagger which found the gap in the fallen knight's throat armour and put an end to all. For him, it would only be an inglorious death. For me it provided a painful awakening to the realisation that what I had been doing was a single-minded pursuit of a pointless Grail, which was only make of pewter and called for the sacrifice of everything and everyone around me in that quest.

It was bad enough to contemplate a lifetime lived to the tempo and with the balanced judgement of a teenager, but to be salvaged yet again by Patrick, for whom I had been a major burden for years, really emphasised how something had to change. My concern was that something of the calibre needed to restore stability may be missing, eroded by all that had gone before. Apart from the brief and heady euphoria of the past week, equally brief but pleasing moment when both driver and car were in tune and the competitors less so, the emotional barometer was almost always low. There are few places lonelier than the cockpit of a racing car and I was only half alive outside it.

Patrick had known for years that big money was needed to compete in a big boy's game and we only had access to a piggy-bank, so I had been dragging them all down with me. It was therefore 'get-real' time, so assuming that he was not going to sack me, some attention was going to be needed in the money-making rather than money-spending department.

There was also the matter of a newly acquired daughter to be accommodated in our already overcrowded lifeboat, since Gwen had already invited me back aboard, to present me with some more real life problems. The thought of the future made the agonising smile almost pleasureable.

Only one silent ghost stood unmoving in a corner of my mind; a shade whose body I would never forget, but whose mind I never knew.

About the Author

ALAN FORSYTH, was born in Wallasey, Cheshire, of Welsh land-owning farming stock, and Scottish/Cumbrian seafarers. After a false start in marine engineering, he joined the Recce Corps in 1945, commissioned in the RAC, the Queen's Bays. He studied Art at Liverpool, was commissioned in the Cheshire Yeomanry, then joined Vickers Supermarine initially in Technical Publications, then as deputy Chief Draughtsman, Chilbolton.

Together with wife, Jennifer, he moved between aircraft and other engineering companies, until joining Furmanite in 1967 as part of a two-man operation, growing to more than 1,500 staff worldwide and sales of £50 million, meanwhile painting, illustrating and writing. Alan was awarded an OBE in 1981 and appointed DL for Cumbria in 1995. His poetry has been published by the University of Wales, Gregynog in 1992 and 1995, and a book of his poems entitled *Waypoints* was published by Hayloft. He and Jennifer have exhibited paintings jointly at Cirencester, Grizedale and Kendal Brewery Arts Centre.